McAFEE COUNTY

McAFEE
COUNTY

A Chronicle

by Mark Steadman

HOLT, RINEHART AND WINSTON

NEW YORK · CHICAGO · SAN FRANCISCO

FIRST EDITION

A number of these stories have appeared elsewhere in a slightly
different form. "Annie's Love Child" appeared in the Winter, 1970
issue of *The Red Clay Reader*. "Anse Starkey at Rest" and "A Worker
of Miracles" have appeared in *Works in Progress*, April and September 1971.

Designer: Victoria Dudley
SBN: 03-080212-1
Printed in the United States of America

For JO

and Our Boys

"We blowed out a cylinder head."

"Good gracious! anybody hurt?"

"No'm. Killed a nigger."

"Well, it's lucky; because sometimes people do get hurt."

—*Huckleberry Finn*

McAFEE COUNTY

Mr. McAllister's
Cigarette Holder

June.

McAfee County, Georgia, the month of June.

Five minutes before eight o'clock in the morning, and already the air is molasses warm and sticky. Summer comes fierce and early into the coastal counties of Georgia. For four months of the year everything seems to be melting down toward the ground like a landscape made of wax. Then, just before it all fuses together into a lump, the wind shifts around to the northeast and fall snaps in, bringing back the brittleness of October, so that things begin to separate and stand up straight again.

But the melting begins in June.

The McAfee County road-grubbing gang is impervious to it. Almost nothing like that bothers them. The slash pines are melting like candles into the flats on either side of the freshly graded road—the black water in the ditches turning to syrup—and they don't pay any attention at all.

One of the men says, "I seen me a fish coming to work this morning."

The other men look at him, waiting.

"About that high." He holds his hand up over his head to show them. "He's headed *up*," he says, fluttering his hand.

The men are waiting for what it will be.

"Says he's going to find him a *dry* place if he's got to swum to the *moon.*"

The men laugh on the *"dry."*

Dropline Richwine, foreman of the gang, stands a hundred yards down the road, squinting under his hand, looks at them milling around, forming up. "Here, Dewey," he says. He hands the small Negro boy a dime. "Dr. Pepper." The boy snatches the coin and runs away. A little over a mile down the road is a filling station owned by Phinesy Wooton. All day the boy will run back and forth fetching cold drinks for Dropline. Alternating Dr. Peppers and Seven-Ups. For every trip that he makes, he gets a penny tip. He won't earn enough during the day to buy a drink for himself, but will have to borrow the three or four cents from Dropline. By the end of the summer he will owe the foreman two and a half, maybe three, dollars.

Dropline holds his pocket watch out like a starter at a track meet, glancing at it, waiting for the big hand to touch twelve. When it does, he puts the watch into the pocket under his belt, cups his hands, and gives the signal.

"Goooo . . . to GRUBBING!" he says.

The gang spreads out, spans the black earth of the roadbed. Seven men. From the back they look like seven half-men—torsoless legs swinging along in an easy, apelike gait. From the front they look like the celebrants of some arcane and strenuous religious sect. Jackknifed at the waist, their arms hanging loose and swinging. They make scooping motions with them as they move along.

Doing their job.

The grubbing gang follows the patrols—the road scrapers—grubbing out the roots and rocks and things from the topsoil that forms the roadbed, before the sheep's-foot rollers come along and pack it down. The work has to be done bending over. A break-your-back position. It is undignified and uncomfortable, but there isn't any choice. If a man keeps at it for more than a year, something snaps. His backbone takes on a permanent set, and he can't get it out. Young boys come along and work at it for a year or even two and don't seem very much bothered by it. They crouch around for a week or so after they quit the gang to go to work in the mill, or at the filling station, or wherever it might be, but soon they straighten up pretty well—or at least work the slump up into their shoulders, where it won't look so bad. But grown men who do it for more than a year take a permanent hitch. It won't ever come out.

"Shad Goety worked five years on the grubbing gang . . . ," it's their favorite story, the men on the grubbing gang— they tell it around, " . . . then he spent thirty-five years picking fruit—most of it off *high* branches. And when they buried him, they had to hinge the coffin and jackknife it to get him in." They laugh every time.

Only Mr. McAllister is the exception to the rule.

He is a great, dignified, bear of a man who has worked nearly twenty years on the grubbing gang, but when quitting time comes he stands up straight as an arrow and walks to the truck like a man in a hurricane with the wind at his back. Dignity personified. And dignity triumphant. Even his clothes don't diminish him.

His bib overalls come from Shotford's Grocery Store and Filling Station, and his snapbrim straw hat from the same place. They are the same that everybody else in McAfee County wears, though Mr. McAllister has decorated his hat with a snakeskin band he made himself. Still, even with the band, it is the same kind of hat that stands on the top counter in Shotford's in nesting stacks three and four feet high. He wears no shirt at all for about half of the year. In the fall and early spring he has a long-sleeved flannel shirt that is red-and-black-checkered. For really cold days he puts on a cardigan sweater that his woman knitted for him out of purple wool. Though most of the men grub barehanded, Mr. McAllister wears white work gloves with blue knit ribbing at the cuffs.

Everyone calls him *Mister* McAllister. That's because of his own manner of speaking. "*Mister* Richwine . . . ," he will say. Or, "*Mister* Glanders . . ." Everyone is *Mister* to Mr. McAllister.

Mr. McAllister himself doesn't understand his own dignity. *He* thinks that the thing that sets him apart is his cigarette holder.

It is a cheap plastic one that he grubbed up in the roadbed one day a year or so after he joined the gang. When he first found it, he didn't know exactly what it was.

"What you reckon, Mister Richwine?" he said.

Dropline looked at the red plastic cylinder, holding it at arm's length, then drawing it up close. He pumped it in and out a couple of times, with the other men standing around watching him. "Cigarette holder," he said.

Mr. McAllister's eyebrows went up. "Shit you say," he said. "Red?"

Dropline pumped it in for another look. "Yes," he said.

Mr. McAllister took it back, holding it at arm's length. "Black," he said. "President Roosevelt. He had him a black one."

The only man Mr. McAllister had ever known to use a cigarette holder was President Franklin Delano Roosevelt, and he had had to go back a good many years to his green salad days to dig up that recollection.

Old Mr. McAllister, Mr. McAllister's father, had not been a churchgoing man, and religion had never been a strong part of his early training as a boy—just what his mother could work in on the sly when the father wasn't around. The old man's main interest had been politics. And, next to Huey Long, Franklin Delano Roosevelt had been his man. They didn't have the Praying Hands picture on the wall, or the Blond Jesus, or any of that kind of thing, but over the mantelpiece there had been a likeness of the President, painted on a cedar slab. Whenever he got drunk, old Mr. McAllister would take down the slab and talk to it—telling it his troubles. Mr. McAllister had the idea that his father was praying, and for a while he had gotten Roosevelt and God mixed up.

But God didn't have a cigarette holder.

After he had found the holder in the road, he took it home and polished it up with wax until it looked like new, and from that time on he was never without it. He kept it in his mouth while he was grubbing, for he was afraid that it would fall out of the pencil pocket of his overalls, and that it might get broken if he kept it in another pocket.

Now and then a young boy, new to the grubbing gang, would try to kid him about it, because most of them weren't used to seeing anybody really using a cigarette holder either. Mr. McAllister never lost his temper when it happened. He took them seriously and tried to answer their chatter rather than fend them off. Generally that worked. Just the same, every now and then a really deep-dyed cretin would come along—one who lived ninety percent of his life out of his spinal column—and he would keep it up and keep it up until even Mr. McAllister couldn't stand to hear it anymore.

"Hey, Mr. McAllister," said Dee Witt Toomey, the young boy on the gang in the summer of 1956, "how come you roll your own cigarettes when you got that fine holder?"

Mr. McAllister put the Bugler packet back into the front pocket of his overalls. He held the cigarette daintily in the fingers of his right hand and licked the seam.

"I seen a picture once," said Mr. McAllister, not looking at Dee Witt, but keeping his eyes on the cigarette, "in a magazine. It showed the inside of one of them cigarette plants. All you could see was cigarettes. Looked like they was a million of them. The words under the picture said they made a hundred thousand of them a day."

He put the cigarette carefully into the holder and lit it with a wooden kitchen match, snapped on his thumbnail.

"Anything that they make a hundred thousand of them a day," he said, "I don't want it."

Dee Witt thought this over for a while. Thinking was mostly a physical act for Dee Witt. He had to get his whole body in on it. You could almost trace the progress of his idea as he worked it up his ganglia, compressing and compacting it and squeezing it up toward his brain—getting it into a shape he could recognize. You finally expected to see something pop out of his mouth—like a Ping-Pong ball in a comic magic act.

"I bet they make a million of them Razorback overalls you're wearing every day," he said at last.

"May be," said Mr. McAllister, "but they's all Shotford's got. I got no choice. Don't count when you got no choice. When I got my choice, one of a thing is what I want."

The reply put Mr. McAllister out of Dee Witt's range, so he had to button up and go off without trying to make a reply. But he brooded about it for the rest of the day, and the next day he worked around until he got a chance, then he snatched the holder out of

Mr. McAllister's mouth and ran off a little ways down the road.

"I got it now," he said. He held it up where Mr. McAllister could see it, in both hands, as if he was going to break it.

"Mr. Toomey . . . ," said Mr. McAllister.

"I got it now," said Dee Witt. "It's mine. Finders keepers." The way he was holding it, it looked like he was going to snap it in two.

Mr. McAllister had a rock in his hand that he had grubbed up. Before anyone could think what he was doing, he reared back and threw it. It caught Dee Witt just over his right eye with a hard, plonking sound. Dee Witt fell over backward, sprawling out, with the cigarette holder still in his right hand.

Mr. McAllister walked up to him, pulling out a marking stake that he kept in his pocket in case of snakes when he had to go into the woods for a piss call. He reached down and took the cigarette holder gently, lifting it out of Dee Witt's hand. Then he looked at the holder and at Dee Witt, back and forth, with his face swelling up and turning red like a balloon. Finally he raised the marking stake high up over his head and brought it down right in the middle of Dee Witt's forehead. The sound was duller—duller but harder— than the sound the rock had made. Dee Witt flinched his arms and legs when Mr. McAllister hit him, then he just lay there with his eyes rolled up into his head.

Mr. McAllister looked up at the other men, who were all watching him. "He oughtn't . . . ," he said. Then he put the holder in his mouth and walked off into the pine trees.

It took three days for them to find him out in the swamp, and another day to convince him that Dee Witt wasn't dead. If the law had come into it, he would have gone to jail. Dee Witt's eyes didn't roll back down to the right place for a month, and he never did see too well afterward, but other than that he wasn't really put out by it. The men on the grubbing gang decided that anything that happened to Dee Witt's head was bound to be an improvement, and when they saw he wasn't going to die, they handled the whole thing so the sheriff never got onto it, bringing Mr. McAllister out of the swamp and back to the grubbing gang. Good grubbing men were hard to find.

And Mr. McAllister was a good man.

He enjoyed his work. Finding the cigarette holder had opened up the possibilities of grubbing for him, and he began to notice the things that he found in the roadbed. Strange-shaped rocks and pieces of roots, buttons, arrowheads, and bones of animals. Best of all, mysterious objects he had to puzzle over and figure at without ever being able to settle *what* they were.

"What you reckon, Mr. Richwine?" he would say, holding up something that he had found, and turning it around for Dropline to see. "Petrified wood?" Petrified wood was his favorite. "See there. Like it's got a grain in it?" He would trace it out with his finger. "And a knot."

Dropline would take it and look at it. "Could be it was petrified wood, Mr. McAllister," he'd say. "I wouldn't want to say."

So Mr. McAllister would drop it into his pocket and take it home to add to his collection. He had a whole cupboard full of cigar boxes filled with things he had found just like that in the roadbed. One box was filled with arrowheads. Another was filled with buttons. Another was filled with teeth. The best one of all was the one that was filled with things that he never could figure out. That was his favorite. He would often take it down at night and go through the things, trying to decide what they were. Every now and then he would finally classify something—a piece of petrified wood that turned out to be just a rock—and it always saddened him to have to take it out of the mystery box and put it into one with a label on it.

Singularity—that was the quality that he prized above all others. It was the key to his character.

Some people said that the most singular thing he had in his whole house was Dora, his albino woman. She was one of a kind too.

The grubbing gang swore that he had grubbed her up out of the bottoms when the county road went through to Fancy Station. The truth is that he found her in the Trailways bus depot at Rainbow, broke and crying, sitting on a cardboard box tied up with string. That had been in the early fall of 1956.

"I ain't never seen no eyes like that before," he said, crouching a little as he stood before her, his cigarette holder gripped in his front teeth, the corners of his mouth pulled up tight in the shape of a smile.

She gave him a long, dead look. "You kiss my ass," she said.

"Miss your bus?" he asked.

She shook her head, then looked away from him.

"Stranded?" he asked.

She nodded.

"Broke?"

She nodded again.

"Shit," he said. "Wouldn't you know?"

He stood looking at her.

"Albino," she said.

"What?" he said.

"I'm a albino," she said.

"Oh," he said.

"I'm a albino, so I got eyes like that."

He nodded.

"You satisfied?" she said.

He nodded again. "Yes'm," he said.

He looked at her for a while. "I got no money to help you with," he said. "I could put you up for the night."

She swung her pale eyes back to his. Her face was streaked from the crying. For a long time they looked at each other straight on.

"I ain't going to fool around with you, lady," he said. "I just wanted to help you out."

She looked at him straight on for a long time again.

"Does it hurt?" he said.

"What?" she said.

"To be a albino," he said. "Does it hurt?"

She looked at him a minute with her eyes wide open. Then she laughed—a high-pitched, tearing sound. "No," she said. "It don't hurt a bit."

He laughed with her. "I thought so," he said.

After a while she wiped her eyes with her handkerchief and stood up. "Well," she said, "it's the best offer I've had. I ain't no Little Miss Fauntleroy. I guess it beats sitting here on my ass watching the cars go by."

"Yes," he said.

She picked up her cardboard box.

"Here," said Mr. McAllister, "I'll take that." He took the box from her arms. "Jesus," he said, "you sure are traveling light. Your clothes don't weigh nothing at all."

"Ain't clothes," she said.

"What is it?"

"Cotton," she said. "Finest long-staple cotton."

"Cotton?" he said. "What for?"

"Stuffing dolls," she said. "I make dolls, and the cotton is what I stuff them with. Good cotton is hard to find."

"I'll be real careful not to drop it," he said.

She looked at him and smiled. "You do that," she said.

"My name's McAllister," he said, shifting the cardboard box under his left arm, and putting out his right.

"Pleased to meet you, Mr. McAllister," she said, shaking his hand. "Mine's Dora."

"Yes," he said.

"How far is it to your house, Mr. McAllister?" she asked.

"Three mile," he said.

"Kiss my ASS," she said, trudging after him.

After they had lived together for about three years—it was the fall of 1959—Mr. McAllister asked Dora what she thought about getting married.

"I don't mind much one way or the other," she said. "I'll do it if it bothers you."

"We going to get married, we got to have us a ring to get married with," he said. He clamped the cigarette holder in his teeth the way Roosevelt used to do it. His head tilted back a little, the corners of his lips pulled up, showing the teeth at the sides of his mouth. His expression came close to being arch—as close as his dignity would let him. He was not an ironic man.

"How we going to get a ring?" asked Dora. "You going to grub one up out of the swamp for me?"

He had.

"Reckon this would do?" he asked. He held out a gold ring with a Masonic signet on it. "It ain't a wedding ring, but it *is* real gold. You could turn it so just the gold part showed."

Dora shrank from the ring. "I ain't going to put that thing on *my* finger," she said.

"What you mean?" he asked.

"That's a Mason ring," she said.

"I know that," he said. "You'd have to turn it around."

"My daddy was a Mason," she said. "He told me what they do to people who learn their secrets and they ain't Masons too."

"You wouldn't be learning no secrets, Dora," he said.

"Same thing," she said, "same thing."

He held the ring out to her, almost in her face. She shrank from it, fending him off with her hand.

"Put it up! Put it up, god damn it!" she said.

"You ain't no Mason!" he said.

"That's it! That's it!" she said.

Mr. McAllister gave the ring a long look, then he put it on the windowsill in the kitchen. He went to bed without saying any more about it.

For a week the ring stayed where he had laid it and for a week barely a word passed between them. Finally, seeing it hurt his feelings so much, Dora braided a cord out of white sewing thread, looped it through the ring, and put it around her neck. She wore it beneath her clothes where no Mason could see it, but it seemed to satisfy Mr. McAllister, and he began to speak to her again.

In the summer of 1963, Dora's birthday fell on a weekend, Saturday, June 22. Mr. McAllister planned a special treat for her.

"Look," he said when he came in from work on Friday evening. In his outstretched right hand were two bus tickets.

"What you got there?" asked Dora.

"Your birthday present," he said. "Two tickets to Tybee Beach. Round trip."

"We can't afford no trip to Tybee Beach," said Dora.

"And that ain't all," said Mr. McAllister. "This is for when we get there." He pulled two five-dollar bills out of his left pocket and waved them before her eyes.

"And this," he said, putting the tickets and the five-dollar bills on the kitchen table, and pulling a half-pint of Hickory Hill bourbon from his hip pocket, "is for when we get back." He put it on top of the tickets and the bills.

Flexing his knees and rocking back and forth slightly, he stood with his hands clasped behind his back.

"Happy Birthday, DORA," he said.

"Kiss my ass," she said.

They walked in the three miles to the Trailways bus depot at Rainbow, starting out at first light, since they weren't sure when the bus would arrive. It came at ten.

Mr. McAllister wore overalls and a red-and-green-checkered sport shirt with a wide collar, buttoned at the neck. Dora wore a purple voile dress. As they walked, Mr. McAllister dropped behind so he could watch her body moving inside the purple nimbus of the dress, silhouetted by the rising sun ahead of her. Every once in a while he would sing the "Happy Birthday Song" to her.

Now and again he would say, "You're a good woman, Dora." And he would add, ". . . for an albino." Then he would laugh.

When the bus came, Mr. McAllister boarded it ahead of her.

"Any special place you want us to sit?" he asked the driver.

"What?" said the driver.

Mr. McAllister took the cigarette holder out of his mouth. "You want us to sit any place special on the bus?" he repeated.

The bus driver looked at him a moment. "No," he said. "You can have any seat you want to."

"Much obliged," said Mr. McAllister.

He walked down the aisle until he found two vacant seats, then he slid into them, taking the one by the window. Dora sat down beside him.

Pretty soon everyone had gotten on the bus. Then the bus driver got on too, closed the door, started the engine, and pulled out onto the highway.

"Tybee Beach," said Mr. McAllister, looking out the window.

The front end of the bus nosed in toward the black shade of the awning outside the drugstore–bus-stop at Butler Avenue and Sixteenth Street. From the cool, green interior of the bus, the passengers stepped out into the yellow-white sunlight, paused for a moment blinking, then slid into the shade.

Mr. McAllister got off first, not looking at Dora behind him. He stepped into the shade and stood looking down the signs over the bars and souvenir shops on Sixteenth Street. At the end of the street, along the seawall-boardwalk, bathers counterflowed slowly in the bright summer sunlight.

"You take this," he said to Dora without looking at her, swinging his forearm back to the left, the palm up. The five-dollar bill was folded tightly and held lightly between the hard, swollen thumb and forefinger of his left hand. "I'll pay for the rides with mine." The sunsquint pulled the corners of his mouth up tight.

"You keep it," said Dora.

"You wouldn't spend it if I do," he said.

"I'll lose it," she said.

It seemed that the breeze might snatch the green bill away, so lightly was it held.

"Put it in your bosom," he said. He pronounced it "*boo*som."

"You keep it," she said.

"It's your birthday," he said.

She took it lightly, holding it away for a moment. Then she made a quick, deft loop with her arm, and the bill disappeared into the front of her dress.

They walked down Sixteenth Street toward the ocean.

"Look!" said Dora.

In the window of the store was a seashell and plastic palm-tree tableau, embedded in plaster of Paris, with a crucifix in the middle.

"Ain't that handsome?" she said.

Mr. McAllister looked down at the pale, watery-colored object, covered with dust in the window. Behind it a gaudy terrycloth towel stood improbably erect. Its colors garish and clashing—bright red and yellow and black. "Tybee Beach, Georgia—Come On In."

"What is it?" he asked.

"A Jesus," said Dora.

They stood contemplating it silently for a minute.

"Let's go look at it inside," he said.

The clerk met them at the door. They were the only customers in the store.

"How much is that there Jesus?" said Mr. McAllister.

"What?" The clerk's hair was dark and shiny, thoroughly combed and parted. In the back a few long strands levered up away from the rest, and when he walked they swayed in a gentle counter-motion, like the tail of a fish.

"The Jesus," said Mr. McAllister. "The Jesus in the window."

"In the window over there," said Dora, pointing.

Together they pointed the clerk to the tableau.

"Ain't it handsome?" said Dora, looking at it in the clerk's hands. He did not offer to let them hold it.

"It's an excellent piece," said the clerk. "Look here"; he pointed to the plastic palm trees with his little finger, holding his hand palm up, the other fingers delicately curled. "And here"; he pointed out each of the features in turn, cradling the Jesus delicately in his left arm.

"And look," he said, leading them over to the counter. He plugged in the cord that extended from the back of the plaster-of-Paris base. Three red Christmas-tree lights lit up behind the shells in the front.

"Oh, that's handsome," said Dora. "That really is handsome."

"How much is it?" asked Mr. McAllister.

"Look what the red lights do to the flamingo," said the clerk, not answering him.

"It's nice, all right," said Mr. McAllister. "How much is it?"

"It's all handmade," said the clerk. "You really don't see many of them these days."

"It's all real pretty," said Dora, "but how much is it?"

"Five dollars," said the clerk. His voice was very quiet and he looked at them steadily, but moving his eyes from one to the other, cradling the tableau in his arm and swaying back and forth at his knees.

"Well," said Dora, bunching her eyebrows together a little, "that's a lot of money."

"It's your birthday," said Mr. McAllister, almost under his breath, drawing his head back a little to look at the Jesus.

"It's a lot of money, though," said Dora, looking at the Jesus, not Mr. McAllister.

"They're hard to get these days," said the clerk, "because they're all handmade. Not many things handmade anymore." He jiggled the plug in and out so the lights flashed on and off.

"It's your birthday, Dora," said Mr. McAllister. "You want it, don't you?"

"But I think we better look around some more," she said. "We just now got off the bus."

"Why don't you just look around some more?" said the clerk, making an expansive gesture with his free hand. "Just go ahead and look around." He slid the Jesus gently onto the checkout counter where they would have to pass it on the way out.

"Oh, it'll be all right for us to just look around," said Dora.

"Don't sell it to nobody before we get back," said Mr. McAllister.

They began to walk slowly down the counters filled with combs and cheap dark glasses and souvenir key chains and ashtrays, spread out in glass-divided compartments in front of the bright beach towels with palm trees and pretty girls and "Tybee Beach, Georgia," printed on them. The clerk hovered along behind them, his shoulders hunched forward, rubbing his hands together.

"Dora!" said Mr. McAllister.

In one of the compartments of the counter in front of them was a pile of plastic cigarette holders, jammed out in different directions—a stiff, shiny nest of them. All with white stems and red, blue, and black barrels. As they looked, Mr. McAllister slowly took his cigarette holder from between his teeth, his mouth going slack. He poised his holder—comparing. They were the same. A pile that would fill two cupped hands.

The sign clipped to the glass divider said "29¢."

"Yes," said the clerk, stepping toward them. "Those are very nice. We sell a lot of those."

Under the awning the wind came in strong and cool from the ocean. Mr. McAllister sat looking at the napkin holder in the middle of the formica-topped table. His hand rested on the edge of the table. Beside his hand lay the cigarette holder.

"Eat your Corn Dog," said Dora.

"They was just like mine, wasn't they?"

"Ain't no two things *exactly* alike," she said.

"Mine ain't as shiny," he said, looking at the holder.

"Your red is prettier," she said.

"But it's just the same, Dora," he said.

"Well," she said, "eat your Corn Dog."

"I ain't hungry," he said, pushing the napkin with the Corn Dog on it over to her.

"I don't want it," she said, "but I hate to see it go to waste."

The napkin fluttered in the breeze, then wrapped around the Corn Dog.

"I ain't having much of a time," she said. "You want to go home?"

"It's your birthday," he said.

"I know," she said. "But I ain't having much of a time."

"Let's get the Jesus," he said.

"I don't want the Jesus," she said.

"I want you to get the Jesus for your birthday," he said.

"I don't want to go back in the store."

"I'll get it for you," he said.

"I don't want *you* to go back in the store either," she said. "Let's just go catch the bus back to town."

"It ain't much of a birthday," he said.

"I ain't never been to Tybee Beach," she said. "And we still got the Hickory Hill when we get back."

As they walked to the bus stop, Mr. McAllister kept talking to her about the Jesus. "We can't just come on down here to Tybee Beach and get you a Jesus anytime you feel like it," he said. "You don't get it now, and you ain't never going to see it again."

They stood under the awning next to the bus, Dora hugging her arms under her breasts, looking down at the sidewalk.

"Will you please go get the Jesus, Dora?" he said. A passenger brushed Mr. McAllister getting on the bus. "Will you please get it for me for your birthday?"

She hesitated, biting her lip.

"You better hurry, lady," said the bus driver. "Bus leaves at two on the dot."

"What time is it?" she said.

"Eight of," said the driver.

"Get us a seat," she said to Mr. McAllister. "I'll be back in a minute."

"Yes . . . ," said Mr. McAllister, nodding, ". . . and the Hickory Hill when we get home."

The bus was just ready to leave when she got back. In her hand she had a brown paper bag.

"That ain't the Jesus," said Mr. McAllister. "What you got in the bag?"

Dora didn't answer him. Instead she leaned out and slapped the man in the seat across the aisle from her. He jumped up in his seat and looked at her.

"You a Mason, mister?" she asked.

"What?" he said.

"I said, 'Are you a Mason?' " she said.

"No," said the man.

"Too bad," said Dora.

She hooked her finger into her dress and flipped out the cord with the ring on it.

"I'm thirty-five years old," she said, turning to Mr. McAllister. She sounded as though she didn't believe it.

Dora snapped the ring off the cord and put it on her finger.

"My daddy was a Mason," she said. She held up her hand, looking at the ring. "Never would tell us no secrets," she said. "The dirty son-of-a-bitch."

The man across the aisle looked out the window.

"What the hell come over you, Dora?" said Mr. McAllister, whispering.

She dumped the contents of the bag into her lap.

"What'd you do *that* for?" he asked.

She didn't answer. Instead she placed the open bag in his lap, then picked up one of the cigarette holders in both of her hands, snapped it, dropping the pieces into the bag. She kept on until she had snapped all of them.

"Seventeen," she said. "Seventeen of them all together. And I got this with the change." She handed him a piece of bubblegum.

He held it limply in his hand, looking at the bag full of broken cigarette holders in his lap.

Dora sat stiffly, her arms folded under her breasts, staring straight ahead at the back of the seat in front of her.

"Happy birthday . . . TO ME!" she said firmly.

She swung her left arm out and tapped the bag lightly with the back of her hand, not looking at it.

"Now," she said. "Throw that piss-ant out the window."

Mr. McAllister rolled a cigarette and put it into his holder. He leaned back in his seat, the corners of his mouth pulled up in a Roosevelt grin. Outside the windows the pines were sliding by under the summer sun, melting into the flats along the highway. Beneath him, the hard, black surface of the road unrolled eastward under the speeding tires of the bus.

Lee Jay's

Chinese-box Mystery

"Why'd you have to do it, Anse?" Dee Witt's voice was whiny and high pitched, like an outraged child's. He sounded like he was going to cry. His face was twisted up in a way that made him look like he was going to cry too.

Anse Starkey didn't answer him. He was sitting on the front-porch steps of his house. Dee Witt stood in the yard, facing him.

"I thought it was going to be just you and me," Dee Witt said, still whining. He twisted his head from side to side as he spoke. "Lee Jay ain't got good sense. He's going to spoil the whole trip for us."

"Lee Jay got money," Anse said. He didn't look at Dee Witt as he spoke. His elbows rested on his thighs, hands lightly clasped together. He was looking at his hands.

"He can't have *that* much money," said Dee Witt, still twisting his head.

"Twenty-five dollars." Anse said it flatly. After he said it he turned his eyes up to Dee Witt. Just his eyes. Not moving his head. His eyes were a light, yellowish green, the color of a seedless grape—a cat-eyed, startling color.

Dee Witt stopped sawing his head around. "Where Lee Jay get twenty-five dollars?" he said. Dee Witt's eyes were blue. White-blue. So light they almost didn't have any color at all.

"Won it on the punchboard down at Shotford's." Anse looked

away again. At his hands. The hands were stubby and strong. Red and puffy with calluses. His forearms had a foreshortened look, tight and heavy. They were red too, with a thick dappling of freckles and a down of curly, orange hair. From under the bill of his baseball cap a lock of hair, darker red, looped down on his forehead. Slick and wet looking, like it was painted on there, just above his right eye.

"You seen him?" Dee Witt asked.

Anse turned his eyes up to Dee Witt again, then back to his hands. "I seen him," he said. His voice was low and quiet, with a raspy edge on it. Out of the back of his throat.

Dee Witt wore overalls that seemed to be too big for him, breaking over the tops of his heavy work shoes, and hanging in loose folds around his waist in the back. He was too tall to get a good fit—even in overalls. The proportions were wrong. Everything about him was drawn out and attenuated—his arms hanging limply at his sides, his waist, which looked to be two or three inches below the place where it should have been. Even his skull was long and narrow. Set at an odd angle on the end of his ropy neck. There was more bone than muscle to him, with thick wrists and big hands. A large man, awkward and angular, with pasty-colorless hair. Too white and powdery. And eyebrows that were nothing more than white spots on his red face.

"That's a lot of money," Dee Witt said, not sawing his head now.

"Yes," said Anse.

"We got to take him too?" Dee Witt asked.

"You want me to knock him in the head?" Anse asked, looking up at Dee Witt.

"Wouldn't be no trouble for you to figure a way if you put your mind to it," Dee Witt said.

"It ain't worth the trouble," Anse said.

"We been planning this trip for a month," Dee Witt said. "Why we got to spoil it dragging Lee Jay around?"

"Lee Jay won't be no trouble," Anse said.

"Lee Jay ain't nothing *but* trouble," said Dee Witt. "He don't know shit from apple butter. We ain't just going to run in to Kose, Anse. We're going to Tybee Beach. First thing Lee Jay is going to do is fuck up everything and spoil the whole trip."

"That's just it," said Anse, looking at Dee Witt.

"I know that's just it," said Dee Witt. "That's what I'm saying. So why'd you have to go and get him to come along with us? What you mean 'That's it'?"

"I mean Lee Jay's always fucking up, but he does it funny," said Anse. "We're going to have us a good time with him."

"Let's save us the good time for when we ain't going to Tybee Beach," said Dee Witt. "You're acting like it was something we all the time doing. I don't want to take no fuck-up with me to Tybee Beach."

Anse closed his eyes and shook his head in a disgusted way. "We're going to have us a good time with Lee Jay," he said.

"He don't always fuck up funny," said Dee Witt.

"More times funny than not," said Anse.

"What if this time ain't funny?" said Dee Witt.

"I'd want to take Lee Jay along even if he didn't have no twenty-five dollars," said Anse.

"But we're going to Tybee Beach," said Dee Witt.

"I'm going to handle it," said Anse. "You leave it all up to me."

"Tybee Beach ain't no place for no fuck-up," said Dee Witt, still sullen.

"You going to leave it up to me or not?" said Anse, the edge coming back into his voice.

"Shit," said Dee Witt.

"Jesus God, Lee Jay," said Dee Witt. His face was screwed up and his voice whinier than ever. "You ain't going to wear *overalls* to Tybee Beach?" Dee Witt looked at Anse. "He's fucking up already," he said.

Lee Jay frowned, pouting his mouth and looking down at his overalls. "Got 'em brand new yestiddy," he said.

"Ain't you got nothing else to wear, Lee Jay?" said Anse, leaning his elbow on the window of the pickup. He was sitting behind the wheel. Dee Witt had opened his door and stepped one foot out onto the runningboard. He spoke to Lee Jay over the top of the cab, ducking his head down to talk to Anse inside.

"Naw," said Lee Jay, taking the seams of his pants legs between his thumb and forefinger and pulling them out to the sides so he could see them better. "'Cept my everday overalls and my church-going suit."

"I seen the suit," said Dee Witt, resting his forearms on the top of the cab and putting his head down on his elbow. "Jesus God."

"How about you wear just the pants?" Anse said.

"Ain't that going to look funny?" said Lee Jay.

"I reckon not," said Anse. "Wear your suit pants and your checkered shirt."

"Oh," said Lee Jay.

"Jesus God," said Dee Witt, his head buried in the crook of his elbow on top of the cab of the truck.

"Go get 'em on," said Anse. "We need to be pulling out pretty soon. Going to take us about two hours to get there."

Lee Jay walked back into his house. He had a hunched, swinging walk, and the same kind of angular body as Dee Witt, only two inches taller. He looked like Dee Witt's big brother, but he was five years younger—nineteen.

Dee Witt stepped down onto the ground, one foot still on the runningboard. "I ain't going," he said. "I told you Lee Jay was going to fuck it up."

"We're going to have us a good time with him," said Anse. "I feel it already."

"That ain't what I feel," said Dee Witt. "I feel like I want to put my number-twelve boot up his ass."

"I told you I'm going to take care of it," said Anse.

"I noticed you was taking care of it just then," said Dee Witt.

"It's going to be all right," said Anse.

While they were talking, Lee Jay came back out of the house. He was tucking in his shirt. Orange-and-red-checkered. His pants were dark blue and shiny, with big, purply spots at the knees and on the seat.

"Got the money?" Anse asked from the cab of the pickup as he came up.

"Yep," said Lee Jay, patting his hip pocket.

"You ain't going down to Shotford's store," said Anse. "Better let me keep it for you." He held his hand out the window of the truck.

Lee Jay hesitated. "I can look after it," he said, holding his hand on his hip pocket.

"Sure you can," said Anse. "I know you can do it. But why don't you give it to me just in case?"

"I can keep it," said Lee Jay.

"But this ain't Shotford's store we going to, Lee Jay. We going to Tybee Beach. Tell you what. You give me ten and Dee Witt there ten and you keep five. We ain't all going to get our pockets picked."

Lee Jay frowned. "How come I only get five?" he asked.

"Well, ten, then," said Anse, "and Dee Witt five."

Dee Witt started to say something, and Anse kicked him.

"Well . . . ," said Lee Jay.

"We're going to Tybee Beach," said Anse. "Better be on the safe side."

Lee Jay drew the money out of his hip pocket. He had folded it up in a handkerchief, and they had to wait while he laid it out on the hood of the pickup and opened it, pulling the folds out carefully. He made three piles of bills. As he laid the bills down one at a time on the hood of the truck, they could see his lips moving.

"Here," said Lee Jay, handing the bills in to Anse.

"Count 'em," Anse said, holding his hand out, palm up. "You might of made a mistake."

Lee Jay counted them into his hand. There were nine.

"How'd that happen?" he said.

"See?" said Anse. "You'd of thought I was trying to cheat you."

Lee Jay started to take the bills back again.

"Lay another one on there," said Anse. "Then count out five for Dee Witt." Dee Witt watched the counting without saying anything.

Lee Jay started to reach into the cab from the driver's side.

"Go around," said Anse.

He counted five ones into Dee Witt's open palm.

"Now see how many you got left," said Anse.

Lee Jay stepped up to the hood again and counted out what was left of the bills. When he finished he looked up at Anse through the windshield. "Ten," he said.

"Get in," said Anse.

Lee Jay walked around to the back of the truck and climbed over the tailgate. He sat down against the window at the back of the cab. Anse rapped on the glass.

"What?" said Lee Jay, turning to look through the glass.

"Move over," said Anse. "I can't see out the back."

Lee Jay slid to one side. Anse rapped on the glass again. Lee Jay's head looked in the window. "What?" he said.

"Button your fly," said Anse.

"I want the white one," said Lee Jay. They were standing by the merry-go-round on the boardwalk, waiting for it to stop so they could get on.

"What the shit difference does it make?" said Dee Witt.

Lee Jay looked at him sullenly. "Lots of difference," he said. "The red one looks funny."

"What you mean?" said Dee Witt, twisting his head and whining.

"I don't know," said Lee Jay. "It just looks funny, is all."

"Jesus God," said Dee Witt.

When the merry-go-round stopped, Dee Witt ran ahead and got on the white horse.

"Get off," said Anse, standing beside him. Lee Jay was climbing onto the merry-go-round.

"I got it first," said Dee Witt.

"You going to keep this shit up too?" Anse said, speaking under his breath. "Get off the goddamn horse."

"The red one looks funny," said Dee Witt, sitting straight up on the white horse and looking ahead. "I told you he was a fuck-up."

Lee Jay came up while they were talking. "I wanted the white one," he said.

"The blue one looks good," said Anse.

"It looks funny," said Lee Jay. "Ain't no such of a thing."

"How about the black one?" said Anse.

"I want the white one," said Lee Jay.

Anse rapped Dee Witt's leg with his fist. Dee Witt didn't move.

"Come on," said Anse. They walked around the merry-go-round looking for another white horse.

"How about the yellow one?" said Anse.

Lee Jay didn't answer.

On the back side of the merry-go-round they found another white horse, but there was a child on it—a little boy about six years old with a candy apple in his hand. Anse didn't ask him. He just lifted him off and put him on the red horse next to it. The child had his hand stuffed in his mouth, and he looked at Anse with big eyes, but he didn't say anything. Lee Jay got up on the white horse, and Anse went and sat down in the swan chariot just as the merry-go-round started. During the whole ride the child kept looking at Anse with his hand stuffed in his mouth. When it stopped and they got off, Anse saw him talking to his mother and pointing at them.

"I ain't been counting on but one fuck-up," he said to Dee Witt as they walked away.

"I told you," said Dee Witt, not looking at him.

All afternoon they walked around the beach looking at the girls in bathing suits, watching them skating at the rink on the pavilion and in the bowling alleys. Two or three times they went into eating places on the boardwalk and got Corn Dogs and beer. Anse and Dee Witt rented bathing suits and went in swimming. Lee Jay wouldn't go with them because he was afraid of the waves. So he squatted on the beach in his orange-and-red-checkered shirt and watched them. Sometimes he walked around looking for shells.

After they had their swim, Anse and Dee Witt took him and let him ride the bump cars and the Ferris wheel. When it started to get dark, they went down to the Brass Rail to see what was going on there.

"This is the best part," said Anse. "Can't come to Tybee Beach and not go in the Brass Rail."

At the entrance to the club was a billboard. On it were thumbtacked glossy photographs of the acts that were performing. There was a rock-'n'-roll band and a piano player and a Chinese dance troupe, "The Dancing Wangs." The photograph of the dance troupe showed one man and three girls, all in very brief costumes. The man was holding one of the girls over his head with one hand, while the other two girls posed with their toes pointed on either side of him.

The three men stood in front of the billboard looking at the picture of the Chinese dance troupe.

"Reminds me of John Fletcher," said Lee Jay.

"What?" said Dee Witt.

"My brother, John Fletcher," said Lee Jay.

"What reminds you of John Fletcher?" said Anse.

"Them Chinese girls," said Lee Jay.

Anse and Dee Witt looked at each other.

"John Fletcher was in the navy," said Lee Jay.

"I know John Fletcher was in the navy," said Anse.

"And them Chinese girls remind you of him?" said Dee Witt.

"John Fletcher is dead," said Lee Jay.

"What are you getting at, Lee Jay?" said Anse.

"When they sent us John Fletcher's things, there was a picture," said Lee Jay.

Anse and Dee Witt looked at each other.

"Yes?" said Anse.

"His buddy sent us his things we'd like to have," said Lee Jay. "His wallet and ring, and all those things like that we'd like to have."

Lee Jay stood looking at the billboard.

"What about the goddamn picture?" said Dee Witt.

Lee Jay frowned. "There was a picture," he said. "Him and a Chinese girl without no clothes on."

"Him and a Chinese girl without no clothes on?" said Anse.

"*He* had clothes on," said Lee Jay, frowning again and raising his voice. "John Fletcher had his navy suit on. The Chinese girl was the one didn't have no clothes on."

"I see," said Anse. He looked at Dee Witt and raised his eyebrows.

"She was kind of squatting down in front of John Fletcher and him standing behind her with his hands on her shoulders with his navy suit on," he said. "She had her legs apart. Just head-on—like that. Pulling at herself with her hands."

"Pulling at herself?" said Dee Witt.

"Yes," said Lee Jay, "pulling at herself. Pulling herself open, you know. It look like it run crostwise."

Anse and Dee Witt looked at each other, waiting for him to go on. Lee Jay didn't say anything. He just stood there looking at the picture of the Dancing Wangs.

"Crostwise?" said Dee Witt.

"Pa said all them Chinese girls got a crostwise cunt," Lee Jay said, looking at the picture.

"I never heard that," said Dee Witt, looking at Anse.

"She wasn't much to look at in the face," said Lee Jay. "Chinese girl. Sure was funny-looking though, with it open crostwise like that. Ma said it were a sin for even a Chinese girl to go showing herself that way."

"John Fletcher's buddy sent the picture to your ma?" said Dee Witt.

"No," said Lee Jay. He sounded exasperated. "He sent it to Pa. In the wallet and things. Ma seen it. She wanted to tear it up, but Pa wouldn't let her. He said he ain't never seen nothing like that before, and, besides, it was good of John Fletcher in his uniform. Ma didn't like it none."

"What did John Fletcher's buddy say?" said Dee Witt.

"He said John Fletcher was dead," said Lee Jay.

"I mean about the goddamn picture," said Dee Witt.

"He didn't say nothing about the picture," said Lee Jay. "He said John Fletcher was dead, and here was his keepsakes."

"What did he die of?" said Anse.

"Caught something in the navy and just died," said Lee Jay. "Pa got a letter telling about it, but we never could none of us make it out. Then Pa wanted to keep the picture and get it framed because John Fletcher was so handsome looking in his uniform. But Ma got the picture and torn it up. We had to all hold him off her when he found out. He ain't got over it even yet."

The three men stood looking at the picture of the Dancing Wangs.

"I'd forgot all about it," said Lee Jay.

"Let's go in," said Anse.

They sat at a table drinking beer and watching the show. After it was over they went outside.

"Could you tell?" Lee Jay asked Anse.

"Looked all right to me," he said.

"They wasn't much to them costumes they was wearing," said Dee Witt, "but it looked all right to me too. Wasn't nothing funny about the man anyways. Did you see the way he throwed them girls around? I wouldn't of thought no Chinaman would have been that strong. Maybe they's a trick to it."

An hour later they were sitting in a Corn Dog place under an open shed on the boardwalk. They had let Lee Jay have two rides on the merry-go-round. Then they had taken him to have his palm read. The gypsy woman had told him that he would take a long trip by water and would meet a dark lady.

"A Chinese lady?" he asked.

Anse and Dee Witt hurried him out of the palm reader's. They had gone into his last five dollars to buy the Corn Dogs and beer.

"Well, look at that," said Anse.

Lee Jay was studying the palm of his hand, tracing out the lines with his finger and mumbling to himself. "What?" he said, looking up.

One of the girls from the Dancing Wangs was passing on the boardwalk. She had on white shorts and a halter, and her hair was in a pony-tail.

"The other two was prettier," said Dee Witt.

"Maybe Lee Jay's going to get his answer now," said Anse, getting up from the table.

"You going to ask her, Anse?" said Lee Jay.

"Maybe better than that," said Anse. "Come on."

They got up and went out on the boardwalk. The girl was a couple of hundred feet in front of them, walking toward the south end of the island where the boardwalk and stores stopped, and the private houses and sand dunes began. It was the place where all the young couples went to do their love-making.

"You going to get your answer, Lee Jay," said Anse as the girl jumped down onto the beach from the low seawall at the end of the parking lot and walked off down the dark beach. Anse's voice sounded excited.

The beach was deserted. Behind the sand dunes the beach houses stood dark and silent. Here and there, through openings between the dunes, they could see a cigarette glowing on a screened porch, or an orange window staring into the dark. The wind and the noise of the waves breaking on the beach drowned out any sounds that might have come from them.

When they got down onto the beach, Anse began to walk faster. There was a half-moon, and they could see the white shorts of the girl ahead of them against the darkness of the dunes. Running in the sand, they didn't make much noise, so she didn't hear them until they were already on top of her. She started to scream, but Anse clapped his hand over her mouth, pulling her down into the sand.

"Help me, God damn it," he said to Dee Witt and Lee Jay, who were standing there watching him. "Grab her legs."

Dee Witt dropped down in the sand, pinning her legs so she couldn't kick them. She was small, but the dancing had made her legs strong. Dee Witt had to hold them hard.

"God damn!" said Anse. "You do that again and I'm going to break your neck."

"What is it?" said Dee Witt.

"She bit me," said Anse.

"What we going to do?" said Lee Jay. He was still standing beside them.

"You don't holler, and we won't hurt you," Anse said to the girl. "Now, you don't holler, you hear?" He removed his hand from her mouth and she started to scream again. He clapped his hand back.

"Give me your handkerchief," Anse said to Lee Jay.

Lee Jay reached into his pocket and took out the handkerchief in which he had folded his money. He knelt down in the sand and began to unfold it slowly. Anse snatched it from him, scattering coins and bills into the sand.

"God damn, Anse," said Lee Jay.

Anse balled up the handkerchief and stuffed it into the girl's mouth.

"Roll her over," he said. Lee Jay and Dee Witt sat on her while Anse got out his handkerchief and tied on the gag.

"Give me your handkerchief," he said, holding out his hand to Dee Witt. He tied her hands together behind her.

"Now," he said. They picked her up, he and Dee Witt, and carried her up into the dunes. They put her down in a bowl between high hills of sand that screened them from the beach on one side and the houses on the other.

"Now we'll see," said Anse. He unzipped the shorts and pulled them off. The girl's body looked pale in the dim light from the moon.

"Come look, Lee Jay," Anse said. He held one of her legs while Dee Witt held the other, spreading them apart.

Lee Jay came up and looked. "No," he said.

"You sure?" said Anse.

Lee Jay looked again, leaning down to make sure. "Yes," he said.

"Let me see," said Anse. "Hold this leg."

Lee Jay stood there looking at the girl.

"Take this leg and let me see," said Anse. He jogged Lee Jay to make him move. Lee Jay took the leg.

"John Fletcher's picture was wrong," said Lee Jay.

"Ain't it pretty, though?" said Anse.

The girl arched her forked body, bending her hips backward.

"Hold her up! Hold her up!" said Anse. "She's trying to get sand in it." Dee Witt and Lee Jay lifted her legs so her whole body was off the ground. She rested on her shoulders and the back of her neck.

"You try that again and I'm going to stuff a cactus up you," Anse said. A bed of them was growing in the side of the dune. He reached down and picked one to show her. It was small and bladderlike, the shape of a little round cushion. With long, needly spines sticking out of it. The girl's eyes were wide as he showed it to her.

"Just you be quiet and ain't nobody going to hurt you," he said, throwing the cactus down, and sucking his thumb where one of the spines had pricked him.

"Maybe we oughtn't," said Lee Jay.

"You done got your answer, now you keep out of it," said Dee Witt.

"Just hold onto that leg," said Anse. He unzipped his pants and hooked his finger inside the fly. The girl made noises behind the gag when Anse tried to penetrate her, guiding himself with his hand. She twisted to move away.

"Don't get ants in your pants," said Dee Witt.

Anse turned to him quickly, glaring.

"I mean, don't get so excited, Anse," said Dee Witt. "Just don't get so excited. That's all."

"Maybe you oughtn't," said Lee Jay.

Anse turned back to the girl. "It's just so pretty," he said. There was a dead smile on his face. "So pretty."

The girl kept twisting and making the noises behind the gag.

"You're hurting her, Anse," said Lee Jay.

"She's going to be all right," Anse said.

"Hurry up, Anse," said Dee Witt. "You're taking too long."

"Make up your mind," said Anse.

"She's too little, Anse," said Lee Jay.

Anse's breath was coming hard now. They could hear his breathing over the noises the girl was making under the gag.

". . . I'm dropping my leg," said Lee Jay flatly. He stepped back. The girl twisted and then kicked, getting her dancer's leg right up into Anse's crotch, catching him squarely. He grabbed himself and staggered backward, bending over. She flicked her leg again, kicking Dee Witt in the stomach, and he backed up too, dropping her leg. Anse was rolling on the ground, holding himself and moaning. The girl turned over on her stomach then got up running and stumbling up the dune with her hands still tied behind her.

"I told you," said Lee Jay. He picked up the girl's shorts and ran after her.

Going down the dune on the other side, she fell, pitching forward and plowing head-first in the loose sand. Lee Jay caught up with her and held out the shorts. "He hadn't ought to have hurt you," he said.

She lay in the sand, looking up at him.

"I'm sorry," he said. "Don't try and kick me, and I'll turn you loose." She lay still, while he rolled her over and untied her hands. When her hands were loose she pulled off the gag.

"Get away from me," she said.

"Here," said Lee Jay, holding out the shorts.

She snatched them from him. "Don't look at me," she said.

He turned his head to the side while she put them on. Then she turned and ran off up the beach with Lee Jay trotting after her. At the end of the boardwalk a policeman was leaning on the rail with his back to the ocean, trying to light a cigarette. The wind kept blowing out his matches.

The girl went up to him. "He raped me," she said, pointing to Lee Jay.

"I never did," said Lee Jay.

"He helped," she said.

The policeman looked at Lee Jay and then at the girl. "Ain't you working down at the Rail?" he said, putting the cigarette back into the pack.

"Yes," she said. "He raped me. Arrest him."

"He don't look like your type, lady," the policeman said.

"There were two others," said the girl.

"Where?" said the policeman, looking over his shoulder down the beach and drawing his pistol.

"Back down the beach there," she said, pointing. "One got his balls busted."

"I never did it," said Lee Jay.

"All right," said the policeman, pointing his pistol at Lee Jay, "you better come with me." He was not as tall as Lee Jay, but he was heavier, with a moony face and pouting, rose-petal lips. His head was enormous, and the hat he wore was two or three sizes too small for him. It was perched high on his head, barely covering his hairline, as if someone had put it there playing a trick on him, and he hadn't yet found it out. It made him look like a man coming home from a New Year's Eve party.

"What about the other two?" said the girl.

"I got to take this one in," said the policeman. "We'll get the other two."

Lee Jay looked down at the pistol, then up at the policeman. "You wouldn't shoot me?" he said. There was a surprised look on his face.

"You just come along and be quiet," said the policeman.

"When you going to get the other two?" asked the girl.

"We'll get the other two," said the policeman. "One thing at a time, sweetie."

"Don't *sweetie* me," she said.

"Let's go," said the policeman.

She turned and they started off down the boardwalk single file. The girl in front, then Lee Jay, then the policeman.

"I ain't done nothing," said Lee Jay.

"Keep your hands up," said the policeman. He raised his voice, talking over Lee Jay's shoulder to the girl in front. "What was you doing out on the beach with three crackers at this time of night anyway?" he said.

She didn't answer.

"Bit off more'n you could chew, sweetie?" he said.

"I never done nothing," said Lee Jay. He had his arms stuck straight up from his shoulders. "You mean you going to take me to the jailhouse?" he said.

"We'll see about that," said the policeman.

"I be damned," said Lee Jay.

They walked along the boardwalk for a while without saying anything.

"Lady," Lee Jay said. The girl didn't answer.

"I'm sorry, lady," he said.

She still didn't answer.

"You ain't going to *apologize* for raping her, are you?" said the policeman.

Lee Jay turned his head back over his shoulder, speaking to the policeman. "I never did," he said. "We just wanted to see if it were crostwise."

"What?" said the policeman.

"She's a Chinese girl," said Lee Jay.

"She is?" said the policeman.

"John Fletcher's picture showed it were."

"Were what?"

"Crostwise."

"Who's John Fletcher?"

"John Fletcher's my brother," said Lee Jay.

"Oh," said the policeman.

"He's dead," said Lee Jay.

"Chinese girl killed him?"

"No," said Lee Jay. "He got sick in the navy."

"Oh," said the policeman.

"He sent Pa a picture," said Lee Jay.

"All right," said the policeman. "That's enough. Crazy talk. I don't want to hear about it no more."

"But I'm trying to tell you," said Lee Jay.

"Well, quit it," said the policeman. "I don't want to hear about it no more."

They walked in silence for a while.

"Listen," said Lee Jay. "I'm sorry."

"I bet you are," said the policeman.

"I knowed it were wrong," said Lee Jay. "Even for a Chinese girl. I knowed that."

"Just keep on walking," said the policeman.

Lee Jay turned his head back over his shoulder again. "But I didn't know it were against the *law*," he said.

The police station was a small, stuccoed building at the end of the parking lot, just off the boardwalk near the pavilion. There was a high counter on one side and a row of chairs against the wall on the other. Behind the counter was the chief, a small, dapper man with gray hair and a neatly trimmed gray moustache. He was wearing a short-sleeved white shirt with shoulder straps. The shirt was open at the neck, and through the shoulder strap on the left side looped the harness of a black Sam Browne belt. When they came in he put down the copy of *Strength and Health* he was reading, snapped on his white police chief's hat, and stood up.

He looked at the girl, then at Lee Jay, then at the policeman. Lee Jay still had his hands stuck straight up over his head. He was holding them so high that his shirttail was pulling out of his pants.

"God damn it, Flatt," said the chief, speaking to the policeman, "you think you bringing in Jesse James? You got the public enemy number one there? I told you it scares shit out of the tourists. How come you didn't shoot him too?"

He turned to Lee Jay. "Put your hands down, son," he said. "He ain't going to shoot you."

Flatt stood looking down at his feet.

"All right, Lone Ranger," said the chief, "what'd he do? Park overtime? Litter a Dixie cup on the beach?"

Flatt didn't say anything.

"Maybe it was something serious, like screwing the Dragon Lady here under the boardwalk."

Flatt was standing with his arm hanging down, holding the pistol.

"And put that goddamned thing up before you hurt somebody," said the chief. "I told you about that before."

Flatt put the pistol into the holster. "She says he raped her," he said.

"I said he helped," said the girl. "There were two others."

The chief's eyebrows went up, and he looked at Flatt. "She kidding you or something?" he said. "You know who she is, don't you?"

"But she *said* he raped her," said Flatt.

"He helped," said the girl. "The others did it."

"Where the others?" said the chief. "I want to see what they look like. Was they climbing trees and eating bananas?"

"Getting away," said the girl.

"It figures," said the chief.

"I had to bring this one in," said Flatt.

"You didn't even try to shoot the other two?" said the chief. He looked at Lee Jay. "Sit down, son," he said, motioning toward the row of chairs along the wall.

"The other two are getting away," said the girl.

"He shoot any tourists?" said the chief, speaking to the girl. "Last time he had it out of his holster he shot himself in the leg."

Flatt's face began to get red. "I ain't never going to hear the end of that, am I?" he said. "I was practicing the quick draw," he said, speaking to Lee Jay and the girl.

"I'd take it away from him altogether," said the chief, "only he'd quit. It makes him feel like Gene Autry."

"Where you from, son?" he said, turning to Lee Jay.

"McAfee County," said Lee Jay.

"How'd you get here?"

"Rode," said Lee Jay.

"Bus?"

"Anse's pickup."

"Who's Anse?" said the chief.

"He's the one owns the pickup," said Lee Jay.

The chief looked at the girl. "He raped you, eh?" he said.

"I said he helped, God damn it," she said. "The other one did it, but he helped."

"You said there was two."

"One did it and the others helped."

"Two helped?" said the chief. "I wouldn't have thought you'd be that much trouble."

The girl didn't say anything.

"Where's it at?" said the chief, talking to Lee Jay again. "The pickup?"

"There," said Lee Jay, pointing out toward the parking lot.

"Ford? Chevy?"

"Ford," said Lee Jay.

"What year?"

"Red one," said Lee Jay.

"Go watch it, Flatt," said the chief. "Go find a red Ford pickup and watch it. Don't shoot it. Just watch it."

Flatt started out the door.

"Flatt," said the chief, "you got any bullets in that thing?"

"Couple," said Flatt.

"You shoot it, Flatt, and it's your ass," said the chief.

Flatt put his hand on the handle of the revolver and started out the door.

"And, Flatt . . . ," said the chief.

Flatt turned back toward him, holding the screen open.

". . . Get someplace they can't see you, will you, Flatt? Hide someplace so you don't fuck it up this time. Please."

Flatt went out without saying anything.

"Looks like pretty slow company for you, honey," said the chief, speaking to the girl. "What happened? The general down at Stewart put your snatch off limits for his soldier boys?"

"Don't call me *honey*," she said. "They jumped me."

"You said they raped you."

"That's right," she said. "Not this one. One of the others."

"Just like that?"

"That's right," she said.

"I don't know if you can make a rape case stick," said the chief. "Might be I could get a judgment on them for screwing a knothole

: *35* :

in the boardwalk out there. Something serious, you know. Judge Lewis ain't going to be too worked up about you getting raped. Couldn't you think up nothing better than that?"

The girl didn't say anything.

"Not this one, you say?" said the chief, nodding at Lee Jay.

"He helped," she said.

"What does that mean?" said the chief. "He hold your pocket-book?"

"Very funny," said the girl.

"I'm just trying to straighten out your case for you," he said. "You know Judge Lewis. He ain't going to buy your story worth a shit. We'll see when Flatt gets back with the others."

"If," she said.

In half an hour Flatt came back with Anse and Dee Witt. There was a satisfied look on his face. Anse was walking spraddle-legged and bent over. Flatt had his pistol in his holster.

"I didn't hear no shots," said the chief, looking at Anse. "What's wrong with that one?"

"I kicked him," said the girl. "He's the one. The red-headed son-of-a-bitch. He's the one that did it."

"I want to see what he looks like," said the chief. "Over here at the desk."

Anse and Dee Witt shuffled over.

"You too," said the chief, motioning to Lee Jay and the girl. When he had them all lined up in front of the counter, he asked the girl again. "Now, once more, honey, what happened?"

"They raped me," she said in an offhand way.

"I know that," said the chief. "You said that before. Details. Describe what happened."

She told him what had happened on the beach.

"He *helped* you," said the chief, nodding to Lee Jay.

"Not at first," said the girl.

"How about that, boys?" said the chief. "What you got to say?"

"I didn't never," said Lee Jay.

"But you was in on it," said the chief.

"He's the one," said the girl, pointing to Anse. "The other two helped."

"Ain't you got nothing to say?" said the chief. Neither Anse nor Dee Witt said anything.

"Say something, Anse," said Dee Witt.

"I got to sit down," said Anse. His voice was so strained they could hardly hear him.

"Okay," said the chief. "You can tell it to the judge. But I ain't going in there with you on no rape charge," he said, speaking to the girl. "Judge Lewis'd throw us out of court. I'm booking them on assault."

"It was rape," said the girl.

"You'll play hell proving it," said the chief, "believe me."

"Can I go?" said the girl.

"Where to?" said the chief. "You going out and try to get raped again? Kind of grows on you, don't it?"

"The motel," she said.

"Should have gone there in the first place," he said. "How come you didn't? You taking a night off or something?"

"To tell the truth," said the girl, not looking at him, "I got a little dose."

The chief arched his eyebrows. "I might have known," he said. "Some people got all the luck. Raped a whore, got his balls busted, and a dose of clap all at the same time." He counted them off, touching his fingers with his thumb. "Now he's got to go to jail too. It's your lucky day, son," he said, talking to Anse.

"Can I go?" said the girl.

"Come back in the morning and sign the complaint," he said.

"You damn right I will," she said.

"Well, boys," said the chief, after she had gone, "you stuck your foot in it this time. She can get you on assault anyway. Maybe she'll cool off by tomorrow. Can you pay her something?"

Lee Jay and Dee Witt looked at Anse, waiting for him to speak.

"Empty your pockets out here on the counter," said the chief.

They put their things on the counter. Lee Jay's pockets were full of sand dollars and seashells that he had picked up on the beach. There was three dollars in cash, but the change had been lost, and the handkerchief, when Anse snatched it.

"What are these for?" said the chief. On top of Lee Jay's shells were three Corn Dog sticks.

"They's nice sticks," said Lee Jay.

"Oh," said the chief. He dropped the sticks on the counter.

"Come on and help me count the money, Flatt," said the chief.

Flatt came up to the counter. They opened the wallets and emptied them.

"I thought you said it was gone, Anse," said Lee Jay, looking at the bills on the counter.

"It is," said Dee Witt. "That's *our* money."

"Christ," said the chief. "How much is it?" He counted the bills. Anse had fifteen and Dee Witt eleven.

"Twenty-nine dollars?" He looked at the three men. "Jesus Christ," he said. "For twenty-nine dollars you could have bought it and had it stuffed." Lee Jay and Dee Witt looked at him.

"What you mean?" said Dee Witt.

"Her going price is ten dollars," said the chief. "Short time."

"You mean she's a *real* whore?" said Dee Witt.

"Son," said the chief, "if she had as many peters sticking out of her as she's had sticking in, she'd look like a porkypine."

"You mean . . ."

"Come around next time it's payday at Stewart and look at them soldier boys lined up outside her motel room. When the tide's in"— he made swimming motions with his arms—"the end of the line is treading water."

"Shit, Anse," said Dee Witt, "couldn't you tell?"

"I got to sit down," said Anse. He went over to one of the chairs and lowered himself into it slowly. Just perching on the lip of the seat. Dee Witt went over and sat down beside him.

"They're going to be blue tomorrow," said the chief.

"I ain't never done nothing," said Lee Jay, still standing at the counter.

"Yes you did," said the chief. "You come to Tybee Beach with a couple of fuck-ups."

Dee Witt looked at Anse. "I told you," he said. "God damn it, I told you." He put his arms on his knees and rested his head on his forearms. "Jesus God," he said.

"Well, anyway, Anse," said Lee Jay, "it ain't so bad."

De Witt looked at him blankly. "What you mean?" he said.

"Leastways we settled it about the Chinese girl," said Lee Jay.

"That makes it all right, eh?" said Dee Witt.

"It makes it better," said Lee Jay.

"What Chinese girl?" said the chief.

"That Chinese girl," said Lee Jay, looking at him, surprised.

"The one that was just now in here?"

"Yes," said Lee Jay.

"The one got raped?"

"Uh-huh," said Lee Jay.

"Boy," said the chief, "that ain't no Chinese girl."

". . . Wang," said Lee Jay.

"The other three is Chinese," said the chief. "That one's a Jap."

"Jap?" said Lee Jay.

"Jap," said the chief.

"Well," said Lee Jay, "what's the difference?"

All three men were looking at the chief. Flatt was looking at him too.

"All the difference in the world, son," said the chief. "All the difference in the world. I thought everybody knew that." His eyebrows were arched, and he looked from one of them to the other. Then he held up his hand, wiggling his finger in a side-to-side motion. "Chinese girls got a crossways cunt," he said.

The Dreamer

1956: SUMMER

Royall Lyme.

John Fletcher unscrewed the cap and held the bottle of cologne to his nose.

He had to smell it twice.

It wasn't like lemons at all.

He put the bottle back into the carton and walked down between the shelves to the prescription counter.

Mr. Lane was waiting on a customer. Filling a prescription. The customer was a tall, straight-backed man, with a red, seamed-up face, and eyes that didn't let go the sunsquint, even inside the drugstore with the sun going down behind the building outside.

Mr. Lane stood waist deep behind the counter. A short, stocky man, with thick-lensed glasses that washed and blurred his eyes when he moved his head. And thin black hair that he plastered down and combed forward to cover the bald part of his head in the front.

John Fletcher stood to one side, waiting for Mr. Lane to finish waiting on the farmer.

"One now. Then one before meals and at bedtime," he said. "It's on the label. Right there." He pointed with his finger, holding the box up between his thumb and index finger. He talked as though he hadn't sold it yet.

The farmer nodded. He stood with his arms folded inside the bib of his overalls. "How much will it be?" he said.

Mr. Lane stood looking at the little box on the counter. He drummed his fingers two or three times. "Three-fifty," he said. His voice went up on the "fifty," and he leaned on the counter stiff-armed with both hands.

The farmer looked at Mr. Lane for a minute without saying anything. Then he picked up the little box, holding it lightly between his thumb and first finger, squinting to read the label. His hands were big, with puffy fingers, but he held the box daintily, seeming almost not to touch it.

"Kind of . . . ," Mr. Lane went hoarse and stopped to clear his throat. "Kind of high," he said, looking at the box in the farmer's hand.

"But that's what Smoaks . . . You know, it's got to be the best there is. Smoaks knows his business." He had shifted his eyes to the customer's while he was talking. Now he looked back at the box, poised lightly between the farmer's thumb and finger.

"Three-fifty . . . ," he said, his voice going down.

"Yes," said the farmer, still looking at the box, but holding it at arm's length, not close enough to be able to read the label.

"Three-fifty is pretty damned . . . high . . . ," Mr. Lane said, leaning stiff-armed, looking down at the counter, "But . . ."

The farmer didn't say anything. He was holding the box at arm's length.

Mr. Lane wrote out the figures on the counter with his finger, coming back to put on the $ with a flourish. "Three-fifty . . . ," he said.

The farmer put the box back down on the counter, then fished a wallet out of the hip pocket of his overalls and counted out four ones on the prescription counter, drawing them out between his fingers to take away the creases, and putting them down in a pile, all the same side up and facing the same way.

Mr. Lane rang up the sale on the cash register and took a half-dollar out of the drawer. He put it down on the counter beside the bills, snapping it down flat like a tiddledywink. The farmer took it and put it into his pocket, ramming his hand all the way to the bottom. Then he picked up the pillbox, holding it in the open palm of his hand, close up to the bib front of his overalls, the way he would carry a baby bird. He was looking down into his hand as he walked away.

After he had gone, Mr. Lane picked up the four bills, put them into the drawer of the cash register, and shoved it closed hard, making it bang.

John Fletcher sidestepped over to the place in front of the counter, holding the aftershave carton in both hands. Then he dropped one hand to his side and put the carton on the counter with the other. Jerky movements, as if he were counting off numbers to himself. As he put it down on the counter, he made a small bow, nodding his head to Mr. Lane.

Mr. Lane stared at the carton without looking up at John Fletcher. He was still leaning stiff-armed on the counter. "Dollar and a half," he said.

"I guess he wanted something for nothing," he said. "Like they always do."

"What?" said John Fletcher.

"You get to be a bleeding heart and you ain't going to be in no business around here," he said. "Not for long you ain't."

"Um," said John Fletcher.

"It ain't my goddamned fault his woman's sick," he said. "Smoaks can kiss my ass anyway." He raised his hands to his mouth, making a megaphone. "Kiss my ass, Smoaks," he said, whispering it like a yell, aiming it out through the front windows of the store. "Kiss my ass, Smoaks . . . ," he whispered a second time, ". . . you mother-fucker."

He dropped his hands to his sides. "Smoaks is a mother-fucking son-of-a-bitch," he said to John Fletcher, not whispering it.

"He is?" said John Fletcher.

"Just write it out and send him on in here," he said. "Then it's Lane's goddamn problem. What he wanted was a bottle of Black Draught anyway. Some B-C powders and a swig of Black Draught to wash it down. And after that a spoonful of sugar with some turpentine in it, and a mustard plaster to sleep on. Smoaks knows that, God damn his ass. But he's got to go and write him a high-class prescription, so he'll take him serious and know she's sick."

"His wife's sick?" said John Fletcher.

"Ain't I heard that before?" said Mr. Lane. "His wife's sick. His wife's sick. I wish Smoaks would come in here right now," he said. "I wish he'd just come right in through that door right there." He pointed to the glass door at the front of the store. John Fletcher turned to look where he was pointing. "You know what I'd do?" he said.

John Fletcher looked at him a minute. "Beat his ass?" he said.

Mr. Lane looked at him. "It ain't my goddamn fault his woman's sick," he said.

"No," said John Fletcher, looking at the carton of aftershave on the counter, "it certainly ain't your fault."

"Them pills I gave him," he said. "You see them goddamn pills I gave him?"

John Fletcher nodded. "I saw the box," he said.

"Five dollars," said Mr. Lane. He held up his hand, the fingers spread apart. "I can show you," he said. "I should have charged him five dollars. I let him have those pills for cost."

John Fletcher nodded again. "Ah," he said. Drawing it out, "Ahhhh . . ."

Mr. Lane dropped his eyes to the counter again. "Maybe I should have asked him for the five. He'd be going to piss and moan about it anyways. All over McAfee County. 'Five dollars. Five dollars.' I could hear him now."

". . . him now," said John Fletcher, nodding.

"I can show you the invoice. Five dollars is what I'm *supposed* to charge him. Just what I paid for them. I could get in trouble letting them go at cost like that. That's a fair-trade item," he said, lowering his voice and nodding his head.

"You certainly wasn't obliged to do it," said John Fletcher, nodding with him. "I could see that, all right."

"He wanted to piss and moan over the three-fifty, too. What does he know? Only he wasn't sure."

"Nobody would expect you to give them away," said John Fletcher.

"He'll be back for a bottle of Black Draught and some B-C tomorrow anyway," he said.

". . . anyway," said John Fletcher.

Mr. Lane looked down at the carton of aftershave on the counter. "Royall Lyme?" he said.

John Fletcher straightened up, giving a little bow and nodding his head. He cleared his throat.

"I don't sell much of that," said Mr. Lane. "You out to get you some pussy?"

John Fletcher jumped when he said it. Then scuttered his eyes from side to side and looked down at the counter. He cleared his throat again, but didn't answer.

Mr. Lane unscrewed the cap and held it to his nose. "Can't hardly smell it," he said. He looked at John Fletcher, then held it to his nose again. "Don't smell like lemons," he said.

"I just thought it might be I would try it," said John Fletcher.

Mr. Lane put the cap back on and then he put the bottle back into the carton.

"Royall Lyme is a dollar and a half," he said.

"Yes, sir," said John Fletcher.

"You want something else?"

John Fletcher looked at the carton of aftershave for a minute. He cleared his throat. "Yes," he said, not looking at Mr. Lane. He looked back over his shoulder. There was no one else in the store.

He leaned on the counter with his elbows, his hands clasped together. "I was going to stop at Kasher's," he said.

"What?" said Mr. Lane loudly. "Speak up."

"Kasher's Shell Station . . . out on Seventeen," said John Fletcher.

Mr. Lane stood leaning on the counter, looking at him.

"He's got a machine . . ."

"What are you talking about, John Fletcher?" said Mr. Lane.

"Kasher's . . . ," said John Fletcher.

"I mean what are you *talking* about?" Mr. Lane said, interrupting him. "I know where Kasher's is at."

"Yes," said John Fletcher, giving a nod and working his lips in and out to wet them. "Well . . . ," he said. He looked up at Mr. Lane, then nodded his head down and looked at the aftershave carton on the counter. He was trying to think of another word. "Listen . . . ," he whispered. He was leaning on the counter and talking into the aftershave carton as if it were a microphone. "Listen . . ."

Mr. Lane looked at him thoughtfully. Suddenly his eyebrows went up, making his eyes blossom behind the glasses. ". . . Rubbers . . . ?" he said. "You want some rubbers, John Fletcher?"

John Fletcher looked up at him quickly, then back at the aftershave carton. He curled the fingers of his left hand around his mouth, nodding. "Yes," he said.

Mr. Lane leaned on the counter with one elbow, bringing his head down to a level with John Fletcher. "What you want rubbers for, John Fletcher?" he said. He spoke in a low tone. Conspiratorial.

John Fletcher spoke into the aftershave carton, not looking at him. "Well . . . ," he said. He didn't say anything else.

Mr. Lane looked down at him for a minute. "No," he said. "No. That ain't what I mean. It wasn't that you couldn't have no rubbers. Only I just was wondering what it was you needed them *for.*"

John Fletcher looked up at him over the aftershave. "Shit, Mr. Lane," he said.

"No," said Mr. Lane. "I mean all of a sudden. Why all of a sudden you got to have a rubber, John Fletcher?"

John Fletcher didn't say anything. Then he cleared his throat and looked up at him. "I'm going in the navy next week," he said. "Thursday. Next Thursday. That's July . . ."—he counted on his fingers with his thumb—". . . July twelfth."

"Yes?" said Mr. Lane.

"I'm going to have to go down to Jacksonville and go in the navy next Thursday," he said.

For a minute neither of them spoke.

"I just wanted to get me a . . . rubber," he said. "If it would be all right."

Mr. Lane looked at him a minute. "How old are you, John Fletcher?" he said.

"Eight . . ."—he had to swallow—". . . teen."

Mr. Lane looked at him for another long minute. He drew an eighteen on the counter with his finger. "Well," he said, "what kind do you want?"

John Fletcher didn't look at him. He frowned, looking down at the counter. "Um . . . ," he said, ". . . um . . ." He looked up at Mr. Lane. "I want the best you got," he said.

"I ain't got nothing *but* the best," said Mr. Lane quickly.

John Fletcher looked at him.

"I got all kind, son," he said. "All kind. You name it. I got it."

John Fletcher stood leaning on the counter with his head tucked down, sucking his lips in and out. ". . . all kinds," he said.

"All kinds," said Mr. Lane. He made flourishes on the counter with his finger. "You name it," he said, punching a dot on the counter, then leaning on his hands with his head tilted back slightly, looking at John Fletcher, ". . . I got it." He thumbed himself on the chest. "I even got some French ticklers," he said, fluttering his finger.

"Ticklers . . . ?" said John Fletcher.

"*French* ticklers," said Mr. Lane.

John Fletcher stared up at him, sucking his lips.

"Listen . . . ," said Mr. Lane, nodding his head and winking, ". . . Trojans."

". . . Trojans?" said John Fletcher, nodding back at him.

"Trojans is a good *man's* rubber," said Mr. Lane.

For a minute neither of them spoke.

"Aaaaa . . . re they made in France, too?" said John Fletcher.

"American made," he said, stabbing the counter with his finger.

John Fletcher looked over his shoulder, sucking his lips.

Mr. Lane waited for him. "You name it. I got it," he said.

"Trojans," said John Fletcher.

Mr. Lane nodded vigorously. "Trojans is good rubbers," he said.

"Trojans will be fine," said John Fletcher.

"Wet or dry?" said Mr. Lane.

John Fletcher looked at him without saying anything. He glanced over his shoulder to see if anyone had come into the store. "What?" he said.

"They come in wet or dry," said Mr. Lane. "Which do you want?"

John Fletcher looked at him. He sucked his lips in and out.

"Wet's messy, but it's good," said Mr. Lane. "Wet's a real treat."

John Fletcher looked up at the ceiling, then down at the after-shave carton. He gave the carton a careful quarter-turn to the right.

"You got to have experience to handle wet," said Mr. Lane. "They're tricky. Why don't you try dry?"

John Fletcher gave the carton another quarter-turn. "Yes," he said.

"That's right," said Mr. Lane. "How many?"

John Fletcher cleared his throat. "One, I reckon," he said.

"One?" said Mr. Lane. "One rubber?" He drew himself up. "I

can't sell you one rubber, John Fletcher. They don't come in *ones*."
He drew a three on the counter with his finger. "They comes
in threes," he said.

"Threes . . . ?" said John Fletcher.

"Threes," said Mr. Lane.

"Well," said John Fletcher, "how much is a three?"

"Fifty cents," said Mr. Lane.

"I'll take a three," said John Fletcher.

"Fifty cents for a three. Dollar and a half for a dozen."

"I don't want no dozen rubbers," he said quickly.

"Fifty cents for a three," said Mr. Lane, "and a dollar and a half
for the aftershave is two dollars with the rubbers." He made a two on
the counter.

Mr. Lane took a small red, white, and blue Lane's Drugstore bag
from the stack beside the register. He worked his hands under the
counter out of sight, not looking at them. Folding sounds came up
from under the counter, and John Fletcher watched off to the side of
Mr. Lane's head as he waited for him to make the package. When
Mr. Lane brought his hands up from behind the counter, he had
made a small packet with the bag folded around on itself, so it didn't
look like anything but just a folded-up paper bag. He sealed it shut
with an American-flag sticker out of a little box beside the stack of
bags, then put it on the counter beside the carton of aftershave.

"That'll be two dollars," he said.

John Fletcher reached back to his hip pocket before he remembered he had his wallet in his coat. He pulled back the lapel to get it,
showing the black lining with a gold embroidered label. The coat
was new. He had bought it earlier that summer when he had moved
out of the house away from the family and his father, but there had
not been many times for him to wear it, and he didn't feel sure of
himself in it yet. It was leopard-skin-patterned, a kind of iridescent
green-orange color under the black spots, depending on the way the
light was hitting it at the time, with the black lining and black lapels.
That was the main part of his moving-away-from-home outfit. The
rest of the things he had acquired under the impetus of the coat. He
had made a clean sweep. Black pants with tight legs and no cuffs.
Black Wellington boots. A black tie, tacked with a golden tiger pin.

French-cuff shirt, with black Swank cufflinks. Everything depended on the coat, which he was still worried about.

"I ain't never seen no coat like that before," said Mr. Lane, looking John Fletcher over. "Is it real?"

"No," said John Fletcher.

"I thought so," said Mr. Lane. "It's hard to tell. You sure do see some funny-looking things these days. Crazy clothes. Crazy clothes." He sounded as though he were talking to himself.

John Fletcher didn't say anything. He fumbled the wallet open and took out a five-dollar bill.

Mr. Lane looked up into John Fletcher's face. "I don't mean *your* coat especially, John Fletcher," he said. "You always been a good boy. I was just thinking about *all* them crazy things the kids is wearing these days."

"Yes," said John Fletcher, putting the five down on the counter beside the aftershave.

"Nigger clothes," he said. "We used to call them nigger clothes." He picked up the bill. ". . . you know?"

"Um," said John Fletcher, waiting for him to make the change.

Mr. Lane held the bill by the ends with both hands, the way he would read a newspaper. Then he laid it down on the counter carefully, pressing it out with the edges of his hands. He made a five with his finger on the counter.

"I seen a kid come in here the other day," he said, underlining the five, then looking up at John Fletcher. "Just a regular high-school kid, you know."

John Fletcher looked down at the bill on the counter, waiting with his wallet sprung open in his hand.

"He had on a pair of pants so tight you could count the change in his pocket," Mr. Lane said.

He paused.

"Forty-five cents," he said.

He paused again.

"Forty-five cents . . . ?" John Fletcher looked at him, starting to frown.

"Well . . . ," said Mr. Lane, ". . . anyway. He had on the pants and one of them strapped-around leather jackets with studs and sparkles and hooks all over it." He paused. "I mean just a regular high-school kid. I seen him in here before. Lots of times."

". . . lots of times," said John Fletcher, looking at the bill on the counter.

"Yes," said Mr. Lane, smoothing the bill again. "He picked up one of those girlie magazines off the rack there." He pointed to the magazine stand at the front of the store. "Used to be they'd read *Titter*, but that ain't nothing now," he said. "They got to *see* it."

John Fletcher looked where he was pointing. ". . . titter," he said.

"Used to be a magazine," said Mr. Lane. "*Titter.* That was the name of the magazine. It showed all you could then, but that ain't nothing now."

John Fletcher looked at him, then down at the bill on the counter.

"It was a pretty good magazine," said Mr. Lane. "But it ain't nothing now." He drew a T on the counter.

"I see," said John Fletcher.

"Anyway . . . ," said Mr. Lane. "I didn't say nothing. Just kept my eye on him. Watching. I knowed what it would be. He was standing there with his leg cocked forward like somebody was going to come around and take his picture. You know how they stand like that. Flipping the pages and looking at the pictures. I didn't say nothing. Just watching him. Sure enough, pretty soon—like that!" He made a fist and held his forearm up. "I didn't say nothing," he said. "It hurt me just to stand here and look at him with it all swole up down his leg that way. Tight pants . . . ," he said, ". . . tight pants." He shook his head. "Halfway down to his knee . . . ," he said. "Big as a nigger's . . . You ever noticed, John Fletcher?" he said.

"No . . . ," said John Fletcher, shaking his head.

"You ever noticed how it is a nigger got all that peter and hardly no balls at all? Little bitty"—he curled his index finger into a circle, holding it to his eye—"like it was a couple of acorns."

He leaned both hands on the counter again. "That's a nigger for you, John Fletcher," he said. "All peter and no balls at all."

John Fletcher looked at him, then down at the five-dollar bill.

"Nigger clothes and nigger peters . . . and that Goddamn shake-your-ass nigger music," he said. "It's getting to be a nigger's world, John Fletcher. Everything is getting to be all niggered up." He shook his head. "I done tried it," he said. "Give them something new and clean, and the only thing they are going to do is take it away and nigger it up for you. If it ain't dirty, and dipped in grease, and got a foxtail tied on it, they don't want it.

"I ain't blaming them for nothing like that you understand," he said. "It's just nigger nature. Only you got to know what it is you can count on in this world. That's one thing I learned a long time ago.

"I have dreams about it sometimes," he said, leaning on the counter and lowering his voice. His eyes bloomed and washed around behind the thick lenses of his glasses as he talked.

"I'm out there at Kasher's, and there ain't hardly no traffic at all. Just me. By myself. And then I can hear a noise coming down the highway like singing.

"Humhumhumhumhum . . ." He made the sound in the back of his throat, pulling his chin into his collar, and keeping his voice like it was far away.

"Always from up toward Fancy Station, on the other side of the viaduct. When I hear it so I can tell what it is, it's always 'Mercy, Mr. Percy,' or some other nigger song like that. Can't tell one from another of them anyway. But they all sound alike, so I know it's nigger music just from the way it sounds.

"Then I see them coming up over the viaduct. And it's a big crowd of bucks, singing 'Mercy, Mr. Percy,' or some other nigger song like that, even if I don't understand the words and can't make them out. Because they are kind of slobbering it so you can't really hear the words anyway, except to know it sure as shit ain't no kind of white man's music like 'Stardust,' or something like that. And then they get close enough so I can see them, and they all have on tight pants, too short so their feet stick out like a paddle blade, and wing-tip shoes with the holes cut out. And red- and yellow- and orange-striped coats with all kinds of colored, candy-striped shirts. And big flowery ties. Just looking at them makes my asshole start to sucking on the seat of my pants. And I want to pick me up a tire iron and coldcock the shit out of them.

"Only there's so *God*damn many of the cocksuckers . . .

"And then I see it. What makes me commence to worry, so I break out in a sweat and want to run away.

"They all got their pants unzipped. With their peters sticking out." He lowered his voice. "Just sticking out there on U.S. Seventeen," he said. His eyes smeared around behind his glasses as he moved his head from side to side. "The dirty cocksuckers . . . And they all got a hard-on. Like a big black baseball bat. A yard long . . . or more . . . with the handle end out. Waving around in front of them when they come marching down the highway."

He took off his glasses to wipe his eyes, and he suddenly looked as though his face had caved in. His eyes receded into his head, congealing into tiny blue agates. Too small for his face, and too close together. He looked blank and stark, the kind of face a child might draw with a pencil that has had too fine a point put on it.

"Ain't that just like niggers?" he said.

"It certainly is," said John Fletcher.

Mr. Lane put his glasses back on and continued with the dream. His voice lowered to a whisper.

"There I am at Kasher's," he said. "All by myself. While them black cocksuckers walk up and surround me, pointing all those nigger peters at me and waving them around.

"And their leader—wouldn't you know? Who do you think their leader is, John Fletcher?"

"No . . . ," said John Fletcher, shaking his head.

"I'll tell you who their leader is. It's John Henry. John Henry Greene."

"John Henry . . . ," said John Fletcher.

"Wouldn't you know?" said Mr. Lane. "He's always their leader. He ties a white flag to his peter and steps into the circle and asks me do I want to surrender or be annihilated. That's what he says. 'Annihilated.' I always wonder where the shit would a nigger like John Henry learn a word like that. But that's what he says. 'Annihilated.' Then he tells me I got just one minute to make up my mind.

"And he starts counting me down. 'One . . . two . . .'

"But I got a trick I learned when I was in the hospital with my hernia. I whip out my pencil (Mr. Lane slid his ball-point pen halfway out of his shirt pocket to show John Fletcher) . . . I whip out my pencil, and tap the head of John Henry's peter with it.

"That's the way the nurses do it when you get a hard-on and they're bathing you up or changing your clothes. I learned that when I was in the hospital with my hernia. The nurses told me they never knew a hernia patient get a hard-on so easy as I did. Just every time they come around me, or tried to fluff up my pillow or anything. They couldn't get over it. I never did have no trouble that way. Even after I had the hernia."

He paused and patted his truss with his hand. "Just don't strain nor lift nothing heavy," he said.

John Fletcher rocked up on tiptoes, looking down behind the counter to see the place where the hernia was.

"When I do that," said Mr. Lane, "tap him with my pencil, John Henry's peter begins to go soft, and he drops down on his knees, kind of biting his lip and looking like he is going to die. Then he says 'It ain't no use, Mr. Lane, boss. You may get me, but my men will get you.' He says, 'my men.' That's exactly what he says.

"But I keep on tapping at the head of his peter with my pencil. I know he's the one I got to handle. So I keep tapping.

". . . Taptaptap . . . ," he said.

"Making it go softer and softer. And he sinks lower and lower. But then he says, 'You done had your chance, Mr. Lane, boss. I tried to make you give it up . . . COLORED MEN . . . ATTEN-TION! . . .' And I look around and all those black peters are point-ing straight at me. So I don't see nothing but white teeth and eye-balls and black, nigger peters. And John Henry, he's stretched out on the ground, with his gone all soft like a big blacksnake between his legs, and the white flag still tied to it. Then he says in a gasping kind of voice, '. . . Ready! . . . Aim! . . . Fire! . . .' And I see the black peters are all pointing at me while I stand there over John Henry with only just my pencil."

Mr. Lane stopped. His voice had gotten loud as he came to the climax of his dream, and his hands were gripping the prescription counter so his knuckles showed white. He looked at John Fletcher for a minute; then he relaxed, letting go of the counter and taking the handkerchief out of his pocket again. He took off his glasses, making his face go tight and sharp, swabbing his eyes and around his mouth with the handkerchief.

"And then I always wake up," he said. "I always wake up just when they are about to . . . to . . ." He put his hand back on the counter with the handkerchief wadded up in his fist. "I always wake up just at that point.

"Someday," he said. His voice trembled. "Someday I reckon I ain't going to make it. Someday I ain't going to wake up in time. Like dreaming you are falling out of a building and you don't wake up before you hit the ground. I know it's going to happen one of these nights. Jesus. And them black bastards will go ahead and get me."

He looked down at the counter, gripping it with his hands.

"Oh, Jesus . . . ," he said, wailing it out. He waved the hand with the handkerchief in it, sweeping it around over the counter. ". . . all over . . ." He put his head down and started to cry. ". . . all over . . . I just won't never wake up again . . . Jesus."

John Fletcher stood there at the prescription counter watching Mr. Lane leaning on his arms and crying. His shoulders heaved as the sobs racked him.

Finally he stopped sobbing and stood up again, taking off his glasses and wiping his eyes with his shirt sleeves. "I want you to promise me something, John Fletcher," he said, pulling his shirt sleeves out and drying his eyes.

"Sir?" said John Fletcher.

"I'm treating you like a man, John Fletcher," he said. "This is just between us. You understand?"

"Yes, sir," said John Fletcher.

"Call me Fred," said Mr. Lane.

John Fletcher leaned down on the counter, speaking into the aftershave carton. "Fred," he said.

"Yes," said Mr. Lane. "I want you to make me a solemn promise and swear you ain't never going to have nothing to do with no niggers when you get in the navy. Man to man," he said. "Will you do that for me?"

"Well, it's not that I wouldn't swear, only that's a hard kind of a thing to tell, the way it is now. They don't make them stay off among themselves like they used to."

"Call me Fred," said Mr. Lane.

"Fred," said John Fletcher.

"I know," said Mr. Lane. "I know what you're saying, John Fletcher. But you still got something to say about it. Just promise me you ain't going to sit down right next to one to eat no meal, nor sleep in the next cot."

"I wouldn't do it unless I had to," said John Fletcher, ". . . Fred."

"That's all I wanted to hear, son," said Mr. Lane. "Just keep away from them all you can, but what the government makes you do."

"Well," said John Fletcher, "I could do that."

"Listen, son," said Mr. Lane, standing up straight, with his glasses on again. "I love my country. I fought the Japs in the Pacific. Little slanty-eyed shitasses. I'd of died too, if it had been that way. It was hell. Jungle rot, and them little slanty-eyed shitasses. Three years . . . ," he said, holding up his fingers. His arm was straining so hard his hand shook. "I seen a lot of my buddies died out there while I watched them. And I'd of died, too, if I'd had to.

"Now it's all going to go down a shithole, just as soon as he can do it." He jerked his thumb at the red, white, and blue "Impeach Earl Warren" sign hanging over the prescription counter. He tilted his head back slightly, and his eyes blurred upward behind the glasses. "The dirty cocksucker," he said.

"But for God's sake, John Fletcher," he said, looking at him across the counter, "you got to promise me just one thing for sure." He drew himself up sternly behind the counter. "I been through it," he said. "I know."

"Yes, sir . . . Fred?" said John Fletcher.

"You listen to me, son," he said. "I been through it. More than anything else above all. There's just one thing I got to hear you say you ain't going to do."

"Well," said John Fletcher, "I wouldn't if I couldn't."

"You listen to me, son," said Mr. Lane. He leaned forward across the prescription counter, making John Fletcher lean forward to meet him. Their heads almost touched over the aftershave carton and the little package of rubbers in the middle of the counter.

"Stay out of the showers with them, John Fletcher." He spoke past John Fletcher's right ear, not looking at him. "I been there, and

I know. Nothing drives them crazy like a white man's asshole. It's almost worse than a white pussy. They'll be on you and up you before you know what happened. I'm telling you, son. I'm telling you for your own good. Watch your asshole, and stay out of the showers with them."

He pushed himself away from the counter, standing up and holding himself at arm's length. "Promise," he said.

John Fletcher stayed bent over the counter, looking up at him from under his raised eyebrows.

"God's listening, son," he said. "God's listening for an answer."

The front door of the store opened, and a woman came in.

"Quick!" Mr. Lane lowered his voice again, bending down toward John Fletcher. "Say it quick."

"Yes," said John Fletcher. "Yes, Fred." His voice was low and whispering, talking into the aftershave carton.

"It'll be all right," Mr. Lane said, slapping him on the shoulder across the prescription counter. "And don't drop the soap for none of them white boys neither," he said. "Some of them got to stick it in every hole they see, too."

He wrote a two on the counter with his finger. "Two dollars," he said. "Two dollars for everything."

With the fingers of his left hand he slid the five-dollar bill back across the counter to John Fletcher.

"This one's on me," he said. "You don't go in the navy every day."

John Fletcher looked at the bill, then up at Mr. Lane.

"Thank you," he said. "Thank you, Fred."

John Fletcher's
Night of Love

"Seaman Williston. Seaman Williston. Seaman Williston."

It wasn't just then that he hated the voice. Earlier, he had. And, later, he would. But this time—not yet. Somewhere under the mucous, adenoidal surface of the words there was a grace note, a musical quality, coming on toward the top. He homed in on it, letting the words float off down the windows of the ward.

He had an ear for grace notes.

"Time to take your temperature, Seaman Williston," she said.

"Up yours, Lieutenant," he thought, ". . . ma'am."

Her hand looked enormous. Man-heavy and freckled. The thermometer—like the kind banks put on billboards, as he would see it from a distance on a hot day. His eyes were squinting. Blurring the hand and the thermometer, and going on up behind them where the high ceilings of the ward receded into the vault of the roof. He could see patches where the plaster had fallen away. And gray continents of mold, like a grainy photograph of the moon. His head rolled sideways on the pillow, making him tighten the squint against the glare from the late-afternoon sun, banging in through the windows on the opposite wall of the ward, like a battery of lemon-yellow klieg lights. A sound of cymbals was in the color.

Still life on chipped porcelain table beside ward bed: Item— glass of water with bent, clear plastic straw leaning; Item—large metal spoon with USN stamped on handle; Item—medicine bottle half full of purplish-pink liquid, handwritten label stuck on crooked.

He framed them in the squint. Watery vermilion of the medicine bottle and the bluish metal of the spoon on the white porcelain tabletop. Part of the spoon handle jagged behind the water glass. The USN magnified through the glass on the offset part.

He moved his eyes toward the foot of the bed, picking up the projectile-shaped container, suspended upside down in a wire frame. Half full, the thick, clear liquid making runs on the sides as the level went down. Rubber tube connected to it underneath into the blocky metal cap. More plastic straws jointing the black rubber tube, with adhesive tape wrapped around the joints. Awkward. But efficient-looking. By tightening the squint he could see a foamy trace of bubbles moving down the clear plastic parts of the siphon into the black rubber tube. The tube falling straight down out of the heavy metal cap of the container, going out of sight toward the floor, then looping back beside the bed where he wasn't seeing it.

He moved his arm slightly, feeling the sting of the needle planted in the vein of his right arm. A vague pain, as if his arm were lying two or three beds away down the ward. He closed his eyes, listening to the sting of the needle in his arm.

"Seamanwillistonseamanwillistonseamanwilliston." Slimy membrane of words, with the grace note lifting and swelling underneath.

The hand and the thermometer came back into focus again. The thermometer looked too big—too big to lift. He was thinking that she might let it fall on him. It would hurt.

"Buh . . . buh . . . buh . . . ," he tried to tell her, pumping his tongue in his mouth aimlessly. A furry Ping-Pong ball he would have liked to spit out.

The thermometer rattled on his lower teeth, jabbing up into the soft, thin place under his tongue. He closed his mouth on it, to stop the jabbing.

His head rolled on the pillow, eyelids fluttering. Everything winging in and out of focus, until he was looking again at the projectile-shaped container hanging in the frame by the bed, and feeling the sting in his arm. A bulletlike container, still half full, with the clear runs down the sides, like a glass of Cointreau half-finished.

A bubble big enough to see by itself floated up from the liquid bottle, the bank of windows on the other side turning it yellow.

Yellow.

Yellow.

Now paling as the sun died, going away. Turning the liquid a pure, translucent lime.

He tightened the squint, moving inside the glass bullet of the container, inside the bubble. Rising and turning. Seeing only the pure, pale, green-yellow of the color itself.

> . . . lime . . .
>   . . . lime . . .
>   . . . lyme . . .
>   . . . ROYALL LYME . . .
>   . . . Royall Lyme . . .
> . . . Royall Lyme.

Not Mennen's. The usual.

Not Old Spice. For special occasions.

This, now. This was a *very* special occasion.

The shape of the bottle. Well, he didn't care much for the shape of the bottle. Too crude-looking where the seams met, and bigger than it should have been for the shape it was. He needed to be ten feet tall before he could use it. Something about the perspective made him feel his size. A small bottle. Better a small bottle, he thought.

And the crown cap looked dull, leadlike. Which worried him. For a crown.

But all the way from the Bahama Islands. He couldn't get over that it was made from limes in the Bahama Islands.

He unscrewed the cap and held the bottle to his nose. It wasn't like lemons at all.

He put the bottle into the carton and started the car. On the way out he stopped by Kose's sometime picture show—the Vanguard Theater—to get his passes signed by Floyd Wehatchett, the manager. The passes went with his usher's job—four a week. He thought that he would put them into the envelope with the money as a kind of bonus for Nettie. The idea of paying her at all worried him—the fact of it. He didn't want to just hand over the money to her—plain bills. So he decided to get around the problem by buying her a greeting card, something with an appropriate verse on it, and putting the money into that. It would make things seem less like a business transaction. The passes to the picture show would be a bonus. He knew she came there a good bit, since he saw her two or three times a week. Never by herself, it's true. But then, if she didn't need them herself, she could pass them on to John Henry as a kind of bonus to him for his part in arranging things.

Floyd's hair was reddish brown, long on the sides and duck-tailed, but crew-cut on top. John Fletcher looked down into the pink shine of his scalp while he waited for him to sign the passes. The manager was thin in an unhealthy, cadaverous way, and to cover it up he bought his coats a size too large, with padded shoulders. If he had worn a big manila envelope, the effect would have been the same—like a two-button sandwich board. He had to walk kind of sideways, with one shoulder down and leading him—as if he couldn't move head-on because of the wind resistance. When he leaned over the desk to sign the passes, his buttoned coat hung away from him so John Fletcher could see right down to his belt buckle.

"Could a colored boy use them?" John Fletcher asked.

Floyd looked up at him from the other side of the desk that filled most of the tiny manager's office. He had a cast in one eye, so his glance forked all over the office. John Fletcher could never tell for sure which eye was doing the looking, and their conversations always made him nervous.

"I don't give a shit who uses them," he said. "Niggers sit in the balcony."

"Yes," said John Fletcher. "I just thought I'd ask."

Selecting the card had taken time. He had canvassed the drugstores in all the towns for twenty miles around. In the end he had gotten one of the first ones he'd looked at in Mr. Lane's Rexall store.

It was a large card with a stuffed red satin heart in an inset. With a good bit of lavender and some yellow, and a dusting of silver glitter scattered all over. Inside there was another heart. Not a stuffed one. There was also a cupid drawing a bow getting ready to shoot an arrow into it.

The verse started with a silver capital, then flowed on down the page in a liquid script. It read:

> *Some girls remind me of mother,*
> *With loving hearts so true.*
> *Some girls remind me of sister,*
> *For the very sweet things they do.*
> *Some girls make me feel sadder*
> *Than a worn-out, discarded old shoe.*
> *Some girls make me feel "gladder"*
> *Than boys could ever do.*
> *There are girls of all stripes and colors*
> *Every kind of hue.*
> *But the girl who is everything to me,*
> *Is the girl who is known as YOU.*

Across the bottom of the card, he had written in purple ink: "*July 3, 1956—A night I will ALWAYS remember.*" He had signed it "*John Fletcher Williston.*" The envelope he had addressed to: "*The Incompareably Lovely Miss Nettie Oatley.*" He slipped the passes into the card, along with the check—he had thought a check more refined than cash money, and had written it out, also in purple ink, tearing up three checks before he got one on which the handwriting suited him just right. The card was in his inside coat pocket, along with the new black Swank wallet.

It was full dark by the time he got home. The headlights of his 1949 Studebaker swept the oaks lining the road. He got a good feeling looking out at the trees as they rushed into the beams of the lights over the nacelles of the hood and fenders which characterized that futuristic automobile. Driving it was like what he imagined it to have been to fly a P-38 in the war.

Some of the trees—the ones leaning out too far into the roadway —had white trunks. The county gang painted them as a warning to drivers. It was a narrow road anyway, and they were dangerous. Everywhere you went at night in McAfee County the low, spreading branches of the water oaks, with the moss hanging down, made you feel like you were driving in a cave. It was lonesome.

As he drove, he sang. ". . . Soooftly . . . as in a MORNNNing

SUNNNrise . . ." He had learned it in the high-school glee club, but had never gotten to sing a solo because Mr. Forne, the director, had kept those to himself—except for the girls. It was his favorite song.

He pulled off the dirt road into his front yard, not swept, but intended to be—bare dirt, with two big oak trees flanking the entrance, and others here and there closing in on the house. He parked his car right up next to the porch, leaving enough room so the second car coming in wouldn't be cramped or have difficulty turning around.

His voice filled the darkness, ". . . SAAWFT—ly, as in an EEEVE—ning SUNNN—set, our love will faaaade aaaa—WAY." He was holding onto the "WAY," but going up the front steps he saw a shadow on the porch. He clipped off the note.

"Who's there?" he said.

"Is she with you, John Fletcher?" The voice out of the shadows of the porch was raspy and high-pitched. The voice of an old man with too few teeth. Slobbery and wet.

"Pa?" said John Fletcher.

"Is she with you?" he said, stepping out of the shadows and into the moonlight of the porch. A small, gnomelike man in overalls. His lower jaw hooked up, caving in his mouth where the teeth were missing—all the uppers. His hair was sparse and wispy, plastered down in sweaty, black tendrils, as if a small octopus was trying to climb over him from the back. His hands were folded inside the bib of his overalls.

"Why'd you have to come over here tonight, Pa?" he said.

"Is she coming on later?" said Pa.

"You got to go home, Pa," said John Fletcher.

John Fletcher and his pa didn't get along. Never had gotten along. Since he was ten years old John Fletcher had known there was some kind of unbridgeable gulf between them, but his pa never found it out. All he knew was that they were father and son—root and branch. "You and me's two of a kind," he would say. He didn't notice that John Fletcher's mouth went tight, and that he always turned around and walked away whenever he said that to him. Most things he didn't notice. His son had been out of the house and gone for more than a week that summer before he missed him. "John Fletcher ain't here, is he?" he said.

No one had ever known Dorcus Williston to have a steady job, though he was pretty good at thinking up get-rich-quick schemes. Some of them were really good in an overall way. But all of them eventually fell through because Dorcus never could get around to working out the details. So it had been Minnie Williston—the mother—who had kept the family together, feeding them and putting clothes on their backs. The old man drove all of them to distraction from time to time. But John Fletcher *stayed* that way. Being the oldest, he had it harder than the other three boys. Dorcus was all the time meddling in his business and getting in the way, putting his arm around his shoulders and offering him homey but stupid advice that he had recognized as disastrous from the very beginning.

So when he got the usher's job at the picture show that summer he talked to Case Deering about the tenant house and moved into it to get some peace and rest.

"I wasn't going to get in the way or nothing," said Dorcus. "I just thought I would stay around and see what she looks like. You know. I had two nights with Maggie Poat once, and I wanted to see if Nettie was like her ma. Maggie was the best there is."

"Pa," said John Fletcher, "this is costing me money."

There was a silence.

"It ain't free, Pa," he said. "I got to pay for it."

"How much a girl like that cost?" said Dorcus.

"Enough," said John Fletcher."Enough so I don't want you sitting around watching us like it was a picture show."

"I wouldn't do no more than just to watch," said Dorcus. "I just ain't never seen a girl like Nettie close to."

"You seen Nettie plenty of times," said John Fletcher.

"With her clothes on," said Dorcus. "I mean I ain't never *seen* her."

"You saw her ma, you said," said John Fletcher.

"Shit, John Fletcher," said Dorcus. "Twenty years ago. Ain't no piece of ass good enough a man is going to keep it in mind *that* long. I just wanted to see what Nettie looked like. You know . . . *tonight*."

John Fletcher looked at him. "I ain't going to share my time with you, Pa," he said. "Get you some money and you can buy her to look at all you want to."

"How much?" said Dorcus.

John Fletcher looked at him. "Twenty dollars," he said.

Dorcus whistled. "Twenty dollars!" he said. "That must be *some* pussy. Maggie was five. I *got* to see what it looks like now."

"Not on *my* time," said John Fletcher.

"I wouldn't disturb nothing," he said.

"Yes, shit," said John Fletcher. "Go home, Pa."

"I ain't only just going to watch," said Dorcus.

"You ain't going to do nothing," said John Fletcher.

"Aw, son," he said.

"Aw, shit, Pa," said John Fletcher. "Save up your money. You can pay for it yourself."

"Twenty dollars?" said Dorcus. "Time I scratched me up that kind of a pile, I wouldn't give a shit no more. It always did take the lead out of my pencil—worrying about money."

John Fletcher didn't answer him.

"Maybe I could get took sick and drop dead tonight, John Fletcher," he said. "Then what?"

"I ain't never been that lucky," said John Fletcher.

"That's a hard thing to say, John Fletcher," he said. "I'm going to be took sometime. It might could be I'd be took this very night. Dead in the morning, and how would you feel then? You got to look at it every way you could. Might be it would happen. You'd be sorry as hell for it in the morning when I was done dead and gone. Too late then."

"Pa," said John Fletcher, "this ain't the kind of a thing that you go and share it with somebody. You sure as hell don't go and share it with your own pa."

There was a long silence.

"It'd be a piss-poor last thought to have of you anyway," said John Fletcher. "I wouldn't want to remember you horny."

"You'd be sorry just the same," he said.

"Go on, Pa," said John Fletcher. "Get the shit out of here. I ain't kidding."

"Jesus, son," said Dorcus. "You got a hard heart."

"I ain't kidding, Pa," said John Fletcher.

"Shit," said Dorcus.

"Pa . . . ," said John Fletcher.

There was a long pause.

"When you going in the navy, son?" he said.

"Jesus wept," said John Fletcher.

"I'm going on home now," he said, though he didn't make a move. "Your ma wants to know. She worries about you, son."

"We talked about it already. She's going to see me off at the bus when I go to Jacksonville."

"She worries about you, son," he said. "The only mother you got."

"Go on home, Pa," said John Fletcher.

"You want me to take a message, son?" he said. "To your ma?"

"Just go on, Pa," said John Fletcher. "I told her already."

For a minute he didn't say anything. "Is this your first time, son?" he said.

"Shit, Pa," said John Fletcher. "Just shit."

"It was just that I thought you might need some advice from an old experienced hand. Somebody to show you the ropes."

"Don't show me no ropes, Pa," said John Fletcher. "Don't show me nothing at all. Just please get the shit out of here."

"All right," he said. "I'm going. Going home right now."

He started down the steps, then paused, scratching his head. "I never told you nothing about none of this," he said, not looking at John Fletcher.

John Fletcher didn't answer him.

"One thing I always found worked for me pretty good. You should blow in her ear. That drives them right out of their mind. I done it to your ma when we was courting . . ."

"Pa," said John Fletcher, "I don't want to hear it about Ma."

". . . She chased me right up that chinaberry tree in her daddy's front yard . . ."

"Pa . . . ," said John Fletcher.

". . . chinaberry," he said. "Lucky. I wouldn't never have made it up no oak. Drove her right out of her mind."

"Pa . . . ," said John Fletcher.

"Just blow in her ear," he said. He tapped his ear with his finger.

"I'm *paying* for this, Pa," said John Fletcher. "I ain't going to have to blow in nothing."

"Yeah," he said. "I just thought you might like to know about it for some other time. In the navy." He paused, looking down off the porch into the yard. "Cigarette ashes," he said. "Cigarette ashes in Coca-Cola. That's high-powered stuff. You got to be careful with that. I knowed a girl torn herself up on a gearshift once." He looked at John Fletcher. "When you get real hard up you can try that. But you got to be careful." He stopped and scratched his head again. "Ain't none of the cars got floor shifts no more anyway," he said.

"Go on, Pa," said John Fletcher.

The old man walked down the steps slowly, putting both feet on each step. When he got to the bottom, he stood there a minute. "Anything you want me to tell your ma?" he said. "She's the only ma you got," he added.

"You going to tell her about this, I suppose," said John Fletcher.

"Jesus, son," he said. "You want me to tell her you're fucking Nettie Oatley?" He looked up at the porch. "I wouldn't of thought you'd of wanted her to find out about that."

"I just figured you was going to do it," said John Fletcher. "It's just about your idea of good news, ain't it?"

"I wouldn't never mention no names or nothing about a thing like that," he said. "I got some sense."

"When did that happen?" said John Fletcher.

"I know how to handle things," he said. "You don't need to worry about me none."

"Just tell her *one* of her sons is fucking Nettie Oatley?" he said.

"I ain't going to tell her nothing," he said.

"Come on, Pa," he said. "You try to hold that in and you'll blow up like a two-dollar tire."

The old man held his finger up to his mouth. "She ain't never going to know," he said.

John Fletcher looked at him standing in the yard at the bottom of the steps. "Just go on, Pa," he said. "Tell Ma I'll be over to see her tomorrow, or the next day."

"Okay, son," he said. "Never a word. Have you a good time." He turned to go, then turned back. "Wash yourself up real good after you finished," he said. "You don't want to go in the navy all clapped up."

"I'll tell you about it, Pa," he said. "Maybe I'll tell you about it."

The old man looked up into the shadows of the porch. "Yes," he said. "That would be nice."

John Fletcher stood looking down at him in the yard. "I might send you twenty dollars, Pa," he said. "After I get in the navy."

Dorcus looked up into the shadows. "You wouldn't really do that, would you, son?"

"You leave me alone tonight," said John Fletcher. "I might do it."

"You could do it with your navy money?" said Dorcus.

"I don't want to be spoiling my evening looking out the windows for you all night," said John Fletcher.

"You got the money?" he said.

"I'll get it," said John Fletcher.

"You figure you going to make you some money in the navy?" he said. "That picture-show job don't pay you enough so you could be taking out high-class whores like Nettie Oatley all the time."

"I'll do it," said John Fletcher.

"Nettie Oatley?" said Dorcus. "You talking about Nettie Oatley? Not some flappy-twatted old fartbag out of one of them piney-woods roadhouses? I done already laid enough pipe in that kind of snatch to run a pissline from here to Daytona Beach."

"I'm talking about twenty dollars," said John Fletcher. "If I see hide or hair of you around this house tonight, you wouldn't get a nickel."

"You wouldn't fuck me up, would you, son?" said Dorcus. "You wouldn't fuck up your own father, would you?"

"You going to fuck *me* up?" said John Fletcher. "I'll do you as I'm done by."

They stood for a minute in silence.

"I don't know whether I'd be up to Nettie Oatley," he said.

"Pa," said John Fletcher, "get the hell out of here. *Now.* Will you, Pa? Before she comes?"

"I trust you, son," he said. He gave an imitation of a salute and began shuffling off toward the road.

"Hey, Pa!" said John Fletcher, shouting from the porch.

"Yeah?" he said, stopping in the yard and turning back toward the house.

"Pa, tell Ma I'll be over for supper tomorrow night, will you?"

"Yes," he said. He put his finger to his mouth again. "Not a word," he said. "Remember. Blow in her ear. Just to prove it works. Don't put no cigarette ashes in her Coca-Cola, though. You wouldn't believe what it would do."

"We ain't going to have no Coca-Colas," said John Fletcher.

"Just as well," he said. "Not the first time, anyways. You got to know what you're doing."

He saluted, then turned and shuffled out of the yard.

John Fletcher watched him out of sight, then turned and went into the house.

All the tenant houses were alike. Functional. This one wasn't in such bad condition, though it was warped over to the side, like it was beginning to want to lie down. Case Deering tried to keep up his houses. Most of the windowpanes were still in, and the front porch sagged only a little. By being just normally careful, you could avoid falling through the rotten planks.

It was built well up off the ground on brick pillars. High enough that a good-sized child could walk under it without stooping over. Outside, it was unpainted clapboard. Inside, the walls were covered with sheet rock, with wide taped joints showing under the paint— salmon pink in the front room, blue in the bedroom, green in the kitchen. All of the colors were pastel and pasty-looking, as though they had been worked into a base of vanilla ice cream. The walls were all furry with a coat of grease and dirt now, with patches here and there where the sheet rock had started to turn to powder and disintegrate. The floors were covered with linoleum rugs—bright yellow, with red and blue triangles that intersected each other. When all the lights were on the glare tended to get up back of your eyes and blind you. In one corner of the living room was a coal stove, painted salmon pink to match the walls. The pipe elbowed out through a flange. It was painted salmon pink too, with weeping black stains at the joints, and more black stains running out from under the flange and down the wall.

The furniture was plain and cast-off looking. An overstuffed couch of coarse cloth, gray with a green fleck in it. One overstuffed chair that looked like the next year's model from the rival company of the one that had made the couch. Darker gray with a brown fleck. End tables at the couch, veneered in some blond wood. One of them had a long sliver of veneer stripped away, leaving the glassy-brown glue showing beneath. Lamps on the end tables. One homemade, from a quart bourbon bottle filled with sand, the shade tan with red and blue ships on it. The other was a vanity lamp, of white plastic that looked like milk glass until you got close enough to see the line of flash along the seam. Potbellied and knobbed. With a white shade, gathered with a pink ribbon at the top. On the wall behind the couch was a large picture in a plastic frame. The lights from the end-table lamps bouncing off it made it difficult to see what it was. A landscape with big patches of blue in it.

John Fletcher had tried to fix the room up a little, though he couldn't afford to spend much money on it. He had draped a crocheted afghan over the back of the couch. His mother had made it, black-bordered squares sewed together, with bright-colored centers. It blotted out pretty much of the gray with green flecks. There were two pillows stuffed into the corners—red and blue satin—souvenirs from Stuckey's, with the "Welcome to Florida" turned to the back. Two ashtrays on the end tables—one from Stuckey's that was chocolate brown with gold lettering, part of the verse to "America the Beautiful," the other from the ten-cent store, a ceramic skull with places in the eye sockets to hold the cigarettes.

He had also added some pictures on the walls—a couple of three-sheet posters from the picture show. One was from a Marilyn Monroe picture that showed her getting her skirts blown up, and trying to hold them down. One was from a Rex Harrison movie, showing him in a dressing gown, with one hand in the pocket, the thumb hooked out. And one was from a Japanese horror movie, showing a giant lizard stepping over a city that was on fire, holding a train over his head in his front paws, and kicking down a bridge with one of his feet. In the foreground a pretty Oriental girl was cringing and looking up at him. The lizard was looking down at her with the red whites of his eyes showing, and a kind of smile on his face. A rapy kind of look.

He had improved on the room as much as he could for this night. Brought a card table out and set it up in the living room for them to eat on, with two kitchen chairs—one straight-backed and wood, the other tubular with yellow formica seat and back—and a checkered tablecloth. He didn't like the color of the room and had decided to cover it up by eating by candlelight. He wanted a wine bottle to hold the candle, but didn't have one, except the wine for supper, which was full. So he used a syrup bottle that had something of the look of a wine bottle about it, he thought. It had a long neck. He soaked the label off, and it didn't look too bad with a red candle in it.

He had set out flowers, red zinnias and marigolds. But the marigolds smelled so bad he had to throw them out. Except for the pink walls, the zinnias looked pretty good. He had sprayed the room with Evening in Paris cologne that he had borrowed from his mother. To cover up the marigolds.

On the end tables he laid out magazines that he had collected for the occasion—*Time, Look, Life, The New Yorker*, and a *National Geographic* that he had found in a trash can behind the library. A couple of paperback books—*Rivers of Glory* by F. Van Wyck Mason and *Sangaree* by Frank Slaughter. Frank Yerby was his favorite, but his copy of *The Foxes of Harrow* had disintegrated and wouldn't make much of a show. On the couch he spread a Sunday edition of the Atlanta *Journal-Constitution*, turned to the book-review page. He had circled a review of a book on Chinese porcelain, making marginal notes like "very good" and "I agree."

He had debated about whether or not to leave the bedroom door open. It wasn't much of a room, and he couldn't afford to re-decorate the whole house for just the one evening, but the blue was the best color of the three. Finally he decided against it, though he hedged by leaving the door cracked open just a little.

The supper menu had given him trouble. Finally he had decided on Salisbury-steak TV dinners. He liked the sound of "Salisbury steak." They would have wine with the meal—Roma burgundy—and coffee after. No dessert. He had a little speech about that. The third draft went: "Sweets I have in great abundance. Nettie Oatley, you are a sugar lump in my eye." He had bought a box of chocolate-covered cherries, in case she wanted something more substantial than the speech.

He lit the oven, then read the directions on the TV-dinner cartons and put them in.

Back in the living room he sat down on the sofa and smoked a cigarette. When he finished, he went into the kitchen and emptied the ashtray and rinsed it out. Then he put it back on the end table. He hadn't thought about it before, but he decided now that he should put out some cigarettes too, so he went and got a juice glass and emptied half of his pack of English Ovals into it, and put that on the end table too. He tuned his transistor until he got some slow music, then put it under the couch, thinking that would be a nice touch—to have the music coming from nowhere.

He lit another cigarette and looked at his watch. Nine-thirty. She had been due at nine o'clock. When he finished his cigarette, he took the ashtray out to the kitchen and washed it again. As he came back into the living room he heard the car and saw the lights sweep the front of the house. He put the ashtray back on the end table and turned off the lamps. Then he lit the candle. It took him two matches to get it burning. Before he finished, Nettie was knocking at the door. She knocked twice, then opened it and let herself in.

John Fletcher was in the middle of the room when she came in. He put his right hand into his coat pocket with the thumb hooked out, dropping the match on the floor and looking at her. He was trying to get a debonair expression onto his face. When Nettie first looked at him she thought he had probably cut a fart.

"Welcome," he said, speaking out of the corner of his mouth, "to my humble abode."

From where she stood at the door, she could see the Rex Harrison picture on the wall behind him. "It ain't so humble," she said, looking at the picture and then at John Fletcher. Her dress was blue. Filmy and low-cut. When she came close to him he smelled magnolias.

Nettie was a good-looking girl. Dark hair, almost black. Thick and long. Her eyes were yellow. Not brown, or light brown, but a golden honey color with sharp green flecks in it. Like a cat's eyes, but not quite as hard. The rest of her facial features were finely drawn, even a little sharp. In fact, her face seemed out of place on her body. Above the neck she was a kind of clingstone-peach soufflé; below it she was all meat and potatoes.

"Come in," he said, going over and closing the door, still keeping his hand in his pocket.

She walked over toward the sofa, pausing at the table for a moment and laying her fingers on it gently. "Very nice," she said.

"Have a seat," said John Fletcher. "And let me get you some wine."

"Wine too?" said Nettie, sweeping the papers into a corner of the couch and sitting down. "You *are* putting it on, ain't you?"

"There is nothing that is too good for a beautiful woman," he said. He didn't look at her when he said it. He looked at the candle. There was a rather long silence, during which he put his left hand into his pocket too, and rocked on his heels slightly, pulling his chin into his collar. "Nothing in this world," he said.

Nettie looked at him. "This is going to be one hell of a night," she said.

John Fletcher stopped rocking and smiled. "I'll get the wine," he said, going out to the kitchen. He still had both of his hands in his coat pockets.

He poured the wine into glasses that he had bought at the ten-cent store, and brought them back out to the living room. Nettie was sitting on the couch smoking one of the cigarettes when he returned.

"I like your coat," she said, taking the glass. "Is it real?"

"No," he said.

"It *looks* real," she said.

"Thank you," he said.

He handed her the glass in his left hand, then put the hand back into his coat pocket. He looked at her for a minute, then raised his glass and toasted her. "To the beautifully . . . To the beautiful Nettie Oatley," he said. He looked down at her. His left eyebrow was raised slightly. She thought he had farted again.

"Shit I reckon," she said. "This is going to be one hell of a night."

She raised her glass to his, tapping it hard enough that some of the wine spilled down her arm. "You can lick it off later," she said, and laughed.

They sipped the wine.

Nettie smacked her lips. "Makes you pucker, don't it?" she said.

John Fletcher gave a number of short smacks. "A little persimmony," he said.

"It's wine right on," she said, taking another sip.

John Fletcher sipped his with his hand in his coat pocket. Every now and then he would take it out, but then he couldn't think of anything to do with it, so he would end up putting it back in again.

"Come on," said Nettie, giving the couch a slap, "sit down and let's us get started."

John Fletcher looked at her. "How about supper first?" he said.

Nettie looked at the table. "Well," she said. "I had me a steak just before I left to come over here. I hate to work on a empty stomach. I get gas something awful." She patted her stomach. "I'm afraid I couldn't eat nothing else. What you got?"

"Salisbury steaks," said John Fletcher. He pronounced it *Sal-is-berry*.

"What kind of a steak is that?" said Nettie. "Something fancy I bet."

"Not really," said John Fletcher. "I thought you might like to try them."

"I'll try anything once, buddy," she said, leaning over and slapping him hard on the thigh.

John Fletcher flinched, spilling wine in her lap.

"You can lick that off later, too," she said.

She reached out and felt his thigh where she had slapped him. "You ain't too solid, are you?" she said. "Kind of pony size."

John Fletcher didn't say anything. He took his hand out of his pocket, then put it back in.

"Don't let it worry you none," she said. "I had all kinds. It don't make no difference to me. Ponies and racehorses and mules. They's all the same."

John Fletcher stood there with his hands in his pockets, looking down at her. He didn't say anything.

"Let's have supper," he said.

He went out into the kitchen and got the TV dinners out of the oven. He wanted to put them on regular plates, but was afraid he would make a mess of it if he tried. So he brought them in to the table in their aluminum trays, with a plate underneath.

"TV dinners?" said Nettie, looking at them.

"Yes," said John Fletcher, smiling with his eyebrow up. "I'm not much of a cook."

"The meat's all right," said Nettie, "but the vegetables taste like shit. I'd as soon eat the box it come in as those green peas there."

"The steaks are good, I hear," said John Fletcher.

"I already had me a steak," she said. She held up her hand, the thumb and forefinger two inches apart. "That thick," she said. "With onions and french fries."

"Well," said John Fletcher. "I hear they're very good."

"Get me some more of that wine," she said. "Maybe a couple more shots of that and I'll get hungry again."

John Fletcher reached for her glass, but she held it away. "Just bring in the bottle," she said. "No need to keep running back and forth."

John Fletcher went out into the kitchen and got the bottle.

She had two more glasses quickly.

"Come on," she said. "We'll try your Salisbury steaks." She got up and went to the table. John Fletcher tried to put his glass down and get there in time to pull the chair out for her. He spilled more wine on the couch, and when he got to her and tried to help, she was already sitting down. She heaved up the chair, getting closer to the table, and put one of the legs down on his foot.

"You got to move fast to keep up with me," she said. She slapped him on the leg again. "Maybe you ought to eat mine too," she said. "Put some meat on your bones. You ever tried taking any kind of a tonic?"

John Fletcher was getting into his chair. He hit the table, and the bottle with the candle turned over. When he lit a match to look for it, it was lying in his plate.

"Now you got to take mine," said Nettie. "I done had me a steak tonight anyway." While John Fletcher got the bottle up and the candle relit, Nettie swapped plates with him.

"How about vitamins?" she said.

"What?" said John Fletcher.

"You ever take vitamins to try and make you gain some weight?"

"I'm bigger than my pa," he said.

"Jesus," said Nettie, "your pa ain't hardly five feet tall."

"But it's in the family," he said.

"Lee Jay is going to be a big man," said Nettie.

"Lee Jay is weak in the head," said John Fletcher.

"Well," said Nettie, "I just wondered. It don't make no difference to me. Big or little. I seen all kinds. You ever tried Hadacol?"

"Pa tried it," he said. "We had to take it away from him."

"It's good stuff," she said.

"Pa quit eating," said John Fletcher. "He was drinking four bottles a day. Staggering around the house telling everybody how good he felt and trying to get Ma in the bedroom with him. We couldn't afford it. He never did put on no weight."

"You ought to try it sometimes," she said. "Or some vitamins. Just to see."

"Well," said John Fletcher.

He began eating his Salisbury steak in silence.

"Give me some more of that wine," said Nettie. "It sort of grows on you. It don't feel like my mouth is turning inside out no more." She held out her glass to him. He poured it full.

While he ate, she sipped the wine and looked around the room. "It ain't much of a place you got here," she said. "The pictures is nice." She raised her glass toward the Rex Harrison picture.

"Yes," said John Fletcher. "I got them at the picture show."

"I can't never remember," she said, nodding toward the Rex Harrison picture, "what's his name?"

John Fletcher looked around at the poster. "Rex Harrison," he said.

"He looks kind of fruity," she said, sipping the wine. "All right in the face, you know, but . . . something . . . fruity is what it is. Like he's got lace on his drawers." She emptied her glass and put it down on the table. "Myself," she said, "John Wayne . . . that's my type. Big Boy Williams . . . he's cute too."

John Fletcher didn't say anything.

She picked up the bottle and poured herself another glass of wine. "Want some more?" she said, looking at John Fletcher. Before he could answer, she poured the rest of the bottle into his glass. "That's all she wrote," she said. She drained her glass and slapped it down onto the table. John Fletcher caught the candle before it toppled over again.

"You go on eating," she said, standing up. "Got to put some meat on your bones. I'm going to get more comfortable."

She walked over to the couch, kicking off her shoes as she went. Then she peeled off her dress, pulling it over her head and dropping it on one of the end tables. She had on black underwear. Across the front of the panties was written in red, "Friday." It was Tuesday. With her back to John Fletcher, she unfastened her brassiere and dropped it on her dress; then she massaged her breasts, kneading them together and pushing them up from underneath. "That feels good," she said, looking back at him.

She took off the panties. Flexed her knees and made a downward motion with her arms; then she was stepping out of them. John Fletcher couldn't follow the motion. Just suddenly she didn't have them on.

He sat at the table watching her with his mouth sprung open, the fork poised in midair, trembling, the peas falling off into his lap.

After she had got her clothes off, Nettie gave an angular pirouettelike spin—she had a baton twirler's grace, had been one in high school—and collapsed backward onto the couch, her legs spread wide apart and sticking out stiff in front of her, her arms raised and hugging the back of her neck.

"You about ready to commence?" she said. Her head was thrown back, and she looked at him under lowered lids.

John Fletcher lowered his fork slowly, not looking where he was putting it. It dropped off the plate and into his lap. He rose slowly from the table, his right hand in his pocket, his left adjusting his tie. He spoke with a croak. "Maybe . . ." He cleared his throat. "Maybe I ought to clear away the dishes," he said.

"Not now, John Fletcher," she said. With her knees locked stiff, she raised and lowered her legs, drumming on the floor with her heels.

John Fletcher took a step, kicking the table and overturning the candle. He lit a match.

"Whyn't you turn on the lights?" said Nettie.

"The pink is shitty looking," he said.

"What?" she said.

"It's a shitty-looking pink," he said. "The walls."

The match went out, burning his fingers. "Jesus," he said. He lit another and set the candle upright on the table again.

"The candle is better," he said.

"Come over here, pony boy," she said.

He walked over with his hand in his pocket.

"Sit down," she said, slapping the sofa.

John Fletcher stood looking down at her. "Why . . ." He cleared his throat. "Why . . ."

She looked down at herself. "Do it every day," she said. "Shave all over. ALL over." She rubbed her hands up her legs and over her belly. "Started with a fella I used to go with once. He said he was paying to see it all, and he was, by God, going to *see* it. He done it himself with a *straight* razor. That was one hell of a sensation, I can tell you. I was afraid I'd twitch the wrong way and he'd put me out of business. But it come out all right. He never even nicked me."

She locked her fingers together and pushed them away, cracking her knuckles. "He had a nice touch," she said.

"When it started to grow back, it scratched so much I had to keep up the shaving. I figure it's a good idea anyway—kind of a conversation piece."

She laughed. "How about that?" she said. "Conversation *piece* . . . Get it?"

John Fletcher rocked on his heels and giggled.

"Anyways," she said, "it keeps down the crabs."

"It certainly does," he said.

She raised her hand and tried to unzip his fly. He looked up at the landscape painting. When she touched him, he flinched his hips backwards, pulling away from her.

"Hadn't we ought to go in the bedroom?" he said.

"You're the doctor," she said.

She stood up, running her hands up her body, massaging her breasts and holding them with her hands cupped under them. "That feels so good," she said. She twisted from side to side, rubbing them against him.

John Fletcher stood with his hands in his coat pockets, jumping his eyes up and down from her face to her breasts and back again. "It certainly does," he said.

They went into the bedroom. It was lit by a bare sixty-watt bulb hanging from a long cord in the middle of the room. The blue walls were better than the pink or the green, but still depressing. The bed was a massive walnut one—a lathe turner's dream come true, with posts that looked like strings of shiny black croquet balls. Festoons of smaller turnings had been worked into every available space. A bulbous tour de force. It filled two-thirds of the room. A matching wardrobe of the same massive design stood on one side. Something about its proportions was reminiscent of a 1940 Wurlitzer jukebox, though not so gaudy, of course. The two pieces of furniture accounted for most of the available floor space. Jammed between the bed and the wall there was an upended orange crate that served as a bedside table. On it was an autographed picture of Rex Harrison. "*Best Wishes*," it said. There was also another chocolate-brown Stuckey's ashtray.

"You know that fruity guy?" Nettie said, pointing to the picture.

"Not really," said John Fletcher.

"How'd you get the picture?" she said. "He wrote on it for you."

"Just sent him a letter and asked him for it," he said.

She leaned over and looked at it closely. "I wonder if John Wayne would send you a picture if you asked him?"

"Yes," said John Fletcher. "They all do."

She stood up, spread-eagled her arms, and fell backward onto the bed. "Let's commence," she said.

John Fletcher turned the picture face down on the table, gently. Then he went over and turned out the light.

"Hey," she said. "You can't see."

"There's enough light from the other room," he said, coming over to the bed. He stood looking down at her. "You're a beautiful woman, Nettie," he said.

She worked her right leg between his and moved it in and out. "You're all right yourself, pony boy," she said.

She sat up on the edge of the bed and unzipped his fly. Then she undid his belt and peeled down his pants and underpants.

"That's as pretty as ever a one I did see," she said, holding him in both her hands. One hand underneath, one on top, stroking him.

". . . thank you," he said.

He cleared his throat. "I thought . . . ," he said, ". . . I was afraid . . ."

She looked up at his face. "What?" she said.

". . . you seen all kinds," he said. ". . . It's . . . little . . . ain't it?"

She looked back down at him. "It's pretty," she said. "It don't go by the yard."

"I thought . . ."

She looked up at his face, then back down. "Don't worry, John Fletcher," she said. "I'd lot rather be tickled to death than choked."

John Fletcher didn't say anything. She went on stroking, sitting on the bed while he stood over her, his hands in his coat pockets, looking across at the wall over her head. With a slow, steady motion he began sinking at the knees, thrusting his hips forward and biting his lower lip. He reached down quickly, grabbing her hands with both of his.

"No," he said, holding her tight.

"Well," she said, looking down at him. "I *said* let's commence."

He looked down at her, opening his eyes. She was sitting with one hand cupped in her lap, the other poised, fingers spread, holding it away.

"Is it over?" he said, licking his lips.

"It's only just started, John Fletcher," she said, looking up at him. "Where's the bathroom?"

"There," he said, pointing.

She got up and walked over to it, still holding her hand cupped. As she went by the door to the living room, she flipped on the light. He heard the water running, then the toilet flushing.

While she was gone, he wiped himself off with a handkerchief and pulled his pants and underpants back up.

She looked at him when she came out of the bathroom. "You ain't had enough?" she said.

"You said we'd only just started."

"Why'd you cover up?" she said.

"It bothers me," he said, not looking at her.

"I know," she said. "You'll get used to it. It's better bare assed."

He looked at her.

"It's pretty as a picture," she said. "Believe me. I know. They don't come no prettier."

She walked over to him. "I'll help," she said, reaching for his fly again.

"I'll do it," he said, catching her hand and holding it.

He began by taking off his coat, getting a coat hanger out of the wardrobe, and hanging it up. He took off his tie and began to unbutton his shirt.

"Why don't you go on back in the other room?" he said.

"I don't bother you, do I?" she said.

"You bother the shit out of me," he said. "Go on back in there, and I'll be along in a minute." He had to go to the bathroom and was afraid she would follow him. He couldn't make water with other people standing around. At the picture show he had to watch the rest room and go when nobody was in there, or go in right behind somebody else and hope he wouldn't use the booth.

"Second time is better," she said, going out of the room.

He went to the bathroom, then came back into the bedroom and undressed down to his underpants and socks. He didn't want to go barefoot, but had nothing else to wear.

Then he went back into the bathroom again and got a towel, wrapping it around his waist to cover up his shorts. When he went back into the living room, he found her dancing around to the transistor music. She had put her high-heel red shoes on, but nothing else. He went to the couch and sat down, watching her.

"I bet you cheated," she said, dancing over to him on the couch. She twitched the towel away, revealing him in his Jockey shorts. John Fletcher sat with his arms resting beside him on the couch, hands gripping the edge.

She danced away from him.

"Nice music," she said. "Where's it at?"

"I thought you'd like it," he said. "Under the couch."

"I like to dance," she said.

"You certainly are a beautiful dancer," he said.

Her dancing was like a provocative calisthenics exercise. As long as she kept her arms and legs in close, it went okay. But she kept flinging them out and striking angular poses, like a cheerleader practicing cheers. She had gotten the wine down a little too fast.

John Fletcher sat watching her. After a while he crossed his legs. Once he drummed with his fingers on the cushion.

"Take your socks off," she said, dancing by him.

"I've got ugly feet," he said.

"They look funny," she said. "Not your feet . . . the socks."

John Fletcher tried to stick his feet under the couch.

She danced over beside the Marilyn Monroe poster and imitated the pose, mashing her breasts together with her arms.

"Sometimes people say I look like her," she said.

"Yes," said John Fletcher, shifting his eyes back and forth from the poster to Nettie. "Better," he said.

"Except for the black hair," she said.

"I like black hair better," he said.

The music changed. A slow tune. "Sentimental Journey." Nettie moved around more gracefully. Not kicking so much.

"How about some coffee?" said John Fletcher.

"Where's it at?" she said, stopping. She weaved a little standing there in the middle of the floor.

"I'll get it," he said.

"Woman's place is in the kitchen," she said.

"Some women," he said.

"Where's it at?" she said.

"It's on the stove," he said.

She went out to the kitchen and turned on the burner; then she came out and danced a fast song and two slow ones until it was ready. She poured it in the kitchen and brought the cups into the living room, sloshing coffee into the saucers.

"Let's sit at the table," he said.

He lit the candle and turned out the end-table lamp. This time he helped her into the chair. Then he sat there across from her, looking at her naked in the candlelight. He wanted to get down and look at her under the table too.

"My table. My house," he said.

"What?" she said.

"Nothing," he said.

"Let's dance," she said. The music was all slow now.

"I don't dance very well," he said.

"I'll teach you," she said.

They tried it once or twice around the floor. She stopped and kicked off her shoes. "Here," she said, holding him at arm's length. "Watch my feet." She did the step for him. Then they tried it together again. "Count," she said. "One-two-three-four . . . one-two-three-four." They moved around the floor. When the music stopped he stepped back from her.

"You'll catch on," she said. "You got rhythm."

"I have?" he said.

"You got natural rhythm," she said.

They tried two more slow dances. "Try counting to yourself," she said.

He stepped on her foot. "I'm sorry," he said.

"Don't apologize," she said. "Keep counting."

He stepped on her foot again. "Let's sit down for a while," he said.

They went to the couch. For a while they just sat there side by side, not talking. Listening to the music. At eleven o'clock the music program went off and the news came on. Then the weather.

"Ninety-eight in Savannah today," said the weatherman. "Humidity eighty-nine percent."

"Ninety-eight degrees," said John Fletcher. "That's hot."

"I'd have died if I'd known it was that hot," said Nettie. " 'Course, I slept most of the day."

"Yes," said John Fletcher.

"It ain't the heat anyway," said Nettie. "It's the humidity gets you down."

"Ninety-eight is pretty hot," said John Fletcher.

"Yes," she said.

"Being in the picture show, I can't tell much about how it is outside," said John Fletcher. "It's always cool in the picture show."

"That's the nice part about working in the picture show," she said. "It's always air-conditioned."

"Sometimes it breaks down," said John Fletcher. "Not very often."

"That must be pretty bad when it does," she said.

"It certainly is," he said.

"It must be bad when you come out at night," she said. "That would make you feel it all the more."

"It certainly does," said John Fletcher.

After the weather report, the farm-and-home news came on. "Cotton is one hundred and sixty-three dollars the bale," said the announcer.

"Did he say a hundred and *sixteen* dollars?" said Nettie.

"Sixty-three," said John Fletcher.

"It sounded like sixteen to me," she said.

"I think it was sixty-three," he said. "I could have been mistaken."

"That's still low," she said.

"Maybe it was *two* hundred," he said.

"That's too high," she said. "Cotton wouldn't be going for no two hundred dollars."

"I thought it was a hundred," he said.

After the farm-and-market news, the obituary program of the day came on.

Organ music swelled in the background, playing "Rock of Ages," then the announcer's voice came on. "On the Other Side . . . ," he said. "Time, ladies and gentlemen, to pause for a moment in the hustle and bustle of weary workaday, and give a thought to those who have left us for a better place . . ."—the music swelled behind him, then died away—". . . on the Other Side. This memorial program is brought to you by Fenway Brothers Mortuary. On the square in Kose. Your grief is in good hands at Fenway Brothers Mortuary." The music swelled again and died away.

"It's creepy-sounding," said Nettie.

"The music is pretty, though," said John Fletcher. "Sometimes they play 'Softly as in a Morning Sunrise.'"

"What?" she said.

"The song," he said, " 'Softly as in a Morning Sunrise.'"

"He sounds happy about the Other Side," she said.

"He's got a good voice, though," said John Fletcher.

"Let's get something else," she said.

"Just a minute," said John Fletcher. "Softly as in a Morning Sunrise" would have made his cup run over. The song did turn up pretty frequently on the program.

The music continued softly behind the announcer's voice. "Mrs. Roscoe Powers passed away this morning at ten-forty-seven," he said, "after a lingering illness. She was in her eighty-ninth year, and had been bedridden since nineteen-forty-nine, in the loving care of her devoted daughter, Miss Glendanna Powers of four-twenty-three Swamp Street in Kose. The body is at rest for viewing at Fenway Brothers Mortuary in Kose. On the square. Graveside services will be held tomorrow at eleven o'clock at Dorchester Memorial Gardens."

"Get something else," said Nettie. "That's creepy-sounding."

"Maybe they'll play 'Softly as in a Morning Sunrise,'" he said.

". . . eight sons and three daughters, twenty-six grandchildren, and seven great-grandchildren . . . ," said the announcer.

"Where's it at, John Fletcher?" said Nettie. "Come on and get something else." She was bending over and reaching under the couch. John Fletcher got down and took out the transistor. She took it away from him, tuning it herself. Bill Haley and "Rock Around the Clock" came on.

"That's more like it," she said.

She got up and began dancing again by herself. "Watch this step," she said. She glided away, keeping her legs close together and wagging her behind at him. John Fletcher watched her going away.

She picked up the coffee cups and wiggled out into the kitchen.

"Nigger work is what I'm best at," she said, dancing back in.

He didn't say anything.

The music changed to a slow one. "Blood will tell," she said, lighting a cigarette from the candle on the table, then sitting down backward in the tubular steel-and-formica chair, facing him.

"Don't talk about it," he said.

"Everybody knows anyway," she said. "Why not?"

"Don't keep doing it," he said.

"I don't keep doing it," she said. "I just said it once."

She inhaled a long drag from the cigarette and tapped the ashes onto the floor. John Fletcher handed her the Stuckey's ashtray.

"You don't need to keep talking about being a nigger," he said.

She took another drag on the cigarette. "You the one's keeping on," she said. "Anyway, I am."

"You're light as I am," he said.

She flipped the ashes off her cigarette, not looking at him. "Shit, John Fletcher," she said.

"You could pass anywheres," he said.

She looked at the burning tip of the cigarette. "Maggie was a sixteenth," she said. "That makes me a thirty-second." She looked at him. "Everybody knows that."

"Everybody in McAfee County," he said. "You're going to be a nigger long as you stay in McAfee County. You could pass anywheres else." He was watching the cigarette smoke. "Anywheres," he said.

"Well?" she said. "What am I going to do that would make it stop?" She drew her hair back over her shoulder by moving her hand beside her neck. The light of the candle behind her made it more black and shiny-looking. Thick. "It's not me that needs to keep it going."

"And it doesn't hurt the business none, does it?" he said.

She looked at him for a long time, tapping her cigarette. "I always did hate a smartass," she said.

"Well," he said, "why don't you move out of McAfee County? Go down to Jacksonville, or Savannah, if it bothers you?"

"It don't bother *me* any," she said. "*You* the one seems to be bringing it up and wanting to talk about it."

"But *that* bothers you, don't it?" he said. "What about Brunswick, maybe? They got a navy base in Brunswick."

"You trying to get me some work lined up, John Fletcher?" she said. "Or you trying to get me straightened out? What the hell are you trying to do for me?"

"I was just thinking," said John Fletcher.

"I don't need no more business," she said. "I'm starting to walk spraddle-legged from the business I got now. Being a white nigger has got its advantages. It kind of helps keep everything under control. You know?"

"It ain't much of a life," he said.

"What ain't?" she said. "It's a hell of a life, buddy. If I was just a plain little white twat, with my looks I'd have been knocked up and married off ten years ago. I wouldn't have had no chance. By now I'd have me a house full of kids. Streaks on my belly from swelling up with them, and my tiddies sucked down so I'd be dumping them in my lap every time I sat down." She hugged her breasts, looking down at them. "No thank you," she said, putting out her cigarette, "I'm doing just fine."

"You'd make more money in a big town."

"I got to hire me an accountant to figure my income taxes now," she said. "If I went to Jacksonville, I'd be clapped up and out of business inside of six months. Don't do me no favors. And quit worrying what it's going to be like the day after tomorrow. You got *this* whole night ahead of you."

"But wouldn't it be better without all this nigger talk?"

"That's part of it," she said. "Besides, nobody don't bring it up but rarely, John Fletcher."

"I couldn't think what it would be like," he said.

"It ain't your problem," she said. "So why don't you just put it out of your mind?"

"But I just can't think what it would be like," he said.

Neither one of them said anything for a while. She kept looking at him, but he looked away.

"What the hell is it, John Fletcher?" she said. "You figure you got it coming for what you're going to pay for this here night of love?"

He didn't say anything.

"It ain't that much *to* being a nigger," she said. "Not if you don't look like one."

"But don't you worry none?" he said. "Think what you could have been."

"I could have been ugly," she said. "Now *there's* something to make you sweat."

He didn't answer.

"How much you figure on giving me, anyway?" she said.

"Forget about it," he said in a low voice, still not looking at her. "Just forget about I ever asked you."

"You going to lay another five on the twenty you was figuring on to make it all worth my while?" she said. "Or maybe you was going to start to fall in love with me to pay it off. Or propose to go and marry me until you leave and join the navy next week? Maybe it was going to be something really serious like that. How much was it going to be worth to you to hear me tell that story about my nigger grandmammy?" She counted off on her fingers. "My great, great, *great*, nigger grandmammy, Coretta?" She looked at him over the back of the chair, resting her chin on her arms. "Coretta was Colonel Fanshawe's nigger slave," she said. "For poontang in particular."

John Fletcher wasn't looking at her. He was looking at the pictures behind her.

"*Pure* nigger," she said.

He flicked his eyes at her, then away.

"It was in December of 'sixty-four," she said. "Sherman was just about to come down and take Fort Moultrie." She stopped and looked at him. "Are you listening?" she said.

He looked at her.

"I ain't going to tell this but one time," she said. "Is it okay so far? That's the way you heard it, ain't it?"

He didn't say anything.

"It was December of 'sixty-four," she said, going on, "Colonel Fanshawe took Bascombe in—that was his youngest son, Bascombe —to let him blow his cherry on Coretta like the other three Fanshawe boys done before they went away to the war. Bascombe was fourteen years old," she said. She took a drag on her cigarette and put it out in the Stucky ashtray. "She got took with his child."

"All right," said John Fletcher. He looked at her, then he looked away. "All *right*," he said.

"But you ain't never heard *me* tell it," she said. "You're paying for it, ain't you?"

He didn't say anything.

"It was December of 'sixty-four. . . . I said that," she said. "Then Fort Moultrie got took the next day by the Yankees, because the Colonel forgot they could come from behind where he couldn't aim his guns. So he had to surrender the fort. Then he took

Bascombe into the magazine and blowed his brains out for him. Just before he blowed out his own brains." She paused. Them Fanshawes was a stupid bunch of farts," she said. "Too stupid to live, if you ask me. I hate to claim kin with a stupid bunch of farts like that."

"All *right*," said John Fletcher. He looked back at her again.

"You wanted it," she said. "What was it you was going to do for me to make it up? Something I wouldn't never forget? Was you going to pay me or thrill me, John Fletcher?"

"Excuse me," he said. His voice was low and courteous, the way he would ask her if there was something he could do for her. He stood up and leaned over toward her. Then his hand swept in a wide motion, coming around hard so that Nettie's head flicked under the impact of the blow. After he slapped her, her head didn't seem to have moved. She sat there staring at him over the back of the chair.

"Shit on your story, Nettie," he said. "I already heard it from everybody *but* you anyways."

"God damn," she said, lifting her hand to her cheek, touching it gently with the fingers. "God damn, you got a heavy hand, John Fletcher."

"Well," he said, not looking at her, "I'll give you five dollars extra." He lit a cigarette. "I'll give you five dollars extra, and I'll marry you to boot." He blew a big mouthful of smoke in her direction. "And if you try to tell me that goddamn story"—he blew another mouthful of smoke in her direction—"I'm going to beat your ass with a hairbrush and wash your mouth out with Octagon soap."

She looked at John Fletcher. "Let's get back in the bed," she said. "We was doing all right before all this ever come up."

John Fletcher looked at her. "Sit down," he said. "We'll get back in the bed directly. I ain't finished smoking my cigarette yet."

"Jesus Christ," said Nettie. "You're a crazy fucker, John Fletcher."

John Fletcher looked at her. She was feeling her cheek with the tips of her fingers.

"Don't call me that," he said.

"Well, you are," she said.

"I don't mean 'crazy,'" he said. "You can call me that. Only don't say 'fucker.' It don't sound right. You ain't got the face to say 'fucker.'"

"What the hell you think I am, John Fletcher? The Rose of Tralee or something? I been saying 'fucker' all my life."

"Well, just don't say it tonight where I can hear it," he said. "You ain't got the face for it. I'm paying you not to say it."

They looked at each other across the back of the chair for a while.

"And don't say 'shit' no more, either," he said. "I'm paying you not to say that too."

"You just got to hear me tell it, ain't you?" she said.

John Fletcher didn't say anything. ". . . Sometime," he said.

"You got any more of that wine?" she said. "I need me a drink."

"No," he said.

"Well, I can't just sit here not saying 'fucker,'" she said. "We got to *do* something."

He didn't answer.

"Come on," she said. "Let's dance." She stood up, reaching over and taking his hands to pull him up.

They danced a couple of slow ones. Then a fast one came on, and they had to go sit on the couch. While he was stooping to sit down, she stripped his shorts off down to his knees.

"Damn!" he said, standing up. "It sticks you, don't it?" He rubbed his backside where the coarse material on the couch had scratched him. Then he sat down, turning to the side slightly and raising his leg to cover himself.

"It's more fun, ain't it?" she said.

"Not yet," he said.

His shorts were still down around his ankles. She bent down, and he let her strip them off. She started to strip off his socks too.

"My feet're ugly," he said, holding her hand.

"But it looks funny," she said, "with just nothing but the socks."

"I could get another color," he said.

She looked at him without saying anything. Still bent over. He let go her hands, and she stripped them off. Then she got up onto the couch beside him and pulled him down on top of her. He tucked his feet down between the cushion and the arm of the couch so they wouldn't show.

"Second time is better," he said after a while.

"Yes," she said.

For a while they didn't say anything. Just lay there holding on and listening to the radio under the couch.

"You going in next week?" she said.

"What?" he said.

"The navy," she said. "You going in next week?"

"Thursday," he said.

"You'll like it," she said. "Navy boys has lots of fun."

"Poontang," he said.

"What?" she said.

"Poontang," he said. "I just had me some poontang."

She didn't say anything.

"I like that word," he said. "Pooooon—taaang."

"That's what you had, John Fletcher," she said. "Like the story says. It's true. I got to tell it to you sometime," she said. "Really tell you."

"Sometime," said John Fletcher. "Maybe I shouldn't have said that," he said.

She didn't say anything.

At two o'clock they had another cup of coffee. Then John Fletcher went and got the envelope, with her card and the check and the passes in it.

"What's this?" she said.

"It's for you," he said.

She opened the envelope and took out the card. The check and the passes fell out in her lap. She picked up the passes.

"Passes to the picture show?" she said.

"Extra," he said.

She looked at the check. "What's this?" she said.

"Your check," said John Fletcher.

"My check?" she said.

"Yes," he said.

"Where's the money?" she said.

"That's it," he said. "I made you a check."

"I don't want no check, buddy," she said. "Cash money. That's what I want."

John Fletcher looked at her. "I ain't got no cash money," he said.

"My business is always cash money," she said, holding out her palm and cutting across it with the edge of her other hand. "Right on the line," she said.

"I don't like that cash money," he said. "Not for this."

"Funny," she said. "I seem to of heard that before." She held out her hand, palm up. "Twenty-five dollars. Lay it right there."

"John Henry said twenty," he said.

"You said five extra," she said. "That's what the check says anyway." She held the check up for him to see.

"I was *giving* you that," he said. "Extra."

"I need the cash," she said.

"I just ain't got it," he said.

"You better have it," she said.

"The check is good," he said.

"Ain't they all?" she said.

"Well," he said, "what're we going to do? I ain't got it. I just ain't got it."

She looked at him a minute. She stood with her weight on one hip, her right hand extended palm up, her left holding her right elbow, bracing under her breasts. Then she turned and went to the couch, getting her things. He watched her as she got dressed.

"I'm going to get me some security," she said. "Not that I don't trust you, John Fletcher." She looked at him for a long minute. "Maybe one of your balls," she said. "Or that pretty little talley-wacker of yours."

John Fletcher stood in the center of the room, one foot lapped over the other, covering it. His hands were clasped in front, hanging down to cover himself there.

She turned on her heel and went to the couch. Getting down on her hands and knees, she reached under and pulled out the transistor radio. The farm-and-market man was back on. ". . . here's good news for hog growers . . . ," he said. She cut it off.

"This'll do for part of it," she said.

She looked around the room. "Jesus God, John Fletcher," she said. She looked at him. "I'm going to need me a bushel basket. Ain't you got nothing *little* that's worth something?" She looked at him for another long minute. "I mean besides your talleywacker," she said. She strode past him into the bedroom. John Fletcher stood there not moving, holding himself.

When she came back out of the bedroom, she had the cufflinks and tie pin in her hand. Also the black Swank wallet. She was holding the wallet open. "Five dollars," she said. "You're right. You ain't got that kind of money. Shit, John Fletcher, you ain't got no money at all." She took out the five and put it into the front of her dress. "For my tip," she said.

While she had been in the bedroom, John Fletcher had gotten his shorts and socks and put them on. He was standing by the couch.

"Turn on the light," she said.

He switched on the bourbon-bottle end-table lamp.

She put the things down on the card table and looked at them —totaling them up. "It ain't enough," she said.

"It cost more than twenty dollars," he said.

"Twenty-five," she said.

"You got the five," he said.

"I thought that was my tip," she said.

He didn't say anything.

"Anyway," she said, "it ain't worth it to me."

She looked at the things for a while. Then she looked at John Fletcher. She turned and went back into the bedroom. When she came out she had his coat.

John Fletcher took a step toward her. "Not the coat," he said.

She held out her hand to stop him. "You'll get it back when you pay me," she said. "It's just for security. Believe me, I'd rather have the money—even if it was real."

"I'll pay you in the morning," he said.

"You'll get your stuff back in the morning," she said.

She put the things in the pockets of the coat, then slung it over her shoulder and started out the door.

"Wait," said John Fletcher.

She stopped and looked at him. "That's all," she said. "You ain't all of a sudden found you some money, have you?"

"Take the card," he said. He picked it up off the table and handed it to her.

She looked at him from the doorway. "Save it for Valentine's," she said.

He held the card out, looking at her. "It's for you," he said.

"I don't want it," she said.

He slipped the passes out of the envelope and held them out to her. "Take these anyways," he said.

She looked at him.

"Give them to John Henry if you don't want to use them," he said.

She stood at the door while he came over and gave them to her. After she took them and put them into the pocket of the coat, she started out the door.

"Maybe I'll see you again," he said.

"I'd better see you in the morning," she said.

"Yes," he said. "Maybe when I come home from the navy."

She looked at him, holding back the screen. "Maybe," she said. "If you save up your money. Ain't all poontang cheap."

"I'll see you in the morning," he said.

"Yes," she said. "You'd better . . ."

Then he thought about the other present he had gotten for her. "Wait," he said.

"What?" she said.

"What would you say about a chocolate-covered cherry?" he said.

She looked at him hard for a minute. "Good night . . . white boy," she said.

She went out the door, letting the screen slam shut behind her.

Six days later he himself walked out of the door to catch the bus for Jacksonville and the navy.

The first move was to the south, but all those that came after were to the west. The remainder of his short life consisted of a series of removes, each more Hesperian than the last.

Great Lakes Naval Training Station and Chicago . . . San Francisco . . . San Diego . . . Tijuana . . . Honolulu . . . Guam . . . At each stopping place he found someone—some girl, each more exotic than the last—who would dally with him at a sailor's price.

A mulatto whore in a red-headed wig in Chicago. In San Francisco a girl who claimed distant Kiowa ancestry, and wore a headband to prove it. A Nisei waitress in San Diego, who kept a naked Samurai sword across the foot of her bed, and made him beat her with the flat of the blade before she would have intercourse with him. A *mestiza* that he bought out of a Tijuana bar (she slept with him one time, and gave him his first dose of clap—he felt a kind of gentle affection for her on account of it). In Honolulu a Chinese girl with a speech impediment. And on Guam a gentle, sarong-wearing Micronesian, who seemed to come to him always fresh from the sea, wearing a hibiscus in her hair.

He missed most of the fine points. But he had the sense that the tendency was the right one. Westering. The Pacific. It was the place he had always wanted to be—in atavistic flight from civilization, like a color-blind Gauguin, without brush or canvas.

Through the whole journey he carried the recollection of Nettie Oatley's honey-yellow eye. Flitting in the darkness of his mind like a spectral firefly, leading him on, to strand and beach him under the high, flaking ceiling of the ward of a navy hospital, set on a green-and-purple island in the middle of the Great South Sea.

As he was lying on the bed in the ward, Nettie's eye would rise behind his retina. A gigantic golden circle—green-flecked, with a center velvet black—like the mouth of a tunnel of love, into which he glided on a float shaped like a swan. Through the yellow gate and into the velvet darkness. The light going away as he drifted through . . . gray . . . gray . . .

. . . the bubble turned slowly, quivering, compressing and elongating as it rose . . . turning gray in the pale green-gray liquid . . . a thick, steady movement . . .

"Seamanwillistonseamanwillistonseamanwilliston . . ." The voice went dying away.

. . . he cartwheeled slowly . . . holding to the bubble . . .

rising through the thick green-gray liquid in the pale lime-gray silence of the dying sun . . . sun dying outside the windows of the
ward . . .

  ". . . willis . . . willis . . . willis . . ."

  . . . turning . . .

  . . . turning . . .

  . . . he wedged himself tightly . . . hearing far away the soft
hissing sound of the trace of bubbles in the tube . . . sighing at the
sun going black outside the windows of the ward . . . leaving
him with only the hissing sound of the trace of bubbles in the tube
going into his arm . . . going out of his arm . . . under the vaulted
moonscape ceiling of the ward . . . coming down onto the bed itself to wrap him around . . . until even the faint hissing of the
bubble trace in the tubing went away . . . leaving only . . . . the
perfect . . . . . velvet . . . . . . blackness . . . . under the
vaulted ceilings of the ward. . . . . . .

Daddy's Girl

"It has to be did," he said, speaking the words under his breath, as if he were afraid someone would hear him.

First light would come soon, the east was just beginning to turn gray, but the low moon still let him see the black outline of the house —dark now. He had turned out the light in the kitchen when he had come into the yard.

He worried about the lantern, was afraid Frances might see it —though he knew she couldn't see it from their bedroom window. She would have to get up and come into the kitchen. But she might do that. She would have been missing him from the bed all night now, and it might have waked her up and started her looking for him.

He began by actually cutting some pieces of kindling—thinking and planning after it was too late to do any good. He had burned a hole in the sheet with a cigarette. Walking the glowing tip around the spot. Tomorrow he would tell Frances it had been an accident, while he was talking to Jackie. She wouldn't think anything about it.

He stood the lightwood on end on the stump that he used for a chopping block, splitting off the pieces in long, jagged splinters, trying to make them come off clean. He had a deft touch, but he was nervous now in spite of himself, thinking ahead. He would have to use his left hand, and he might blink, too.

"It's got to be did," he said again.

He had trouble getting the position right, at first propping it up over a piece of the lightwood. But it didn't feel steady enough to him, so he put it down on the block itself, curling the other fingers back out of the way, extending them along the sides of the stump.

He held the ax close to the head, not raising it very high because he was afraid that he wouldn't be able to control it. Then he thought that it might not come clean, and he would have to try more than once. He braced the handle of the ax along the inside of his arm, clamping it into his side with his elbow, still thinking he was going to miss. He was afraid that if he thought about it too much he would begin to tremble, that he might falter at the last minute. The main thing was to make it clean—a single stroke. It would be hard enough to explain anyway, but he thought he could manage if he did it clean.

He counted to steady himself. "One . . . two . . . three . . ."

The blood welled at the stump of the finger, a swollen red bubble, shiny, pumping off big, slow drops. He closed his eyes, holding the wrist tightly in his left hand, squeezing it to stanch the flow of blood and slow the pumping of the bubble. Behind the lids he could see the other eyes, staring at him open and wide in the moon-filled room. He could feel the other hands on his wrist, locked and still. Holding on—the way you would hold on to a spear thrust into your body, not wanting it to move. Just about able to bear it, if only it wouldn't work in the wound. Not even wanting it out, but just wanting it not to move.

He let the bubble drop onto the block, then another, and another. Covering it. Covering the block and the ax head.

"Call Dr. Smoaks, Frances," he said. His face was chalky white and dead looking, and his eyes seemed to be receding into their sockets, like lead cooling in a mold.

"Good God, Henry! What you done?" said Mrs. Sipple.

"Call Dr. Smoaks," he said. "Then get me a rag or something to tie it up."

When she left, he took it quickly from the block. Still holding the wrist tightly. He went to the pumphouse and put it on the shelf where he kept the tools for the pump, laying it in the back where it wouldn't be seen. Then he walked back to the house and sat down on the steps to the back porch, not wanting to drip blood on the floors inside the house. He was sitting there when the sun came up.

Later, in the afternoon, he went back down to the pumphouse. He worried about putting it there, thinking he should have left it on the stump. The ants had gotten to it, and he let them take it. He didn't know what to do about it now anyway. Frances hadn't asked. She had been too worried about him for that. The next time he looked, it was gone. A rat probably. He had seen one at the pumphouse now and then.

And so it ended like that. With the rat taking it away.

"It's a girl." Dr. Smoaks stood in the Sipple kitchen. It was a cold October night and the windows were sweating, running in black streaks on the black panes.

Mr. Sipple stood by the table, frowning slightly. "Well . . . ," he said.

"Don't act that way, Henry," said Dr. Smoaks. "And don't let Frances see you. It takes a real man to blow the balls clean off."

"First one ought to be a boy," said Henry, not looking at him.

"First one ought to be what it is," said Dr. Smoaks. "It ain't for you to say."

"I was counting on a boy," said Henry.

"You ain't got no right to count on nothing," said Dr. Smoaks. "Now give me one of them cigars and a cup of coffee." He sat down at the table. Henry pushed the box of King Edwards toward him. Dr. Smoaks opened it and took out a cigar. He rolled it around the edge of the flame to get it started even, puffing the smoke up toward the ceiling. Mr. Sipple brought the coffeepot from the stove and poured.

"Frances had a hard time, Henry," said Dr. Smoaks, fanning at the blue cloud that enveloped his head.

"She's all right, ain't she?" said Henry. He stood holding the pot in his hard, balled fist.

"Well, but she had a very hard time." Dr. Smoaks took another pull at the cigar, then sipped the coffee, holding the cup in both hands.

"Is she tore?"

"Always tears a little."

"But is she tore bad?"

"Pretty bad," said Dr. Smoaks, sipping the coffee. "I want you to stay away from her till I tell you not to."

"How long?"

"Can't tell exactly. Seven or eight weeks anyway."

"Well, but she's going to be all right?"

"I think she's going to be all right, but you got to keep away from her. Till I say so."

The two men sat at the kitchen table drinking coffee and not looking at each other.

"It ain't going to be *that* long," said Dr. Smoaks. "It was going to be six weeks anyway. It's always six weeks."

Mr. Sipple didn't say anything.

"It could have been worse," said Dr. Smoaks. "Think about Dero Mullins. Mae nearly died when Annie came last spring. Dero ain't been able to lay a finger on her . . . not nothing else either . . . for,"—he counted on his fingers—"six months now. Six months, Henry. You think about that."

"You sure she's going to be all right?"

"I'm sure. I just don't know how long, is all. I'll tell you what," said Dr. Smoaks, "if it's got to be longer than seven weeks, I'll get you fixed up with Maggie Poat."

Mr. Sipple looked at him.

" 'Course, you needn't go telling Frances I said that," he added. "That's privileged information. I'm *your* doctor too."

The corners of Mr. Sipple's mouth were pulling up in a little smile. "You think you could maybe arrange that?" he said. "Pull some strings and fix it up? Maggie ain't bad. You going to fix it so I wouldn't have to stand in line or something?"

"I'm not talking about what I'd do for Maggie. I'm talking about what I'd do for *you*. Maggie's the best there is," said Dr. Smoaks.

"Reckon it's the nigger blood?" said Mr. Sipple.

"I wouldn't say so," said Dr. Smoaks, "though I wouldn't say no, either."

"She's a lot of woman," said Mr. Sipple.

"She's the best there is," said Dr. Smoaks.

"I'd of thought when Nettie come it'd of loosened her up too much. Put her out of business."

"Needn't be," said Dr. Smoaks.

"Nettie was a big baby."

"Don't make no difference," said Dr. Smoaks. He looked at Mr. Sipple. "You ain't worried about Frances that way?" he said.

"Well, no," said Mr. Sipple. "It crossed my mind."

"Don't you worry about Frances," Dr. Smoaks said. "Just stay away from her till I tell you to. You couldn't even tell the difference. It's going to be better than ever. Maybe by Christmas."

"Is this one big as Nettie?"

"Nettie was a big baby."

"How big is this one?"

"Seven and a half, I'd say. Just guessing. Seven and a half or seven and three-quarters, something like that."

"She look all right?"

"Ain't none of them look too good just at first. She's all right."

"Nettie is going to be a better-looking woman than her ma."

"Looks ain't all."

"She's going to have some of the other, too. Plenty of it."

"God damn, Henry, how you think you can tell that? She ain't but five years old."

"You can tell."

"Not me," said Dr. Smoaks. "I can't tell nothing at all. Just looks like a five-year-old girl to me. Little skinny."

"Look at her face," said Mr. Sipple.

"Freckled," said Dr. Smoaks. He looked at Mr. Sipple for a minute without saying anything. "I didn't know you had the gift of prophesy, Henry," he said. "I sure as hell didn't know about that. You speak in tongues too?"

Mr. Sipple didn't say anything.

"Good," said Dr. Smoaks.

"What?" said Mr. Sipple.

"I said, 'Good,'" said Dr. Smoaks. "When Osie brings that daughter of yours down here for you to look at, you can show me how you do it."

Mr. Sipple looked at him.

"You know," said Dr. Smoaks. "Look at her face—or whatever it is you got to look at to get it straight—and tell me how she's going to be when she gets to be a grown-up woman."

Mr. Sipple looked away. "Anyway . . . you can tell," he said.

"Oh, I believe it," said Dr. Smoaks. "I ain't doubting your word. Only I just ain't never seen it done before."

"All right," said Mr. Sipple.

"Yes," said Dr. Smoaks.

They sat in silence for a while.

"While we're just sitting here waiting for Osie to bring her down so you can settle all this business for her and set my mind to rest, would you care to tell me just one other little thing? It ain't hardly worth your time, I know, it being so simple and all, but you got to get it cleared up sometime."

"What?" said Mr. Sipple.

"Would you care to tell me what your child's name is going to be? Or is that kind of fortune-telling too easy for you, and you only pay attention to the hard stuff, like how she's going to be in the bed when she gets to be a grown-up woman?"

Mr. Sipple looked at him. "What?" he said.

"What you going to name her?" said Dr. Smoaks.

"I ain't thought about no names for girls," he said. "I knowed it were going to be a boy."

"Well, you better start," said Dr. Smoaks. "She ain't. You wasn't telling that fortune worth a shit."

"If it were a boy I was going to call him Jack," Mr. Sipple said. "You know, John. John Sipple. Jack for short."

"That won't do," said Dr. Smoaks, sipping his coffee and pulling on the cigar.

"Jackie is all right," said Mr. Sipple. "Jackie Sipple. Sounds all right to me."

"Why don't you give her a real girl's name?" said Dr. Smoaks. "Annie, or Sue Marie, or something like that?"

"What's the matter with Jackie? There was Jackie Fitzgerald. And Jackie Sue Womack. I've knowed lots of Jackies."

"But you're still thinking like it was a boy," said Dr. Smoaks. "Think like she's a girl. Which she is. How about Sue Marie Sipple? Sounds good to me."

"Jackie," said Mr. Sipple. "I like Jackie Sipple."

"What kind of a middle name you going to put with that? Sue Marie goes together real good. What you going to put with Jackie?"

"Jackie Sue," said Mr. Sipple. "How's Jackie Sue?"

"Sounds tacky to me," said Dr. Smoaks. "I never could stand that Womack child. Can't you do no better?"

"Well, why don't *you* try then?"

"I ain't interested. If it's *Jackie*, it's going to be up to you. How about Caroline Ann?"

"How about Caroline? Jackie Caroline Sipple. Caroline was Frances' mother's name. They come from Carolina, too."

"Too long," said Dr. Smoaks.

"But they come from Carolina," said Mr. Sipple.

"And she come from Two-Oak," said Dr. Smoaks. "If information is all you're after, why don't you name her *Two-Oak, October twenty-seventh nineteen-forty female Sipple?* It's got to *sound* right too, Henry."

"It don't hurt none to show where you come from."

"Better you'd show where she's going," said Dr. Smoaks. "But I forgot. You already taking care of that too."

"Jackie Caroline. Jackie Caroline," he said.

"See?" said Dr. Smoaks.

"Jackie Lou?"

"Sounds too close to Jackie Sue. How about Sue Ann?"

"Jackie Ann," said Mr. Sipple. "Jackie Ann Sipple."

Dr. Smoaks didn't say anything. He blew a ring with the cigar smoke, and then tried to blow another ring through it.

"Jackie Ann Sipple," said Mr. Sipple. "Sounds all right to me. I don't care about nothing but the *Jackie* anyway."

"Do what you want about it," said Dr. Smoaks. "You owe me five dollars for my fee."

"I'll pay you Saturday," said Mr. Sipple.

"That's tomorrow," said Dr. Smoaks.

"I mean *next* Saturday."

"See you do," said Dr. Smoaks. He took out his prescription pad and scribbled something on it.

"What's this?" said Mr. Sipple, looking at the piece of paper.

"MAGGIE POAT—ONE TIME," the prescription said.

"Just in case," said Dr. Smoaks, smiling. "But you got to wait seven weeks first. It'll be my Christmas present to you if Frances ain't right by then."

Mr. Sipple folded the piece of paper and put it into the pocket of his overalls.

"Hide that where Frances ain't going to see it," said Dr. Smoaks. "I don't like my patients discussing their treatments with each other."

They sat there in the kitchen, waiting for Osie to bring the baby down, listening to the radio and smoking cigars, trying to blow smoke rings. Smoaks was better at it than Mr. Sipple. The news came on, and the announcer told about how the Battle of Britain was going.

"Look at that one," said Mr. Sipple.

The two men watched the smoke ring float off wiggling toward the ceiling. It went all the way.

"That's the best one I ever seen," said Mr. Sipple.

"Ain't she little, though?" Mr. Sipple had paused on his way through the kitchen and stood looking over his wife's shoulder at the tiny girl in the basin on the kitchen table. Frances cradled the child's head gently in her left hand, leaning over to make it more comfortable for her, and giving more support with the forearm along her side. With her right hand she would scoop water and let it run down on her, sometimes holding her fingers and thumb together, pointing down, and letting the water drip, to be more gentle.

Henry was amazed at the tiny, female body in the basin. The small, inverted purse of flesh between her legs, hairless and naked, made him embarrassed, so that he would look away and then back again and away. She took him unawares. He had never seen her naked before that. It was too much of a revelation, because he hadn't been prepared for a girl anyway. But it fascinated him and worried him both, and he never again stopped to watch her having her bath. The nakedness of the girl child jangled his nerves.

When the sons came, they didn't distract him from the daughter, though he actually spent more time with them than he did with her. But wherever she was around the place, he seemed to be always aware of her. In part that was a response to her awareness of him.

From the very beginning, Jackie seemed to know how to have her way with her father. When the younger brothers began to appear, three of them, in stepped progression, regularly every two years or eighteen months, her tie with her father seemed to be strengthened with each new addition. And this without separation from the mother—nor division between them. They were the women of the house and he the man; the one Henry's woman, the other daddy's girl.

At first none of the sons were there to run and meet him when he came home from work in the evenings. Then it was Jackie who won the race to his outstretched arms. When the boys got big enough to beat her, she would stand on the porch, outrunning them with the look in her eyes, one finger poised on her lower lip, taking the prize as the father collected the boys into his arms and onto his shoulders and walked across the swept dirt of the yard up to the porch. Then unloading them and stooping to let her put her arms around his neck and kiss him on the cheek and walk with him into the house.

Once, when she was ten, Mrs. Sipple caught her playing doctor with her brothers—two of them. She told Henry when he came home. It was his duty as man of the house to punish them, and he took the boys into the bedroom and beat them on their bare behinds with a belt. He had done it—had to do it—many times before, and he was comfortable at it, though he didn't enjoy doing it. But Frances insisted that Jackie had to be punished too, which was true. She was the oldest, and she had started the game. It was the first time that Mr. Sipple had ever had to do that, and he took her into the bedroom too, without thinking, before he realized what it was. That this was Jackie, and that he couldn't carry it through. He left her standing by the bed and went back out to talk to Frances.

"You got to do it," he said. "It ain't fit I should beat a daughter."

"You the one swings the belt in this house," said Frances. "You got to cut her too. 'Twouldn't be fair doing it to the boys and not her too. They'd never get over it. It were her doing. They ain't old enough."

"Couldn't you?" he said. The belt was still in his hand, and it wiggled limply at the gestures he made as he talked.

"It wouldn't be the same. Just go on in there and get it over with. You ain't going to really hurt her."

"But I can't," he said, pleading.

"Well, you got to," Frances said.

He looked at her helplessly.

"Face up to it, Henry," she said. "You got two minutes to take it onto yourself and do what you got to do. Then I'm going to take the belt and go in there and do it for you. And you wouldn't never get over that. You the man of the house. And it's got to be did."

He couldn't face up to his wife too, so he went back into the room and closed the door. The late sun was coming in through the window, and it lit up Jackie's hair in a gold nimbus where she was still standing by the bed.

"It's got to be did," he said. "It wouldn't be fair to your brothers."

"I know it," she said. She was sniffling and crying, and the tears were already running down her cheeks.

"I'd give anything not to, but I got to do it," he said.

She nodded. "I know it," she said. "Just get it over with."

"Lean across the bed," he said. She did as he told her. To make it proper, so the blows wouldn't be softened, he raised her skirt a little, carefully, baring the backs of her legs and tucking it under her to hold it just right. Her legs were skinny and frail looking, and he tried not to look at them. The tendons behind her knees stood out where she had drawn up waiting for the blow.

He swung the belt, bringing it down with a fast swishing sound, not looking at the place where the blow fell. In his nervousness he hit her much harder than he had meant to. A great red welt marked the place where the belt had struck. Jackie let out a long wail, then buried her face in the bed clothes. He looked at the red streak on the backs of her legs. The scream startled him, and he couldn't raise the belt again.

"That's all," he said, throwing the belt on the bed. "Don't never do it again."

She looked at him over her shoulder. One side of the skirt came untucked, and it fell down, covering the welt on one side. She was still teary eyed, but she wasn't crying now.

"You give Sid and Gilmore eight apiece," she said. "I counted them."

"I hit you harder," he said. "It's your first time. Now, tell me you ain't never going to do it again." The other side of her skirt came untucked, covering the welt completely.

"I won't never," she said. "Ain't Sid and Gilmore going to be mad?"

"It's your first time," he said. "I made you holler louder. Counting the licks ain't all there is to it."

She nodded, wiping her eyes.

"Now, mean it when you say you ain't never going to do it again, he said. "I couldn't stand to give you another beating, and if you do it, I'll have to."

"Not never," she said. "I promise not never."

"Nor nothing like it neither," he said.

"No," she said.

"Mean it, honey," he said. He leaned down, and she put her arms around his neck, hugging him.

"I do," she said.

He went back out to the kitchen and sat down at the table. "I kept my part of the contract," he said, digging the heels of his hands into his eyes. "I couldn't do no more. If it ain't enough, you got to go in there and finish it up yourself."

"It had to be did," she said, drying her hands and coming over to him. She put her arms around his neck and kissed him. "It were the only fair thing."

He rested his hand on her arm. "Yes," he said, "but I hope to God she don't never do it again. I couldn't carry it off no second time."

"You done what you had to," she said.

"But not no more," he said.

"Yes," she said. She stood behind him with her arms around his neck, putting her cheek against his while he rested his hand on her arm.

As Jackie passed into her teens, her relationship with her father underwent a subtle change, which he wasn't fully aware of at first, though he noticed something and started to puzzle out what it might be. She still sought him out for his approval, was loving and attentive to him, but her interests were widening, turning outward and away from him, to boys nearer her own age. It was a hard time for Henry, for she would alternately be his and not his—aware and coquettish, distant and unconcerned. It made him love her more than ever.

She would come to him for reassurance and approval, putting her arms around his neck and sitting in his lap—playfully, as she had done when she was a little girl. But he began to see more and more that she was practicing on him—at least that was partly it—while saving a secret part of herself for others, whom Mr. Sipple could almost see and hear and smell waiting for her in the darkness outside the house. He grieved for the secret part.

First he forbade her to cross U.S. 17 to the Camp Stewart side —hoping to forestall that calamity—the bane of all the fathers of daughters in the six counties surrounding the army base. But he couldn't lock her into the house and forbid her to go out with the sons of neighbors—people he had known for years and saw every day. Though the very sight of their pimply faces and the sound of their high-pitched, cracking voices made him grit his teeth and talk out of the back of his throat. He wanted to chase them off with a hoe. Finally he began to worry that he might forget himself and kill one of them.

And Jackie seemed to distinguish among them, showing preferences. That was the worst of all. It made him realize how little he knew his own daughter—how unbridgeable was the gulf that separated them. She liked some better than others. What was the basis of her choice? To him they were an aggregate, a concatenation of fluty, prancing gamecocks, dressed in too-tight Levis and T shirts—a constant, undifferentiated presence ringing the house, homing in on his daughter like a pack of hounds on a bitch in heat. And Jackie, whom he could not conceive to be aware of it, was being driven, aware or not, along the periphery of that dance of life, despite all he could do to thwart and prevent it. He had never seen a chastity belt, never even heard of one, but he groped for the concept, and, given enough time, might have conjured it up and locked her into it out of the depth and desperation of his anguish. Only time was the one thing he did not have.

And the thought that made him most frantic was the suspicion, enforced by his wife's equanimity, contrasted with his own anguish, that Jackie did have a woman's awareness, below or beyond conscious recognition of that awareness, of what it all meant and led to. And not only that, but that she was enthusiastic about it. There came to him the realization that woman's knowledge was going to beat him in spite of all that he might plan and actually worry into fruition. If he had been able to conjure into substance the chastity belt, he would have found that they, his wife and his daughter, would have already conjured into substance the key.

"Ain't it nice Jackie is so popular?" Frances said to him as his daughter left on a walking date to BYPU, going out of the yard on the arm of one of the pimply-faced, tight-Levied, cracked-voiced bantams, whose neck he had wanted to wring.

He realized that it was a losing battle, but that he would have to fight it anyway.

Frances didn't even notice that he had not answered her.

His anguish turned to agony when Jackie accepted a date with John Fletcher Williston, an older boy who told her that he would be around to pick her up in an automobile.

"You got to talk to her, Frances," he said.

"About what?"

"About not getting in trouble. About how the boys are going to act and what she needs to do."

"We done had that out before."

"But you need to do it again."

"Jackie knows about it. We talked it over."

"But she ain't only fifteen. And she's going out in a automobile."

"It'll be all right. John Fletcher is a good boy."

"Ain't none of them that good. Don't I remember about it myself? And in a automobile."

"It'll be all right. She's rode in a automobile before."

"You ought to remind her."

"You going to put her in mind of it anyway if you keep on talking about it all the time."

"Won't you talk to her?"

"All right. But the talk ain't going to do no good one way or the other if she ain't got sense enough by now anyway."

"It'll remind her."

"Maybe it'll remind her of the wrong thing."

"I'm going to telephone Dorcus Williston and tell him I'm holding him accountable for that boy of his."

"You out of your mind, Henry? You ain't going to do no such

of a thing. John Fletcher is a good boy. I told you. It's going to be up to Jackie with him. If she ain't got sense enough, it'll be her own fault. But talking to her tonight ain't going to make her sensible, though I'll do it just to calm you down. You stay away from that telephone."

"I wish I could talk to her."

"Why don't you?"

"I wouldn't know what to say."

"You wouldn't know how to say it, you mean."

"And what to say, too."

"You go on out in the kitchen and get you some coffee and a piece of pie or something. I'll go speak to her."

Mr. Sipple was sitting at the table in the kitchen when she came back. He had cut himself a piece of pie and was stirring a spoon in a full cup of black coffee.

"What'd you say to her?"

"We talked it over."

"But what'd you say to her?"

"I couldn't say it to you. It's woman's talk."

"But what did you say?"

She looked at him. "You say what you wanted me to say, and I'll tell you if I said it."

They looked at each other a minute, and then he went back to stirring the coffee. He wished he had put his ear to the door and listened.

"You think she understands what we mean?" he said.

"She understood already. Like I told you. I just reminded her about it."

He didn't reply.

She came over and put her arms around his neck. "Don't worry, Henry," she said. "Jackie's a good girl."

Mr. Sipple wouldn't come out of the kitchen to speak to John Fletcher when he came to the house, so Mrs. Sipple had to sit in the front room and talk to him while Jackie finished getting ready. Before she left with him, she came into the kitchen and kissed her father good-bye, pecking him on the cheek.

"You be in by eleven o'clock," he said.

"Eleven-thirty, Daddy," she said.

"You be careful, and make him drive that car right," he said.

"Don't worry, Daddy," she said. "John Fletcher is a good driver."

"Eleven-thirty," he said.

She kissed him on the cheek again and went out of the kitchen, half running.

"You be careful," he said.

The swinging door flap-flapped, fluttering closed.

When he heard the screen slam he got up and went into the front room, looking out the window at Jackie and John Fletcher going out of the yard together.

"Where the hell he get a coat like that?" he said. "Zebra skin?"

"Leopard," Mrs. Sipple said. "It ain't real. All of them wear crazy things these days."

"Looks like it ought to be hanging on the wall," he said. "And him with it."

John Fletcher opened the door for Jackie and helped her into the car.

"He's got good manners," Mrs. Sipple said.

"He knows I'm watching," said Mr. Sipple. "I ain't worried about what he's going to do when he knows I'm watching."

"Come on, Henry," she said. "Don't worry about Jackie. She's a good girl. And John Fletcher is a good boy."

Mr. Sipple didn't answer. He stood behind the curtained window, watching the car going out of his yard.

"I'm going on to bed," she said. It was nine o'clock. "You going to wait up to see she gets in on time?"

"She better get in on time," he said.

"Well, no sense both of us losing sleep. I'm going on to bed."

"I couldn't sleep nohow."

"Don't shame her in front of John Fletcher, Henry. You got anything to say, you wait till he's gone."

She kissed him and went into the back of the house.

He sat in the front room listening to the radio. At ten-forty-five he cut out the lights, sitting in the dark. The car pulled up at eleven o'clock, but Jackie and John Fletcher didn't get out. Through the open window he could hear the occasional murmurings as they talked. He saw a match flare inside the car, lighting up their faces —Jackie was smiling—then the glowing ends of two cigarettes, moving in the darkness. At eleven-thirty-one the door on the driver's side opened and John Fletcher got out. He was not wearing his coat, and had taken off his tie. He went around and opened the door on Jackie's side, taking her hand as she got out. They walked up to the house holding hands and swinging their arms between them, like two small children. Midway to the house John Fletcher stooped and picked up a stone from the yard. He threw it away over the oak tree in the front by the road; then he said something to Jackie, and they both laughed. All the way across the yard they were mumbling to each other, but Mr. Sipple couldn't make out what it was they were saying.

They came up the steps onto the porch and out of his line of sight. There was no talking now, though he could hear their breathing and every now and then a shoe scraping on the boards of the porch. He tiptoed out of the front room and into the hall. Through the curtained window in the front door he thought he could make out Jackie. She was leaning her back against the door. John Fletcher stood on the other side of her. Their arms and hands seemed to be moving, but he couldn't tell about the movements through the curtain of the window.

At last Jackie moved forward and turned to open the door. Mr. Sipple stepped quietly into the front room.

"All right," she said. "Good night."

He couldn't hear what John Fletcher said.

Jackie came into the house quietly, closing the front door behind her without making any noise. He barely heard the click as the latch fell.

Mr. Sipple stepped into the hall.

"You're late," he said.

"What time is it?" she said.

"Quarter to twelve," he said.

"We was back at eleven," she said.

"I said in the house," he said.

She didn't say anything.

"You been smoking cigarettes," he said.

"No I ain't," she said.

"Don't lie to me," he said.

"I ain't smoked no cigarettes," she said.

"I seen you," he said.

She didn't answer.

They stood facing each other in the darkness for a minute. Neither one spoke.

"What else you been doing you wouldn't want to tell me about?" he said.

"I ain't been doing nothing I wouldn't want to tell you about," she said. "I ain't been doing nothing at all."

"Like you ain't been smoking cigarettes?" he said.

She didn't reply.

"Didn't your mother talk to you about how you was to behave?"

"Yes," she said.

"She say it was all right for you to go smoking cigarettes and standing around on the porch in the dark?"

"No," she said.

"What else was you doing out there on the porch anyways? Something else you wouldn't be wanting me nor your mother to know about?"

"We wasn't doing nothing."

"Like you wasn't smoking no cigarettes?"

She didn't say anything.

"You tell me," he said. "Tell me what else your mother said you wasn't supposed to be doing."

He could hear her breathing in the darkness of the hall. She didn't reply.

"You done told me one lie, which I wouldn't have known no better than believe, except I seen it with my own eyes. How many more lies you going to tell me tonight?"

"No lies, Daddy," she said.

"I couldn't trust you," he said. "I wanted to trust you, but I couldn't do it no more. You shouldn't have said 'No' about the cigarettes."

"That's the only time," she said. "I'm sorry about that. But it's the only time."

"But I can't believe you no more," he said. "I just got to see for myself from now on. I ain't going to be able to ask you no more."

She didn't reply for a minute.

"I'm sorry," she said.

"Be quiet and come in your room," he said.

He tiptoed down the hall behind her. When they had gone into her room, he closed the door gently so as not to wake his wife. She turned on the light, and the room was lit by a bare bulb, hanging at the end of a long cord from the ceiling.

"Turn that light out!" he said.

She flicked the switch, and the room was dark again, except for the patches of moonlight falling onto the floors through the windows.

"Now," he said, "get your clothes off and get in the bed."

She didn't speak.

"I ain't going to watch," he said. "I can't see nothing in here anyway, but I'm going to turn my back. You do as I say."

"What you going to do?" she said.

"You just do as I say," he said.

In the darkness of the room he could hear the sounds her clothes made as she undressed. The sounds made him nervous, and he talked to cover them up.

"I want you to be a good girl, Jackie," he said. "You go telling lies, and I can't believe nothing you say. Why'd you have to lie to me about that cigarette? You must have knowed I seen you?"

She didn't reply. He began to be aware of something trying to come around from the back side of his mind, but he didn't know what it was. He listened for it for a minute. Then the silence began to make him nervous again, and he started talking to cover it up.

"Just one lie, and now I can't believe what you tell me. I ought to just ask you, and now I can't."

"I'm ready," she said.

"You got your gown on?" he said, not turning around.

"Pajamas," she said.

"Where's your gown?" he said.

"I don't wear a gown now," she said.

For a minute he didn't speak. "Take off the bottoms," he said.

"Why?" she said.

"Take them off," he said. "I ain't going to look. Then get in the bed and pull the covers up."

He heard the clothes sounds again, then the squeaking of the bed and the rustle of the sheets as she got in. It was still trying to come around, but he didn't know what it was.

"You ready now?" he said.

"Yes," she said.

He turned and went to the bed in the darkness. The moonlight came in through the windows, giving enough light for him to see the objects in the room. He took her clothes from the chair and went to the window with them, examining them in the moonlight. She watched him from the bed as he came back from the window, laying the things carefully across the back of the chair.

He sat on the side of the bed, not touching her.

"I'm going to try one time," he said. "You answer me and tell me the truth."

"Yes," she said. She had the sheet pulled up, holding it tight around her neck.

"What happened in that car?"

"Nothing," she said.

"You smoked a cigarette," he said. "That happened."

"But nothing else," she said.

"I'm trying to believe you, girl," he said. "Now, you tell me the truth. Didn't nothing else happen?"

"No," she said.

He sat in silence for a while. The thing was still trying to come around out of the back side of his mind, and he was listening for it, but it wasn't there yet.

"Why'd you have to lie about the cigarette?" he said. "Maybe I'd have believed you if you hadn't lied about that."

"I'm sorry about the cigarette," she said. "But ain't nothing else happened. That's the God's truth."

He sat in silence for a while. "What else you know about that might have happened?" he said. "Why don't you tell me that? What'd your mother tell you about?"

She didn't answer.

"He had the zebra coat off, and his tie, when you got out and come in the house," he said.

"It's hot out tonight," she said.

"What else he have off in that automobile?" he said.

"What you mean?" she said. "He didn't have nothing else off. What you think?"

"And what did you have off?" he said. "Anything you had off in that automobile?"

"Pa," she said. She touched his hand with hers. He took the hand and squeezed it, hurting her. He thought he could feel it coming around again—but then it wasn't—and he squeezed her hand.

"You hurting me, Pa," she said.

"I just got to know," he said.

"Turn loose, Pa. You hurting me," she said.

He let go her hand. "Tell me again," he said. "Tell me ain't nothing happened in that automobile tonight. One more time, so I might believe it."

"I told you," she said. "I told you—I told you—I told you." She started to cry.

"You lied," he said. It was coming around again—almost . . . Almost—and then it wasn't. "You lied," he said.

He put his hands on her shoulders and pumped them up and down on the bed. She fought back, neither of them making any sounds in the dark stillness of the room. Only the creaking and groaning of the springs of the bed, going faster and faster.

His hands were still on her, not just her shoulders, and they were thrashing around on the bed together, fighting each other, the sheets twirling and billowing, wrapping them around and tangling. She moved under him and against him, fighting his hands. Not scratching or trying to hurt him, but reaching and countering his moving hands, fending them off.

He caught one of her hands and held it. Then the other. Holding both of them in his one, his other hand free. Only for a moment. He could have counted to five, just that long before she broke the one hand free and caught his wrist, squeezing it tight so it wouldn't move.

She gave a small, sharp cry.

"Pa," she said, speaking just the one word. And then the movement stopped.

He saw the wide, staring eyes in the darkness of the room and the underlip held in the teeth. He hadn't felt it. But then he did. Like putting his hand into a spider's web and not knowing he had touched it until the hand drew back, collapsing the latticed pattern. He felt her hands locked on his wrist, frozen there while they looked at each other, staring through the dark. The billowing sheet settled around them as they knelt facing each other in the disorder of the bed.

His eyes slid off to the side, going out of focus, and he could feel it beginning to come around now, almost swinging into his consciousness. He moved slowly, twisting his wrist out of her grip, pulling her arms up toward him before the fingers came loose and she fell over on her side with her knees drawn up, locking her hands between her legs.

He rose beside the bed, standing quiet in the dark. "It was . . . ," he said, ". . . you lied about the cigarettes. You know you done that." He cupped his hands together over his nose and mouth, rubbing his fingers along the sides of his nose. Then he put his hands on his hips, standing with his shoulders hunched forward and his head hanging down.

"Well . . . ," he said, ". . . well . . ." He laced his fingers together in front, pushing them away, cracking his knuckles.

Then he went out of the room into the kitchen. He sat in the dark in the kitchen for a long time, staring out the moonlit windows. Sitting at the table, he felt it again, swinging around on the dark side—not there yet, but coming.

He turned on the light and lit the burner under the coffeepot. While it was heating, he went to the shelf to get the sugar bowl. Beside the bowl he saw the cigar box. There were three others, scattered around the house, filled with old Christmas cards and sewing things, buttons and the like. This one had been the first.

When he saw the box, it came swinging around out of the darkness, and he knew what it was.

"Smoaks . . . ," he said, croaking it out of the back of his throat. He was looking at the King Edward box. "Call Smoaks," he said. "God damn it to hell. I should have called Smoaks."

He lifted the cigar box gently from the shelf and put it on the kitchen table. With his little finger he lifted the lid, turning it back gently. A thimble, a pincushion—like a furry, red tomato, studded with the heads of straight pins—and a tangle of ribbons. He looked at it for a minute, then he went and cut off the burner under the coffeepot and came back to sit down at the table. He pulled the open box over in front of him and took the things out of it, putting them on the table.

"Smoaks . . . ," he said, looking into the empty box, ". . . Jesus God."

After a while he went back into her room and burned the spot out of the sheet. Not a large hole—a half-dollar would have covered it. When he put out his hand to move her, she scurried away from his touch. He didn't look at her when he lit the match so he could find the spot.

"I'm . . . ," he said. He didn't finish.

"Go away, Pa," she said.

He went back into the kitchen and sat down at the table with the empty box in front of him. Afterward he shook a single ribbon out of the tangle. It was a pink one, twisted and creased. He dropped it into the box and closed the lid. Then he turned off the light and went out of the house, carrying the box in both hands.

On the back porch he stopped to take the lantern from the nail. He didn't light it, worrying about Frances. At the pumphouse he stopped again to get the shovel. Then he went on into the woods.

When he was far enough from the house that the trees would hide him, he lit the lantern and hung it from the limb of a pin oak, putting the box down gently to one side. Then he scooped a shallow hole in the ground and put the box into it. With the first scoop of dirt on the shovel, he stopped, looking down at the box, pausing. He shot the dirt out of the shovel to the side of the hole and slid the blade under the box, lifting it out gently and putting it down on firm ground beside the hole. He raised the shovel high over his head, holding it by the very end of the handle in both hands and arching his body to keep from going off balance backward. Then he snapped forward, doubling up and bringing the flat of the blade down on the box, smashing it, so that it made a sound like a paper bag bursting, a small, brittle explosion.

He hit it two more times, splintery-sounding swats. Then he scraped the pieces into the hole and covered them over with dirt, pressing it down with his foot and kicking pine needles over the fresh earth to cover the place.

He took the lantern off the limb and walked back to the house, not putting it out this time. When he got back to the pumphouse, he leaned the shovel against it and took the ax. The woodpile was on the opposite side of the house, where he didn't think Frances would see him.

"She's staying out too late, Henry," Frances said. Jackie had just left the house, going off in a pickup with two boys from Kose. They had said there would be another girl—Annie Mullins. They would pick her up going out.

"Well," said Mr. Sipple, "maybe you better talk to her some more. I don't see nothing else I can do."

"You could tell her to come in earlier," she said. "Or not to go out at all."

"But, like you said, it's still up to her," he said.

"Well, but it seems like there ought to be something you could do."

"Nothing for me," he said. "I already done everything I could do. It's up to her now."

"But she's only just fifteen," she said.

"Yes," he said. "Nearly sixteen. But we can't do it for her. She's a big girl now."

They sat across from each other at the kitchen table. Both of them sitting very straight and looking into the center of the table. It was quiet in the kitchen. The coffeepot was sputtering on the stove. Then, across the ceiling, over their heads, they could hear a rat scurrying in the attic.

Mr. Sipple folded his arms and hugged himself, his eyes turned up toward the ceiling, listening to the rat. The bandage was off the stump of his finger, but it was still angry-looking, red and purple. Dr. Smoaks had said it was going to be all right. But for now the empty space between his fingers, splayed out against his upper arms, was very noticeable. He worked the fingers, feeling the ab-

sence of the missing one in the empty space there on his arm. A posi-
tive feeling of nothing where something ought to be He sat straight
in the chair, feeling the loss in the space between his fingers and
listening to the rat scurrying in the attic.

Smoaks, Deering,
Maggie Poat, and the Shark

1934: SUMMER

The Rainbow Fishing Camp is located one and two-tenths miles from Kallisaw Sound—that's as the crow flies. But you can't go that way, not without webbed feet you can't. It's straight across the marsh. Nothing but slick, blue-brown mud and marsh grass. Like wading through lard. Every step, you sink in up to your crotch. It won't suck you under like quicksand, but you can't do anything with it. You have to go out in a boat through Half Moon Creek, a tidal estuary that takes its time—over four miles—swinging in a wide, arcing turn through the brownish-green spears of the grass. At low tide the creek is just a trickle of water between mud banks, pocked with the holes of fiddler crabs. The banks look and smell like putrified black flesh.

There isn't much to the camp itself. Just one clapboard building with a shed over the front. Coca-Cola signs nailed all over it, a couple of NuGrape Soda ones—they sell more Dr. Pepper than anything else in the soft-drink line, but there isn't a single Dr. Pepper sign on the place—and some Roosevelt posters left over from the campaign of year before last. McAfee County always goes Democrat, but in nineteen-thirty-two everybody voted.

The Rainbow Fishing Camp is owned and operated—half-heartedly—by Mansfield Whitmire. No enterpreneur. A small, peppery man, with gray hair, a stubble of beard, gray too, and a face that looks like it was stuffed in a cheesecloth bag and baked in a brick kiln. The business end of the enterprise consists of a rickety dock that spans the marsh on the rim of the creek and juts out into the stream itself for perhaps twenty feet. A treacherous causeway of weathered, gray wood, most of it rotten looking, with a floating dock bobbing at the end. There is a walkway down to the floating dock—a ramp with rollers on the bottom end, and hinges on the upper, narrow cleats nailed across for steps. But at low tide it hangs almost straight up and down, and is impossible to use. It is easier to jump. Around the floating dock are tied six flat-bottomed bateaux, all painted dark green, with the paint flecking off, and white numbers on the bows where the names ought to be.

At the end of the bluff, where it drops down into the marsh and the dock begins, there is a sixty-gallon drum with a hose draped into it for fishermen to flush out their outboard motors when they come in. Inside the wooden building with the Coca-Cola and Nu-Grape signs is a room that takes up most of the space of the building. There are two long trestle tables with benches on either side, and along one wall is a counter, about half of it taken up by glass display cases containing hooks and lines and various patented gadgets guaranteed to help catch fish. Mansfield doesn't try to sell them, so over the years the cases have taken on the forlorn and neglected appearance of a display of artifacts in a museum of natural history.

Mansfield isn't married. It would have cramped his style. Occasionally he will have in a woman for a while to cook for him and keep him company—generally in cold weather, when the camp isn't doing much business anyway. Sometimes she will stay on for a month or two. "Trying her out," Mansfield says. But it never works. Always there is a fight over something trivial, and the girl—they are mostly women now—will be off for the parts unknown from which she came, or toward which she was heading when Mansfield waylaid her. When this happens, Mansfield will begin to show up at Maggie Poat's roadhouse again on Friday and Saturday nights. For two years now he hasn't had anyone in there with him at the fish camp at all. The Depression has slowed everything down.

Number-four bateau nosed in toward the floating dock. Standing in the bow, ready to fend her off when she bumped the edge of the dock, was a tall, William S. Hart-ish man. Six feet two or three, with a healthy-weary leanness. Slightly round shouldered, in profile he was reminiscent of the Indian in *The End of the Trail*. He wore a gray felt hat with the brim flopped down all around.

The man at the oars backed water carefully, trying to bring the boat up to the dock gently. So gently that the tall man in the bow wouldn't be able to feel the moment of impact. Not the slightest jolt.

When the bow touched, the tall man flinched slightly, rocking down on his leg braced in the bow. He stepped onto the dock with the line and dropped it over a bollard. The second man shipped the dockside oar, then pulled on the other, moving the boat ahead against the line secured to the bollard, and bringing it in alongside the dock. The tall man stooped down and put his hand on the gunwale, drawing it up against the fender. While he held the boat, the second man shipped the outboard oar, then stood up. He had the body of an overblown two-year-old. Chubby and rotund and spraddle legged. But a big man too. Just over six feet. He looked a lot like Wallace Beery, with a fleshy, lopsided face. On his head was a battered white yachting cap.

"You hold the boat," he said. "I'll get them out."

"Don't show off, Case," said the tall man. "I'll give you a hand."

"Just hold the boat, Smoaks," he said. "I can get them out."

He stooped over, reaching down into the bottom of the bateau, then stood up with a galvanized washtub in his arms. It was half full of water, which sloshed around, making it hard to balance. Staggering a little, he stepped out of the boat, took three choppy, waddling steps, then put the washtub down carefully on the dock. The shrimp made zinging sounds against the sides of the tub.

"Get the net," he said.

Smoaks reached into the boat and took out the shrimp net. It had been carefully folded, the line wrapped around it neatly and tied. When he dropped it, the sinkers on the skirt made a loud thump on the dock.

"Think they'll be enough?" said Deering.

Smoaks looked at the tub. "The three of us couldn't eat all those shrimp in a week," he said.

"I hate to run short," said Deering.

They heard an outboard motor in the creek.

"Mansfield," said Smoaks.

"Yes," said Deering. "He ain't never going to tune that Johnson."

They looked up toward the sweeping curve in the creek where the Sound was. Mansfield came around the curve, crouched in the stern of number six. The bow of the bateau canted high out of the water, so it came plowing along on its transom, rolling the water up in front, until Mansfield seemed to be pushing the whole creek ahead of him as he came in. He half-stood in the rear of the boat when he saw them, not letting go of the steering arm of the motor, and began waving. They could see his mouth working too, but the sound of the motor blotted out whatever it was he was saying.

"Worked up as hell about something," said Deering.

They made fast the stern line of number four to another piling off to the side of the floating dock, then stood looking at him as he came up. He cut the motor and coasted in to the side of the dock.

"Big bastard," he said, standing up, and then sitting down again before the bateau bumped the piling.

"What?" said Deering.

"Big bastard," said Mansfield. "Biggest one I ever seen."

"Biggest what?" said Smoaks.

"Shark," said Mansfield. He stood up again and grabbed the dock, beginning to walk the boat around to the cleat on the end.

"Give me the line," said Smoaks.

"What?" said Mansfield.

"Give me the line and I'll bring you around," said Smoaks.

Mansfield gave him the line and stood up while they led it around to the front of the dock. Smoaks began to make it fast to the cleat.

"Don't do that," said Mansfield.

Smoaks looked at him.

"What?" said Deering.

"Get in," said Mansfield. "We got to go get him out."

"We can't go now," said Deering. "We got to get the shrimp down to Maggie's."

"Shit on the shrimp," said Mansfield. "I tell you, this is a big bastard."

"Maggie's expecting us," said Smoaks.

"I can't get the bastard out by myself," said Mansfield.

Smoaks and Deering looked at each other.

"They'll be all right," said Smoaks. "We'll fill the tub with water."

"I hate to keep Maggie waiting," said Deering.

"You don't catch a big bastard like this every day," said Smoaks.

Smoaks took a bucket that Mansfield used for bailing the boats and scooped water into the tub. Deering stood on the dock watching him. When he finished filling the tub, they got into the boat, Smoaks first, then Deering. Before they could sit down, Mansfield gave the starting rope a pull. The Johnson didn't catch.

"Shit," said Mansfield, "wouldn't you know?"

He wound the rope around the starter again and gave it a second pull. It caught with a roar, nearly dumping Mansfield out of the boat. He never would sit down to start a motor.

Getting out of the creek was slower than coming in—the tide was on the flood. With Smoaks and Deering in the bow, the bateau plowed into the water, washing waves up onto the banks as they passed, making the marsh grass whip and sway. They had to work out against the tide. A curve to the left, then a long, widening curve to the right, and around the last bank of marsh grass they saw the open gray-green expanse of Kallisaw Sound. Mansfield turned to the right, heading for the public landing. He put his shark line out there, anchoring it to a piling that he had driven into the sand.

Smoaks and Deering could see the line stretched out from the shore. It wasn't moving much—just stretched out taut. They tried to follow it out into the water, but lost it against the movement of the waves. So they looked for the gallon jug that was the standard float for a shark line. While they were looking, they saw it bob to the surface with a blue-green wink. The line dropped into the water for a moment, then sprang taut again as the jug went under.

"Big bastard," said Mansfield.

He ran the boat up onto the shells at the public landing, and they got out. The line was three-quarter-inch manila. Bigger than it needed to be, but Mansfield didn't want to take any chances of losing one when he did get him on the hook. The jug would bob to the surface every now and then and the line would go slack. The movement wasn't frantic, just strong and regular. He had been on the hook for several hours.

"Help me," said Mansfield, going over to the line and taking it in his hands. The two men went over and took hold.

"When I count three," said Mansfield. He wasn't looking at them. He was looking at the piling in the sand behind them.

"One . . . two . . . three. . . ." On the "three" they all put their backs into it and started off up the beach. They made three steps before the line went taut again and stopped them. They could feel the size of the thing on the other end.

Smoaks and Deering looked at each other. "Jesus," said Deering, "it *is* a big bastard."

Mansfield grunted behind them. "I told you," he said. "I told you it was a big one."

For a minute they stood there, all three of them, straining as the big fish stood them off. Then they began to gain on him slightly. The feet that had been poised in the air went down onto the ground, and they made two more steps before it stopped them again.

"How big?" said Deering. They were all straining on the line.

"What?" said Mansfield. He was leaning back on the line, his face going red, while he looked toward the piling in the sand where the end was tied.

"How big?" said Deering.

"You feel him," said Mansfield. "That's how big. Big bastard."

"You ain't seen him?" said Deering.

"I *felt* him," said Mansfield.

They made four more steps.

"What the shit is he doing?" said Mansfield. "He ain't really fighting us none. Just ain't moving."

"You sure it's a shark?" said Smoaks.

"He ain't even seen it," said Deering.

Mansfield looked away from the piling at them. "What the shit else would it be?" he said.

"A big ray will sound like that. Lay himself down on the bottom, and there ain't no way to get him loose," said Deering.

"I hadn't thought about no ray," said Mansfield. "He's moving around too much for that. A ray sucks himself down on the bottom."

"A shark ought to move around more," said Deering.

"I think it's a shark," said Mansfield.

"Well," said Smoaks, "let's get it out. You don't ever know for sure till you get it out so you can look at it."

"Anyway, it's a big bastard," said Mansfield. "Something that big, I'd want him out of the water just the same. Whatever it is."

"Yes," said Smoaks. "You're right about that."

They took two more steps; then the line went taut again, and they lost two.

"Hold it good," said Mansfield. He let them brace themselves; then he dropped the line and ran to the piling, where he took up the slack and put a clove hitch around the piling to hold it. Then he went back and helped them walk six more steps of slack into the line.

"Hold it good," he said.

"How much line you got?" said Smoaks, his face red, leaning back against the pull on the line.

"Thousand feet," said Mansfield.

"Jesus," said Deering. "It ain't going to take but all summer."

"Why don't you go get your car?" said Smoaks. "We'll tie it to the bumper, and you can just drive off and haul him out that way."

"Pull my bumper off, you mean," said Deering.

"You said it was going to take all summer to do it this way," said Smoaks. "You're right."

"What time is it?" said Deering.

Smoaks pulled out his pocket watch. "Five-thirteen," he said.

"Maggie's going to think we died," said Deering.

"Maybe you'll see somebody back at the camp," said Smoaks. "Get them to tell her we'll be late."

"Shit," said Deering.

They left Smoaks to watch the line while they went back to the fishing camp in the boat to get the car.

After they had gone, Smoaks sat down on the beach beside the taut line. The gallon jug would dip under from time to time, catching glints from the sun going down behind him, and winking its blue-green eye at him. Between the dark line of trees on Kallisaw Island and the beach where he sat, the gray-green water of the Sound moved in a gentle, restless chop. It was a hot day, and working on the line had drenched him with sweat, but he didn't even think about going into the water to cool off. No one in McAfee County went swimming in the open sea. Not that Smoaks was a spooky man. Not at all. He was steady and solid. But he had seen the things that got dragged out of the water on the ends of fishing lines. No one who had seen would want to get down into the water with them.

He sat motionless, watching the jug at the end of the line and trying to form an air-lighted image of what was going on in the depths of the gray-green water. Trying to see the great, silent shape moving there in the darkness under the water. Pulsing like the heart of the Sound itself on the end of the line.

He gave it up. It wasn't dark, but it was getting dark. The trees on Kallisaw Island were turning black.

He thought of the other lines like this one, scattered up and down the coast. Catching them at the back of his eye and seeing them wave slowly in the gray-green darkness of the seabed. Each baited with the pale body of a chicken, or a great chunk of rotten meat. Inside the bait, the hook, buried like a hard, inverted question mark. Many of them forged by hand and big as a man's arm from elbow to wrist.

Every one of the brutes fished out of the water was one less to worry about—one to the good. He and Deering had had a moral duty to help Mansfield get his out, a duty that increased in direct proportion to the size of the beast. They had known that at the beginning. The other had just been talk.

But there was no end to it, this fishing for monsters. No matter how many they caught, they could be sure that another—maybe even bigger, maybe a thing more unspeakably obscene—would be waiting for them under the green water. Perhaps next time it would rise to the bait and be pulsing there on the end of the line when they came back—in a day, or a week, or a month—to pull it out.

Smoaks lit a cigarette and hugged his knees. The sweat drying out of his shirt made him cold.

It was over an hour before he heard the sound of the Ford's engine coming down the oyster-shell road toward the landing. Twenty-eight minutes after six. At ten minutes to seven Mansfield arrived in the bateau, keeping in as close to shore as possible, staying away from the jug, where it winked in the water. The sun was getting low behind the marsh to the west, but there were two hours of light left before dark.

Mansfield made Deering back the car up to the piling; then he took the loose end of the line and looped it over the bumper.

"No, you don't," said Deering. "He'll pull the bumper off." He cut the engine and got out of the car. "Give it to me," he said. He took the end of the line and passed it through the rear windows of the Ford, making a harness. "He ain't going to pull off the whole top of the car," he said. "He ain't that big of a bastard."

"Okay," said Mansfield. "Now you-all get a good hold on it while I let off the end from the piling here. Then we'll just walk out the slack until the Ford is taking the whole load."

Deering and Smoaks took up their positions, digging their heels in and hauling back so the end of the line between them and the piling fell slack. Mansfield lifted the clove hitch off the piling in two deft movements, then ran up and took his place in front of them on the taut part of the line.

"Now," he said, "we'll walk out the slack easy and let him pull on the Ford for a while."

Deering kept looking back at his car as they walked it out. It rocked when it took the whole strain, but it didn't move.

They had to get out into the water a little way before the line was taut again.

"I don't like it," said Mansfield.

Deering went and got in the Ford. He started it, put it in gear, and began to roll up the oyster-shell road.

"Hold it," said Mansfield. "Let me look at the line. I don't want to break it and lose the son-of-a-bitch."

He satisfied himself that it was going to hold. "Pull away," he said.

"It ain't scraping the paint, is it?" said Deering.

"No," said Mansfield.

Deering eased the Ford off in first, bringing the line with him.

It came out of the water hissing, squeezing the water off in a mist as the shark surged on the end. The Ford rolled off slowly down the road.

"There he is!" said Mansfield. He and Smoaks both saw the big fin as the fish rolled, coming into the shallower water. "I told you it was a shark," he said.

"He's a big bastard," said Smoaks, speaking low, looking at the great fish pulsing at the other end of the line.

"Help me guide the line," said Mansfield. "He's going to tear himself open on the shell rake out there. Stop the car!" he yelled to Deering. Deering had the door open, watching as the line came in. He stopped the car and put on the brake.

"He's a big bastard," he said, looking at the water, where they could see the big fish rolling.

"We'd better bring him in the rest of the way ourselves," said Mansfield. "He's going to cut himself to pieces on the shell rake out there."

In shallow water now the big fish had lost most of his fight. But he was so big that as he came out of the water he got harder and harder to move.

"You got a gun in your car?" said Mansfield.

"Pistol," said Deering.

"Get it," said Mansfield. "We got to get too close to him. I want him dead before we drag him out."

Deering walked back to the car and got the pistol.

"Want me to do it?" he said as he gave the pistol to Mansfield.

"He's my fish," said Mansfield.

"I know that," said Deering. "Do you want me to shoot him?"

"I'll shoot him," said Mansfield.

He took the pistol and went to his boat, shoving it off the sand and into the water. "Hold the line," he said, "and keep him headed away from me if he tries to go for the boat."

"He's worn out," said Smoaks.

"He's a big bastard anyway," said Mansfield. "Don't fuck around, now."

The boat was drifting, and Mansfield took an oar and paddled out to the shark. The boat bumped him, and he thrashed his tail, rolling over and splashing water into the boat.

"Sit down," said Smoaks. "You want him to knock you out of the boat?"

Mansfield sat down. He pointed the pistol, holding it with both hands, and fired all six bullets into the head of the shark. There was a thrashing and rolling; then the water was still. The gray-green turning red.

"Okay," said Mansfield. "Pull him in."

"What?" said Smoaks.

"Pull him on in," said Mansfield.

"You going to leave him here?" said Smoaks.

"I want to *see* him," said Mansfield. "Then we can take him back to the camp."

"We got to get him out twice?" said Smoaks. "How much you think he weighs?"

"He's a big bastard," said Mansfield. "You felt him on the line. How much you think?"

"Once is enough," said Smoaks. "You can see him when we get back to the camp. We can all see him."

Mansfield looked at him for a minute.

"Bring the boat on in," said Smoaks.

Mansfield paddled the boat back to the landing. Smoaks got in and pushed it off, coasting out toward the shark.

"What you better do is tie him on behind the bateau and tow him back to the camp," he said.

"Um . . . ," said Mansfield, looking at the shark. "Ain't there no other way?"

"No other way I can think of tonight," said Smoaks.

Mansfield looked up at the sky, then back at the shark in the water. "It's coming on dark," he said.

"Yes," said Smoaks. "Won't be anything left of him by tomorrow if you don't get him out of the water."

Mansfield stood in the boat looking at the hulk of the shark. "I don't want to be towing that thing in the water in the dark," he said. "No telling what might come after it."

"I'll be riding with you," said Smoaks.

"Can't you think of no other way?" said Mansfield.

"He's dead, Mansfield," said Smoaks.

"I know he's dead," said Mansfield. "I just don't like it with it coming on dark and all."

"I'll be with you," said Smoaks. "He's not going to get us."

Smoaks took the hook out of the side of the shark's jaw and put it back in the center, so he would tow more easily. Mansfield made the chain leader fast to the stern of the boat.

"Not too short," said Smoaks. "Give him the whole chain. He'll tow easier."

"We'll see you back at the camp, Case," he said to Deering.

"What if you don't make it back?" said Deering.

"That's the kind of talk we need," said Smoaks. "You want to get to Maggie's tonight?"

"See you back at the camp," said Deering. He got into the Ford, started it up, and drove off down the oyster-shell road.

"Come on," said Smoaks.

Mansfield pulled the starter rope. The Johnson kicked off on the first pull.

"It's an omen," said Smoaks.

"Sit down," Smoaks said.

Mansfield kept standing up to look at the shark in the water behind the bateau. The hook in his lower jaw pulled his head up, holding his snout out of the water. A little wave rolled up and went streaming off out of the corners of his mouth. The tail waved slowly from side to side in the wake of the boat. It looked like he was reaching up out of the water toward the boat.

"He looks like he's trying to bite the boat," said Mansfield.

"What?" said Smoaks. He couldn't hear over the sound of the motor. "Sit down before you fall out."

Mansfield looked at him, then twisted the arm of the motor, cutting it off. The bow of the bateau dropped into the water, and it rapidly lost way. The shark nosed ahead, gliding toward the boat, bumping into it, its head slowly sliding under the water as the strain on the leader went off. The boat lurched when it hit, and Mansfield lost his balance, almost toppling over the stern on top of it. He caught himself on the motor, burning his hand.

"God damn," he said, jerking his hand away.

"It's dead, Mansfield," said Smoaks.

"It looks like he's chasing us," he said.

"*You* shot him," said Smoaks.

Mansfield stood looking over the stern at the hulk of the shark in the water. He held his left hand to his mouth with his right hand, licking it to stop the burning.

"All right," said Smoaks. "I'll show you." He moved to the stern. "Sit down," he said. "Sit down, and I'll show you."

He put his hand on Mansfield's shoulder, pressing gently. Mansfield sank onto the seat, still sucking on his hand. Smoaks sat down on the seat opposite him, looking at him.

"Now, watch," Smoaks said.

He pulled on the chain of the leader until the shark's snout came out of the water. Streams of water rushed out of the corners of its mouth. Smoaks snubbed the chain over the stern with his left hand, then thrust his right hand into the shark's mouth, pushing it all the way to the elbow. He had to lean out over the stern, so his forehead was resting on the tip of the snout.

Mansfield watched him, his eyes going big.

"See?" said Smoaks. "He's dead. He's a big bastard, but he's dead, Mansfield."

"I know he's dead," said Mansfield, his voice loud and whiny. He took his hand out of his mouth. "I shot him, God damn it."

"Well?" said Smoaks.

"He just looks like he's going to take a bite out of the boat when we're pulling him."

Smoaks took his arm out of the shark's mouth and let go the leader. "Get up in the front," he said.

Mansfield put his hand back to his mouth, then stood up and moved to the bow.

"Sit down," said Smoaks.

Mansfield stood looking over the stern of the boat. "I wish it wasn't coming on dark," he said. "I can't make out none of the trees on the shore."

"Sit down where you can't see it," said Smoaks. "I'll take it in the rest of the way."

Deering was waiting for them on the floating dock when they got back to the Rainbow Camp. They rigged a block and tackle to a davit that Mansfield used to haul his boats out of the water to clean and paint them. Putting the hook of the tackle through the eye of the shark hook, the three of them got on the fall of the tackle and hoisted the shark out of the water.

It was the first time they had seen all of it. It was enormous. Gray-white and sleek—not like the brown, wide-headed sand sharks they usually caught. From nose to tail, it must have measured nearly twelve feet. Because of the block and tackle, they couldn't tell how much it weighed. Half a ton perhaps.

"Look at them teeth," said Mansfield. "Nothing but teeth. He's got a hundred of them."

Deering looked up at the great crescent mouth, standing on the belly side of the fish—not too close. "Makes you cold just to look at it, don't it?" he said.

"He's a big bastard, all right," said Smoaks. "Biggest one I ever saw."

It was getting very dark now. Seventeen minutes after eight. The sun was down, the marsh going black.

"Look," said Mansfield. Hanging from the davit, the shark was eviscerating through his anus. On the dock was a pile of slippery-looking intestines, like a mound of wet, purple macaroni.

"No bones," said Smoaks. "Turn him up like that, and everything just drops out where it can."

"He's shitting his guts out," said Mansfield.

"In a manner of speaking," said Smoaks. "Hang him the other way, and they'd come out through his mouth."

"Ain't he a big bastard, though?" said Mansfield.

"We get us a piece of him tomorrow," said Deering. "Don't forget to tell everybody we helped."

"What you want?" said Mansfield.

"I want me some teeth," said Deering.

"You name it. You got it," said Mansfield. "What you want, Smoaks?"

"I'll think it over," said Smoaks. "I'll think it over and let you know in the morning."

They gathered up their washtub and the shrimp net, emptied most of the water out of the tub, then carried the shrimp out and put them in the back seat of the Ford.

"Don't let him get away from you," said Deering. "I want a picture of me with him in the morning."

Mansfield wasn't listening to him.

"How's your hand?" said Smoaks.

"What?" said Mansfield.

"Let me see your hand."

Mansfield held it out, and Smoaks looked at it. "Not too bad," he said. "Put some butter on it. You'll have a blister there in the morning."

They got into the Ford and drove off. Mansfield stood on the edge of the bluff, by the sixty-gallon drum, looking down at the dock, where the enormous fish hung pale silver in the moonlight.

Maggie Poat's roadhouse—that was all anyone in McAfee County ever called it; no one from outside McAfee County ever had any occasion to refer to it at all—was a wooden building set back off U.S. 17 in the live oaks. It had been there for fifteen years or so. No one recalled just exactly when it had been built. Sometime after World War I. Nineteen-eighteen or -nineteen. Its original purpose wasn't very clear, because there had been no U.S. 17 at the time. Just a dirt road that wandered around in the pines and oaks, starting at Midway and eventually ending up at Darien. The building was a monument to some forgotten and misguided entrepreneur—an unsuccessful visionary—who had tried to set up a business in this unlikely spot. Whatever the building had been intended for originally, it was not a dwelling. The rooms were too big for that, and it had no screened porch in front. Probably it had been a store—with the big room for merchandise in front, and rooms at the back where the family lived. Only a family man would have been desperate enough to plan and pursue his fortune in such an out-of-the-way spot. It had to be a project born of desperation.

Subsequently, it had served for a store—so its appearance might have been due to alterations made by Bancroft Davis. He had moved into it sometime around nineteen-twenty-four or -five. Then he had moved out after the stock-market crash of nineteen-twenty-nine. Not that the crash had anything to do with the move, really. People in McAfee County kept hearing about how terrible it was over the two or three radios that served the county in those days. It made some of them nervous to think that something terrible was going on, but actual repercussions were very dim there. It certainly didn't affect Bancroft's business, which had never amounted to much anyway. But Bancroft had a feeling for dramatic moments, and he was fed up with the business, which was really no business at all. So when the crash came along, he took it as an opportunity to go ahead and unload—the way he had been planning to do.

Maggie Poat bought it off him for two hundred dollars cash and a Model T Ford. She had been operating around the county for four or five years—she must have been about twenty-one or -two at the time—and had just gotten tired of moving so much. It looked like an ideal setup to her. The big room for entertainment, and the little rooms in the back where she could take the customers. She kept the kitchen the same size, but partitioned the other rooms, so she had four small ones. On weekends she would have in two or three girls to help her out with the customers. During the week she worked the whole thing by herself, with only one Negro girl to do the cooking and housework.

Maggie took over the business at a bad time, considering. But President Roosevelt helped her along in nineteen-thirty-three by setting up a CCC Camp down in the woods near Fancy Station— about three miles away. Once the word about her place got out, she drew the payroll for the whole camp every Saturday night. Incidental customers would wander in from time to time, whenever luck went their way and they got their hands onto some money. Business became so brisk that she would have a little band come in on Saturday nights to liven things up.

The Dorchester Swamp Stompers was a three-piece outfit— drums, accordion, and banjo—played by Gordon and Folger Gramling and Hewlitt Gay. Folger actually carried the melody on his accordion, but Hewlitt had gotten the group together, and he insisted on fronting it. He was the one with the artistic temperament—high strung and nervous, with a permanent note of insistence in his cackling voice. Gordon and Folger didn't much care. The brothers were phlegmatic to the point of imbecility, and as long as they made a little money on Saturday nights, and got to perform to an appreciative audience, they didn't notice that Hewlitt was having his way. His banjo had a palm-tree beach scene painted on the head in black; and red, yellow, and green light bulbs inside that would blink off and on while he played. "Red Sails in the Sunset" was his showpiece. He would wrap himself around his instrument, playing with his left hand way up on the frets near the head, and his right whipping up and down in a blur, drawing out the chords *legato e molto espressivo*. Sometimes he would get himself so worked up there would be tears in his eyes when he finished.

Smoaks and Deering stayed away on weekends, but they put in a good deal of time around the place from Monday to Thursday —especially Thursday, which was usually quiet, since payday was Saturday, and everyone would be broke by that late in the week. They didn't either one of them have much money to spend—doctors were paid with goodwill and produce in McAfee County, and farming had gone to hell everywhere—but they were good company. And they were always bringing her little presents of one kind or another—fresh vegetables out of Case's garden, or some shrimp or crabs they had caught. Every now and then a bottle of perfume from Smoaks, who did get a cash fee from a patient once in a while. They would take her out to ride in their cars. And she liked tooling around on the dirt roads, scaring the niggers and raising hell.

They had all known each other for a long time. Since they were children. And had gone through school together.

Smoaks and Deering pulled around into the back yard and parked the Ford under one of the big oaks. They still had their fishing clothes on. Maggie was sitting on the kitchen steps, waiting for them when they got there, and the pot was already going, with a fire under it, out in the middle of the yard. Two Negro children, boys, eight or nine, stood near the pot.

"Thought you wasn't coming," she said from the steps, not getting up.

"Mansfield caught a shark," Deering said, getting out of the Ford.

"What?" she said.

"Mansfield Whitmire caught him a shark on his line. We had to help him bring it in," Deering said.

"Mansfield's crazy," she said.

"It's a big one," said Deering. "Biggest bastard of a shark I ever seen."

"How big?" said Maggie.

"Fifty feet?" said Smoaks, talking to Deering. "You reckon it was more than that?"

"What you mean?" said Deering. "Sixty at least. I seen shrimp boats wasn't that big."

"At least sixty," said Smoaks, talking to Maggie.

"You boys got the beer, I see," she said.

"I swear," said Deering. "Ain't that right, Smoaks?"

"He's not lying to you, Maggie," said Smoaks. "Biggest bastard I ever saw."

"Did you get the shrimp, too?" she said.

"Let's get it out, Smoaks," said Deering. Together they got the washtub and brought it over to the fire. They poured off the water onto the ground, then started scooping up handfuls of shrimp and throwing them into the pot. The two Negro boys helped them.

"What's Mansfield going to do with it?" said Maggie.

"Maybe he ain't going to do nothing with it," said Deering. "He's scared of it. He was only looking at it when we left him."

"It's dead, ain't it?" said Maggie.

"Hanging up on his dock," said Smoaks. "But that don't matter to Mansfield."

"I bet he locks his doors tonight when he goes to bed," said Deering.

"Really, now," said Maggie, "how big?"

Deering and Smoaks looked at each other. "We'll go over and look at it after we eat the shrimp," said Smoaks.

"I always wanted a sharktooth necklace," she said.

"Why didn't you tell us about that before?" said Deering. "Smoaks and me would have gone out there to Kallisaw Sound and got you one with our bare hands."

"I never thought to bring it up before," she said. "First time."

"How about a whole jawboneful?" said Smoaks. "You could wear it on your head for a hat, or a crown maybe."

"Well, but what I always wanted was a necklace," said Maggie. "I never thought about a whole jawbone."

"Smoaks and me helped Mansfield get him in. We got a claim on him for anything like that, I reckon."

"Besides," said Smoaks, "he won't go near the thing by himself anyway. We'll just go down there after we finish eating and get you whatever pieces you want off him."

Smoaks went and got the beer out of the car. "It's not cold," he said. "We stopped for the ice on the way from Mansfield's."

"Long as it's not hot," said Maggie.

Smoaks opened the bottles with an opener he had on his key chain. Then they all three sat down on the steps to drink their beer and wait for the shrimp to get done. Maggie sat on the top step. Deering and Smoaks sat on the bottom one, where they could see up her dress.

They talked of various things. The weather: Hot and dry. Roosevelt: He was the first President the three of them had actually voted for, and they felt a personal interest and responsibility for what he did. So far they were satisfied with him.

They also talked about the upcoming Baer-Carnera fight.

"The wop's just so goddamn big," said Deering. "How you going to knock out a man as big as that?"

"Size isn't that important," said Smoaks. "Look at Dempsey. Carnera's too big to handle himself right. Baer is going to kill him."

When the shrimp were ready, they scooped them out of the pot with a dipper, putting them on newspapers, then shelling them by hand and dipping them in the sauce made with Worcestershire and catsup. Smoaks opened more beer.

"Mansfield sure as shit was scared," said Deering, chuckling.

"How big was he, really?". said Maggie, holding the bottle in both hands and resting her elbows on her knees.

"Sixty feet," said Smoaks. "I told you."

"Okay," she said. "I was just asking."

"Big enough to scare the shit out of Mansfield," said Deering.

"He was a big bastard," said Smoaks, sipping his beer.

"Yeah," said Deering, laughing and slapping his leg. "Scared the shit out of Mansfield. He'll lock his doors tonight."

"Well, it *is* scary," said Smoaks. "I got to thinking about it sitting there on the beach while you and Mansfield went to get your car."

"Mansfield sure had the shit scared out of him," said Deering, slapping his leg again and taking a swig out of his bottle of beer.

"Okay," said Smoaks.

"You notice how he wouldn't get close to him when we got him back at the dock?" said Deering. "Poor old Mansfield. Scared of his shadder."

"Wasn't his shadow he was scared of," said Smoaks, not looking at Deering.

"Wouldn't no man take on like that over no dead shark," said Deering. "Not no *real* man wouldn't do it. Not over no live one neither, for that matter."

Smoaks didn't say anything. The light from the fire lit up the festoons of Spanish moss above the pot and around. They hung suspended, dropping out of the darkness into which the light from the fire did not penetrate—like stalactites in a grotto.

"Mansfield's crazy," said Maggie.

"Mansfield thinks funny," said Smoaks, "but he's not crazy."

"Scared the shit out of him," said Deering, taking another pull on the beer.

"Mansfield's been fishing the sound for a long time," said Smoaks.

Deering looked at him. "What's that supposed to mean?" he said.

"Nothing," said Smoaks. "Just that he has."

"Okay?" said Deering.

"Nothing," said Smoaks. "Mansfield had the shit scared out of him."

"That's all I said," said Deering.

"Yes," said Smoaks.

"Well, God damn it, he did."

"I said he did," said Smoaks. "Just let it go."

"What are you getting at, Smoaks?" said Deering.

"Nothing," said Smoaks. He looked into the fire for a minute. "I was scared, too, God damn it," he said.

"What of?" said Deering. "It was dead."

"I know the shark was dead," said Smoaks. "It wasn't the shark so much I was scared of." He looked into the fire for a minute again. "He was a big bastard, though."

"Shit," said Deering. "You sound crazy as Mansfield."

"You ever been swimming out in the Sound?" said Smoaks. "I mean, right out in the middle?"

"What the shit has that got to do with it?" said Deering.

"Have you?" said Smoaks.

"No," said Deering, looking into the fire.

They sat for a while without saying anything. Deering looked at Maggie. "You think I'd be scared?" he said.

"What?" said Smoaks.

"You think I'd be scared to go out there in the Sound, don't you?" said Deering.

Smoaks didn't answer him for a minute. "I never really thought about it, Case," he said. "I wasn't thinking about you. You *ought* to be scared."

"Shit if that's so," said Deering. "I wouldn't be scared worth a *God* damn."

"Okay," said Smoaks.

"No," said Deering. "You think I'd be scared, don't you?"

"I told you I wasn't thinking about you anyway," said Smoaks. "Why don't you just let it go?"

"Yes," said Maggie. "Let's talk about something else."

"No," said Deering. "No, I ain't going to just let it go." He stood up. "I ain't scared, Smoaks," he said. His assertion had the air of a challenge.

Smoaks looked up at him in the firelight. "Sit down, Case," he said. "Sit down and shut up."

"Don't say 'shut up' to me, Smoaks," said Deering. "I ain't scared."

"Just sit down," said Smoaks.

"For Christ's sake, yes," said Maggie. "Sit down, Case. We've heard about enough of it."

"Say it," said Deering.

"Say what?" said Smoaks.

"Say I ain't scared." Deering weaved a little from side to side as he stood there above them. The fire lit up his face from below, making black holes where his eyes should have been.

"Sit down," said Smoaks.

"Say it," said Deering.

Smoaks looked into the fire. "Okay," he said at last. "Okay. You ain't scared. Now, will you sit down?"

Deering looked at him. "You don't believe it, though," he said. "You don't really think I wouldn't be scared."

Smoaks didn't say anything.

"Come on," said Deering. He began walking away from the fire.

"What?" said Smoaks.

"Come on," said Deering.

"Where?" said Smoaks.

"So I can show you I ain't scared."

"Jesus, Case," said Maggie. "Won't you let it go?"

"No," said Smoaks. "No, he ain't going to do that." He stood up and started after Deering. "Come on," he said to Maggie. "You're through eating, ain't you? You can see the shark anyway."

"This is crazy," said Maggie.

"Yes," said Smoaks. "Yes, it is."

"I hate it when he gets his ass on his shoulders that way," she said.

Deering had the engine of the Ford running. "Come on," he said.

They got into the car and drove to the camp. Mansfield's house was dark, and no lights came on when they pulled up in front.

"He's got his doors locked," said Deering.

"Drive on down there closer to the dock," said Smoaks.

Deering pulled down where the path went out onto the causeway leading to the dock, cut off the engine, and pulled up the brake.

"Come on," said Deering, getting out of the car. "We got to get us a boat."

"Jesus," said Maggie.

"It's a nice night," said Smoaks. "Come on, Maggie. You and me can neck. Case likes to show how good he can row."

They walked down to the dock. The moon was bright, and they

could see the great silvery hulk of the shark still hanging on the davit. The pile of intestines glistened in the moonlight.

"He's a big one, all right," said Maggie.

"Sixty feet," said Deering. "Just like we said."

They walked out onto the dock.

"Jesus," said Smoaks. "Look at that. Why'd he want to go and do that?"

A hatchet stuck out of the shark's head. They could see a number of great, bruised gashes where Mansfield had hacked at him. There must have been fifteen or twenty of them.

"What the hell got into him?" said Maggie.

"I told you it scared the shit out of him," said Deering. He stood beside the shark, looking up at its mouth and patting it with his hand.

"Must have stuck in the cartilage in his head, and he couldn't get it out," said Smoaks.

"Maybe he got scared and just ran away," said Deering.

"Maybe," said Smoaks.

"I ain't scared," said Deering. He slapped the great fish with his open hand. A sharp, solid sound. The fish didn't move. "Come on," he said, and walked out onto the floating dock. When they didn't follow him, he made a big follow-me motion with his whole arm. "Come on," he said, "follow me."

"We got to do this, Smoaks?" said Maggie.

"It's a nice night," said Smoaks. "Not too much of a moon, but it's a nice night."

They walked down onto the floating dock.

"Help me get it loose," Deering said, working on the line to number-four bateau.

Smoaks helped him get the bowline off; then they all got into the boat, and Deering took the oars and started to turn the bow out into the stream.

"Let me cast off the other line," said Smoaks.

Deering rowed them out of the creek and into the Sound. He headed for the public landing, keeping well out from the shore. When they got to the public landing, he turned the bow into the Sound and rowed it straight out for two or three hundred yards.

"Is this it?" he said.

"Is this what?" said Smoaks.

"Where the jug was," said Deering. "Mansfield's line?"

Smoaks looked back toward the shore, then around at the Sound, getting his bearings.

"Okay," said Deering. He shipped the oars, then stood up and stumbled into the bow. He fumbled around for a minute before he got the flywheel that served for an anchor; then he swung it over the side, slinging it into the water.

He watched the line as it paid out. "Won't reach bottom," he said, looking at the line hanging off the bow. "Okay," he said, turning to Smoaks, who was sitting in the stern with Maggie. "This is about the right place."

"Okay," said Smoaks, looking around. "Looks like about the place to me."

"I'm ready if you are," said Deering.

"Me ready?" said Smoaks. "Ready for what?"

"We'll see who the yellowbelly is," said Deering.

"I ain't in no contest with you," said Smoaks. "This was all your own idea. You just go right ahead."

"Ain't you man enough for it?" said Deering.

Smoaks didn't say anything.

"Calling me yellow, when you ain't man enough for it your own self," he said.

"Nobody called you yellow, Case," said Smoaks. "This whole thing is your own idea. The Sound scares the shit out of me in the *daytime*."

"Are you coming or not?" said Deering.

Smoaks sat looking at him for a long time. "He's crazy as hell, Maggie," he said. "We never should have let him have the beer."

"Come on, Case," she said. "I'm getting cold out here."

"It's me and you, Smoaks," said Deering. "You got the guts for it?"

"Maggie's cold," said Smoaks. "Do it. Or let's go on back and finish the beer."

"It takes a yellowbelly to call a yellowbelly," said Deering.

"That's not quite the way you ought to put it," said Smoaks.

"You're a yellowbelly, Smoaks," said Deering. "Don't tell me. I may be going to have to beat your ass too, after we get back."

"Yellowbelly . . . ," said Smoaks. He stood up in the stern, rocking the boat. "That's the kind of a mind he's got," he said, speaking to Maggie. "I'm not ever going to hear the end of it if I don't. You know?"

"It's crazy as hell," said Maggie. "Let's go on back in. I'm getting cold."

Smoaks patted his stomach with both hands, looking up at the sky. "It's a nice night," he said. "I'd lots rather neck."

"Yellowbelly," said Deering. With both of them standing up, the boat had begun to rock, so it was difficult to keep their feet.

"You see?" said Smoaks. "He's going to remember this tomorrow. He wouldn't never let me forget about it. It wouldn't be a joke after a while. I'm just not up to hearing him run his mouth for the rest of my life."

"We'll see who the yellowbelly is," said Deering. He began to take off his clothes. "We'll both of us go in the water"—the boat rocked and he nearly fell out—"we'll swim out from the boat a ways. Last one has to get back in the boat wins."

"You know . . . this whole thing is crazy as hell," said Smoaks. "Let's go on back and finish the shrimp and beer. The Sound scares the hell out of me in the *daytime*." He looked around him at the black water. The boat rose and fell gently in the swell.

Deering didn't say anything. He swayed, pulling off his undershirt, and almost fell out of the boat.

"Turn your back, Maggie," said Smoaks.

"Jesus Christ," said Maggie. "After all these years."

The men stripped off their clothes, then jumped into the water.

"Kind of warm once you're in," said Smoaks, swimming away from the boat.

"Can I look now?" said Maggie.

"I saw you peeking," said Smoaks.

"This far enough, Case?" he said. They could see the boat, but they couldn't see each other.

"I can't see you, yellowbelly," said Deering.

"You let us know, Maggie," said Smoaks.

"Out a little further, Case," she said.

"This okay?" said Case.

"Little further," said Maggie.

The water was dark and warm. When he moved, Case could see his limbs outlined in phosphorus. Now and then a small fish would dart by, making a phosphor trail in the water—coming up to him, then darting off. The water was very warm.

"Wonder what the little fish are?" said Smoaks, yelling so Case could hear him.

"Don't say nothing," said Deering. "That's part of it."

The gentle swell lifted them from time to time—a rhythmic, pulsing movement. The moonlight made the boat, with Maggie in it, look bigger than it was. But it also made it look farther away.

"This is what I call a hell of a way to spend an evening," said Maggie from the boat.

"No talking," said Smoaks. "We got to concentrate on all those sharks that're swimming around here trying to get us."

Deering didn't say anything. He was treading water, watching the phosphor trails that his legs made in the water beneath him. He didn't like that sparkly light. Moving his arms in paddling motions, he saw them outlined in the silver bubbles too. Now and then more small fish would dart up to him for a moment, hover, then dart away. He moved his hands to fend them off. Looking down into the water, he could see other trails of phosphorus moving below him. Whether they were little fish just beneath his legs, or big ones farther down, he couldn't make out for sure. He didn't want to watch them, but he couldn't make himself look away. He began to remember the shark's crescent mouth.

Case had the skin of a farmer. Red face and V at the neck. Red arms to the elbows. Everything else was dead white. His legs pumping the water below him had the waxy paleness of a plucked chicken—pieces of dead meat.

A shrimp nipped his back, and he thrashed in the water.

"Don't splash," said Smoaks, his voice floating in over the crest of a swell; "that's what gets them interested."

Deering didn't answer him. He moved his arms and legs more slowly. Another shrimp nipped him on the back, and he jumped— trying not to splash. He watched his white feet moving, trying to look behind them, still seeing the row on row of triangular teeth, stuffed in the white gums.

He looked up into the sky, pale violet, lit by the moon. But then he looked back down into the water again. He couldn't help himself.

He felt his stomach muscles contract. His breathing began to be labored. The water was warm, but it sapped him, drawing the heat out of his body. He felt a chill coming on, hitting him in the stomach in waves. His teeth began to chatter, and his stomach muscles contracted, making him pull his head down into the water. He threw his head back, doubling up his legs, trying to float that way, keeping his nose and mouth out of the water. The spasms of the chill kept hitting him, faster and faster, drawing him into a ball to hold in the heat. His head kept going under water. When it did, he would see the mouth. A hard, white crescent. Open eyes, big as silver dollars, staring into him with a cruel, glazed idiocy. The shape of the fin and the tail waving slowly in the water.

And behind all of these, there was another shape. Which was not the shark, but something else. Moving in a gray-green light, with no real shape at all.

"What's the matter, Case?" Maggie was standing in the boat.

"Something wrong?" said Smoaks.

"Something's the matter with Case. He's rolling around in the water."

"Row the boat over and see if he's all right," said Smoaks.

"I can't row the boat," she said.

"Where is he?"

"Over there," she said, pointing.

Smoaks began swimming in that direction, climbing the black swells.

"That way," she said.

He looked where she was pointing, then corrected his direction. He heard him, and swam to the sound.

"You all right, Case?" he said.

"Chchchchiilll . . . ," said Case. His teeth were chattering, so he could hardly talk at all.

"We got to get you back in the boat," said Smoaks. "You'll have a cramp if you keep balling up like that."

"IIIIIImmmmmm aaaallll rrrrrright," said Deering, barely getting the words out through his clenched teeth.

"Like hell you are," said Smoaks. "You're going to drown. I got to get you out right now." The swells rolled under them, throwing them up toward the pale half-moon, bringing the horizon into view all around, then pulling them back down into the black trough.

Smoaks got his hand under Deering's chin and began to tow him toward the boat.

"LLLLeeeeaaaavvvveeee mmmmeeee aaaalllloooonnnneeee," said Deering.

"You lose," said Smoaks. "Face it like a man."

Deering didn't say anything.

Smoaks towed him in toward the boat.

"Is he all right?" said Maggie.

"Help me get him in the boat," said Smoaks. "Hold him." He started to pull himself over the side, but Deering held on to him.

"MMMMeeeeffffiiiirrrrssssstttt," he said.

"Come on, Case," said Smoaks.

"IIII . . . llllooossseee . . . ," said Deering.

Smoaks looked at him for a minute, then hoisted himself into the boat. Together he and Maggie lifted him in.

They went back out through the fishing camp, up the ramp from the floating dock, by the dead shark without looking, to the car. Mansfield didn't wake up, or at least didn't come out to speak to them. His house was a dark shadow under the trees.

When they got back to Maggie's, Smoaks fanned the embers of the fire back into flame and piled wood on until they had it roaring. Maggie went into the house and got a blanket to wrap around Deering. Then they all sat down in the red light of the fire under the festoons of Spanish moss hanging down out of the darkness, and Smoaks opened bottles of beer for them.

"I seen the mouth," Deering said, holding his bottle of beer and looking into the fire.

"What?" said Smoaks, not looking at him.

"I seen the mouth," said Deering. "The shark's mouth."

No one spoke.

"It was white," he said.

Smoaks took a sip of beer, looking into the fire.

"First time I ever been in the water out in the Sound," Deering said. "Not even in daylight."

"It was bad," said Smoaks.

"You wasn't scared," said Deering.

"Who said?" said Smoaks. "I was pissing in my pants the whole time."

Deering looked at him, then back at the fire. "I seen something else, too," he said.

"What?" said Smoaks.

Deering didn't speak for a minute. "It wasn't the shark," he said.

"Oh," said Smoaks. "You shouldn't have had those beers before."

Deering looked at Maggie. "It wouldn't have made no difference. Would it, Maggie?" he said.

She didn't answer.

"Maybe I wouldn't have gone at all without the beers," he said.

He stood up, holding the blanket around him; then he reached out the one hand holding the bottle of beer, turned it over, and poured the beer onto the ground. When it stopped splashing, he opened his fingers and let the bottle drop. "Well," he said, throwing off the blanket. He turned and started walking toward the car.

"Where you going?" said Smoaks.

"I reckon I'd better be getting along," he said.

"How am I going to get home, then?" said Smoaks.

Deering stopped, turning back to look at him. "Come on," he said.

"Let me finish my beer," said Smoaks.

"Finish it," said Deering. He stood looking back at them by the fire. Not moving.

Smoaks looked at him, then back at the fire. "Go on," he said. "I'll walk." He tilted the bottle up and took a swig, popping it away from his lips.

Deering turned and walked to the car. Neither Maggie nor Smoaks watched him as he started the car and drove away. Both of them were sitting looking into the fire.

When Smoaks got home, he didn't go to bed. He sat around for a while on his front steps. Then he got into his car and drove down to Mansfield's fishing camp. The house was still dark, and Mansfield didn't come out to meet him. He took his black bag, getting out of the car and walking down to the dock where the shark was. It looked huge and silver in the moonlight.

He cast off the clove hitch on the tackle and slowly lowered the big fish onto the dock, snubbing the fall around the davit. It was a struggle to do it by himself, keeping the thing from sliding off into the water. He grabbed the hatchet handle and used it to lever him into position. Finally getting him down and stretched out on the dock.

Bright as the moon was, there still wasn't enough light. So he went up to the house and rummaged around until he found a kerosene lantern. He took it back down on the dock and lit it, putting it down by the big fish's head. It made him look orange, with a red point in his eye.

He heaved the shark over onto its back.

Then he took his tools from his bag and went to work inside the mouth. Not just taking the first ones he came to, but picking and choosing—so he got what looked like the three best teeth in the bunch. There were so many of them, it was hard to tell which were *the* three best. But he got three good ones, cutting them loose until he could pull them out with his hands. It took a little while for him to do it.

After he had gotten them out, he swabbed them with alcohol and wrapped them in cotton. Then he put them away into his bag, and put the bag into his car.

He pulled out his watch and looked at it. Five-twelve. He went to the house and banged on the door until Mansfield stumbled out and answered.

"I got my teeth," he said.

"What?" said Mansfield. His mouth sounded dry and sleepy.

"I said, 'I got my teeth,'" he said.

"Smoaks?"

"Yes," said Smoaks. "I got my shark's teeth. I just took three of them."

"Take all you want," said Mansfield.

"Three's enough," said Smoaks.

There was a silence.

"Is that all?" said Mansfield.

"I wanted you to know who'd done it," said Smoaks.

"Help yourself," said Mansfield. "The bastard's got enough of them." He was yawning as he spoke.

Later Smoaks took the teeth into Savannah to a jeweler's, where he got them set as key chains—sterling silver. He gave one to Maggie, and one to Deering, and he kept one for himself.

"I know you wanted a necklace," said Smoaks. "Maybe Case can get some more for you. The carcass is still down there in the marsh somewhere. Mansfield just rolled it off the dock for the crabs to get."

"It don't make any difference," said Maggie. "I shouldn't have said anything. The key chain's fine. I'll wait on the next one for the necklace."

"I'll go look and see if I can find it," said Deering.

"The key chain's fine," she said. "Thank you."

They kept on seeing each other from time to time during the summer, but they didn't have the good times they used to have. Smoaks was the only one going into the house with Maggie now. It was embarrassing. In August a new roadhouse opened up, closer to Fancy Station, and the CCC Camp men didn't come around to Maggie's so much. She had to let the Dorchester Swamp Stompers go, and it worried her so that she stayed preoccupied most of the time and wasn't much company, even for Smoaks. When the cotton started to come in, Case had to spend all of his time seeing to it, and getting in his other crops. And Smoaks got busy with a flu epidemic, so they just kind of drifted away from each other.

By fall it was pretty well over. Then the wind shifted to the northeast, and the winter came in with the rain.

Just after New Year's, Maggie moved to Jacksonville. In April Smoaks went down to help her with the baby. Just before that— toward the end of March—Case began keeping company with Cora Dekle in a serious way. He proposed, and they were married in the following fall.

Maggie came back two years later with the baby, moved into her old roadhouse, and started up her business again.

They would meet occasionally here and there around McAfee County, and they were always too hearty with each other. Self-conscious and forced.

Smoaks kept his sharktooth key chain in his doctor's bag and used it for the ignition keys to his car. He still has it, worn and yellow now, and no longer sharp. Maggie lost hers while she was in Jacksonville. The day before Case Deering married Cora Dekle, he rented bateau number four from Mansfield Whitmire, rowed it out into the middle of Kallisaw Sound, and dropped his over the side into the deep green water.

After John Henry

"Put it down, honey. You drop it and break it, and I have to punish you."

"I wouldn't never. You know I wouldn't." The voice had a sullen quality. It had been corrected too many times.

"You wouldn't never mean to do it. And you'd be sorry when you did. Then I'd have to go and do something mean and ugly. That would make us both mad. So you just put it down. Set it on the table there. You can look at it, and I won't have to worry you'll drop it. Come on, now, honey. Do as I say."

He put the mason jar on the porcelain-topped kitchen table. Leaning on the edge, his chin propped on his forearms, he watched the suspended helix of the objects in the colorless liquid.

The light from the window came in golden yellow through the liquid in the mason jar. It cast a translucent orange shadow on the porcelain of the tabletop.

The road gang from the county farm was working on the bridge. It was a small bridge, just big enough for the logging trucks coming in and out to go one at the time.

Most of the men just stood around leaning on the concrete railing. A few of them with swing blades moved their blades with listless, pendulum motions, brushing the weeds on the shoulders of the fill. It was hot now. They had been out since just after sunup. Dinnertime was coming soon. Back down the dirt logging road, under some trees, the cook, Jessie, had two fires going. On one of them was a pot of beans, on the other was a pot of grits. Jessie was a trusty, an old man who was no longer any good for road work. He was doing five years for stealing a pig from Case Deering—the fourth time he had been on the road gang. The men could see him moving in the shade under the oaks and tending the pots. The day was too still to smell the beans.

Sweat poured off John Henry. He was digging with posthole diggers. A hole to put the supports for the forms in. The muscles in his upper arms bunched and jumped as he worked the diggers. He grunted softly as he speared them down into the hole. When they hit the bottom, his muscles locked; then they strained and locked again as he spread the handles and raised them out of the hole. Some of the men leaning on the railing were looking at him. They liked to watch John Henry work.

In the middle of the road, just off the bridge, Gunther Coleman stood. He was a small man, five-feet-six or -seven, but he stood with his shoulders pulled back and erect. Most of his face was lost in the shadow under the brim of his straw hat, but his chin shot out forward and up. It was square and firm, with a dimple in the middle. There was a stubble of gray hair on it. The thumb of his left hand hooked into his belt, and a double-barreled shotgun was cradled in his left arm, the muzzle tilted down toward the road. His right hand rested on the handle of a pistol slung low on his right hip. The holster of the pistol was tied down with a piece of leather bootlace around his right thigh. He stood with his left leg shot, resting his weight on his right.

He was watching John Henry too.

Suddenly Gunther drew the pistol. A whispery blur of a motion, and there it was in his hand. "Okay, boy," he said, "you be careful of them diggers."

John Henry looked at him between the spread handles of the posthole diggers. His arm muscles bunched, and the sweat dripped off his elbows. He was smiling. The blue-black skin made his teeth look very white. He liked Mr. Coleman, but he could never tell for sure. Mr. Coleman was holding it too lightly. It was a big gun—he couldn't shoot it with his arm bent that way. But the black muzzle looked very big, even at that distance. He could see the shells in the cylinders.

"Yes, boss," he said, not moving.

Gunther eased the hammer down with his thumb and put the pistol back in its holster. He continued to rest his hand on the handle. Under the brim of his straw hat, his eyes squinted out of the shade. Light blue eyes—young looking—set in a face that was red and crinkled from the sun. Kind eyes, too. The kind, youthful eyes of a boy.

Gunther loved the pistol more than anything else he owned. It had cost him a month's pay to buy it, and he couldn't shoot it very often because the bullets cost so much—the county wouldn't give him anything but shells for the shotgun—but he loved to wear it and take it out and point it around every once in a while. It was a Colt .45. Nickel-plated, with pearl handles. He had wanted one ever since the Gene Autry movies at the theater in Kose on Saturdays. But he had never actually shot anyone with it. Not a person.

The sound of the dinner gong came out of the trees down the hot, dusty road. The men lined up and filed back where Jessie had the fires going. They walked on the shoulder. Gunther and the other guards walked behind them and to the side.

They sat around under the trees eating the beans and grits. The guards ate beans and grits, too, but for dessert they had bowls of blueberries that Jessie had picked for them, and cold milk. The men in the gang sat on the ground. The guards sat on boxes that Jessie had gotten out of the truck for them. After they finished, the men lay around on the ground, some of them smoking. Jessie sat between the roots of a big oak tree, his legs spraddled out in front of him, his back resting against the trunk of the tree.

"Look out!" Gunther yelled. He was looking at Jessie. His voice was so sudden that everybody jumped. Before Jessie could move, Gunther had quick-drawn his gun and let off a shot at the tree trunk just above his head. The bullet knocked a chunk of bark and wood off as big as a man's fist.

"Lord God, boss," said Jessie, "I ain't done nothing."

"Not you," said Gunther. He walked over beside the tree and picked something up off the ground. It wiggled in a stiff kind of way and then went limp. A lizard. His head and one of his front legs were gone. He was light tan and a little longer than a man's hand.

"Thought it was a scorpion," said Gunther. "It's just a plain old lizard."

"That was some shooting," said Jack Inabinet, the chief of the gang. "Took his head clean off. Clean as a whistle. God damn, that was *some* shooting. I ain't never seen nothing that quick."

Jessie giggled, and the other men on the gang murmured to each other. All of them kept looking at the scar where the bullet had hit the trunk—a big white pit in the gray bark of the tree.

"If it had of been a scorpion, he'd of sure saved your life, Jessie," said Jack Inabinet. "One of them bites you, it's worse than a moccasin."

"Yes, sir, boss," said Jessie. "I sure am much obliged to you, boss."

Gunther put his hand back on the handle of the gun and walked around in circles looking at the ground. Every now and then he would look back at the scar on the tree trunk. When he walked he swung his right hip lower, almost limping on the gun side. It had been a good shot, and he didn't get to shoot often—not at anything *real*, he didn't.

"I hope all you boys seen that," said Jack Inabinet. "In case you got any ideas about slipping off sometime, just remember Mr. Coleman here and what he done to that lizard." He patted Gunther on the shoulder, then pointed with his long, angular arm to the scar in the tree trunk. Jack always rolled the sleeves of his shirts up too high, way up above his elbows, nearly to his shoulders. He was proud of his arms. The muscles on the front looked good, but on the back they were dished-out and stringy, and his elbows stuck out too far.

John Henry looked at Gunther and smiled a big smile. Gunther looked off to the side, like there was something way off down the road that he was trying to see. The corners of his mouth turned up a little, and he had to keep swallowing to help pull them back down.

Riding back to the camp that night, Skoad Farley talked to Jack Inabinet. Gunther was in the trailer that hooked on behind the truck. It was his job to be sure that none of the gang got out through the wire doors. The trailer was a little box, like an outhouse on bicycle wheels, open in the front so he could watch the back of the truck. It wasn't very comfortable to ride in it.

"I never seen no shot like that," said Skoad. Skoad was thirty, just starting out, the youngest guard in the camp.

"Best shot I ever seen," said Jack, nodding gravely. "Coleman is a damn good man." Jack was a good, steady driver, and riding the trailer wasn't too bad when he was at the wheel.

"Did you see how them niggers rolled their eyes when he made that shot?" said Skoad. "Even John Henry, too."

"They'll think about that for a long time," said Jack, holding the steering wheel in his right hand and leaning his left arm on the window. "A shot like that keeps the itch out of their feet for a long, long time."

"Even John Henry," said Skoad.

"John Henry get the itchy foot, he gets his ass blowed off same as any other nigger," said Jack.

"I was watching him work the diggers today," said Skoad. "He got a hell of a arm on him. He throwed them diggers like they's a couple of toothpicks. Up and down and up and down. And them arms just a-working."

"John Henry's a good worker," Jack said flatly, whipping the wheel a little to make his arm muscles jump.

"And ain't he got a hell of a arm on him?" said Skoad. Then added flatly, looking out the window on his side. "For a nigger, I mean."

"Shot me a lizard today," Gunther said to his son, Ransome, that night when he got home. "Good, fast shot. Right off the hip." He demonstrated, using his hand.

"Uh-huh," said Ransome, putting the dishes on the table. He looked up at his father for a moment.

"Right in the eye," said Gunther, laying his finger on his cheek under his eye.

Ransome didn't say anything. He went to the stove and stirred the pot of grits, then opened the door of the oven and looked at the biscuits.

"Little bitty one," said Gunther. "Right in the eye."

Ransome stood beside the stove looking at his father. He wiped his hands on his apron, working them slowly in the stained and greasy folds. He was a big man, but shapeless—a head taller than his bantam father, with a high waistline, and most of his weight in his hips. The apron seemed to be tied halfway up his chest, and when he turned around his pants showed puckered and gathered under the belt. His hips were so big that he couldn't get a good fit in the waist, and he had to pull his belt in tight to keep them from falling off. He had on a white, short-sleeved shirt, open at the neck, with collars that fanned out wide, like the collars on the shirt of a small boy. His eyes were blue and darting—piglike—protruding a little and surrounded by small, puffy lobes of fat, set in a face that was too round and babylike. The lashes were so long he looked like he was wearing eye makeup. His skin had a dirty pallor, like biscuit dough that has been kneaded too much, and his face and arms glowed with a faint, waxy sheen. The dome of his head was plastered with a sparse thatch of greasy hair. In another five years he would be bald—now he had the head of a newborn black-haired baby. About him wafted an aura of Evening in Paris cologne, which almost overcame a thick, rank undertone of creased and folded flesh and dirty underwear.

"Right in the eye," said Gunther again, turning over his plate without looking at his son.

Ransome served them out of the pots, mincing back and forth from the table to the stove. Gunther watched him moving about the kitchen. Somehow Ransome gave the impression he was skipping. It made Gunther tired to watch him.

"Lord . . . ," said Gunther, resting his forehead on his clasped hands, his elbows on the table, ". . . for what we are about to receive, make us truly thankful. In Jesus' name. Amen."

"Amen," said Ransome. He sat with his head bowed on his chest, his hands folded in his lap.

After grace, they ate in silence, Gunther hunching forward over his plate, his face almost in it, scooping the food into his mouth with his fork—held the way he would hold a poker to stroke up a fire. Ransome sat straight in his chair, taking small, dainty mouthfuls.

"You're a good cook, son," Gunther said flatly. "And that's a fact." He sat sucking a toothpick and watching Ransome clearing away the supper dishes. He seemed to walk on tiptoe, making movements that were too light and airy for such a big man. Ransome didn't answer.

"It's about the best shot I ever made," Gunther said at last.

"That's good, Pa," said Ransome. He was washing the dishes at the sink, and his back was to his father as he spoke. He didn't turn around.

Gunther pulled the toothpick out of his mouth and looked at it. "You don't give a good God damn, do you, boy?" he said. His voice was soft and even, without tightness. There was no tone of accusation in it. He was just stating a matter of fact.

Ransome didn't answer.

Gunther put the toothpick back into his mouth and leaned on the table with his elbows. "Where your balls, boy?" he said.

Ransome stopped washing the dishes and turned his head to him over his shoulder. His pale, dimpled face was smooth under the overhead light in the kitchen, cupid lips sucked up in a red pout. Gunther wasn't looking at him. Ransome's face flushed, and he turned away.

"No," he said softly, talking into the window above the sink. "No, Pa, I don't . . . give a damn," he said.

"What *do* you care about, son?" he said. "Not my shooting. Not nothing I can talk to you about—like my shooting—nor nothing else we could talk about. Not women . . ." The inflection on the last word went up, as though he expected his son to interrupt him.

Ransome stopped moving his hands in the water in the sink.

"Why couldn't you have some kind of meanness in you I could understand and we could talk about it sometimes? Some kind of meanness I could figure out," he said, going on. His voice was flat, toneless. "Wrecking cars, or shooting niggers, or chasing women . . ."

He sat at the table, leaning on his elbow. Folding the napkin into smaller and smaller triangles with his right hand. Turning it down and creasing it to make it stay.

"I just don't know, Ranse," he said, looking at the napkin. "I just don't know what to do for a pussy."

Ransome stopped moving his hands in the water. "Don't call me that," he said, talking out the window. His mouth pulled up tight and the words coming hard.

Gunther looked up at his son's back, then down at the napkin again. "You like pussy things, you got to be a pussy," he said. "I don't know no other word for it, son. It's just the only word I know." His voice was quiet.

For a while neither of them spoke. The water in the sink made a heavy, sloshing sound.

"What am I going to do, boy?" Gunther said, his voice quiet, talking down to the napkin on the table. "What am I going to do, son? Get you a dress and marry you off?"

Ransome turned from the sink, looking his father in the eye. He leaned back against the rim of the sink, kneading his hands in the apron.

"I'm sorry I'm a fat ass," he said. "I'm sorry I ain't got no big muscles and I'm a fat ass, Pa. Me and my fat ass, we're sorry for it all." His eyebrows were drawn up like he was hurting somewhere and was going to cry about it. "But don't call me a pussy," he said. "Think of something else."

They looked at each other across the kitchen table for a minute.

"That's all," said Ransome, shrugging his shoulders. "There ain't nothing else to say about it," he said. "There just ain't . . . nothing else to say about it."

He turned back to the sink.

Gunther looked at the back of his son's neck with his dead, blue eyes. There were two grayish-pink rolls of fat just above the boy's shirt collar. Dark sweat stains spread below his armpits, and his hips jiggled as he stirred his hands in the water of the sink.

"It ain't just no fat ass," said Gunther.

Ransome didn't answer him.

Gunther rose from the table, scraping the chair backward. "No," he said. "No, there ain't nothing else to say." He put his hands in his pockets and went out of the room. The water in the sink sounded heavy and oily.

Gunther watched the gang taking their Saturday bath under the bucket shower in the yard. John Henry's muscles bunched and jumped as he soaped himself under the cold water. It was warm in the yard, but the water was from an artesian well. John Henry danced and jiggled, first on one foot, then on the other. The muscles in his arms balled up like oranges.

"Hey, boy," said Gunther as John Henry started back to the shed, drying his head. "Hey, boy, come over here.

"You a good strong hand, boy," he said. "How much time you got left?"

"Two weeks, boss."

John Henry's eyes were black. The whites were clear, and he looked at Gunther with his eyes straight on and open. A look that was too steady.

"When you finish your time, you come around and see me," he said. "You come around and see me, and I see about you getting a job. A little time on the gang won't hurt you none. Do you good if you let it. A real strong hand don't have to go hungry in McAfee County."

"Yes, sir, boss," said John Henry. "Yes, sir, I sure will do that."

He walked away, rubbing his head with the towel.

Gunther watched him going away. He watched John Henry's shoulders and arms moving the towel around on his head. Big bunches of muscles jumped out on his neck and shoulders.

"Biggest arms I ever seen on a buck," said Skoad.

"He's a good boy," said Gunther.

After two weeks they turned John Henry loose. Gunther waited for him to come around and see him.

Case Deering had done well as a farmer—he was a little more successful than the average for McAfee County, at least. He had some money, and worked hands on his place, so that most people in the county, the ones who didn't live in Kose, looked up to him. He was stable, deliberate, and generally respected—he was also a fair man, after his own sense of justice—though he was not universally well liked. Positions of authority came to him naturally as a result of his status and manner—both of them inspired confidence. Whenever an organization of any kind began to form up, Case had the refusal of head man for it. During the nearly twenty-one years of his childless marriage, he had been forced more or less to look for outside interests to keep himself going. Cora was a dull, dry woman—proper and selfish.

Two of the many positions that had come to him he took more seriously than the others: deacon and treasurer of the Two-Oak Missionary Baptist Church, and Grand Cyclops of the Two-Oak Klavern of the Ku Klux Klan.

"John Henry been peeping on white women," Mrs. Deering said to him at supper.

Mr. Deering looked at his wife. "Who said?" he asked.

"Grace June Folsom seen him," she said. "And Aggie Dekle." She sopped a piece of bread around her plate on the end of her fork. "I seen him, too," she said.

Mr. Deering pushed his plate away and put his glass of buttermilk in front of him. He was crumbling cornbread into the glass.

"When?" he asked, looking at the glass.

"Yesterday evening," she said.

He looked up at her, then back at the glass.

"I took me a sponge bath in the kitchen. John Henry come up to the window by the stove. I hollered at him, and he run off. I seen him out the window."

Mr. Deering turned the glass slowly between his thumb and index finger.

Mr. Sipple was panting hard as he lifted the shotgun down from its rack in the living room.

"What you doing, Henry?" said Mrs. Sipple, coming in from the kitchen, wiping her hands in her apron.

Mr. Sipple didn't answer her. His breath came in hard, heaving gasps, and he seemed to be about to collapse.

"You been running, ain't you?" she said. "Man your age running around here like that. You sit down and get your breath, Henry. Then you tell me what you been running for."

Mr. Sipple fumbled for the shells. His missing finger made him clumsy. He wasn't adjusted to it yet. Finally he got two shells out, spilling others on the shelf and floor. He held the two between the fingers of his hand, the gun cradled under his arm.

"Sit down, Henry," Mrs. Sipple said again.

"Get back," Mr. Sipple said, his voice dry, panting, with his mouth open. "Get back in the kitchen."

He brushed the catch, and the gun broke across his forearm. He dropped the two shells into the chambers and snapped it closed. Then he went out of the house. At the foot of the front steps he stopped, pressed his hand to his chest, and sat down heavily on the bottom step. He tried to get up, straining, and flopped back on the step.

"Henry . . . ," said Mrs. Sipple, coming out onto the porch.

"Get back in the house," he said, his voice strained and panting. "Get back in the goddamned house."

Mrs. Sipple hesitated a moment, holding the screen door back with her hand. Then she stepped backward over the threshold and let the door slam to in front of her.

He was still sitting balled up on the bottom step when the girl came into the yard. She was young, but nondescript, with lank, colorless hair. When she saw him huddled on the step, the gun across his knees, she stopped. "Pa," she said. "What's the matter, Pa?"

Mr. Sipple looked up at her. His voice was still dry and strained, but he wasn't panting so much. Mrs. Sipple stood behind the screen door.

"I seen it," he said. "I seen you down there by the bottoms."

The man and the girl looked at each other across the swept dirt of the yard.

"Oh," she said. "Seen what?"

"I'd a been back and blowed his brains out," said Mr. Sipple, looking down at the ground, "only I got a catch in me—here. . . ." He still hugged his chest, pressing in with his left elbow and right hand.

The girl didn't say anything.

"He raped you, didn't he?" he said, looking down at the dirt between his shoes.

The girl looked at her father, then at her mother behind the screen door. Her arms folded, hugging her breasts, her fingers biting hard into the flesh of her upper arms.

Mr. Sipple raised the gun until it was level with his daughter's chest, staring at her out of his tight, blue eyes. His nerve failed him, and he lowered the gun again, looking at the ground.

"He raped you, didn't he?" he said, louder this time. ". . . Jackie?"

"I ain't the first one, Pa," she said, her voice going up, beginning to sound like she would start to cry.

"Frances," he said over his shoulder, "get your daughter inside the house and see to her."

Mrs. Sipple came out of the house, closing the screen door quietly behind her. She put her arm around her daughter, who was crying now, and went back into the house with her. Mr. Sipple staggered to his feet, and he and his wife looked at each other as she went by him into the house with their daughter. She didn't understand yet.

"He raped her," Mr. Sipple said. There was a tone of finality in his voice. He stood bent over, hugging his chest with his left elbow and right hand, the shotgun tilted toward the ground.

"Where you going, James Lee?" she said. The air in the shack was close and rank, smelling of kerosene. The light from the lamp made the newspapers in the windows look orange.

"I just going out for a while," said James Lee. He was tall and lanky, with a long, skinny neck. His skull was long and gourdlike, and the back of his head protruded grotesquely.

"You better stay home after dark," she said, looking at the kerosense lamp by the bed. "Ain't nothing good for you out there in the dark."

James Lee hesitated at the door. "I just be going to get me a Co-Cola," he said. "We just going to go down to Shotford's and get us a Co-Cola. I be back directly."

"You better stay away from John Henry," said the woman. She sat stiffly in her chair, looking at the lantern and talking to her son behind her.

"We just going to get us a Co-Cola down to Shotford's, Ma," he said, his voice whining. "I be back directly."

"You go out in the dark with John Henry sometime and you ain't never coming back," she said, sitting straight in the chair, her voice low and level. "John Henry have hisself a big time, you and John Henry. He have hisself a fine big time. And all the colored folks going to pay up for him sometime. John Henry be gone pretty soon now. Very soon. And we be paying up his good times after he gone."

"Ma," said James Lee, wavering.

"You come back and stay with your ma, James Lee," she said. "I make you a glass of sugar water, and you stay here with me."

"I don't want no sugar water," said James Lee sullenly. "I want me a Co-Cola."

"White man going to get John Henry," she said, her voice dropping lower. "You go in the dark with John Henry, white man going to get you too."

"Aw, Ma," said James Lee, whining. He came back into the room and sat down on the bed. "Aw, Ma . . . ," he said. ". . . I want me a Co-Cola. . . ."

Behind the Two-Oak Missionary Baptist Church is a grove of oak trees. In the grove is a picnic area. Almost every Sunday the church has a picnic, until the weather gets too cold in the winter. The oaks are tall, with big, spreading limbs, and the ground underneath is open and sandy. Under the trees are four big tables, made of concrete slabs, gray and heavy. The men's Sunday-school class made them as a project one summer, and the forms they used weren't fancy. But they are very sturdy tables. Every now and then somebody after church will back a pickup into one of them and just bounce right off, with maybe a little chip knocked out. It took the whole county gang all of an afternoon to set them up. Before the concrete hardened in the forms, Brother Fisco wrote a motto on each one: "Blessed *are* the meek," "Blessed *are* the merciful," "Blessed *are* the pure in heart," and "Blessed *are* the peacemakers."

"They's there to stay, boys," said Brother Fisco the afternoon he held the dedication.

To this grove they brought John Henry.

They pulled some cars and pickup trucks up under the trees and parked them with their lights on, facing toward the tables.

John Henry had a gag in his mouth, and his hands were tied behind him. His eyes were open and staring, and his muscles bunched and twisted under their hands. Four of them carried him and put him down on the "Blessed *are* the pure in heart" table—on his back. Some others stepped up to help hold him down.

"Get his pants off," said Mr. Deering in a dull, matter-of-fact voice. He had a toothpick in his mouth.

They pulled them off, then tied his legs down, passing the rope under the heavy slab of the table so that the edges cut the backs of his knees.

"Let Mr. Sipple up front," somebody said, and they pushed him up to the table. He looked down at John Henry without saying anything.

John Henry made strained, grunting noises inside the gag. He tried to roll off the slab, but they held him down.

"Let's get it over with," said Mr. Deering. He took the toothpick out of his mouth and spat between his shoes.

Anse Starkey stepped up to the table. In his hands he held a pair of long-handled pruning shears. He opened the handles into a wide V and put the bill carefully down between John Henry's legs. John Henry strained and twisted away just a little.

"You better be still, boy," said Anse. "You going to lose more than you need to."

John Henry kept on twisting. Choked, straining noises came from behind the gag. The muscles of his legs flicked and jumped.

"Somebody better hold them," said Anse. "I can't see nothing in this goddamn light anyway." He looked around at the crowd. "Stand back," he said. "Get off them tables and stand back so I can see what the hell I'm doing. . . . Hold them, Dee Witt," he said.

"Don't cut my finger off," Dee Witt said.

"You wouldn't miss it that much," said Anse, putting the bill of the shears in again. "Keep it out the way."

He levered down on the handles of the shears carefully, moving them partway closed and holding them. Then he looked closely at the bill of the shears, putting his head down so he could see better. He rocked back, braced himself, then flexed his arms, pushing the handles. They closed smoothly. The men bore down on John Henry to keep him still.

Anse looked at Mr. Deering. "That all?" he asked.

"Leave him something to play with, God damn it," said a voice from somewhere in the crowd.

Mr. Deering nodded his head and spat between his shoes.

"Ain't enough," said Anse. "Where's Mr. Sipple? Mr. Sipple!" he yelled.

Mr. Sipple had moved back behind the lights. They pushed him up to the table again.

"Ain't enough?" asked Anse. He worked the shear open and closed.

Mr. Sipple didn't say anything. He just stood looking down at John Henry on the slab.

"Take it all," said Anse. "Take it all, and he won't never forget it."

"It's enough," said Mr. Deering, looking at Anse.

"Mr. Sipple's to say," said Anse. Mr. Sipple stood by the table staring at John Henry.

"Hold it up, Dee Witt," said Anse, opening the shears again.

"That's enough," said Mr. Deering, taking a step forward.

Anse levered the handles closed again, and John Henry strained and croaked in his throat under the gag.

Mr. Deering came up and jerked the shears away from Anse. "You wasn't going to be satisfied, was you?" he said.

"You getting to be a nigger-lover, Mr. Deering?" said Anse, a faint smile on his face. He jumped away into the darkness behind the lights when Mr. Deering raised the shears as if to hit him.

Mr. Deering looked down at John Henry, holding the open shears by one handle. "Put some turpentine on him," he said. "Then untie him."

He turned to go.

"You want them?" Dee Witt asked.

Mr. Deering looked at him in a cold sort of way. "Leave them there," he said. "Leave them there on the table."

They untied John Henry. He lay there with his legs hanging off the sides of the slab. His breath was heavy and rasping in the back of his throat. When they untied his arms, he moved them down slowly and held himself.

"It had to be did," said Mr. Deering, looking down at him. "It's just one of them things had to be did." He turned and went away. The cars and pickups backed out and drove off down the road in front of the church.

Gunther met the line of cars coming down the road from the church.

Mr. Deering came into the house through the kitchen door and sat down at the table without taking off his hat. He was still chewing on the toothpick.

"Where you been?" Mrs. Deering asked.

He looked at his wife, then back at the table in front of him.

"I wondered where you was off to," Mrs. Deering said. "Where you been?"

"Don't talk to me, Cora," he said, not looking up at her. "I'll be all right after a while. Just don't talk to me right now."

"John Henry?" she said.

"God damn it, Cora, I said don't talk to me." He got up and went out of the kitchen into the yard. At the foot of the steps he saw a toad hop. He drew back his foot and kicked it into the darkness.

Gunther found him spread out on his back, holding himself, the blood dripping off the end of the slab and soaking into the sand.

"Come on, boy," he said quietly, trying to get his arm under John Henry's shoulders to help him up. "Come on, so we can get you to a doctor."

"Don't move me." John Henry's voice was a low, rasping croak. "It hurts."

"You don't get to a doctor, you going to bleed to death," he said.

"I can't move," said John Henry. "Don't make me move."

Gunther leaned both hands on the slab, looking down at John Henry.

"Boss," John Henry whispered.

"What?" said Gunther. John Henry spoke so strained and low he couldn't hear him.

"Boss," said John Henry, "I going to die."

"You ain't going to die, John Henry," said Gunther. "Doctor fix you up. Doctor fix you up good as new. . . ." His voice trailed off.

"I going to die. And I need to do it. Let me do it, boss," said John Henry, holding himself.

"You ain't going to die," said Gunther.

"Give me your gun, boss, so I can do it," said John Henry.

Gunther looked down at him on the slab.

"Boy," he said at last, "ain't no nigger never had that gun in his hand. Ain't but one white man had it, and never no nigger."

"Please, boss," said John Henry, with his eyes closed.

Gunther looked at him for a long time. Then he drew the pistol out of his holster. He held it in front of him and looked at it.

"You ain't no good for a cut shoat," he said. "Not you, John Henry. . . . *I'll* do it," he said, holding the gun to John Henry's head.

John Henry opened his eyes, staring straight up into the branches of the trees over the table. "Yes," he said, "but I need to do it. Me. Let me have the gun, and I can do it. . . . I ain't no shoat, boss," he said.

Gunther looked at him on the slab for a minute. Then he turned the gun and held it to John Henry, handle first.

"You wasn't going to die, boy," he said. "But you be better off anyway."

John Henry looked at the pistol with his eyes, not moving his head. He reached up to take it in his hand, holding himself with the other hand.

Gunther held the gun away. "Wipe the blood off your hand," he said.

John Henry wiped his hand on his shirt, then took the gun.

"You always was good to me, boss," he said. "I sure did always admire your gun and the way you treated me nice."

He lay with the gun in his hand, resting on his chest.

"You sure was good to me, boss," he said again.

Gunther turned to step back from the table. As he did so, John Henry raised the revolver and fired into his chest. Gunther reeled backward under the impact of the bullet. The second shot hit him in the shoulder and spun him around. The third knocked off his hat. The last three whistled off into the branches of the tree.

"I sorry, boss," he said. "I sorry it you . . . I had to get me one . . . I had to get me one."

They found him off to the side of the table next day, lying on his face. John Henry was gone. After they moved him away, there were two dark spots in the sand made by the blood. They never did get it cleaned out where it had pooled in the "Blessed *are* the pure in heart."

John Henry still had the gun with him when they found him.

They gave it to Ransome.

The light from the window came in golden yellow through the liquid in the mason jar.

"They look kind of purply and gray," said James Lee. "I'd have thought they'd been bigger, too."

"Maybe they've shrank. I don't think so. That's probably just the way they look, honey. Like that, I mean."

"They don't move at all," he said. "Just stay there." He took the mason jar in his hand and swirled it.

"God damn it, honey, I told you to leave it alone. You going to go and break it, and I'll have to do something mean to you."

"I just can't stand it when they stay there like that."

"I'm going to put it up so you'll quit worrying about it."

"Not yet, Mr. Ransome," he said. "Don't put it up yet. I won't touch it no more."

"Get temptation out of the way, is what I say. Get temptation out of the way, and then you don't never have to be sorry."

He took the mason jar from the kitchen table and opened the cupboard.

"Let me see the gun, Mr. Ransome," he said.

"Jesus God," said Ransome, "ain't you never going to be satisfied, James Lee?"

"Just let me see it a minute, Mr. Ransome. All I want is to see it just a minute."

"James Lee, honey, I don't even like you looking at that gun. It makes me nervous for you to just look at it."

"Just a little look, Mr. Ransome. Just one little look, and I wouldn't ask you no more. Not no more at all."

Ransome hesitated, with the cupboard door open. He didn't like to look at the gun himself. It made him nervous just to open the cupboard door and see the bundle of rags wrapped around it. It made him go all cold inside, just seeing the rags and knowing that the gun was wrapped up inside them.

"Just one look, James Lee," he said, putting the mason jar on the counter. "Just one look, and then I better not hear no more about that gun. Not no more never. You hear, honey?"

James Lee nodded stupidly, his lower jaw sprung and his mouth hanging open.

Ransome took down the bundle of rags and opened them up on the counter under the cupboard, his back to James Lee. James Lee leaned against the edge of the kitchen table, his hands gripping it tight.

"There," said Ransome, turning. The fingers of his right hand were extended together. The pistol lay on his fingers in his open palm.

"Lawd, ain't it pretty?" said James Lee under his breath. "It looks just like Mr. Autry's. . . . Lemme hold it just a minute, Mr. Ransome," he said. "I give it right back. I just got to hold it in my hand a minute, Mr. Ransome."

"God damn it!" said Ransome. "Didn't I know it? You and every other nigger in McAfee County just got to get this gun in his hand."

James Lee made a tentative move forward from the table.

"Right there!" he said. "You hold it right there, honey."

"Please, Mr. Ransome," he said. "I be real friendly for you, do you let me hold that silver gun in my hand."

"I love your black ass, James Lee," said Ransome, "but I'll blow it off for you, first step you take for this gun."

"Don't you try to fool me now, Mr. Ransome," said James Lee. "Ain't no bullets in that gun. I see it from here."

"Maybe just one you don't see," he said.

They looked at each other for a minute, then Ransome wrapped the gun back up in the rags and put it on the shelf. Then he put the mason jar back on the shelf beside the gun and closed the cupboard.

He sat down on the couch.

"Now, you just forget about that old gun, and come sit down here by me, honey," he said, patting the couch beside him. "Come on over here and sit down and be friendly, James Lee, honey."

James Lee stood looking out the window. The back of his long head swelled out above his thin neck. "Time I be getting home," he said.

"You ain't going to leave me now, are you, honey?" said Ransome. "After I done showed you the gun and all. Come on over and sit here by me."

James Lee stood looking out the window. "Coming on sundown," he said. "Ma don't like I should be out after it get dark."

"Just a minute, honey," said Ransome. "I show you something else. Something better than the gun. Get you a Coca-Cola."

Ransome went into the bedroom. When he came back, he had a deck of cards in his hand.

"Come here, honey," he said, patting the couch.

James Lee came over, wiping the mouth of the Coca-Cola bottle, and sat down beside him. Ransome flipped the deck of cards and looked at James Lee. Then he turned over the deck of cards and showed James Lee the top card.

"Jesus God, Mr. Ransome," said James Lee, staring at the card. "Where'd you get them picture cards at?"

"Ain't never seen nothing like that before, have you, James Lee, honey?" said Ransome. He put his arm around James Lee's shoulder. With his other hand he patted his knee. "You forget about that old gun and John Henry's jewels," he said, squeezing James Lee's shoulder, his cheek almost touching the boy's.

James Lee's mouth was hanging open as he looked at the cards. One by one he slipped them over, carefully, making a new pile on the couch beside him.

"Just look at them pictures, James Lee, honey," he said. "Just look at them pictures and forget all about that gun."

The smell of Evening in Paris cologne was strong in the room.

James Lee didn't say anything. He just kept turning the cards.

Annie's Love Child

"Best your ma didn't live," he said, looking at the girl sitting across the kitchen table from him. "Best your ma died before ever she should live to see that this day should come."

The girl sat with her hands in her lap, motionless; her torso also motionless above the yellow-oilcloth cover of the table. She was a healthy-looking girl, sturdy and well formed. Her breasts were large and pendulous, outlined under the limp cloth of her dress. The dress itself was shapeless, of purple cloth with pink flowers on it. She wore nothing underneath it, and the limp material crested at her nipples, falling straight down in two small, peaked folds. She was a tranquil, healthy-looking girl.

"And you ain't going to say?" he said. The girl didn't answer. "Just somebody come along and it happened. Just somehow it happened—and you ain't going to say."

"Wouldn't do no good," the girl said. "He's long gone anyway. It wouldn't do no good."

"It would do me some good," he said. "It really would do me a whole lot of good." The girl didn't answer. "Where is he long gone to?" he said. "Where to, and where from? Annie, you answer me. You answer me and tell me who."

The girl didn't speak.

"Somebody from the carnival through here in August?" he said. "Some soldier boy from Stewart, maybe? Some kind of a traveling man selling things out of a suitcase, with black, shiny shoes and a automobile?"

The girl didn't speak.

"I'm going to find out sometime, Annie," he said. "You might as well tell me. Sometime I'm going to find it out anyway. Make it easy on yourself."

She didn't answer.

Everything about her tended downward. The small, indistinct festoons of the purple and pink flowers falling from the nipples of her breasts; her shoulders, downward-sloping but sturdy; her lank, colorless hair, hanging straight down along the sides of her head, breaking into thin cascades at her shoulders and fanning slightly over the swell of her breasts. Her arms immobile at her sides, disappearing under the table.

Her eyes, too, were downcast. Fixed on a spot in the middle of the yellow-oilcloth table cover in front of her.

The father sat across from her. Not looking her in the eye, but meeting her gaze at the spot she had selected on the yellow-oilcloth cover of the table and bouncing his father's indignation up under her lowered lids off the shiny yellow surface of the table. He sat with his elbows and forearms on the table before him, his hands clasped. His voice was high, with an edge on it.

"If she had of lived, she would have died this day," he said, talking into the yellow shine of the oilcloth. "This day, and the shame of it, would have been her last, had she lived to see it."

The girl's lips were relaxed. They looked like the soft, relaxed lips of a sleeping child. The man's mouth was hard, his lips thin. His lower lip projected slightly, as if he had an undershot jaw, curving back to meet the thin upper one. His mouth looked hard and dry. When he talked, his lower teeth showed.

"How could you have done it, Annie?" he said. "How could you have done such a thing like that? Such a sinful thing?"

She pursed her lips slightly. Not nervously, but just pursing them slightly.

"I ain't real sure yet," she said. Her voice was low, with a masculine tone in it. "Just almost two months," she said. Her lips barely moved when she spoke. "Just hardly two months. It ain't enough to tell," she said. "Not for sure."

"Tell what?" he said in his high voice. He raised his watery blue eyes to look at her face. She continued to stare at the spot in the center of the yellow table. "Tell what, when you done already told? Ain't no more telling to it. You done it, and that's all. You done it, and the shame ain't going to go away. Not in two months, not in three months, not in three years. Annie, it ain't never going to go away."

He moved his eyes down to the table again. Trying to get at her. Trying to get under the lids of her eyes to move against that rooted and vegetable passiveness.

"You think it's going to be all right if you don't have the child?" he said. "You think you can come up with your woman's blood, and it just late a little, and that woman's blood is going to wash it all away?" He worked the fingers of his hands as he talked, clasping and unclasping them on the table. "Woman's blood wouldn't do it," he said. "Woman's blood wouldn't wash it away like it never was. You can bleed yourself out for the next ten years, and it wouldn't do it.

"You sinned," he said. "You sinned, Annie, and wallowed in the filth of it. Ain't nothing going to take that away. Ain't nothing going to make it clean and take that away like it just hadn't never been.

"That's too easy," he said. "That's just too easy. If it were so, I'd go get me a swab and boil me some lye and swab the filth out of you. Swab it out and scrape it clean with a wire brush and boiling lye. I'd open you up and scrub the corruption out of you till you was white and dry inside. White and dry and dead, and clean of the corruption." His fingers bit white into the backs of his hands. "If it were only so. If it were only so, and just so easy."

When he finished speaking his shoulders drooped and he began sawing his head from side to side. For a long while he sat like that, looking down at his hands clasped on the table, his head sawing from side to side.

The girl looked at him calmly across the yellow oilcloth of the table. "You sound like a preacher, Pa," she said. "Church talk."

He looked up at her, working his mouth, compressing the lips. Then he looked back down at the table without saying anything.

She rose from the table and began to clear away the dishes. Her hands moved surely as she picked up the plates. The movements of her hands and arms were deliberate and unhurried as she cleared away the table things, taking them to the sink. Her eyes were still downcast. Not out of shame, and not out of remorse, but out of an inwardness. As if she were looking into herself and listening to something inside, something that spoke a secret to her that she already knew but wanted to hear anyway.

The man sat at the table, not looking at her.

"Leave the dishes alone," he said. "Leave the dishes alone and listen to what I got to say."

"Got to be did sometime," she said, not looking at him.

"Sometime. Some other time," he said. "Sit down, Annie. Sit down and listen to me."

She sat down in the chair across the table.

"What're we going to do?" he said. "What're we going to do if the baby is going to come?"

She looked at him a moment. He was still looking at the table, not seeing her eyes. Her eyes were calm, the lids not raised and not lowered now. Just looking at him calmly. "We're going to wait and see," she said flatly. "We're going to wait and see, and if the baby is going to come, that's all there is. We'll just have to wait and see."

"You ain't going to have no love child, Annie," he said, his mouth tight. "For your mother's sake and her rest and peace, I wouldn't let you do it."

She didn't reply.

"We're going to wait a little while more," he said. "Just a little while more to be sure. And if the baby is still going to come, we are going to do something and stop it."

He looked at her, and their eyes met.

"You ain't never going to have no love child, Annie," he said. "It ain't never going to happen."

Josey stood on one side of the kitchen table, her arms folded under her breasts. Mr. Mullins sat at the table on the other side. He looked at the spot in the center of the table. Sometimes he looked up at her. She stood erect, her head wrapped in a blue headcloth, thrown back a little, looking at him steadily.

"You too late," she said, her voice flat but distinct, not loud. "Three months is too late."

"I had to be sure," Mr. Mullins said. "Can't hardly be sure in three months."

"I could of done it with a coat hanger," said Josey. "Boiled it and scraped it right out, and no trouble. But not now, it's too late." Small, wiry gray hairs had sprung from under the headcloth around her ears. Her apron was worn but clean. A big yellowish-brown stain splotched under the pocket, but the folds were crisp and pressed looking. She wore men's high-topped work shoes. Out of the tops of the shoes her thin shanks rose, bowing slightly up under the crisp apron.

"Three months is too long," she said. "Two is bad enough."

"We done tried the quinine," said Mr. Mullins. "And chopping wood. And I run her up and down the steps till I got tired watching her."

"Ain't nothing I going to be able to do," said Josey. "Ain't nothing I going to be able to do, 'cept the quinine. And that ain't going to work."

He sat looking into his hands on the tabletop as if he had the answer cupped inside them.

"Go get me Dr. Smoaks," he said, talking to the top of the table, then looking at her. "Go get me Dr. Smoaks and bring him out here, and we'll see what he's got to say."

"Same thing," said Josey. "He ain't going to do nothing neither. It too late for me, and too late for him too."

"I done got your say," he said. "Three months may be right. But you go get Dr. Smoaks anyway. I want to see what a white man's got to say."

Josey didn't reply. She turned and walked to the kitchen door, knocking the screen open with her shoulder without unfolding her arms.

"Three months is too late," said Dr. Smoaks. He and Mr. Mullins sat at the yellow kitchen table. They were drinking coffee. Beside his cup was his black bag. Josey stood at the end of the table, her arms still folded under her breasts, moving her eyes slowly from side to side as the talk shifted between the two men.

"Maybe we could give her more quinine," said Mr. Mullins.

Dr. Smoaks lifted his cup smoothly but daintily. He sipped it, taking small sips, watching Mr. Mullins over the rim of the cup.

"Quinine ain't enough," he said. "Quinine ain't enough, and it won't do it." He held the cup by the handle, bracing it lightly between the thumb and forefinger of the other hand. "You can give her a gallon of it a day," he said. "Pour it into her with a funnel. And chopping wood won't do it. And running her up the steps. Ain't nothing going to do it," he said. "Why don't you just face it, Dero? Annie's going to have that baby."

"No she ain't," said Mr. Mullins. "It ain't never going to happen."

Dr. Smoaks put the coffee cup back into the saucer, resting his forearm on the table. "Look at her, Dero," he said. "Just look at her and think about it. Nothing we're going to do would make her turn loose of it. Can't you just look at her and see that? You couldn't even stick your hand in there and grab it and pull it out. Like as not, if you tried to do it, she'd just pull down on your arm, and hold on, and bring it to term along with the baby."

Dr. Smoaks pulled his watch out of his vest pocket and looked at it perfunctorily. Then he wound it and put it back into the pocket.

"Only way to get it out is to cut it out," he said. "And I wouldn't be able to do that."

Mr. Mullins looked at him. "You could do it that way?" he said.

"No," said Dr. Smoaks. "I said to cut it out was the only way it can be done. But I couldn't do it."

"She ain't but just barely sixteen," said Mr. Mullins.

"God damn it, Dero, it's against the law," said Dr. Smoaks. "I wouldn't care if she was just twelve. The law won't let you go and cut out a baby just because you feel bad about it."

He stood up and put his hand on the handle of his bag, looking down at Mr. Mullins on the other side of the yellow table. "I feel bad about it," he said. "I really do feel bad about it, but I can't cut her for you just for that."

Josey watched the two men, standing at the end of the table with her arms folded.

"What if she's going to have trouble?" said Mr. Mullins.

"She ain't," said Dr. Smoaks. "I can tell about that too. She ain't going to have no trouble at all."

"But she ain't never going to get over it," said Mr. Mullins.

"You mean *you* ain't never going to get over it," said Dr. Smoaks.

"I mean she ain't never going to get over it too," said Mr. Mullins. "Her with a baby and just barely sixteen."

"Don't nobody have to know," said Dr. Smoaks.

"How is it nobody is going to know?" said Mr. Mullins. "You can't keep no secret like that."

"Maybe," said Dr. Smoaks. "Maybe so."

"How you going to keep something like that a secret?"

"I would say she had the rheumatic fever," said Dr. Smoaks. "Josey could look after her. You would keep her up in the house."

The two men looked at the woman.

"Can't no nigger keep her mouth shut," said Mr. Mullins. "I don't mean you in particular, Josey," he said, talking across the table to Dr. Smoaks, not looking at her. "Just that it ain't possible for no nigger to do it."

"Well," said Dr. Smoaks, "what choice you got? I can't do no better than that. You better think on it awhile."

"And what're we going to do after?" he asked.

"I'll take care of after," said Dr. Smoaks.

"And ain't that against the law, too?" asked Mr. Mullins.

"Well, yes," said Dr. Smoaks. "Well, yes, it is, only not as much. I would take care of after for you. I would do that."

For a while neither of them spoke.

"No," said Mr. Mullins at last. "No, it won't do. It's too risky. I guess you better cut her."

"I told you I can't cut her," said Dr. Smoaks. "God damn it, Dero, get your head out of your ass and listen to me. There's a law says I can't cut her. And if I go ahead and cut her anyway, there's another law says I go to jail for it. And it probably says you go to jail for it too. And Annie."

"And the law don't care that she ain't hardly sixteen?"

"Dero," said Dr. Smoaks, "the law don't give a God damn how old she is. Nor me. Nor you. Nor Josey there."

Mr. Mullins sat thinking for a minute. "Then," he said, "I don't give a God damn for the law.

"I want you to cut her, Smoaks," he said, his hands clasped on the table in front of him. "I want you to cut her and take the child."

"I told you I can't do it," said Dr. Smoaks. "It's against the god-damn law."

"If you don't do it . . . I will," said Mr. Mullins quietly.

Dr. Smoaks looked at him across the table. A quick, sharp look. "You want to kill her?" he said.

"She'd be better off, if it come to that," said Mr. Mullins, not looking at him.

"That's crazy talk, Dero," said Dr. Smoaks. "A strong, healthy girl like Annie. You sound like it ain't never happened before. Like Annie done outraged the whole of McAfee County this way."

"It ain't never happened before in *this* house," said Mr. Mullins. "I mean it, Smoaks. If you don't cut her, I will."

Dr. Smoaks looked at Mr. Mullins across the table, gauging him. Mr. Mullins had his head down, not looking at him. His hands were clasped hard in the middle of the table.

"You reckon he means it, Josey?" he said, not looking up at the woman.

She looked at Mr. Mullins. When she spoke, her voice was flat and low. "He might could do it," she said. "He feel it enough so he might could do it. I wouldn't want to say."

"You're just about that crazy," said Dr. Smoaks. "Just about crazy enough to get it started anyway. That would be enough. You might change your mind, and then she would bleed out right there in the bed. And you standing by wringing your hands, and wishing to hell you hadn't never started in on it in the first place. And being sorry as hell after."

Mr. Mullins and Josey didn't speak.

"He might could do it," said Josey.

Dr. Smoaks didn't look at her. "You know what it looks like on the inside?" he asked. "You'd sure wish to hell you hadn't never started on it. I know that's the way it would be after it was too late. And I know you are sure as hell going to do it too, ain't you? God damn it, I told you it's against the law. You want me to get my license taken away?"

"No," said Mr. Mullins. "Only I'm going to do it if you don't. Josey here will help me."

He didn't look at her, and she didn't speak.

"Yes," said Dr. Smoaks. "Oh hell yes. That'll be a fine team, sure enough. Then you can both of you stand there and keep each other company while you watch her bleed to death. That'll fix it up all right."

He stood with his hand still on the handle of his bag for a minute. Then he took it off and put it in his pocket.

"Just keep him at the table till I get back," he said, speaking to Josey. "Ain't no rush," he said. "You got six months to go."

He went out of the kitchen screen door into the dark, leaving the black bag on the yellow-oilcloth table.

Mr. Mullins and Josey waited in the kitchen while he walked it out. He sitting at the table, his hands clasped in front of him. She standing at the end with her arms folded.

"All right," Dr. Smoaks said, letting the screen door slam to behind him. "All right, God damn it. But if it ever gets out, I'm going to come down here some night and do me some more cutting . . ." —he pointed his finger at Mr. Mullins—". . . on *you*.

"And the same for you, Josey," he said. "I mean that thing."

They both looked at him, their eyes dead and waiting.

"Get some water boiling," he said to Josey. "I got to go back to my office and get the things. And make him understand he's going to watch it. He's going to watch every bit of it. He'll get himself a lesson out of this anyway. If he don't watch it—and I mean watch every bit of it—I ain't going to do nothing."

He picked up his black bag and went out the screen door, letting it slam to behind him. They heard the motor of his car roar when he started it, and the wheels spun and slung stones as he lurched it out of the yard.

Annie didn't think too well of it when Dr. Smoaks came back to see her the second time that night. And when he pulled out the needle and wanted to give her a shot, she didn't like that at all. So Mr. Mullins and Josey and Dr. Smoaks—all three of them—had to sit on her to hold her down while he put the needle in and gave her the anaesthetic. It took effect almost right away.

"All right," Dr. Smoaks said, dropping the syringe back into his bag. "All right, Dero, you're going to have a front-row seat.

Right there where you can see all the blood and everything." Mr. Mullins was standing beside the bed. Between the bed and the wall. "All the blood and everything else. And when I cut it out, I'm going to put it in your hand, and you're going to take it out in your hand in the back yard, and dig a hole and bury it. And first time you close your eyes not to see, or say something, or just even make a noise, I'm going to stop right there and sew her back up, and that'll be the end of it. You understand?"

Mr. Mullins didn't say anything. He stood in the small space between the bed and the wall, looking down at his daughter on the bed. She looked like she was asleep, except her face was pulled down a little bit more than usual.

"You stand right there, Josey," Dr. Smoaks said. "And when I ask for something, you give it to me right away." He looked at her. "And you listen good so I ain't going to have to say it but one time."

Josey stood at the head of the bed, on Dr. Smoaks's right-hand side. A chair was pulled up with its back against the wall at the very head of the bed. The instruments were laid out on it on a towel.

Dr. Smoaks leaned over and raised Annie's nightgown. Josey had to help him, lifting her legs so they could work it up over her stomach. Josey turned it back down again at the top, tucking it under her chin so her face wouldn't be covered.

Mr. Mullins stood by the bed, looking down at his daughter. His hands were clasped in front, hanging down, and he leaned backward slightly, bracing his shoulders against the wall.

"I ought to shave her," said Dr. Smoaks, "but I ain't got the time. Get some of that boiled water and a rag, Josey, and wash her off good with soap."

Mr. Mullins watched.

Annie's thighs were full and slightly apart. He could see the soft rolls of flesh high up and inside them. Her stomach rose in a gentle swell. Over the fronts of her thighs and on her lower abdomen there was a down of fine white hair. The light from the lamp beside the bed caught it from the side and turned it silver. Under Josey's scrubbing the skin turned pink, and the blond patch between her thighs turned dark from the wet, dark golden brown, with glinting highlights from the bedside lamp.

Josey toweled her dry, and her skin had a soft, powdery texture.

"Go get some more water," said Dr. Smoaks. Josey left the room. "You swab her down with this," he said to Mr. Mullins, handing him a wad of cotton and a bottle of alcohol.

Mr. Mullins clamped the cotton to the mouth of the bottle, then upended it. He swabbed in small, rapid circles, having to lean far over the bed, because they had moved Annie near the edge on the opposite side, where Dr. Smoaks could work on her better. The circles grew larger and slower. Every now and then Mr. Mullins would douse the cotton from the bottle of alcohol. When he had swabbed her good with the circular motion, he began at the top of her abdomen, working down with overlapping swipes across from the side. He had moved one knee up onto the bed, leaning on his left hand. When he finished, he stuffed the saturated ball of cotton into the mouth of the bottle.

"Just like Mae," he said, looking down at his daughter.

"What?" said Dr. Smoaks.

Mr. Mullins looked down at his daughter's body on the bed. It was shining a little in the places where the alcohol hadn't dried yet. It had turned more pink than ever under his swabbing.

"My wife, Mae," he said. "She looked just like that. I'd forgot. Same white hair and all." He leaned back on his heel, bracing both arms on the bed. "Twelve years," he said. "I wouldn't of thought I'd forgot." He reached out his hand as if to lay it on his daughter's stomach.

Dr. Smoaks caught it quickly. "Not no more," he said. "Nothing that ain't been sterilized. Give me the bottle, and stand back there against the wall."

Mr. Mullins stood between the bed and the wall, slouching his shoulders and bracing them lightly against the wall, his hands held together in front.

Josey came back into the room with a pan of water which she set down on a second chair, beside the one with the instruments on it. Steam rose from the pan.

She and Dr. Smoaks washed their hands in the pan, lathering them and rinsing them, then lathering them and rinsing them again. After he dried his hands, Dr. Smoaks took a bottle of Merthiolate with a glass wand on the cap and drew a long red line with the wand diagonally across Annie's stomach. It was a very long line, and Mr. Mullins looked at it intently. The pink in Annie's skin was fading now. She began to look pale. The red scar across her stomach was vivid against the paleness.

"What's that?" asked Mr. Mullins.

"I cut to that line," said Dr. Smoaks. "I put the line there and cut to it so I don't forget what I'm supposed to do in the middle of it." He looked at Mr. Mullins across the bed. "I ain't no goddamned surgeon," he said. "I ain't no goddamned high-price surgeon, and it ain't every day I get to cut somebody. I figured I better draw me a picture to go by."

Mr. Mullins looked at the long red scar. "Ain't no growed man you got to take out of there," he said, his hands clasping tightly as he held them together. "Just a little bitty one. Hardly just big enough to see."

"You going to tell me all about it?" Dr. Smoaks asked, looking at him hard across the bed. "Why don't I just sit here and listen while you explain all about it to me?"

"It just don't hardly seem like you got to cut her that much," said Mr. Mullins.

"No telling what I might have to take out after I get her open," said Dr. Smoaks. "Might be I got to take out all kind of things after I see what she looks like inside there."

"You ain't never said nothing about that," said Mr. Mullins.

"I told you I didn't want to cut her," said Dr. Smoaks.

"But only the baby," said Mr. Mullins. "You never said nothing about taking something else."

"Can't tell," said Dr. Smoaks. "Might be I got to take out lots of things when I open her up. You never can tell about that kind of a thing."

Mr. Mullins looked down at his daughter's body on the bed. The red line was very long and ugly. Sweat beaded his upper lip, and he swallowed as though his throat was dry. Annie's skin had gone white again, powdery soft looking, except where it was raked by the red line of the Merthiolate.

He reached his right hand out toward her stomach, an involuntary movement. Dr. Smoaks struck it away hard, firmly and quickly.

"I told you, 'No,' " he said.

"She's *my* daughter," said Mr. Mullins, looking down at Annie, not at Dr. Smoaks.

"You give her to me," said Dr. Smoaks. "I didn't want her, but you give her to me."

Mr. Mullins looked up at him. "When you get through with her, she's going to look like the end of a feed sack," he said.

"You wanted her fixed for the baby," said Dr. Smoaks. "I didn't never say I was going to make her look pretty."

Mr. Mullins looked down at the white, dry belly of his daughter. The fine, pale hair glowed again silver in the light from the bedside lamp. "She's just like her ma," he said. "Just like Mae used to be. I never seen it till now."

"Give me the scalpel." Dr. Smoaks spoke to Josey. She looked at him as he spoke, not moving. "That there," he said, pointing to the instruments on the chair.

The shaft of the bright silver instrument was poised in his hand. He held it deftly, seeming to touch it only with the tips of his fingers. Mr. Mullins clasped and unclasped his hands, licking his lips and swallowing as he watched the hand, and the instrument in the hand. The dainty silver point came to rest at the upper end of the long, red slash, making a tiny dimple in the skin. Dr. Smoaks's left hand moved to rest on Annie's hip, bracing to steady himself. He held that position, not moving for a moment. Then he made a sudden, sweeping stroke, the scalpel point just barely touching her skin. Blood started all along the red line. A string of darker beads inside the bright red of the Merthiolate.

"No . . . ," said Mr. Mullins.

He looked up and found Dr. Smoaks looking at him hard. "I ain't hardly started yet," he said. "That's just to mark the place."

"No," Mr. Mullins said. He reached down, and his fingers closed around the hand that held the instrument, lifting it away.

Dr. Smoaks didn't speak.

"You get through with her, and she's going to have a belly looks like a goddamn feed sack," he said. "Stitched and puckered like a goddamn feed sack."

"You going to change your mind, Dero?" said Dr. Smoaks. "You think you're going to change your mind now?"

"Put them up," said Mr. Mullins. "Put them back in your bag and just go on."

"You wanted it, and I'm doing it," said Dr. Smoaks.

Mr. Mullins still held his hand. He tightened his grip. "You move it, and I break it," he said. "You start to move it, and I break it right off."

They stood like that for a long time, reaching each other across the bed, and across the dry, white belly of the daughter. Across the long scar, stepped off with beads of dark blood inside the brighter red of the Merthiolate. Josey had folded her arms under her breasts, and she stood to one side, looking at them.

"It's going to cost you anyway," Dr. Smoaks said at last. "You wanted it, and I was set to do it. I would have done it, too. So you're going to pay for it."

"Put them in your bag and go," said Mr. Mullins.

"But it's going to cost you," said Dr. Smoaks.

"Yes," said Mr. Mullins. He let go of the hand. Dr. Smoaks tossed the scalpel lightly back onto the chair. "Bring them downstairs, Josey," he said. "Bring them downstairs and get me a cup of coffee." As he walked out of the room, he rolled his sleeves down. He didn't look back at Mr. Mullins.

Mr. Mullins lowered his open hand, placing it on his daughter's stomach. The red Merthiolate scar and the dark beads of blood ran out from under his fingers. Under his palm, her skin was soft and dry. He removed his hand and wiped the blood on the leg of his pants.

Josey was collecting the things and putting them into the bag.

"Give me the rag," he said to her. She handed him the rag from the basin.

"Get some soap on it," he said, handing it back to her.

She soaped it and handed it back.

Mr. Mullins took the soapy rag and rubbed it along the Merthiolate scar. The beads of blood disappeared, and the bright red of the mark faded a little. But it did not disappear. Her skin turned pink again under the scrubbing.

"It go away after a while," said Josey, looking down at him.

He looked up at her and nodded. She handed him the towel, and he gave her the rag. After he dried Annie, she helped him get her nightgown back down and pull up the covers. When she took the black bag and went downstairs, she left him sitting on the edge of the bed patting the covers over his daughter's stomach. He didn't look at her as she went out of the room.

When she got to the kitchen, Dr. Smoaks was sitting at the table. He had gotten his own coffee.

"Hardest case of rheumatic fever I ever diagnosed," he said, holding the cup in both hands as he sipped. "And rheumatic fever is always hard," he added.

Josey put the bag down on the end of the table and looked at him. She didn't say anything. When he finished, he rose, taking his black bag, and went to the door. Going out, he stopped, holding the screen open with his hand.

"Tell him that's going to be five dollars," he said. "Five dollars, whether I did it or not. Just for my time," he added. "I would have done it, too," he said, not looking at her.

Josey watched him as he went out the door.

Annie took her confinement calmly, growing even more passive as the weeks went by. Mr. Mullins insisted first that she not go out of the house, and then that she not go out of the bedroom, for fear someone would see her. Neighbors' houses were not nearby, and the loblollies screened the house from all save the few who took it in mind to make a deliberate visit, so that keeping the secret was not so difficult after all. One or two delegations of women from the neighborhood came to call, being met once by Mr. Mullins when he was home, and then by Josey when he wasn't. Holding them there on the porch and explaining that Miss Annie was *poorly*, and that Dr. Smoaks wouldn't allow her to have any visitors, since what she had might be catching. The delegations were curious, but not persistent. They soon dropped away and didn't come back.

Josey saw to the house and fixed the meals.

After she was confined to her room, Annie sat for long hours in a chair pulled back from the window—Mr. Mullins wouldn't let her come too close even there, for fear she would show herself and let the secret get away—in an attitude of listening. Tracing the progress of the thing closed up inside her. Concentrated and intent on the augmentation going on inside herself, as if she were to be called on later to give an accounting for it, cell by cell.

Mr. Mullins did not try to break in on her. The night in the bedroom seemed to have cast the die for him, and he was now resigned to the fact of his daughter's condition, sin and all. But her air of listening and waiting quickened him to expectation himself, and his expectation increased as her term drew to a close. Perhaps that too came out of a remembrance of what he had gone through, with Mae, sixteen years before.

"A week, maybe," said Dr. Smoaks. They sat again at the kitchen table, covered with the yellow oilcloth, Josey standing at the end of the table with her arms folded.

"She's not to have nothing," said Mr. Mullins. "No shot nor nothing to help the pain. This will be for her to learn her lesson."

Dr. Smoaks looked at him over the coffee cup. "She'll learn her lesson," he said, looking into the tilted cup. "Don't you worry about that."

"Not real hard," said Mr. Mullins. "Not real hard, so as to hurt her bad. But enough for her to remember it. Just so she will learn her lesson and remember it for a while."

"She'll remember," said Dr. Smoaks.

They wouldn't let him into the room. So he sat at the kitchen table with a cup of black coffee getting cold in front of him, his hands clasped in front of him on the table, the cup of coffee between his forearms getting cold with a film of oil on top.

Every so often Josey would come down into the kitchen to do something—get some more hot water, or some towels, or something, and they would look at each other, but without speaking.

Finally he heard the crying. A sharp cry once, then a couple of little ones. Then nothing. He never did hear Annie making any noise.

Josey came down into the kitchen and got some more water, cold water this time, and some more towels. They looked at each other hard as she turned from the sink to go back upstairs.

"She be all right," Josey said in a flat, low voice. She didn't look at him when she spoke. From the foot of the stairs she gave him a second long look. Then she went on up to the bedroom.

In a few minutes Dr. Smoaks came down the steps. He came down them slowly, rolling down his sleeves, and walked over to the table and sat down across from Mr. Mullins.

"Coffee?" Mr. Mullins asked.

Dr. Smoaks looked up at him briefly, then back down at the table. He nodded.

Mr. Mullins got up and poured a cup of coffee at the stove. Then he put it down in front of Dr. Smoaks and went around and sat down across the table from him.

"Was it hard?" Mr. Mullins asked.

Dr. Smoaks looked up at him, then back at the table. "No," he said. "It wasn't hard. I didn't deliver it. Just caught it. It just dropped right out in my hand."

"I never did hear Annie," said Mr. Mullins.

"Annie's all right," said Dr. Smoaks. "I told you that. I told you Annie would be all right."

"I'm glad she's all right," said Mr. Mullins.

They both sipped their coffee.

"Dero," said Dr. Smoaks.

"Yes?" said Mr. Mullins. "Yes, what is it?"

Dr. Smoaks didn't speak for a minute. "It's a boy, Dero," he said, sipping his coffee. He put the cup down in the saucer carefully, looking into it. They sat for a while across the table.

"God damn it, Dero," Dr. Smoaks said. He swung himself sideways in the chair, looking out the screen door of the kitchen.

"God damn it, Dero . . . ," he said again, looking down toward the floor, ". . . it was a nigger."

Mr. Mullins looked at the side of his face across the table. "What?" he said.

Dr. Smoaks didn't look at him. He was looking out the screen door again. "I said it's a nigger," he said. "A fine, bouncing nigger baby," he said. "Annie gave birth to a fine, bouncing nigger baby," he repeated, ". . . a nigger baby boy."

Mr. Mullins looked at him across the table. His hands were stretched out in front of him limply, and his mouth was hanging open.

"What . . . ," he said, his jaw working slowly, ". . . what did you say . . . ?"

Josey came down the stairs and into the room. She stopped at the foot of the stairs and looked at the two men.

"She wants to know can she have something to drink," she said.

"What?" said Dr. Smoaks, looking at her.

"Miss Annie want to know can she have something to drink. She say she thirsty, and she want to have something to drink," she said. "Something cool."

"Get her a glass of water," said Dr. Smoaks. "She can have a glass of water." He was looking out the screen door again.

"Why'd you do it?" said Mr. Mullins, his voice almost too low to hear. "Couldn't you just dropped it or something?" he said. "Couldn't you just dropped it on the floor?"

"I didn't think to do it," said Dr. Smoaks. "I would have done it if I had thought to do it. But I was too surprised to think about it, I reckon," he said. "It was just that I had it in my hands, and then it was breathing on its own. And it started to holler, so I couldn't think what I had to do until it was too late. It was already hollering, and it was too late."

"What you mean, it was too late?" said Mr. Mullins.

Dr. Smoaks looked at him. "I mean it was *too late*," he said. He didn't explain.

"It ain't too late for me," said Mr. Mullins. He scraped back his chair and rose from the table.

Dr. Smoaks looked up at him across the table. "She ain't asleep," he said. "You said she wasn't to have nothing, so she ain't asleep. You're going to play hell getting it away from her."

Mr. Mullins stood in front of his chair.

"Anyway," said Dr. Smoaks, looking away again, "it ain't that easy. Even if you do get it away from her," he said. "It ain't that easy."

He rose, scraping back his chair. "Well," he said, "anyway, I'm through with it—finally."

"What?" said Mr. Mullins. "You said you was going to take care of it." He looked at Dr. Smoaks.

"I can't get rid of no nigger baby," he said.

"You said you was going to fix it up and take care of it," Mr. Mullins said.

"Not no nigger baby," said Dr. Smoaks. "I can't get rid of no nigger baby. See Josey," he said. "Maybe she'll get rid of it for you."

"I'll get rid of it," Mr. Mullins said, not looking at Josey.

"All right, if you can," said Dr. Smoaks. "You take care of it if you can. It ain't that easy. Not even a nigger baby is that easy."

He rose, taking his black bag in his hand and going to the door. He stood with the door held open a little, not looking back at Mr. Mullins.

"You owe me a dollar," he said, standing in the door. "My fee for delivering a nigger baby is one dollar," he said. "So you owe me one dollar."

He went out of the house, letting the screen door slam behind him.

He bowed the hickory stick between his hands, standing at the foot of the bed, watching Annie nurse the baby. She watched the baby, not looking at him.

"You going to give it up," he said. Bowing the stick out in front of him. "I don't mean you going to give it up next week," he said, his voice breaking into the darkness of the room. "Not next week, nor some other time," he said. "I mean you going to give it up *now*."

Annie watched the brown head against her breast. It made her breast look even whiter, with the pale blue veins just under the skin.

Mr. Mullins whipped the stick across the end of the bed. It sounded like a rifle going off in the still room. Annie flinched, but she didn't look at him.

"I mean *now*," he said, louder.

He struck the bed again. Not hitting anything, just the bed. He whipped the stick down again and again, the tempo increasing and the noise of the slaps getting louder. Saying, "Now . . . Now . . . Now!" And the stick hitting in between. Annie flinched every time the stick hit the bed. But she didn't look up at her father. The stick broke, and Mr. Mullins tried to whip the bed with the stump. It was too short, and he threw it against the wall.

"NOW!" he said.

"Let her finish with the baby." Josey spoke from the doorway of the bedroom. "She be through in a while," she said. "That be time enough."

He stood at the foot of the bed watching. His eyes held tight on the brown head against the blue-white of Annie's breast.

Josey spoke again from the doorway. "Whyn't you wait till she be sleep? She got to go to sleep sometime," she said.

Mr. Mullins paid no attention to her. "He's through," he said after a while. He came around to the side of the bed, keeping his eyes on the brown head as he moved. "He's through, ain't he?" he said, looking down as he stood by the side of the bed.

Annie didn't look at him. The baby didn't move. The nipple had come half out of his mouth, and his eyes were closed.

"You got to take him?" Annie's voice was low, and there was just a little quaver in it. She didn't look up at him.

"Yes," he said. "I got to take him now," he said.

He reached down and lifted him up. Annie's arms were limp outside the covers. She didn't move to cover her breast, and after he moved the baby away, Mr. Mullins stood looking down at the whiteness of his daughter's breast, with the nipple still moist and pink from the sucking, the veins pale blue just under the skin. He held the baby away, one hand under its head, and the other under its hips, looking down at her in the bed.

"He's too little," she said.

"Cover yourself," he said.

She drew the sheet over her breast, pulling it up to her chin. "He's too little," she said again.

"You got to give him up," he said, holding the baby away and looking down at her. "You got to give him up now, because you ain't going to want to do it no more tomorrow, nor the day after, nor any other time. Now is the best time," he said.

"Same as killing him," she said.

"It'll be on me," he said. "All of it'll be on me."

He continued to look down at her.

"You knowed you wasn't going to keep it anyway," he said. "Not if it had been like I thought, you wasn't going to keep it. And you sure as hell knowed you wasn't going to get to keep it like it is."

He started toward the door, still holding the baby away from him. Holding it in his hands so it wouldn't lie against him and touch him.

"Pa," she said from the bed. He turned, and she was looking at him now. "Pa," she said again, still looking at him. "His name is John Henry." After she said it, she looked away from him.

Mr. Mullins looked at her for a long minute, then shook his head slowly from side to side. "Jesus God," he said.

"Pa," she said, looking at him again. "Josey," she said, looking away. "Make him put the bunting on him, Josey. So he don't catch cold."

"Yes, child," said Josey from the doorway.

He walked out of the room and down the stairs, still holding the baby away in his hands to keep it from touching him.

It was getting lighter all the time, and still he hadn't made up his mind. He would have to make it up soon, though, since he had to get done with it and back to the house before it was good light.

The bank dropped off steeply in front of him. The black water undercut the bank, and little eddies floated by in an arc, reaching in toward the roots hanging down into the water. Mr. Mullins was sitting and looking down into the water, his back propped against a tree. Beside him the baby lay on the sack. The sack was spread out on the ground, but there was a bulge in the bottom of it where he had put the rocks. The baby fidgeted, but it didn't cry. Every now and then it would flinch its arm or its leg and screw its face up, but so far it hadn't cried. Mr. Mullins kept thinking that if it would only cry he could do it. And he got mad, since the baby wouldn't cry. He sat there leaning against the tree and getting madder all the time. Looking at the black water swirling past under the bank.

Mr. Mullins would look at the water, and then he would look at the baby beside him. Streaks of mist hung under the trees along the opposite bank. The water looked cold, but he knew it was warm. He had reached down and put his hand in it to see.

"Shit," he said finally, standing up. "Shit on it anyway."

"Out of the county," he said, handing the baby to Josey in the kitchen. It was full light now. He had taken a long time getting back, because he had to stay away from the cleared land for fear someone would see him. "That's all I give a good God damn about," he said. "Just make sure you get him out of McAfee County."

"Yes, suh," said Josey flatly, taking the baby from him and cradling it in her arms. "I see to it," she said.

He went to the cupboard and took out a Prince Albert tobacco can. "Here," he said, handing her the money. "Two dollars is all I can spare. You do it for the two dollars, you hear?"

Josey took the money without speaking, but she nodded her head.

"I ever see him again," he said, "and I'm going back to the river. I'm going to take him back to the river and do it," he said. "Wouldn't happen twice."

Josey nodded and turned to leave, the baby cradled in her arms.

"And, Josey," he said. She turned to him. "Better not nobody ever find out," he said. "Better not nobody ever find out, or I take you with me when I go back to the river."

She looked at him for a minute, then turned and went out the kitchen door.

"You better get back in that bed," he said. Annie stood at the foot of the stairs. He sat at the kitchen table, his forearms stretched out on the yellow-oilcloth top, his hands clasped together. He looked at her, then back at the table. "You get back in the bed, you hear?" he said. "You get back there and stay till you get your strength back. Then we see what we're going to do."

"He was too little," she said, looking at him from the foot of the stairs. "You wasn't even going to use the bunting till I said it," she said. "If you just could have waited a little bit."

He didn't look at her. "Won't you *please* get back in the bed, Annie?" he said. "We're going to have to talk about it later on. But won't you please get back in the bed right now?"

She looked at him from the foot of the stairs. Her bare feet were planted on the floor firmly, and with her hand she reached out, just barely touching the newel. Her lank hair was hanging down over her breasts, and she looked pale. Under her hair the milk was making two long, weeping stains down the front of her nightgown.

"His name is John Henry, Pa," she said, her voice low and level, from the bottom of the stairs. "I give him his name," she said, "and his name is John Henry."

He didn't look at her. "Won't you *please* get back in the god-damned bed?" he said. He put his head down on the edge of the table between his elbows. His voice was muffled and low. "Won't you *please*, Annie, get back in the goddamned bed?"

She looked at him a minute, then turned and walked slowly up the stairs. Leaving him resting his head on the shiny yellow table in the kitchen.

John Henry's Promise

1956: SUMMER

A shutter was clicking away inside Nettie's head, keeping time with the slap of the tires on the asphalt of the highway. Sixty-five . . . seventy . . . the toes of her bare right foot curling around the top of the gas pedal, jamming it down, making the yellow Pontiac stretch itself out and lay down on the highway. It was a good road car, heavy and steady. She liked to run it hard.

"Niggers," she said. "*God* damn. What are you going to do about niggers anyway?"

She had had to argue with Josey every step of the way. First about the coffin. Fifteen hundred dollars for mahogany.

"I don't know, Miss Nettie . . . ," said Josey, her voice getting whiny, making Nettie's hair prickle along the back of her neck.

"Shit on you, Josey." She hadn't said it. The shutter clicked open, black on an empty frame. "It's *my* goddamn money. What is it *you* don't know, anyway?"

She had gone ahead and gotten it just the same—mahogany, with a bronze plate and handles. Beckworth had made a special trip in to Savannah to bring it out in the hearse—not charging the fifty cents a mile. All Josey could do was shake her head and whine. "I don't know, Miss Nettie . . . I just don't know . . ."

"Niggers . . ."

She didn't see the speedometer. Curling the toes of her bare right foot over the top of the gas pedal, laying the yellow Pontiac down on U.S. 17 until she could almost feel it stretching itself out, streaking into Savannah through the pine flats and marsh. There were things floating around inside her head with the clicking. Scenes that would suddenly stop and come into focus like pictures in a frame.

The colors were bright blue and green—the muddy brown of the river and marsh—and the shiny blue and red of the crabs.

Nettie thirteen years old. Standing on the Altamahatchee River bridge, watching as the crane hauled the white Ford out of the marsh, with the water pouring down from the half open windows. Then moving along the rail closer to watch as they pried open the doors and pulled Maggie out of the car—Smoaks cursing and picking off the blueshell crabs with his hands, throwing them down onto the bridge and stomping them with his feet. The Ford had gone over into the water the night before. There wasn't much left of Maggie to claim, because of the blueshell crabs. Nettie had gotten sick watching Smoaks pulling them off.

Then they wouldn't let her bury Maggie in any of the white cemeteries, since the sixteenth part of nigger blood was too much.

"I be *God* damn if I'm going to put her out in a nigger grave-yard," said Nettie.

So she and Josey took Maggie in to Savannah to have her cremated, and she went by herself to sprinkle the ashes into Famous Creek, down in the woods behind the house. Afterwards, she kept the urn to put on the mantlepiece in the front room, filled with a spray of sea oats.

The shutter clicked again, and she was seeing the trees and the moss of the cemetery. John Henry's mahogany coffin, with the dull-shining yellow of the bronze plate, spooling down into the open grave. Beckworth himself had been there to help with the fifteen-hundred-dollar coffin, his foot tapping the lever that started the spools to spinning as the coffin went sucking down between the chrome bars on the edges of the grave.

She had been hugging Josey and crying. Both of them crying. Watching the big red-brown box going away.

Then, later, she had had to argue with Josey all over again about the stone. After the funeral, after the red-brown box had sucked down into the black shaft of the grave with the mechanism whirring inside the chrome bars, after Beckworth had taken his equipment away—after it had all been over, she had remembered. There weren't any markers on the graves. Just homemade things that fell apart and got stepped on until the weeds and honeysuckle grew over them. She had remembered that later. And then she had had to argue about it.

"I don't know, Miss Nettie." Josey shaking her head.

"Shit." Not saying it. "What is it *you* don't know, Josey? It's *my* goddamn money. Mine for the coffin and mine for the stone."

Saying instead, "We owe him that, Josey. That much. I'll pay for it."

"I don't know, Miss Nettie. Folks might . . . I don't know . . ."

Thinking, "Folks will . . . John Henry? Yes, yes, you're goddamn right . . . Folks sure as shit will . . ."

"I'll buy it, Josey," she said. "Wouldn't nobody say nothing, because I'll be the one to buy it. Everybody knows about me and John Henry. It'll be all right."

"I don't know, Miss Nettie . . . I just don't know . . ."

"Shit . . . ," she thought, ". . . niggers . . ."

Too late Saturday when she thought about it after the funeral on Friday. She had to wait for Monday, with the stone getting bigger and bigger inside her head all day Sunday. "Gigantic . . . something gigantic," she was thinking. "It's going to be . . . oh, God damn . . . gigantic."

She put all the money she had into the barrel of the flashlight. Three battery-sized rolls. Twenties, mostly twenties. Two thousand, one hundred and eighty dollars. Then she jammed the flashlight under the front seat of the Pontiac and wedged it with rags.

The Oconee River bridge was a blur. Going over it at seventy miles an hour, the tires whining up at her from the metal plates of the center span. Mist hung blue-gray along the shore, rolling up under the branches of the trees. The river hardly seemed to be moving at all. There were great sick-looking patches of algae, lying green-yellow on the still surface.

It was beginning to get hot. Six-fifteen. The Negro men were starting to come up out of the woods to the highway. She passed two of them walking on the shoulder of the road. Their shacks were built back out of sight in the woods, at the ends of the two sandy tire tracks, parallel traces with stunted Bermuda grass plats in between, running off into the pines and Spanish bayonets. Now and then something like little settlements had crept up out of the woods to the highway. A compound of three or four houses, with hard, swept yards, a sagging cat's cradle of clothesline wires running back and forth from house to house, holding the settlement together. In the open spaces between the houses, the big black iron pot would be sitting on a pile of ashes.

The houses were unpainted, some covered with brick-patterned tar paper, leaning and collapsing off the brick and piled stone piers, with dark open rectangles where the doors should have been and floursack curtains waving out of the open windows. Traces of blue breakfast smoke were rising out of the chimneys.

In one of the settlements—three houses set close together, two breasting the highway up close, the third set farther back between them—there was a woman tending a fire at the pot, stuffing pieces of wood under it, turning her face away from the heat of the fire. On the porch of the middle house was a mound of faded clothing.

There were children in the yard—small, toddling age, a few older—stirring up swirls of dust as they chased each other around among the houses. A boy toddled toward the pot with the fire under it. The woman rammed the fire with a piece of yellow kindling, her head turned toward the highway, shielding her face from the heat of the fire with her hand—not seeing the child. He must have been about two or three years old. His shirt was too big for him—red and white checkered, flapping under the blue-black shine of his morning-washed face.

Nettie caught him out of the corner of her eye. He couldn't have been closer than fifteen feet to the pot. There wasn't any danger. The woman would see him, or he would feel the heat of the fire and would veer off himself before he got too close.

The shutter clicked, framing the picture there inside her head —checkered shirt and the black iron pot with the fire going underneath, pink flame licks beginning to curl up the sides, the woman with her face turned away, her hand up, yellow palm outward, shielding her face.

Nettie hit the brake, and the car veered sharply, catching the right-front tire in the rut formed by the edge of the asphalt on the shoulder of the road. She whipped the wheel back to the left to break the wheel out and onto the road, her right hip jammed against the back of the seat, locking her leg on the brake. The car hopped, making a long, looping skid. It came to rest in the left-hand lane, facing back toward McAfee County.

The shutter closed—black—and the picture was gone again.

Over the hood of the car she saw the boy stop and look at her; then he put his hand into his mouth and ran away toward the house, going in under the front steps standing up. The woman tending the fire was standing beside the pot looking at her, the stick of yellow wood in her hand held slightly away from her body in a limp gesture.

Nettie rested her head on the steering wheel for a minute; then she looked up to see that the Negro woman had started walking toward her. There was no trace of the boy. She ground the gears into reverse and backed off onto the shoulder, turning the car at right angles to the highway. Without looking to see if the highway was clear, she slapped the car into low and gunned the engine, leaping onto the road and heading for Savannah again. When she looked into the rearview mirror to see where the woman was, she saw her standing on the shoulder, still holding the piece of wood in the dainty way.

Nettie watched her in the mirror for a long time as she pressed her bare foot down on the gas pedal.

Josey jammed the piece of wood under the pot, shielding her face with her hand. Then she stood up and walked away, going to get the clothes off the back porch. The water in the pot bubbled and steamed, the steam mixing with the blue smoke from the fire.

"Look out, John Henry!" Nettie was only four, but a year older than the boy. She was bossy, and she treated him as if he were her child, ordering him around and laying hands on him because she had made him her care. There were just the two of them to roam around the yard together, and looking after him gave her something to do. He didn't like it.

She rushed over to stop him, making a big show of it. In trying to help him, she knocked him down, and he started to cry.

"Nettie help you," said Josey. "You ain't going to cry, and Nettie trying to help you? Hush up that crying, John Henry."

Nettie forced herself onto him, straddling him and trying to help as he was getting up, but getting in the way and keeping him from doing it. He bawled, wrestling around in the dirt, getting his checkered shirt dirty, the shirt riding up and exposing the shiny black swell of his belly. He fought to pull it down, covering himself.

"Hush up, John Henry," said Josey. "Hush up that bawling. Don't no manchild cry like that." She came over and helped Nettie, getting her out of the way so John Henry could get up. He ran off toward the porch, with Nettie following along with him, trying to put her arm around his shoulder to comfort him.

"Fire," she said. "Burn up John Henry."

When she said that, John Henry bawled louder than ever, twisting and trying to get away from her. She hugged him harder, mothering him anyway.

"Nettie," said Josey, "come here, Nettie. You help me put in these here clothes."

The girl looked at her, her arm still around the boy, holding him back, the boy twisting to get away.

"Come on now, Nettie," said Josey. "You be a good girl and help me with these here clothes."

She looked at Josey. "Nigger job," she said. "That there's a nigger job."

Josey looked at her. "Come on now, Nettie," she said. "Don't you talk to Josey thataway. I going to tell you mama about how you was talking to Josey."

"That there's a nigger job," she said. She kept her arm around John Henry's shoulder. "I'm taking care of John Henry."

"I be going to tell you mama on you," said Josey. "What you said." She started toward the back porch of the house.

Nettie took her arm away from John Henry's shoulder and gave Josey's back a hard look. "Nigger job, Josey," she said, yelling.

Josey kept walking toward the house, not looking at her.

Nettie dropped her arm and called. "Josey." Josey kept walking toward the house. "I'm coming, Josey," she said, her voice going up. "Don't tell Mama." John Henry started to run away toward the porch steps of the shack. Nettie reached out and gave him a slap on the back of the head. "Bad boy," she said. John Henry gave a loud bawl. Josey stopped and turned toward her.

"I'm coming, Josey," she said. "I don't care. I don't care when John Henry burn up in the fire."

"You be a sweet girl, Nettie," said Josey. "You be a sweet girl and help me with them clothes."

"I be sweet," said Nettie.

"And, Nettie," said Josey.

"Yes," said Nettie.

"Don't you say 'nigger.' "

"Yes," said Nettie.

" 'Nigger' is a hard word, Nettie," said Josey. "Don't you never say that word no more. You hear?"

"Yes, Josey," said Nettie. "Never no more." She walked slowly toward the pot as the woman came back with the clothes.

"Niggerniggerniggerniggernigger . . . ," she whispered.

"You be a sweet girl, Nettie," said Josey.

"I be sweet," she said.

The Pontiac sped down the highway, the yellow-white-yellow stripes of the centerline snaking in and out under the left fender.

A boot in the right-front tire clicked on the asphalt, the whirring clicks of the boot working with the clicks of the shutter inside her head, framing pictures. . . .

Playing at Famous Creek that ran into the Dorchester Swamp, down in the woods behind the house. Nettie eleven. John Henry ten.

She had the story about Cleopatra. She had gotten onto it in the tent show. Seven days of double features—Charlie Chan seven times, Charles Starrett and Lash LaRue five times, building to the climax of the last two nights, *Cleopatra* and *The Sign of the Cross* by Cecil B. De Mille. *The Sign of the Cross* playing on Sunday night by special permission.

That summer they played Cleopatra.

"We got to have us a barge," said Nettie. "You reckon you could build us a barge, John Henry?"

"What kind?"

"Cleopatra had her a barge."

"Would something like a raft be a barge?" he said. He was getting taller than she was now. Beginning to fill out with muscles that weren't little boy looking anymore. He could swing an ax and cut kindling as well as Josey could. Next winter he would start splitting the logs for the fireplace.

"Something like," said Nettie. "You could make it fancy?"

"We could fix it up some," he said.

"I'll draw you a picture," she said.

"Not real fancy," he said. "Some."

He made the raft for her, trimming the logs so the front end came to a point. Then she wanted a divan on it, so he made a border of logs and they filled it up with moss and covered it with a quilt. He made a roof for it out of bamboo; and they covered that with a sheet.

Nettie had him cut a palm frond for himself to fan her with, and he used a long bamboo pole to push the barge around in the creek. They spent the first week just getting ready to play Cleopatra. Nettie had to collect some things for herself—earrings and bracelets and necklaces. Then she had to make herself a crown and paint it out of a bottle of gold paint she got at the ten-cent store in Kose. When she had finished with her own costume, she worked up one for John Henry.

"These go on your arms—up here," she said. She handed him bracelets made of strips cut out of tin cans and painted gold.

"What for?" he said.

"Because that's what you wear," she said.

"Oh," he said. "It ain't going to do much good wearing them up there."

"Well," she said, "all I know is what I seen in the picture show."

"Why you reckon I got to wear them?" he said. "It ain't going to do no good wearing them way up there."

"I don't know," she said. "That's the way they showed it. You're going to be the eunuch. Eunuchs always wears them gold bracelets on their arms."

"I see," said John Henry. "Does the eunuchs wear beads?"

"No," she said. "I'm the one wears the beads."

"Oh," said John Henry. "What else does the eunuchs wear?"

"What?" said Nettie.

"What else does the eunuchs wear to push the barge around?"

"Well," she said. She hesitated. "You're going to wear you a piece of white cloth out of a sheet," she said. "I'll show you." She drew him a picture of a big black man in a turban and a white loincloth like a diaper. "It's pure white, John Henry," she said.

"That's two pieces," he said.

"What?" said Nettie.

"One on my head, and the . . . other one."

Nettie looked at the picture. "Yes," she said. "I forgot. Two pieces."

"What about my overalls?" he said.

She looked at him. "You ain't going to wear no overalls," she said.

He looked at the picture. "Just that there little bitty thing is all?"

"Two pieces," she said.

"I need to wear my overalls too," he said.

"That'd spoil it," she said. "Didn't no eunuch wear no overalls."

He looked at her a minute. "I ain't going to be no eunuch," he said.

"I ain't never heard nothing about no eunuch that he was wearing overalls," she said. "I ain't never heard that in my life, John Henry," she said. "We're talking about Egypt. Wasn't no overalls in Egypt. No such of a thing."

He didn't say anything. "What if somebody is going to see us?" he said.

"You got the cloth on," she said. "There ain't nothing to that. Wouldn't nothing show."

"It ain't like overalls," he said. "I wouldn't want nobody to see me."

"Ain't nothing going to show," she said.

"You ain't seeing what it is I'm trying to tell you," he said. "I better wear my overalls."

She looked at him. "We can't play Cleopatra then," she said. "I ain't going to do it half-assed."

"I done made the barge," he said.

"Too bad," she said.

"Well," he said.

"It's pure white," she said. "You going to look good in it."

John Henry didn't say anything.

"You ain't seen what it is I'll be going to wear," she said. "I gone to lots of trouble."

He looked at her. "What were you going to wear?" he said.

"Beads," she said.

"I know," he said. "What else?"

"Hardly nothing," she said.

"Maybe we ought not be playing Cleopatra," he said. "What else you going to wear?"

"Hardly nothing except the beads," she said. "A crown. It's hard to tell about it. You'd have to see it."

"I don't know," he said.

"We got to play it like it was," she said. "Or I ain't going to play it at all."

"You going to wear beads?" he said.

"Lots of beads," she said. "We're going to play 'Going to Meet Mark Anthony.' That's the way she done it. Mostly beads—and the crown."

"Who's Mark Anthony?" said John Henry.

"He's the one she went to meet," she said. "He couldn't hardly believe it."

"I reckon not," said John Henry. "Was he a eunuch?"

"No," said Nettie. "He was a Roman."

"What did he wear?"

"Mark Anthony wore him a uniform. He had on a helmet."

"How come I couldn't be the Mark Anthony?" he said. "A helmet sounds better than the eunuch suit. I look good in a helmet."

"We got to playlike for Mark Anthony," she said.

"Oh," said John Henry. "How come it was I couldn't be the Mark Anthony?"

"I'm trying to tell you," said Nettie. "He was a Roman. Mark Anthony was a Roman general."

"Oh," said John Henry.

"You couldn't be Mark Anthony," she said. "You got to be the eunuch."

"Oh," he said. "I couldn't be Mark Anthony?"

"A Roman is like a white man, John Henry," she said.

"Oh," he said.

"A eunuch is a Egyptian," she said. "They stand around and wear a pure white cloth and wave a fan over me and push my barge around. The eunuch is more important than Mark Anthony, really," she said.

"Yes," said John Henry.

"No," said Nettie. "I mean it. We can playlike for Mark Anthony, but I got to have me a real eunuch to push the barge around and fan me with the palm leaf."

"A eunuch is a colored man?" said John Henry.

"A *Egyptian* colored man," said Nettie.

"Yes," said John Henry. "A eunuch couldn't wear no helmet," he said.

"That's what the Roman generals wears," she said.

"Yes," he said.

John Henry pushed the barge. Sometimes he fanned her with the palm leaf. There wasn't much to her costume—the bottom piece from her bathing suit, a hollow rubber ball cut in half and the halves painted gold, with a lot of beads and bracelets.

They would meet down at Famous Creek, going off from the house separate ways. The game itself caused them to do that, and the costumes, though pushing the barge around was all there was to it.

The third week they had been playing Cleopatra John Henry came down and found Nettie waiting for him on the barge. She was lying on her side on the divan, her head propped up with an elbow.

He looked at her, then he looked around to see if anyone might be coming out of the woods down where they were.

"Put your clothes back on," he said. "What if somebody was to come around down here and seen us? These here little white pants is bad enough."

"*That's* the way to catch you a Roman," she said. "They couldn't put it in the picture show."

"I reckon not," he said, turning away from her, not looking. "That's the way to get me kilt," he said. "Put your clothes back on. It's bad enough anyway. Please, Miss Nettie."

She rolled over onto her stomach, pouting. There weren't many beads in the back. John Henry looked down at her lying on the divan. From the back Nettie was beginning to look like a woman.

"We got to play something else," she said, not looking up at him. "I need me a real Mark Anthony. This here has done played out."

"I ain't going to stay around you like that," he said. "I got to get on back to the house and get my overalls on."

"Ain't nothing going to happen to you, John Henry," she said. She got up and put on her bathing-suit bottom and the rubber-ball halves. "A eunuch just ain't enough. We got to get us a Mark Anthony too."

She brought Vincent Demott, a thirteen-year-old who lived down the road, getting him to be the Mark Anthony. There wasn't time to make a real costume, so she got him to wrap a towel around his waist, and he used a gold-painted football helmet and a sword she had John Henry make for him.

They played "Going to Meet Mark Anthony" for a while, and then Vincent called John Henry a nigger instead of a eunuch, and they started to wrestle. But Vincent was too much older and bigger, and Nettie helped him so they could hold John Henry down and take off his loincloth.

"They ain't much of it," Vincent said when they had gotten the loincloth off.

"He ain't but ten," said Nettie.

"He's a nigger, though," said Vincent. "I'd of thought a nigger had a bigger one than that."

"Let him up, Vincent," said Nettie.

Vincent looked at her; then he reached across and grabbed one of the rubber-ball halves and yanked. Both of them came off. A necklace broke, and beads poured down on John Henry's chest.

"Look out," said Nettie, "you broke my beads."

"Maybe I would be going to break something else," said Vincent.

Nettie looked at him. "Don't break my beads," she said. She stood up and took off the bathing-suit bottom and the beads; then she ran into the water of the creek. Vincent chased her, and they came out on the opposite bank and ran into the bushes. John Henry put on his loincloth and sat on the bank to wait for them. While he was waiting, he picked up Nettie's beads. After about a half an hour, Nettie came out by herself, wading across the creek.

She and John Henry talked it over sitting on the bank.

"You was gone pretty long," he said.

"Yes," she said.

"Just you and Vincent."

"Yes," she said. "I didn't mean to help Vincent against you."

"I hope you had yourself a good time. You and Vincent," he said. "It took you long enough."

"You ain't old enough," she said. "Vincent is thirteen. I told you I was sorry."

"You don't think so?" he said.

"I'll tell you about it sometime," she said. "You wouldn't understand nohow. You ain't old enough."

"I ain't?" he said. "You had to help Vincent. Just a Roman was all you needed. You couldn't use no eunuch."

"We wasn't playing Cleopatra," she said.

"I know you wasn't," he said. "You got to have you a eunuch for that."

"Yes," she said.

"You better put your clothes on," he said. "Vincent done gone home now."

She put on the bathing suit and the rubber-ball halves.

"Here," said John Henry. He held out his hand to her.

"What?" she said.

"I picked up your beads for you while you was over there with Vincent."

She took them from him, pouring them back and forth from one hand to the other. "I let Vincent pee a baby in me," she said.

John Henry looked at her. "What did you say?" he said.

"That's the way you do it," said Nettie. "The boy takes his, and he pees a baby inside you."

"Yes," said John Henry.

"It hurts some," she said.

John Henry looked down at himself. The loincloth was dirty where she and Vincent had wrestled him around on the bank pulling it off. He looked back at Nettie. "He pees?" he said.

Nettie nodded her head. "Yes," she said. "That's the way to make a baby."

"Pees?" said John Henry.

"Vincent peed a baby in me," she said. "I told you."

"Well," said John Henry, "what is Maggie going to say?"

"Maggie ain't going to find out about it," she said. "I ain't old enough to really have a baby. That's the way you do it."

"Did it hurt Vincent?" he asked.

"No," she said. "It didn't seem to hurt him none."

For a while John Henry didn't say anything. "Would you let me?" he said.

Nettie looked at him. Then she looked away. "You ain't old enough," she said.

"I can pee," he said.

"That ain't all there is to it," she said. "You ain't old enough anyway."

"Maybe you could let me try and see if I was old enough," he said.

She shook her head. "It wouldn't be right," she said.

"I known you better than Vincent," he said. "How come it's all right for him and it ain't all right for me?"

"That ain't it," she said. "I know Vincent don't know me the way you do. But it wouldn't be right. I told you, you wasn't old enough."

"I'm old enough to pee," he said.

"That ain't it," she said.

"I pushed your barge around," he said. "I pushed your barge around and fanned you with the fan. I done all that. Let me do it, Nettie," he said.

She was still sifting the beads from one hand to the other. She didn't look at him. "I couldn't let you," she said. "I couldn't let you pee no nigger baby in me, John Henry."

"Oh," he said.

"It wouldn't be right. You see that, don't you?"

"I hadn't thought," he said.

"Maybe we can find you a colored girl so you could pee a baby in her."

"Yes," he said.

"I could help you find one."

"Yes," he said.

"Come on," she said. "Get the palm leaf and fan me. We got to play Cleopatra some more."

John Henry got the palm leaf.

"Don't feel bad," said Nettie. "You're a good eunuch, John Henry."

"Thank you," he said.

"The Romans got to be the Eye-talians," she said. "They ain't much no more."

"Yes," he said.

They didn't play Cleopatra anymore after that. Nettie got to meeting Vincent down at the creek on a regular basis, and then he brought along some friends. She never did help John Henry find himself the colored girl.

That was their last summer of playacting. Nettie grew up the next winter and began keeping company with boys out in the open. Wearing lipstick and high-heel shoes. Maggie didn't care for it, but she wasn't able to do anything about it. Then John Henry went to work for Case Deering, so he and Nettie became just good friends.

In the spring of 1954, just before he was eighteen, John Henry got arrested on suspicion of stealing forty-nine dollars from the Harold Brown Esso Station in Kose. After the trial, he took his turn on the county road gang. His sentence was for two years. While he was doing his time, Nettie would come down with Josey occasionally and bring him things to eat. Once she knitted him a white wool cock warmer with a red head, but he hid it from the other boys on the gang because he was afraid the guards would find out. Most of the time it was too hot to wear it, and even in cold weather the wool tickled and made him itch.

Two years; most of his friends were doing time too. It kept him out of the draft. When they let him go in June of 1956, Nettie and Josey came down to meet him at the gate. Nettie drove him home in her new Pontiac.

At the house Nettie got him aside and told him of her plan. She had been thinking it over and had decided that she owed it to him one way or another. She had never helped him find the colored girl like she promised—and she always tried to keep her promises. That time was past now, but she had thought of something better.

"What picture show you seen that at?" he said, after she explained it to him.

"I got it all fixed," she said. "You got to go through with it. I done it for you mostly, anyway."

"I couldn't do nothing like that, Nettie," he said. "I couldn't go through with it nohow. Somebody would find out pretty soon."

"I tell you, I got it all set up," she said. "You got to go through with it. How many times you reckon a colored boy is going to get him a chance like that?"

"I couldn't go through with it," he said. "You better go see you another picture show. I just couldn't go through with it."

"Ain't a jigaboo in McAfee County wouldn't give his right ball for a chance like that," she said. "It's all set up."

"You going to have to set it down," he said. "I couldn't go through with it."

"No?" she said.

"No," he said.

"Let me explain it to you," she said.

"You done explained it to me already," he said.

"I been working on it all spring," she said.

After she showed him the costumes, explaining it over twice, he said, "What am I going to do when I couldn't go through with it?"

"I got it all figured out," she said. "You're going to wear this. I had Fred vulcanize it out of a inner tube down at Kasher's. He sure as hell couldn't figure it out. I told him it was for a horse I was going to buy. He looked at me funny, but he let it go. You strap it on. If you get buck fever and can't get up yourself, you can use it instead. If it's all right, you can pull it to the side and go ahead anyway. It's the idea that's important."

"What idea?" he said.

"Fixing you up," she said.

John Henry looked at the black tube in his hand. "Ain't that going to hurt them?" he said.

"They'll know they been screwed," she said.

"You going to get me killed, Nettie," he said.

"I'm going to get you a white piece of ass," she said. "Two pieces. What kind of nigger are you going to be to turn down two pieces of white ass? I been working on it all spring. You never did appreciate nothing I done for you, John Henry."

"It ain't going to be like you think," he said. "Why don't you take that thing and use it on them yourself?"

"I told you," she said. "It's the idea of it. You got to be the one."

He looked at the black tube in his hand. "Where you see a picture show like that anyway?"

"It's all set up now," she said. "You can't back out."

He didn't answer.

She got him to carry the black iron pot down into the woods at the place she had set up. Then she got the costumes and the white bantam rooster and took those down herself. At sundown she and John Henry went together and got the fire started under the pot so the water would be boiling when the girls got there. They put in some big pieces of moss to make it look better when the water started to boil. Then Nettie put in some mint and sage and other spices she had brought with her, and a packet of red Rit dye.

"I got them so worked up they couldn't hardly wait for you to get off the gang," she said. "They're stupid, but they're white. White every way there is. I was being careful about that. You ain't going to have that many chances. Not for two, you ain't."

"I ain't sure I can go through with it, Nettie," he said. "Even with this here rubber thing." He held the tube in his hand.

"Stuff it with moss," she said. "It looks like its ninety years old."

"It ain't that easy for a man," he said.

"It'll be all right," she said. "It's the idea cf it, anyway. That rubber doohickey is going to let you bring it off."

They got into their costumes. Long black robes that Nettie had gotten up for them. Just before St. Patrick's Day she had found a shamrock-green top hat—they were selling them in stacks in the ten-cent stores in Savannah. John Henry was wearing the hat in addition to the robe.

"How come a green one?" he said.

"They didn't have nothing else," she said.

"I don't like it," he said.

"I couldn't get nothing else," she said. "That's all they had."

"I don't mean the hat," he said. "I mean all of it."

"You look fine," she said. "You're a fine-looking Lord Redwine."

He didn't say anything, trying to get the hat adjusted on his head.

"That's your name to do it with," she said. "You'll be Lord Redwine."

"Lord Redwine?" he said.

"Yes," she said. "Can you remember?"

"How does the hat look?" he said.

"Fine," she said.

"Ain't it too small?" he said.

"It looks just fine," she said.

"I better wear my pants," he said.

"You ain't going to have time to take them off," she said.

"It don't feel right without my pants," he said.

"You can hold the cloak to in the front," she said. "It would take you too much time to get the pants off."

"You got it all figured out, ain't you, Nettie?" he said.

"I been working on it three months," she said. She looked at him steadily. "I'm going to take care of you, John Henry," she said. "I promised myself. I ain't going to run out on you. I keep my promises."

"Yes," he said.

She gave him instructions about the ceremony, telling him where he was to stand, the way he was going to fold his arms and hold his head up, not looking. And when he was to raise up his arms and throw back the robe. She made him walk through the motions twice. Except for throwing back the robe.

The sun was down and the pot was at a hard, rolling boil when the girls arrived. Over their arms they carried the white robes that Nettie had instructed them to make. John Henry sat on a stump before the fire, his arms folded, not speaking, the way Nettie had told him.

"You can go over there to get dressed," said Nettie, pointing to the big oak tree. The girls looked at John Henry without speaking.

"Get your robes on," said Nettie.

They went behind the tree. Nettie and John Henry could hear Jackie talking.

After a while they came out from behind the tree in their robes. John Henry cut his eyes toward them once; then he stared into the fire under the big clothes pot. Nettie arranged them facing each other across the boiling pot, standing in front of John Henry. Their faces and the robes were orange-red in the firelight.

"Now, you all got to do what I say," she said. She stood on the far side of the kettle, facing John Henry. "For this ceremony, we're going to change names. That there"—she pointed to John Henry— "he's Lord Redwine, Prince of the Outer Darkness." The girls looked at John Henry. He sat with his arms folded, not saying anything.

"John Henry?" said Jackie.

"Lord Redwine," said Nettie.

"Yes," said Jackie.

"I"—Nettie gestured to herself, making the black cape billow and swirl—"I am Sheena, Queen of the Night."

"Sheena is Queen of the Jungle," said Jackie.

"I'm giving the names," said Nettie. "You ain't supposed to talk."

"Did you get this out of a *funny* book?" said Jackie.

"There ain't going to be nothing funny about this," said Nettie. "You'll be seeing about that. Don't you say nothing else."

She waited for a minute to make sure that they were paying attention to her. Then she gestured again. "You"—she pointed to Annie—"you're going to be Nefertiti, Goddess of Virtue." Annie nodded solemnly.

"And you"—she gestured to Jackie—"will be Hatshepsut, Goddess of Virtue too."

"Hot-shit-what?" said Jackie.

"Hot SHEP . . . Hot SHEP . . . ," said Nettie. "Hatshep*sut*. You going to keep this up?"

"Suit," said Jackie.

Nettie looked at her sharply.

"I ain't never heard of Hatshepsut," said Jackie. "How come I couldn't be Nefertiti?"

"I'm going to call the whole thing off if you don't shut your mouth," said Nettie. "I looked for them names all last spring. Hatshepsut is plenty good. Too good for you."

"I heard of Nefertiti once," said Jackie. "How come I ain't never heard of Hatshepsut?"

"Lots of people never heard of Nefertiti," said Nettie.

"I heard of Nefertiti," said Jackie.

Nettie looked at her for a long time without speaking.

"Hot-shit . . . ," said Jackie, ". . . suit."

For a while nobody said anything.

Nettie went on, talking to Annie. "First I got to rub you with oil and spices," she said. "Hold up your gowns."

The girls obeyed.

"Hold it up dainty, Hatshepsut," she said. "Not like you was going to take a crap."

She went to Jackie first. "Hatshepsut, I put this oil on you in the name of the Powers of Outer Darkness. Hocus . . . pocus . . . diamond ocus." She poured oil on Jackie's head, then massaged her body with it. Jackie squirmed.

"Tickles," she said.

"Hold still," said Nettie.

"My daddy'd shit a brick," said Jackie. "Hot shit."

"Hold still," said Nettie.

"Suit," said Jackie.

"I ain't going to tell you again," said Nettie.

Then she rubbed Annie with oil.

"Now," she said, throwing away the oil bottle, "you got to light candles and make your oath to the Dark One."

Jackie looked at John Henry. "He sure is," she said. "Black as the ace of spades. He ain't Lord Redwine. He's Lord *Black*wine."

"You going to be sorry when I turn him loose on you," said Nettie.

"He is," said Jackie. "How long before you're going to turn him loose? It ain't been nothing to it up to now. I didn't know you was going to have so much ceremony."

"Shut your mouth," said Nettie.

"I'm getting tired," said Jackie. "I want to *do* something."

"Repeat after me," said Nettie.

"How am I going to repeat with my mouth shut?" said Jackie.

"Figure it out," said Nettie. "You're smart enough to hear about Nefertiti, you're smart enough to figure it out."

The girls stood holding candles in both hands. "I ain't never heard of Hatshepsut," said Jackie.

"Repeat after me," said Nettie. She hesitated a moment, looking at them. " 'Flesh and blood, muscle and bone, body and soul, heart and hand and all I am, I give to the Prince of Outer Darkness. Lord Redwine, to thee.' Then you bow down."

The girls repeated.

"Now we got to sacrifice the rooster," she said.

"Jesus," said Jackie, "couldn't we skip the rooster?"

Nettie went and got it, holding it by its wings to keep it from flapping. She gave the butcher knife to John Henry, then held the bird's neck out so he could cut it. "To Lord Redwine," she said, bowing her head. John Henry sliced it neatly, and the head came off, Nettie spreading her arms wide, then holding up her hands, letting the blood run down her arm.

"Now you got to anoint the virgins," she said, speaking to John Henry. "On your knees," she said, speaking to the girls.

"You getting ready to turn him loose?" said Jackie.

"On your knees," said Nettie.

"He going to put the chicken blood on us?" said Jackie.

"More ways than one," said Nettie. "More ways than one."

"You're pretty strong on rubbing, ain't you?" said Jackie. "Got to be the chicken blood, I reckon?"

"Just get down on your knees and keep your mouth shut," said Nettie. "We're just about through getting ready."

"What about the candles?" said Jackie.

"Keep hold of the candles," said Nettie.

They knelt down.

"Hands and knees," said Nettie. "Facing each other." She threw their robes up over their heads. Then she helped John Henry, motioning him what he was supposed to do, and he smeared the girls with blood from the rooster.

"Lord Redwine?" said Jackie, her voice muffled by the robe. John Henry didn't say anything. "It's getting better," she said. "You got a nice touch."

"Just a minute now," said Nettie. "You going to be sick, Annie?"

"I'll be all right," said Annie.

"You let me know if you feel like you're going to be sick, you hear?"

She waited a few minutes.

"Well?" said Jackie, looking back over her shoulder.

"Just a minute," said Nettie.

"Turn him loose," said Jackie. "We done had enough hocus pocus. I'm done wore out and rubbed out too. Turn that black man loose and let's get on with it."

"Now we're ready," she said.

"Hot shit," said Jackie.

She blindfolded them and made them lie down on their backs, head to head.

"Can you do it?" she said to John Henry, whispering.

"I think so," he said. "They going to stay blindfold?"

"Yes," she said. "Rub them some more with the blood if it'll help."

"I'd rather rub them with the oil," he said.

"Oil's gone," she said.

"It'll be all right," he said, "if they's going to be blindfold."

"What you whispering about?" said Jackie. "Stop that whispering and turn him loose."

"Jackie first," said Nettie.

"Yes," said John Henry. "You can go now," he said, speaking to Nettie.

Nettie looked at him. "What?" she said.

"I be all right," he said. "You can go on. 'Bout a half-hour. Maybe forty-five minutes."

Nettie looked at him. "I set it up," she said.

"Yes," he said. "Much obliged. I couldn't never done it by myself."

"Yes," she said. She made no motion to leave.

"Better make it forty-five minutes," he said.

"I set it *up*, John Henry," she said.

John Henry stood looking at her. His skin gleamed orange in the firelight. "What you mean?" he said.

"Get on with it," she said.

"You wasn't going away?" he said.

"I set it up," she said.

"*You* ain't blindfold," he said.

"Wouldn't none of this happen, except I set it up," she said. "I had to work on it all spring. I worked on it like a dog."

"You mean you going to *watch?*" he said.

"Not you," she said. "Them."

"You going to close one eye?" he said. "What you mean *them?*"
She didn't answer.

"I couldn't figure that," he said. "What kind of a man you think I am, taking them women and you standing around watching?"

"It ain't *you*," she said. "It's *them*."

"I'll have to tell you about it later," he said.

"I known you all my life, John Henry," she said.

"Jesus Christ, Nettie," he said. They had been whispering, but John Henry's voice was beginning to rise. "You got to go off and leave it to me. You got to leave this to me."

"Good God Almighty," Jackie said, "it ain't going to take this long to get me into heaven. What the hell part of a ceremony is this?"

"Put that blindfold down," said Nettie.

"You think I'm some kind of a prize bull that you got to make sure about the bloodlines?" said John Henry.

"I told you," she said. "*They's* the important ones."

"You got to go," he said. "You got to go off and leave it to me." Nettie looked at him. She made no move to leave.

"I might have knowed," he said. He reached inside the black robe. "Here," he said. He handed her the rubber tube. "You going to have to do it yourself. Then you can be sure."

"What?" said Jackie. "What did you say?"

Nettie looked at it without speaking. John Henry dropped it onto the ground. "Lord Redwine is through," he said. "Go get your clothes on," he said, speaking to the girls.

Jackie sat up, pulling the blindfold away from her eyes. "Jesus Christ," she said. "You mean you're calling it off? Now? After you done rubbed the chicken blood on me?"

"Put that blindfold back on," said Nettie.

"Why don't you go off and leave us alone anyway?" said Jackie. "You ain't doing nothing but holding things up."

"Ain't Lord Redwine," said John Henry. "You wouldn't want to do it with John Henry Greene."

"I knowed it was you, John Henry," said Jackie. "I knowed it was you all along."

"Get back down," said Nettie. "I'll leave you alone. You ain't going to walk out on me?"

"I got to get my pants on," said John Henry. "I told you it wasn't going to be the way you thought."

"I worked on them three months," she said. "You ain't going to get buck fever and walk out on me now?"

"You girls get your clothes and go home," he said. "It wasn't what you thought."

"It sure as hell wasn't," said Jackie, getting up.

"Stay where you are," said Nettie. "John Henry . . ."

"You going to set it up again," he said. "Work on it some more. Next time you hang that thing between your legs and do it yourself so you can be sure. It's a black one too."

"You ain't walking out?" she said.

"I need to get my pants," he said.

"That's all she wrote," said Jackie. "I wouldn't care if he had to carry it around in a wheelbarrow. It just ain't worth it. Come on, Annie, let's you and me go get us a bath."

"I ain't going to let you walk out," said Nettie.

"You ain't going to do nothing else," he said. He turned to the fire, put his foot against the pot, and shoved it over. The red water and moss splashed onto the ground with a hissing noise. The moss looked like a possum after the cars have been running over it on the highway for two days. "This here ceremony is done over," he said. "No more Redwine."

"John Henry . . . ," said Nettie.

"Stay away," he said. "You stay away from me. I ain't your boy no more."

She looked at him across what was left of the fire.

"This here is John Henry Greene," he said, speaking to the girls. "This ain't Lord Redwine, this is John Henry Greene. I'm going to tell you. Tuesday night. I be down to this very spot on Tuesday night." He looked at Nettie. "By myself," he said. "You ain't swore nothing to John Henry Greene."

"John Henry," said Nettie.

He walked away into the dark.

Jackie watched him across the fire as he walked away. "That's *some* nigger," she said.

Nettie was sitting on the steps waiting for him when he came into the yard.

"John Henry," she said.

"Yes," he said.

"I kept my promise, John Henry?" she said.

For a minute he didn't answer. "Yes," he said. "Yes, you did, Nettie."

"I ain't never broke a promise," she said.

"I ain't never said you did," he said.

"I ain't never," she said.

For a while neither of them spoke.

"It wasn't them, was it?" he said.

"What?" she said.

"It wasn't them, was it?"

She didn't answer. After a while she said. "I meant to keep my promise."

"Yes," he said.

Then she went into the house and left him sitting on the back steps in the dark.

The yellow-white-yellow centerline snaked in under the left fender. "He had it," she said, speaking out loud to herself. "I kept my promise, and he had it. But he ain't never had it all."

Far ahead down the road she saw a figure, a Negro man in overalls. He was walking on the right shoulder, carrying a brown-paper lunch bag in his hand. "Can't teach them," she said, looking at the figure as it got bigger with the car speeding into it. "Right shoulder."

She passed the man, slowing down, and he looked into the car. The shutter inside her head clicked, opening a blank frame, catching the look from the man on the shoulder of the road. She put her foot on the brake and cut the car onto the edge of the road. The man came up on the highway side of the car, going past. While she was watching him in the rearview mirror, she could see him looking at her through the back window of the Pontiac.

"Hey, boy," she said. She was resting her elbow on the window, looking off down the highway as she spoke. "Where you going?"

After she spoke, she looked at him, tilting her head to one side and hanging it down, looking up at him out of the window.

He stopped beside the car, looking into the empty back seat behind her, over her shoulder; then he took off the railroad cap he was wearing. "Down the road," he said. He pulled his eyes back out of the car, looking down at the edge of the road at his feet.

"Hot to walk," she said.

"Yes, ma'am," he said. He looked up and down the highway, then back at his feet again. "Gonna be hot today," he said.

"Get in," she said. "I'm going that way."

He looked up and down the road again, then back at Nettie, over her shoulder at the back seat. "Much obliged," he said. He started to open the back door on the highway side.

"Come around," she said. "You better sit in front."

He looked at her, looking into her eyes this time. "No, ma'am," he said. He took his hand off the door handle.

"Come around," she said.

"Thank you, ma'am," he said. He put his railroad cap back on and started to walk away down the road.

Nettie blew the horn, and he flinched.

"Get in," she said. "Sit on the other side where I can see you."

He went around the car and got into the back seat.

She put the car into gear, then pulled out onto the highway, not driving as fast—forty-five and fifty. About half a mile down the highway she came to a dirt road running off into the pines and Spanish bayonets. She slowed and pulled off onto the dirt road. The man looked at her, watching her face in the rearview mirror. She was looking at him with her head tilted slightly. He turned and looked out of the window at the pines on his side of the car. "I ain't going thisaway," he said. Saying it low, whispering. Nettie didn't answer. The road was rutted and narrow. As the car moved along down it, it lurched and bumped, scraping the sides on the spikes of the Spanish bayonets. They didn't come to any houses.

"You going to ruin . . . your car," he said. The lurching made it difficult to talk.

Nettie didn't answer.

"Scratching the paint off with them baynets."

"You know where this road goes?" she asked, looking in the rearview mirror.

"Down to the landing," he said. He couldn't open the door and jump out into the bayonets. The sound was like fingernails scraping across glass.

"Is there a store or something down there?" she said.

"No'm," he said. "Ain't nothing. Just where they goes fishing."

"Colored folks?" she said.

"Mostly," he said.

"Trash fish?" she asked.

He didn't say anything.

After a while she came to a little clear place where she could pull off. She turned the car into the pines and cut off the motor. The man was sitting forward on the edge of the back seat, with one hand on the back of the front seat and the other hand on the door handle. He watched her watching him in the rearview mirror. Then he looked out the window on his side into the pines.

"You got to do something for me," said Nettie.

The man sat looking out the window. "This ain't the way I go," he said. "I got to be to work at seven-thirty."

"You *got* to do it for me," she said. He wasn't looking at her.

"What time is it?" he said.

"Listen to me," she said. "I said you *got* to do it."

She took his hand, pulling it over the back of the seat and putting it over her breast outside her dress. His hand touched her for a moment; then he pulled it back. He opened the door and stepped out of the car.

"Not me, white lady," he said. "I got to be to work."

"Get back in the car," she said.

"It's broad daylight," he said. He pulled the bill of his railroad cap. "Time I be getting on to work," he said.

She got out on her side, looking at him over the top of the car. "You ain't going to say no to *me*," she said.

He looked back for a minute, then he looked away.

"I'll pay you," she said.

He didn't answer.

She hiked her dress up and pulled it over her head.

"No," he said, not looking at her. Then he looked at her over the top of the car.

"I mean what I'm saying," she said. "I got to have me a black man."

He looked away, then flicked his eyes toward her over the top of the car. She walked around behind the car, getting between him and the road.

"Not me," he said.

"Twenty dollars," she said. She reached both arms up behind her, taking off her brassiere as she came around the car. He stared at her sliding it down her arms and dropping it off on the ground.

"Listen," she said, "I got colored blood in me too. Nigger blood."

He flicked his eyes away, then back, looking at her breasts. "Not . . . not . . . not me, white lady," he said. Her nipples were pink-brown—large.

"Look at me," she said. He looked at her. "I got nigger blood— couldn't you tell?"

His eyes went up and down, looking at her. "All right," he said. "I ain't your man. You ain't nigger enough."

"Black man," she said, coming toward him, "you got to screw me." She moved up to him, standing toe to toe. He wouldn't look at her. She put her arms around his neck and pulled herself up, kissing him on the mouth. "I'm good poontang," she said.

When they were starting to get back into the car, she stopped him. "I ain't paid you," she said. "Twenty dollars."

He looked at her, standing with the back door of the car open, his foot inside. "You don't owe me no twenty dollars," he said. "You don't owe me nothing. I got to get to work."

"You can use it, can't you?" she said.

"Always use twenty dollars," he said. "What time is it?"

"I said I'd pay you," she said. "I keep my promises." She reached into the car and got her pocketbook. "How much nigger blood you think I got?"

"Some," he said. "It'll do."

"Not enough to show," she said. "Enough to make it?"

"That's right," he said. "What time you say it getting to be? I got to be to work at seven-thirty."

She took the automatic out of her purse. When he saw it he stepped back away from the car, not trying to run. She put three shots into him before he knew what was happening. After he flinched his hands down to protect himself, she put three more shots through the backs of his hands, keeping count. She saved the last shot until after he was down on the ground; then she stepped up close and drilled him right between the eyes.

"Not that much nigger blood," she said. "You wasn't nothing of a Roman, neither, boy."

Then she got into the car and drove back to the highway and on into Savannah.

She didn't know just where she was going, but she seemed to home in on it like she was following a radar beam—the Savannah Monument and Stone Works. The yard in front looked like a fore-shortened graveyard, the stones and monuments on display crowded up on the grass with just enough space to walk between. They had what she was looking for at the back of the yard. A small obelisk, black granite, with a shaft about four feet tall, rising off a big solid base where the inscription would go. Altogether it was about six or seven feet tall.

She made a cash deal with the man on the condition that it would be delivered right away.

"Can't be tomorrow," he said. "That's Tuesday."

"What about Tuesday?" she said.

"My man don't work on Tuesday," he said.

"Wednesday, then," she said.

"He'd have to work Tuesday for you to get it Wednesday."

"He's going to have to work tomorrow," she said.

"I told you," he said. "He don't work on Tuesday. That'd be extra."

"Why Tuesday?" she said.

"It's his religion," he said.

"What the hell kind of a religion is it won't let him work on Tuesday?" she said.

"I don't know," he said. "He says it's his religion. Stonecutters ain't that easy to find. I can't afford to ask him. He works first-class the rest of the time."

"Does he work Sunday?" she said.

"That's *my* religion," he said.

"You got a red-hot business going here, mister," she said.

"It works out pretty good," he said.

"He's going to have to work *this* Tuesday," she said. "I got to have it Wednesday."

"That'll be extra," he said. "I can't guarantee it, but it'll be extra."

"You're getting enough now," she said.

"I can't make it Wednesday," he said.

"How often you sell one of them?" she said. "I mean a big one like that. Fancy."

He looked at the stone without answering her.

"I just can't make it Wednesday," he said. "I couldn't afford to make him mad. Stonecutters ain't that easy to find."

"There ain't that much lettering," she said.

"Too much for Wednesday," he said. "It's his temperment. You try to push him, and you can't get him to do nothing at all."

"Here's ten extra," she said, handing him the bill. "You can handle him. Tell him you *got* to have it by Wednesday."

"He thinks he's an artist," he said.

"It's got to be done good," she said. "Twenty?"

"Well," he said.

"I ain't going to be took too much, mister," she said. "Twenty is tops. You get his ass moving for twenty, or that thing can set out there for another year. You ain't going to tell me you sell one every day."

He looked at the bills. "Wednesday afternoon," he said.

"Just so it's Wednesday," she said.

She wrote out the inscription on a piece of paper he gave her.

"With an *e*?" he said.

She looked at him. "What else you think it might be?" she said. "You ain't going to screw this up, mister?"

"That's the reason I wanted to be sure," he said. "It's a hell of a job erasing."

"Just the way I got it down there," she said, giving him the paper. "Space it out so it looks pretty."

He took the paper and put it into his vest pocket. "I told you he was a artist, madam," he said.

After she left the monument works, she drove to the sheriff's office. The deputy on duty was a young man with a tanned face. He was wearing a Stetson tilted back on his head.

"Yes, ma'am?" he said, coming up to the counter.

"I want to see the sheriff," she said.

"He ain't in right now," said the deputy. "He's out on a call. What could I do for you?"

"I'd rather see the sheriff," she said.

"He ain't going to be back before this evening," he said.

"Well," she said. "I really thought I better see the sheriff."

"I could do the same thing for you," he said.

She looked at him for a minute. "You next in line to him?" she said.

"You might say," he said. "I been here two years."

"Well," she said, "all right. It's serious."

"I been here two years," he said.

"I killed a nigger," she said. She looked him in the eye when she said it.

The deputy looked at her. "How'd it happen?" he said. "Hit him with your car?"

"I shot him," she said.

He looked out the window; then he pulled his hat down on his forehead and looked at the counter. "You shot him?" he said. He looked back up at her.

"Seven times," she said. She reached into her purse and got the Beretta, putting it up onto the counter. "That there is what I shot him with."

The deputy looked at the automatic, then back at her. "Seven times?" he said.

Nettie dropped her eyes. "He tried to rape me," she said.

The deputy looked at her across the counter. "I better get the sheriff," he said.

The monument was delivered late Wednesday afternoon. Nettie met the truck to direct them where to set it up.

"That's a nigger graveyard," said the man who was driving the truck.

"I got it marked off with string," she said. "You set it up over there where I marked it off with the string."

"I ain't never set up no monument for no nigger graveyard," said the driver.

"You put it down easy," she said. "If you chip it, I ain't going to pay for it. The writing faces this way."

On Wednesday night she got John Fletcher to take her picture on it. She sent him a copy, and used it to pass around for advertising. Finally just about every man in McAfee County got hold of one.

The flashbulb lit up Nettie and the obelisk, but it didn't reach into the background, which was black, except for some pieces of moss hanging down into the top of the picture. Nettie was standing with her side to the camera, one foot on the base, and the other leg lifted and wrapped around the shaft of the obelisk, hugging it with her arms. She had high-heel shoes on, but nothing else. Her arms were reaching up, so her right breast was mashed against the granite, swelling it out, with the nipple showing. Her head was tilted to one side, and she was looking into the camera and smiling.

John Fletcher took the picture on Wednesday night before he left to go in the navy, using up two rolls of film getting it right. More than half of the prints were blurred where the camera shook.

After the pictures were developed, seeing herself and the monument framed by the open blackness of the flash, the clicking in Nettie's head went away—freezing the shutter on an open frame.

For a week after the monument was set up, people from all over the county made special trips to the Golden Rainbow African Baptist Church graveyard just to look at it. Blacks and whites coming together. Finally the novelty wore off, and they stopped coming. But it is still the biggest monument in any of the McAfee County graveyards, except the big Baptist graveyard in Kose.

It is still a fine-looking monument, though the color is graying out in the weather, and the shaft of the obelisk is almost covered with honeysuckle. Jessie Wight keeps the vines pulled back off the base so the inscription will show.

It is very impressive.

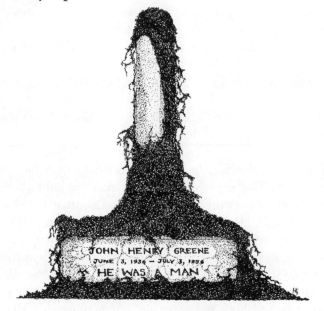

JOHN HENRY GREENE
JUNE 3, 1936 — JULY 3, 1936
HE WAS A MAN

Dorcus

and the Fat Lady

The Ferris wheel spun over the midway—pinwheels of light, going around and around. Behind it the night sky swelled high and black, making the spinning lights stand out—red and white—wheeling over and collapsing in on themselves.

Lee Jay stood watching it with his mouth open. Beside him, just inside the entrance, Dorcus stood counting the change from the tickets. He slid the coins out between his thumb and index finger, milking them off into the open purse. The last one dropped, and he flourished his empty hand open.

"Sixty-five cent is a lot of money for a carnival," he said. "Just to get inside. You be sure you ain't going to miss nothing, Lee Jay. Don't no carnival come around just anytime."

"Yessir," said Lee Jay. The top of his head came almost to his father's shoulder—powdery white hair that stayed in his face most of the time. He had developed a permanent crouch trying to see out from under it.

"What's that, Pa?" he asked, pointing to the Ferris wheel.

"We'll see it all," said Dorcus. "That's the Ferris wheel. You ride it."

"Yes," said Lee Jay. "Yes*sir*."

"Here," said Dorcus, putting four quarters into the boy's hand. "That's four big rides, or six little ones. Spread them out. I can't give you no more."

Lee Jay looked down at the four coins in his hand. He had never had more than fifteen cents to himself at one time in his life. "All of it?" he said, looking at his father.

"Yes," said Dorcus. He tried to pat him on the head, but the boy was so tall that he had to reach up to do it. It was awkward. Lee Jay's hair waggled into his eyes under the patting.

"That's a dollar," said Lee Jay, holding his palm out flat with the coins spread on it.

"Don't no carnival come to McAfee County just every day. You got to pay for it," said Dorcus.

"Yessir," said Lee Jay. He closed his hand on the coins.

Together they started down the midway toward the Ferris wheel. Everything was bright and noisy—loud, popping music that changed every thirty feet they walked. Now and then somebody would lean at them out of a red-and-white-painted stall and ask them to step up and do something.

"Keep walking, son," said Dorcus. "They'll get your money, and you wouldn't see doodley shit. I done tried them games."

Lee Jay hooked his finger through the hammer loop on his father's overalls and put his hand with the money in it into his pocket.

"What's they for, Pa?" asked Lee Jay. He pointed to a row of Kewpie dolls on a shelf back of the counter of one of the red-and-white stalls.

"You win them," said Dorcus.

Lee Jay looked at them for a minute. "How you going to win them?" he said.

Dorcus looked into the stall. "See yonder?" He pointed to a pyramid of three wooden milk bottles at the end of the tent. "You knock them down."

"Them bottle things?" said Lee Jay.

"Yes," said Dorcus. "You thow a baseball and knock them down, and you get you one of them there dolls. They ain't real bottles. They's made of wood."

"Just for thowing a baseball?" said Lee Jay. He was looking at the dolls.

"You think that's real easy, don't you?" said Dorcus.

"Just for thowing a baseball?" said Lee Jay.

"You thinking about how easy it looks, ain't you?" said Dorcus. He closed his eyes and shook his head slowly. "You going to be able to shit a yaller posthole digger sooner than you going to hit them there bottles," he said.

Lee Jay looked at the bottles. They were so close it seemed to him that he could almost reach out and knock them over with his hand.

"It don't look like they's nothing to it," he said.

"That's the way they *want* it to look," said Dorcus, nodding again. He looked at the man in the booth. "How much is it for a try?" he asked.

"Fifteen cents," said the man, who looked like he didn't much care whether they tried or not. His right hand throbbed in the pocket of his seersucker pants where he was scratching himself. He didn't look like he cared much about that either.

Dorcus looked down at Lee Jay; then he reached into his pocket and took out his purse. "I'm going to learn you a lesson," he said, slapping the fifteen cents down on the counter. "Give him a ball and let him try."

The throbbing stopped while the man took his hand out of his pocket and put two baseballs on the counter.

"I get *two* balls?" said Lee Jay, looking back at Dorcus over his shoulder.

"That's a man's share," said Dorcus. He laughed and looked at the man behind the counter. The man had his hand back in his pocket again, and he acted as though he hadn't heard anything.

"Just go ahead and thow 'em," said Dorcus to Lee Jay. "You going to see."

Lee Jay picked up one of the baseballs, holding it between his thumb and the first two fingers of his right hand. He rolled it around looking at it. "Looks all right," he said.

"Just go ahead and thow it," said Dorcus. He folded his arms and looked at the pyramid of milk bottles.

Lee Jay twisted the baseball in the palm of his hand and leaned over to take a long look at the pyramid, crouching down to see under his hair. Then he placed his left foot and turned side-on. He wound up very slowly and elaborately before starting his delivery. As his swing developed, he hopped up into the air and untwisted his body with the motion of his arm coming around, making the shift with both feet up off the ground and coming down squarely with them just reversed—right foot forward and left foot back. It was a crazy, spastic kind of a motion, and a person seeing him do it from a long way off would have thought he was trying to not step on a snake. Sometime before he came back down on the ground, his arm gave a whiplike motion, and the ball went zinging off—right through the center of the pyramid. The two bottom bottles leaped off to the sides—left and right, and the upper one spun in the air while Dorcus could have counted to five.

"Son-of-a-bitch!" said Dorcus, looking at the place where the bottles had been. Lee Jay was frozen in his follow-through position—feet planted firmly on the ground, his arm still extended out toward the bottles, looking down in front of his right foot. His stance was something like that of *The Discus Thrower.*

"Son-of-a-bitch!" said Dorcus again. "You hit 'em!" He slapped the counter with his hand. "Hot damn!" he said.

"I was feeling it," said Lee Jay. He looked up at the place where the bottles had been.

"Right on. Right on," said Dorcus. "Hit 'em right on."

The man behind the counter looked at the bottles sourly; then he went and set them up again.

Lee Jay looked at Dorcus.

"You got another ball," said Dorcus. "But it'll never happen. They got it all figured out." He folded his arms again.

Lee Jay picked up the ball and went through his windup. The second ball went into the pyramid more solidly than the first one had, bouncing bottles off both sides of the tent and the ceiling.

"I be *God* damned," said Dorcus. "Twict. I be God damned."

"What am I going to do now?" said Lee Jay.

"Give him his doll, mister," said Dorcus.

The man was looking at the bottles with the sour expression still on his face.

"I want that one," said Lee Jay. He pointed to a golden, glittery doll, with blond hair and a crown. "That there princess doll."

The man slouched over to the shelf and got it down for him.

"Let me see that there doll," said Dorcus. Lee Jay handed it to him. "Sometimes they's cracked," he whispered. "Yes," he said, holding the doll off and looking at it. He gave it back to Lee Jay. "You wouldn't do it again in a hundred years, Lee Jay," he said. "I hope you done learnt your lesson."

"Yessir," said Lee Jay.

"That's a nice-looking doll," said Dorcus.

"Yessir, it is," said Lee Jay.

Dorcus and Lee Jay walked down the midway, Lee Jay holding the doll in both arms to keep from breaking it. A few booths down from the baseball stall they came to a "Dunk-the-Nigger" booth. As they were passing, the man throwing hit the target on the arm of the seat, and the black man collapsed into the tank of water. When he stood up in the tank he held his skinny arms out limply, blinking his eyes to get the water out of them.

"Ain't that James Lee?" said Lee Jay, pointing.

The Negro was trying to set the trap on the seat, but he couldn't figure it out, so finally the man who ran the booth had to come over and do it for him. When he climbed back onto the seat over the tank, his arms and legs were thin and spidery in the wet clothes, and he looked like a big cricket sitting there inside the chicken-wire cage.

Dorcus stopped and looked. "James Lee?" he said.

James Lee blinked out of the chicken wire, looking to see who was calling him.

"What you doing, James Lee?" said Dorcus.

"Dunkin'," said James Lee. He smiled broadly and waved. "I get me fawty-five centa hour," he said.

"Jesus God," said Dorcus. "Fawty-five centa hour? How'd you get you a job like that, James Lee?"

"Just got it," said James Lee.

"Fawty-five centa hour?" said Dorcus, talking to the man behind the counter.

The man looked at Dorcus, but he didn't say anything.

"He ain't *doing* nothing," said Dorcus.

"You want to throw a ball at him?" said the man.

"No," said Dorcus. "How much is it?"

"Twenty cent for three," said the man.

"No," said Dorcus.

"I done made me two dollahs awready," said James Lee. He gave a high, cackling laugh. "Fawty-five centa hour and free Co-Colas too." He had begun to shiver a little, but he gripped the ends of the slat on which he was sitting, and smiled. "I done had me three Co-Colas and a cigyrette," he said.

Lee Jay held up his princess doll. "Look, James Lee," he said. "I won me a doll."

"That all he does?" said Dorcus. "And you paying him fawty-five centa hour . . . for that?"

"Used to be we could get them for thirty-five," said the man, "but they won't none of them work for that no more. Everthing come high these days. Generally they want fifty."

"How deep is that there tank?" said Dorcus.

"Thirty inches," said the man.

"Couldn't nobody drownd in nothing that shaller," said Dorcus.

"Not hardly," said the man.

For a minute neither of them spoke.

"Lost a nigger once in Folkston," said the man. "Hit his head on the side of the tank, I reckon. Never did come up again. I reckon he hit his head on the side of the tank. Couldn't even a nigger drownd hisself in no thirty-inch-deep tank of water."

"No," said Dorcus. "Not even no nigger couldn't do that."

For a while neither of them spoke.

Dorcus cleared his throat. "Got to be a nigger, I reckon?" he said.

"What?" said the man.

"I said, I reckon it's got to be a nigger," said Dorcus. "You wouldn't want a white man for no job like that?"

"No," said the man. "I couldn't use no white man."

"No," said Dorcus. "Not even though he'd work for *fawty* centa hour?"

The man looked at him. "No," he said.

"Yes," said Dorcus.

He looked at James Lee in the cage for a minute. "He doing all right?" he said.

"What?" said the man.

"He doing all right with the job?" said Dorcus.

"Yes," said the man. "Why?"

"If you want to know the truth," said Dorcus, "he's the dumbest shitass in McAfee County."

The man looked at James Lee. "If *you* want to know the truth," he said, "I figure he's the dumbest shitass in the *world*."

Dorcus looked at James Lee and nodded. "You seen a lot, I reckon," he said.

"I thought I'd done seen them all," said the man.

"Yes," said Dorcus.

"He's doing all right now," said the man. "He wanted to hang on the bar so he wouldn't fall in the water at first. What you reckon he thought the forty-five centa hour was for?"

"Takes a while to catch on, I reckon," said Dorcus.

The man didn't say anything.

"Yes," said Dorcus. "It takes a while to catch on, I reckon."

"Not much to it," said the man. "You know how a nigger is. Don't want to go in the water. You got to kind of get them used to it."

"Yes," said Dorcus. "It's too bad you couldn't use no white man. Then you wouldn't have to worry."

"Yes," said the man.

While they were talking, James Lee got down off the bar and started to get out of the cage.

"Where you think you going?" said the man.

"I just be going to get me a Co-Cola," said James Lee.

"Get your ass back in that cage," said the man. "You done had four Co-Colas already."

"Three," said James Lee.

"Get your ass back in that cage," said the man.

Dorcus looked at James Lee getting up on his perch like a big, shiny spider. "Don't drownd yourself, James Lee," he said.

"Can I thow a ball at James Lee, Pa?" said Lee Jay.

Dorcus looked at him. "Not for no twenty cent for three you can't," he said. "After this here carnival is gone, you can give him a nickle and he'll let you thow at him all day long."

He and Lee Jay started off down the midway.

: 233 :

James Lee waved to them. "Fawty-five centa hour," he said. "Co-Colas extra, too."

"Niggers got to rub it in," said Dorcus to Lee Jay.

After they had gone, a stocky red-haired teenager with pale green eyes stepped up to the counter. "Give me some balls," he said.

The midway was laid out in an elongated horseshoe. At one end was the entrance and a line of concession stands selling hot dogs and candy apples and cotton candy. At the opposite end, on the inside of the horseshoe, were the most spectacular rides—the ASTRO-ROCKET and the MOONTRAIN ROCKET and the DYNONFET ROCKET. On the outside of the horseshoe were shows like PARIS REVUE and BLACK AND TAN FANTASY and GIRLS-GIRLS-GIRLS. On the near side of these was the giant Ferris wheel, folding over on itself outside the pin-wheels of red and white lights.

Standing underneath it, Lee Jay thought it seemed to go up for-ever into the black sky overhead. He hugged the doll to him and looked up at the big machine cartwheeling into the blackness. It made his stomach turn over to watch it, and he thought how it would be if it came loose and rolled away over McAfee County with every-body in it sitting right side up.

"We're going to give it a ride later," said Dorcus. "Not now. We're going to save it for last."

Opposite the Ferris wheel was the freak show. A long platform with pictures behind it of the various freaks that were on display inside. The barker had a little stand in the middle, and next to him on the platform stood a man in blue tights with red trunks on. There was a Band-Aid on his lip, and he was eating a glass lightbulb— just nibbling off pieces of it while the barker explained to everyone what he was doing. He had a careful look on his face, and didn't seem to be enjoying it very much.

"Come on," said Dorcus. "Let's go see us them freaks."

He went up to buy the tickets, which were fifty cents and twenty-five cents for children. At first the barker wanted to sell Dorcus two fifty-cent tickets.

"He ain't but only eleven," said Dorcus.

The barker looked at Lee Jay narrowly. "If he's eleven, he ought to be inside where people could see him," he said, hooking his thumb toward the tent behind him.

"That's the truth," said Dorcus.

"He's too big for eleven," said the barker. "Twelve is fifty cents."

"He ain't going to be twelve until his next birthday," said Dorcus. "That's November sixteenth."

"You mean he's going to be sixteen on November twelfth, don't you?" said the barker.

"No," said Dorcus.

The barker looked at Lee Jay. "How old are you, boy?" he said.

"Tell him how old you are," said Dorcus.

"You stay out of it," said the barker.

Lee Jay looked the barker in the eye. "Eleven," he said. He hooked the doll under his elbow and held up both hands with the fingers spread.

"How many fingers he think he's got?" said the barker.

"He'll be twelve in November," said Dorcus, holding up both his hands with the fingers spread.

"Oh," said the barker. He tore off a child's ticket and handed it to Dorcus. "Seventy-five cents," he said.

Inside the tent there was a platform that was separated into sections by canvas partitions. In each section was a freak sitting on a stool—except that there weren't enough sections to go around, and the Giant and Midget had to share the same one. There was a Monkey Lady, the Giant and the Midget, an Alligator Lady, a Fire Eater who was a Negro, a Thin Man, and an old blue-haired lady in a long red sarong with purple flowers on it who had a big snake wrapped around her neck. After the Snake Lady there was an empty section for the Glass Eater, who was also the Sword Swallower. He hadn't come in from the platform yet.

All of them but the Midget looked sad and mopey and worn out—like they were waiting to be vaccinated in a county health clinic. Even the snake looked droopy—or asleep—with his head flopped upside down and his tongue lolling out of his mouth. He kept sliding off the lady's neck, so she had to be all the time hiking him up and wrapping him back around.

In the middle of the tent was a low platform with a velvet-covered chain around it. In the middle of the platform was the fattest lady Dorcus had ever seen. She sat on a kind of throne made out of gilded four-by-fours, and over her head was a banner—blue cloth with white lettering. It said: FLORINE THE FAT LADY—SIX HUNDRED AND THIRTY-FOUR POUNDS OF *WOMAN*.

Florine had on the sort of short, no-shape dress that Shirley Temple used to wear in the movies, and her hair was done up in the same kind of ringlets. The dress was made of blue satin, cut low and straight across at the top to leave a lot of skin showing, so people would know she was real. Her arms and legs rolled out of the tiny blue dress in wads and folds of flesh like mounds of vanilla ice cream that was starting to melt.

Braced on the floor and leaning back into her lap was a stalk of bananas from which about half of the bananas were missing. Florine hugged it with her left hand. With her right hand she carried a banana back and forth to her mouth in a teeter-totter pumping motion. She wasn't paying any attention to what she was doing —her eyes had a glassy, transfixed look in them—but the motion had the precision and regularity of a metronome. Only her forearm moved, rocking the banana up into her mouth dead center every time. Each time her arm rocked up, about a third of the banana disappeared.

When she finished the banana, she moved her right arm off to the side in another mechanical motion—without looking—and dropped the skin into a galvanized washtub that was sitting on the platform beside her throne. The tub was almost a third full of banana skins. Some of them had caught on the rim, and hung out in looping, yellow festoons.

Dorcus stood watching her with his mouth sprung open and his eyes staring wide. "Look at that, Lee Jay," he said, pointing. "Just like a goat eating string."

The barker and the Glass Eater came into the tent, and the barker began getting the people together to see the show. He introduced himself as Garvin Treecastle, and said that he would explain the freaks to them.

Treecastle was a tall, knobby man, with a face like a melancholy bag filled with golf balls. A thin black moustache came winging out from under his nose, V-ing high over his mouth—which looked as though it had been cut with a single stroke of a scratch awl.

He was the saddest-looking person in the tent.

And though the freaks had been despondent enough before, the moment he stepped onto the platform their spirits flagged visibly a further notch or two.

He began his explanations in a mournful voice—not meeting the eyes of the customers, but looking out over their heads toward the front of the tent. His explanations were all scientific and nugatory, as if he were trying to undermine and contradict the promise of the gaudy posters outside. Three of the freaks—the Monkey Lady, the Alligator Lady, and the Fire Eater—were described as victims of "rare skin disorders." Whether it was true of the others or not, the Alligator Lady at least seemed to confirm his diagnosis. The whole time he was explaining her, she stood at the front of the platform, scratching herself and sprinkling the upturned faces of the first row of customers with a fine, flaky dust.

Two other freaks—the Giant and the Midget—he described as having "rare hormone deficiencies," and the Thin Man as the victim of a high metabolic rate.

When he came to the Snake Lady and the Sword Swallower, he seemed to have run out of scientific explanations, but it didn't matter much. By that time his undertaker's voice and the sullen attitude of the freaks had caused most of the customers to lose interest anyway, and they had begun to drift around the tent on their own. Some of them left altogether and went back out on the midway. Only Dorcus and Lee Jay and one or two others stayed on until the end.

For Florine, who was the last of the freaks, the best he could do was to muster up the one word "Glands" and point to the sign over the platform. After which he mopped his face with the red handkerchief that lapped out of the breast pocket of his coat like an inflamed tongue, then screwed a cigar into an amber holder and lit it.

The smoke seemed to revive him, and he turned to Dorcus and Lee Jay. "Poke her if you want to," he said. "She's real."

Dorcus looked at him in surprise. "You mean I can feel her?" he said.

Treecastle blew out a cloud of smoke. "That's what I said, ain't it?" he said. He looked at Florine for a minute. "Anything that big ought to have five legs and a crutch," he said.

Dorcus walked up and poked his finger into her stomach. It sank up to the knuckles. He watched her face to see what would happen. Nothing happened. Her arm with the banana rocked back and forth without a break in the rhythm.

"Come here, Lee Jay," said Dorcus. Lee Jay stepped up, and Dorcus took his hand to guide it into the fat lady. "Feel that?" he said. Lee Jay nodded, his eyes round, looking up at the fat lady. "That's a fat lady," said Dorcus.

"Yessir," said Lee Jay, nodding his head. "That's what it is."

Dorcus poked his finger into Florine again—farther down in her stomach. Florine rocked a banana up to her mouth for the last nip, paused long enough to belch, then dropped the peeling into the washtub.

"I swan," said Dorcus.

After he had felt her, Lee Jay went back to watch the Sword Swallower. Dorcus walked two or three times around Florine's platform, looking at her from all angles. "I seen one before," he said, talking to Treecastle, "but I ain't never got to *feel* one. Don't she mind it none?"

Treecastle looked at Florine for a minute. "Does she look like she minds it?" he said.

Dorcus watched her while she rocked her arm four times and a banana and a half disappeared. "No," he said. "Not hardly."

"Long as you don't get in the way of the banana," said Treecastle, taking another pull on the cigar.

"How many bunches of bananas she eat a day?" said Dorcus.

Treecastle looked at him. "What?" he said.

"I was wondering how many bunches of bananas a fat lady like that would eat a day," said Dorcus.

"Five," said Treecastle, looking at Florine. "Five goddamn bunches of bananas a day. I ought to be running a banana boat."

"That's a lot of bananas," said Dorcus.

"If the price goes up a dollar a bunch, I'm out of business," said Treecastle. "She eats seven when she's upset."

"What?" said Dorcus.

"When she's upset about something, she eats seven stalks a day."

"Seven?" said Dorcus.

"Seven," said Treecastle.

Together they looked at Florine for a minute without speaking.

"Seven goddamn stalks," said Treecastle.

"I swan," said Dorcus.

"Dolly weighed seven-forty-eight, and she only eat four."

"Dolly?" said Dorcus.

"Dolly was my last one," said Treecastle. "Seven hundred and forty-eight pounds. She didn't never get upset."

"This ain't the only one you got?" said Dorcus.

"Dolly's dead," said Treecastle. "This one's the only one I got now. They don't live long."

"Oh," said Dorcus.

"Glands," said Treecastle. He patted his side.

"Yes," said Dorcus.

"Glands gets them every time."

Dorcus looked at Florine. "How can you tell when she's upset?" he said.

"She eats seven bunches of bananas a day," said Treecastle. "I told you."

"You mad about something?" said Dorcus.

"No," said Treecastle. "I ain't mad. I'm happy as a goddamn lark."

"I thought you sounded like you was mad," said Dorcus.

Treecastle looked at Florine. "I used to kind of like bananas," he said.

"Yes," said Dorcus. "Bananas is pretty good."

"I'd as soon eat a turd now," said Treecastle.

"I see," said Dorcus. "You can get too much of anything."

"I can't even stand to smell them no more," said Treecastle.

For a minute neither of them spoke.

"It's interesting, though," said Dorcus.

Treecastle looked at him.

"I said it must be interesting working around fat ladies and freaks like that," said Dorcus.

"Used to be," said Treecastle. "I ain't got the balls for it no more. It's driving me shithouse."

"How come?" said Dorcus. "I would have thought it would have to be interesting."

"Well," said Treecastle, "the freak part *is* pretty interesting. Only that ain't all there is to it."

"I see," said Dorcus. "What do you mean?"

"Freaks is easy enough to get along with mostly," said Treecastle, "but you let one of them get his ass in a sling about something, and right away it works around to everybody else."

Dorcus looked along the platform at the freaks. "They look sort of droopy-assed," he said.

"Take Inez there," said Treecastle. He pointed to the Monkey Lady. "She and Harry"—he pointed to the Sword Swallower—"they're engaged."

"Yes," said Dorcus, nodding. "That's interesting."

"Harry tried to eat a forty-watt fluorescent bar a while back. Said he was going to do it in fifteen minutes. Harry's got more sense than that, but he had to show off in front of Inez, I reckon. It like to killed him."

"*Forty*-watt?" said Dorcus.

"That's a yard of glass," said Treecastle. "He had the hiccups for five days. It blowed his nerve. Even after he got over the hiccups he would get to thinking about them coming back on him again— while he had that sword rammed down his throat—and he had to lay off for two weeks. Harry couldn't give it up that long. If he don't stick something down his throat every day, he gets moody. Well, he *couldn't* stick nothing down his throat for nearabout three weeks. It was awful. He took it out on Inez, and now Inez's taking it out on the rest of us."

"That's the way it is," said Dorcus.

"She said she was going to shave all her hair off and get her a straight job." Treecastle shook his head. "Inez couldn't hold no straight job. She's shittier looking with her hair shaved off than what she is with it on. I seen her. She looked like a ugly shaved monkey."

"I see," said Dorcus.

"Something like that throws the whole show off," said Tree-

castle. "It works around to everybody after a while. Grace there"—
he pointed to the Alligator Lady—"she's been talking about going
to see a skin doctor. Jesus. She's had them scabs on her since her
baby hair fell out, and now she thinks she can go see some quack
and get a penicillin shot and it'll go away. You don't never
get through with them goddamn skin doctors anyway. They can
keep a dose of poison ivy scratching for fifteen years. I seen it happen. One of them sons-of-bitches gets ahold of Grace, he'll be handing her down to his grandbabies to work on. I told her to try Ivory
soap and some Vasoline and sulfur ointment I'd make up for her for
nothing. I meant it, but she took it wrong and ain't spoke a word
to me for three days."

"Skin doctors is bad news," said Dorcus.

"Yes," said Treecastle.

"The sulfur is good though. I mix mine with lard," said Dorcus.

"Lard?" said Treecastle.

"We got plenty of lard," said Dorcus. "You don't hardly notice
the smell because of the sulfur."

"You ought to try Vasoline," said Treecastle. "It's neutral."

"Yes," said Dorcus. "The sulfur is the main thing, though. Sulfur
is good."

"Yes," said Treecastle.

He looked back at the platform. "Doloris there—" He pointed
to the Snake Lady. "Doloris is scared Jupiter—that's the snake, Jupiter—is going to die. She says she's too old to train her a new one. It
ain't nothing only she's feeding him too much to eat. She stuffs him
all day long, then can't figure out why he won't wake up for her to
do the show. The Goddamn snake wasn't worth a shit in the first
place. He ain't worth killing now. But you can't talk no sense to
Doloris about it."

"It's a nice-looking snake," said Dorcus. "I ain't too much on
snakes myself, but I'd say that was a pretty nice-looking snake."

"Handsome *is* as handsome *does*, is what I say," said Treecastle.
He took a pull on his cigar.

"Well," said Dorcus. "Is that all?"

"What?" said Treecastle.

"Is that all the trouble you got?" said Dorcus.

"Mister," said Treecastle, taking the cigar out of his mouth. "I ain't only started to tell you my troubles. This here ten-in-one's a trouble *factory*."

"Well," said Dorcus, "I reckon you must have your share. But it's interesting, though."

"Fred"—Treecastle pointed to the Fire Eater—"that's the nigger there, Fred been reading some of that Black Muslim horseshit. Now he says we got to all call him Ali Baba. *Ali Baba*. Jesus. He says we're all prejudiced and he can't stand working around no prejudiced white trash that they don't know how to treat a nigger right. He says he's going to find him a all-nigger carnival and go to work for it. If he can't do that, he's going to be a missionary out to Africa and save the heathen. I ast him what the shit kind of a church is looking for a halfwit nigger missionary, but he just keeps on saying how prejudiced I am and what would I know about it. He won't hardly talk to me no more. Even when I call him Ali Baba."

"Ain't that just like a nigger?" said Dorcus.

"Fred's all right," said Treecastle, "only I got to get them books away from him."

"A reading nigger ain't worth a shit," said Dorcus.

Treecastle took another pull at the cigar. "Linville"—he pointed to the Thin Man—"Linville's queer."

"The skinny feller?" said Dorcus.

"He run off the Strong Man I used to have, following him around and hanging on him, telling him how pretty his eyes was, and asting him to let him feel his muscles, till he just couldn't stand it no more and he quit the show. Now Linville's gone moody and says he's hungry all the time."

"The tall skinny feller is a queer?" said Dorcus.

"I ain't going to fuck around with Linville none," said Treecastle. "A Thin Man just ain't that hard to find. I'll beat his ass and ram him up a tailpipe is what I'll do."

"I wouldn't blame you for that," said Dorcus.

Treecastle took several deep drags on the cigar, calming himself down.

"Well," said Dorcus, "leastways the Giant and the Midget is all right."

"Yes," said Treecastle, "they's just fine. Only except Goliath is scared shitless of Tiny." He pointed to the platform. "Look how he keeps his eye on him."

Dorcus looked.

"How the hell do you figure that?" said Treecastle. "Something like the way an elephant is scared of a mouse? Maybe Goliath thinks Tiny is going to run up his pants leg and bite his peter off."

"I swan," said Dorcus.

For a minute neither of them spoke.

"Sounds like trouble to me," said Dorcus.

Treecastle didn't answer.

"What about the Fat Lady?" said Dorcus.

"What?" said Treecastle.

"The Fat Lady," said Dorcus.

Treecastle looked at Florine. "Yes, shit," he said, "Florine too."

"What's her trouble?" said Dorcus.

"Well," said Treecastle. Florine dropped a peeling that hit on the rim of the washtub and flopped onto the platform. Treecastle lifted it with the tip of his cane and dropped it into the tub. "Florine ain't been serviced for over three weeks," he said.

"What?" said Dorcus.

"Used to be we'd kind of pass it around the people in the show," he said. "But we can't do that no more. Inez told Harry she didn't care if the whole carny went under, he had to stay away from Florine. I was depending on Harry, but you know how a woman is when she gets like that."

"Yes," said Dorcus.

"And Linville's queer," said Treecastle, counting them off on his fingers, "and Fred's a nigger, and Tiny—well, you can see how that would be."

"Yes," said Dorcus. "I can see that."

"You ever noticed how it is the women go crazy over midgets?" said Treecastle.

"No," said Dorcus.

"I can't understand it," said Treecastle. "It seems preverted to me."

"Yes," said Dorcus. "I wonder what they see in them?"

Treecastle shook his head. "I never could understand it," he said.

For a minute neither of them spoke.

"What about the Giant?" said Dorcus.

"What?" said Treecastle, "Goliath?"

"The Giant there," said Dorcus, pointing.

"Goliath's *strange*," said Treecastle. "I mean fucked-up strange. I don't have no more to do with him than just what I have to. You don't never know how it is he's going to take something. I'd be afraid to ast him."

"I see," said Dorcus.

"Besides," said Treecastle, "he don't seem to be interested in no women. Probably he just had to give it up. On account of his size, you know."

"Yes," said Dorcus.

"I had me a canvasman used to come in and take care of Florine for me ever once in a while for a dollar. But he quit the show in Pembroke. Now ain't nobody else I can turn to."

Dorcus looked at him for a minute. "Wait a minute," he said. "You mean . . . you mean don't nobody want to fuck the Fat Lady?" he said.

"I mean if don't nobody do it soon, I'm out of business," said Treecastle. "I can't stand no seven bunches of bananas a day." He looked at Dorcus. "How'd you like to be in a business where you had a two-bunches-of-bananas-a-day profit margin?"

"And you got to *pay* somebody to do it?" said Dorcus.

"I tried it myself," said Treecastle, "but it weren't no good. I ain't the man I used to be. Besides, like I said, I can't stand the smell of them bananas."

"You mean you got to *pay* somebody?" said Dorcus. "What kind of a man would it be that you'd have to pay him to do it to a Fat Lady?"

"They's all kinds in this world, mister," said Treecastle. "Believe me, they's all kinds."

"I wouldn't have thought it," said Dorcus. "You wouldn't have to pay *me* to do it to no Fat Lady. You wouldn't have to pay me nothing at all."

"You mean you'd like to screw Florine there?" said Treecastle.

Dorcus looked at Florine narrowly, squinting his eyes. "She's *unusual*," he said. "That's the thing."

Treecastle nodded his head. "Yes," he said.

"I done it to a cross-eyed nigger gal had a clubfoot in Jacksonville once," said Dorcus. "She made me buy her a gold tooth first, but it were worth it. That was *some* foot, mister. I ain't *never* seen nothing like that before."

"You did?" said Treecastle.

"And a redheaded hunchback in Waynesboro with a sister was a halfwit. We had to pay her thirty dollars and keep telling her we loved her, but it was worth it too. That hump made *all* the difference."

"*We?*" said Treecastle.

"Yes," said Dorcus, "I had to go halves on that one. That special stuff is too high for me by myself."

"God damn," said Treecastle.

"They's plenty of ugly girls in McAfee County," said Dorcus. "But they ain't any *unusual* ones."

"I see," said Treecastle. "What's your name, mister?"

"Dorcus," said Dorcus.

"Well, Mr. Dorcus . . . ," said Treecastle.

"Dorcus Williston," said Dorcus.

"Well, Mr. Williston . . . ," said Treecastle.

"Mr. Treecastle," said Dorcus, "ain't nobody else in McAfee County ever done it to a Fat Lady. I bet you, ain't nobody ever done it."

"I reckon you're right about that, Mr. Dilliston," said Treecastle.

"Williston," said Dorcus.

"Williston," said Treecastle.

"Well," said Dorcus, "I'd be the only one could say he'd fucked a Fat Lady."

"Well," said Treecastle, "yes, you would." For a minute he stood watching Florine eating a banana. She was getting down toward the end of the stalk. "You mean you want to do it?" he said.

"Fuck the Fat Lady?" said Dorcus. "They ain't nothing in this world I'd rather do," he said, looking at Florine. "Nothing in this world."

"Well," said Treecastle, "once you got started on it, you'd have to go through with it. You understand that, don't you? Jesus God, if you didn't go through with it, she'd be eating *ten* bunches a day."

"Mister," said Dorcus, "I ain't never gone back on my word in my life. If I say I'll fuck the Fat Lady, I'll fuck the Fat Lady. What kind of a shithead you think I am?"

"And you say you'll really do it?" said Treecastle.

"I said it'd be a *honor* to do it," said Dorcus. "I'll do it," he added.

"Well," said Treecastle. "It ain't really that bad. I reckon *finding* it is the hardest part."

"Yes," said Dorcus. "I'd be the only man in McAfee County ever done it to a Fat Lady. Think of that."

Treecastle looked at him. "I ain't looking at this from just your side," he said. "The main thing is, you got to promise me you ain't going to try to get out of it at the last minute."

Dorcus looked at him. "You think I'm crazy or something?" he said.

Treecastle looked at Florine for another long minute. "Okay," he said. "But you better not try to get out of it."

"You ain't never going to be sorry," said Dorcus. "I can promise you, you ain't never going to be sorry."

While they were talking, Lee Jay came back from watching the Glass Eater. "He eat a whole light bub, Pa," he said. " 'Cept the screw end. He give it to me for a keepsake." He held up the bulb end for Dorcus to see.

Treecastle looked down at him. "What we going to do about the boy?" he said.

"I hadn't thought," said Dorcus.

"Whyn't you send him on home?" said Treecastle.

"I can't send him home by hisself," said Dorcus. "He ain't but eleven."

"He sure does look older than that," said Treecastle.

Lee Jay held up his hands with the fingers spread. "Eleven," he said.

"He's big for his age," said Dorcus. "Everybody notices that."

"Well," said Treecastle, "we got to do something about him."

"Well," said Dorcus.

"I'm eleven, mister," said Lee Jay, holding up his hands. "Eleven."

"Put your hands down, Lee Jay," said Dorcus. "He knows you're eleven."

Lee Jay put his hands down.

Treecastle looked at Lee Jay for a minute. Then he turned to Dorcus. "There's a fireworks show at ten-thirty. Could you get him to watch that while you come on back here?"

"How much does it cost?" said Dorcus. "We're nearbout out of money."

"It's free," said Treecastle.

"It is . . . ," said Dorcus, ". . . free?" He scratched his chin and looked at Lee Jay, then back at Treecastle.

"Yes," said Treecastle.

"Generally a fireworks show ain't free," said Dorcus. "Generally you got to pay to see a fireworks show."

"This one's free," said Treecastle.

"I ain't never heard of no free fireworks show," said Dorcus. "I sure would hate to miss a free fireworks show . . . if it's free."

"Shit," said Treecastle.

"Well . . . ," said Dorcus.

"Forget it," said Treecastle. "I might of knowed."

"You sure it's free?" said Dorcus. "Generally you got to pay to see a fireworks show."

"Forget it," said Treecastle. He turned to go.

"Well," said Dorcus. "I might get me a chance to see a free fireworks show sometime." He looked at Treecastle. "I hate to miss a free fireworks show. What time did you say it started?"

"Ten-thirty," said Treecastle. "You better go on and see the show. You can't make up your mind. I can't take no chance on you if you can't make up your mind."

"No," said Dorcus. "I hate not to see the fireworks show, but it's just everything coming at me at once. I'll take Lee Jay and be back."

Treecastle looked at him. "How do I know you ain't going to change your mind on me again? I couldn't afford the *two* extra banana stalks I'm buying now. I can't take no chance on *five*."

"You could count on me," said Dorcus. "I'm all right now. I wasn't thinking a minute ago." He put out his hand. "Shake on it," he said.

Treecastle came back, and they shook hands.

"I ain't never gone back on my word when I shook on it," said Dorcus.

"The show starts at ten-thirty," said Treecastle. "You be back here then, and I'll have her ready to go in the truck."

"Ten-thirty?" said Dorcus.

"Come around to the back of the tent," said Treecastle. "I got the truck parked out back of the tent. I'll have her ready to go in, but you'll have to help me."

"Ten-thirty," said Dorcus.

"At the back of the tent," said Treecastle.

"Come on, Lee Jay," said Dorcus.

"And, Dilliston. . ."

"Williston," said Dorcus.

"Williston . . . ," said Treecastle.

"Yes," said Dorcus.

"Don't you be late, Williston," said Treecastle.

"Yes," said Dorcus.

"If you're late, it's off," said Treecastle.

"I shook on it," said Dorcus.

Dorcus got Lee Jay settled at the grandstand where the fireworks show was to take place. "It's ten now," he said. "They'll start at ten-thirty, so you'll be able to see real good. Meet me at the freak-show tent when it's over."

The lights were on, but there were not many people in the grandstand yet. Just a dozen or so. Dorcus patted Lee Jay on the head and went away.

Lee Jay sat alone in the stands holding the princess doll in both hands and looking at the screw end of the light bulb that Harry had given him.

Dorcus was waiting at the back of the freak-show tent at ten-fifteen. At ten-twenty-five he heard a sound inside the tent like a steam locomotive pulling into a station. The flap of the tent flew back and Florine waddled into the opening—puffing and sucking, and holding the banana stalk in front of her with both hands, the way a bridesmaid would hold a bouquet. At her side Treecastle staggered, his hat askew, the cigar holder gripped in his teeth.

"Give me a hand, God damn it," he panted when he saw Dorcus. "This ain't no one-man job."

Dorcus helped him get her to the loading ramp of the truck. Beside the ramp they stopped, and Treecastle stood aside to wipe his brow. Florine let the stalk slide to the ground and pulled off a banana.

"Jesus, she's hard to move," said Treecastle. "It's all dead weight."

He put the handkerchief back into his coat pocket and went up the ramp into the body of the truck. Dorcus heard him moving around inside. When he reappeared at the tailgate, he had something in his arms.

"I made it myself," he said. "You should have seen us trying to load her on the truck before."

When he laid it out, Dorcus saw that it was a harness, made up of a heavy leather yoke, which was buckled onto Florine, and ropes that extended from the yoke to pulleys on either side of the tailgate.

When Treecastle tried to buckle the yoke onto Florine, she began making grunting noises and made as if to hit him with the banana stalk.

"She's scared of the ramp," he said. "Come on, Florine. Don't give me no trouble now. We're almost there."

He dropped the harness and took hold of the banana stalk. Florine clung to it, and the grunting noises turned into squeals.

"Come on, God damn it," said Treecastle. He was sweating and panting again. "Give me the goddamn banana stalk." He finally tore it out of Florine's hands and heaved it up onto the tailgate. It struck with a soft, squashy thump.

Florine let out a wail and stretched her arms toward the spot where the stalk lay.

"Now," said Treecastle. He slipped the yoke on and buckled it. "All right," he said to Dorcus, "take the other rope and keep it tight. We got to guide her up. If she falls, I'll have to shoot her."

With Dorcus on one side and Treecastle on the other, they got Florine underway. She walked with her arms outstretched and her

legs stiff at the knees, swinging them out to the sides instead of lifting them—like a great mechanical doll. As she waddled up the ramp,
she made small, whimpering sounds.

At the top she stopped and tried to reach down for the banana
stalk. The whimpering grew louder. Treecastle picked up the stalk
and heaved it farther into the body of the truck. The thump
echoed off the metal sides, and Florine toddled off after it with her
arms outstretched.

Treecastle paused and turned to Dorcus. He pulled the handkerchief out of his coat pocket and mopped his face. "Jesus," he said.
"If I ever get anything ahead, I'm going to buy me a fork lift. I ain't
up to this kind of shit no more."

"It would of been a help," said Dorcus.

"Okay," said Treecastle when his breathing was normal again,
"let's get her clothes off."

They went into the van of the truck, where Florine stood whimpering, trying to reach down to the banana stalk, and Treecastle
began unsnapping snaps. After a while Dorcus sat down to wait for
him to finish.

"I think that's all of them," said Treecastle at last, working his
fingers to get the cramps out. "Give me a hand."

Taking off Florine's clothes was like striking a tent. What had
seemed to be a brief costume when it had been on her took on the
dimensions of an awning when they had gotten it off. It covered
the whole tailgate of the truck.

Florine stood revealed in all her creased and folded glory.

"Jesus Christ," said Dorcus in a low voice. "I ain't never going
to live to see nothing like that again."

"I don't know how to take that," said Treecastle. "You ain't running out on me, are you?"

"I just ain't never seen nothing like it before," said Dorcus.
"Honest to God."

"We got to get her down," said Treecastle.

At the front end of the truck the floor was covered with straw.
It was piled high and loose on the sides, but in the center it was
packed into a gigantic crater of a nest. The stalk of bananas lay on
the floor at the edge of the straw.

"Now," said Treecastle, picking up the stalk with one hand, and fending Florine off with the other, "be ready. I'm going to throw the banana stalk into the hay. When she starts after it, we'll give her a push. Try to guide her so she falls in the loose part. Be careful. She's got to hit right."

"What?" said Dorcus.

"If she don't hit right, it's over," said Treecastle.

"How come?" said Dorcus.

Treecastle looked at him. "This is a *Fat Lady*, buster," he said. "If she don't go down right, there ain't no way you're going to be able to get *at* her—not unless you got you a spare yard of peter to snake around. If she lands on her stomach, you couldn't get at her with a drain auger."

"Oh," said Dorcus.

"Just be careful," said Treecastle. "I'll do the guiding."

He fluffed up the hay with his foot. "I'm going to throw it now," he said.

Dorcus crouched behind her, tense and waiting. He gave a short nod of his head.

"Now!" said Treecastle. He tossed the stalk. As Florine started after it, he and Dorcus gave her a push. They were a little off center, and she spun as she fell—daintily, with one leg raised slightly, like a ballerina. Then she toppled sideways, seeming to fall in slow motion. For a moment she lay on her side, thrashing. She could have rolled either way. But Treecastle put his foot on her and gave a shove, and she rolled onto her back.

The two men walked over and inspected her. She lay waving her arms around and trying to lift her legs off the floor.

"Looks okay to me," said Treecastle.

Dorcus was unhooking the straps of his overalls.

"I'll be out by the tailgate if you need any help," said Treecastle. "If you can't manage it by yourself, you call me. You understand, Dilliston?"

"Williston," said Dorcus.

"Williston," said Treecastle. "You understand?"

"I'll manage," said Dorcus. "Ain't nothing to it now."

"There's plenty to it," said Treecastle. "That's what I mean. The light ain't too good in here, and it ain't that easy to tell no way. The way she bunches up down there, it looks like a cunt convention. You be sure you get it in the right place. I can't afford no ten stalks a day," he said.

"What you want to do, paint a circle around it?" said Dorcus. He sounded hurt. "I'm forty-six year old, mister. I reckon I know what a pussy looks like."

"I didn't mean to hurt your feelings none," said Treecastle. "But I got a lot riding on this. It ain't that easy—even when you got a good light it ain't. Try to be sure. Call me if you ain't." He walked to the tailgate and down the ramp.

In a minute or two Dorcus called out. "Mr. Treecastle . . ."

"Oh, shit," said Treecastle. "Ohshitohshitohshit."

He looked up to see Dorcus standing stark naked on the tailgate of the truck.

"Mr. Treecastle . . . ," said Dorcus.

Treecastle stood with his head in his hands. "Oh, shit," he said.

"Mr. Treecastle," said Dorcus. "Looks like we done run out of bananas."

The Ferris wheel spun high up into the night, bucking backward as it started climbing, then collapsing in on itself as it came over the curving glide at the top and started down. For a moment before it began to come down, Lee Jay had the feeling that he was going to fly off into the night and roll away over McAfee County. He sat beside Dorcus in the gondola, his eyes wide as two pale blue saucers, wrapping the princess doll in his arms and trying to hold on at the same time. Dorcus sat as he would sit in the glider on his front porch at home—one hand stretched out along the back of the seat, holding Lee Jay, the elbow of the other arm crooked over the side.

"Nothing like riding the Ferris wheel," he said. "Ferris wheels is the way to go."

Lee Jay nodded. His breath was coming in deep gasps that he had to hold on to. He couldn't speak to answer his father.

"I done something tonight you wouldn't believe, Lee Jay," said Dorcus.

Lee Jay held on, trying not to look down.

"I done something tonight I got to tell you about when you get growed," he said.

Lee Jay was holding on to the crossbar. As they started down, his eyes rolled up, looking at the darkness above him.

"I done something tonight even better'n riding the Ferris wheel," said Dorcus. "Better'n a free fireworks show."

Lee Jay was looking up at the gondola above them as they came curving down, sliding backward.

Dorcus reached into his pocket. "Lee Jay," he said, ". . . have a banana."

Anse Starkey at Rest

1962: SUMMER

The raccoon moved back and forth at the end of the tether. Back and forth and back and forth. If you watched it too long, it made you tired. The scope of the chain allowed him a run of only six or seven feet, and he moved back and forth inside it with a continuous motion, anticipating the turns at the ends, and swinging into them almost before he got to them. He moved as if he had contracted to perform a certain number of circuits and was now somewhere past half through—a contract which he felt he had to honor, but had long ago lost interest in. Occasionally he would stop at the end of the run and sit, not resting, just sitting for a short minute— as if the resting too were a part of the contract.

The tether was a piece of light chain, fastened to the raccoon's collar at one end, and at the other to a looped eye in the end of a galvanized grounding rod that had been driven into the ground. He could have roamed all over a circle fourteen feet in diameter— but he didn't do it. Instead he kept his run parallel to the road that passed in front of the store, always holding just enough tension on the chain to keep it from dragging on the ground.

Billy Coon didn't look unhappy. He just looked busy. If he had looked unhappy, Walt Shotford would never have left him out there, because Walt set great store by Billy Coon, and wouldn't keep him doing anything if it made him look unhappy.

Maybe Billy kept so busy on the run because he thought that was what Walt expected of him. The relationship between Walt Shotford and Billy Coon was crazy any way you looked at it, and one explanation was as likely as another.

To begin with, Walt had started to stake Billy out in front of
the store because he said it was good for business. But that didn't
make much sense. The business he had was going to keep coming,
no matter what he did. Shotford's store was the only one in the Two-
Oak community—an institution. There wasn't any reasonable way
he could have kept his customers *from* coming. If he had locked the
door to the store and just wouldn't let them in, it would have *dis-
couraged* them. But, likely as not, they would have stood around
until he gave in and opened it up again and let them come, because
there was nowhere else to go anyway. The fact was that there was
no logical business reason for Shotford to put Billy out there, no
matter what he said. Some people had come down to look at Billy
and make comments to each other about him at first, but, after all,
everybody in the Two-Oak community already knew what a coon
looked like, so even that little bit of interest had died out after a
week or so, and they almost stepped on him going back and forth to
the store, because they had forgotten he was there in the first place.

The real reason Walt kept Billy out there was probably because he had the idea that Billy enjoyed it, although he admitted
himself that he couldn't ever really tell what the coon did enjoy.
But at least he didn't fight *not* to be put on the leash, the way he
had fought not to be put in the pen that Walt had spent two weeks
building for him out in the back behind the store. The fact that
Billy more or less let it go had to be taken as a sign to the good—
Walt interpreted it that the coon enjoyed the chain and stake.

After Walt put him out, it was a couple of weeks before Billy
got his routine adjusted like he wanted it. Whenever anything went
a way he didn't want it to, he would bristle up and fuss about it,
until Walt figured out what he was getting at and adjusted things to
his liking.

Billy would get out in the morning and walk the run for about
an hour and a half, and again in the evening for a couple of hours.
Those were the times that Shotford did most of his business, and it
was as if the arrival of the customers put Billy in mind of doing
something to earn his keep. In between times, he would loll around
in the shade, snatching at flies and bugs, or sleeping on top of the
house Walt had built for him. He was never known to set foot inside

it, but he liked to climb up on top and straddle the peak of the roof and go to sleep there. At about noon he would start to fussing and squawking, and Maude—Mrs. Shotford—would have to come out and get him and take him into the kitchen and feed him some tidbit—a piece of cheese or a Lorna Doone cracker—to make him stop. Then Billy would climb up in an old rocking chair that was kept on the back porch, with a folded rug in it for a cushion, and go to sleep for a while. When he woke up, the customers would be arriving, so he had to be taken back out front and put on the leash again.

Walt had more patience than sense with the coon. It took him a month to work out the schedule that Billy liked. When he was sure that the arrangement was going to stick, he went in to Darien and got him a nice collar and chain at the ten-cent store—a red leather collar, with silver studs on it. Walt thought it made Billy look very handsome. Billy didn't seem to care.

Leaving the coon out there on the chain at night worried Walt, because he was afraid that sometime the hounds might gang up on him and kill him. But Billy didn't like to stay in the house at night, so Walt gave in and went and got a big Heinz 57 bitch out of the dog pound in Savannah, and put her out with Billy to protect him.

Even though he had wanted a yard dog—one that would stay close to the store and not be following her nose all over McAfee County—Walt was afraid at first that he had made a mistake about Blanche. She was big enough, all right; if she got up on her hind legs, she could have put her front paws on Walt's shoulders and look him in the eye—a kind of cross between a pit bull and a Shetland pony, with short white hair and a big black spot over one eye. But the trouble with Blanche was that she was even lazier than she was big.

For a while it looked like Walt never was going to see what she looked like standing up. Every time he would shoot a glance at her out the window, or when he went into the yard, she would be stretched out on the ground asleep with her hind legs sticking straight out behind her and her head down on her front paws. Or rolled over on her back with her mouth open and her tongue lolling out and her paws flopped up in the air, the flies buzzing in and out of her mouth. When Walt finally got mad about it, and lost his temper and went out and kicked her, she woke up moaning a little. But when she saw who it was, she wagged her stump of a tail, and that was all there was to it. She seemed to be ready for him to kick her to death, and no offense taken. Walt figured that when the other dogs got onto what her nature was, it would be all up with Billy.

Just the same, she had taken up with the coon right away, moving into the house which he didn't use—or rather, moving partway in, since it was too small for all of her, so she had to sleep with just her head and front paws inside the door, and her rear end sticking out in the yard. She ate five pounds of meat scraps a day, and wouldn't have been worth killing for anything else except the job Walt had gotten her for. As it turned out, she was just right for that.

The only thing she took a real interest in was other dogs, and there wasn't a hound in the whole Two-Oak community that could get within five hundred yards of Shotford's store. Whenever she smelled one coming, she would be up on her feet, with the hair down her spine standing straight up like she'd backed under a rake, and a noise in her throat like a dump truck unloading gravel. It made Walt's mouth go dry and his palms sweat the first time he heard it.

He ran out of the store to see what kind of a four-toed throwback had gotten spit up into his yard out of the Dorchester Swamp. He never even thought of Blanche. When he got out there, there she stood, with her back hair up, and the muscles in her shoulders bunched, looking off down the road. About a hundred yards away, in the middle of the road, stood a blue-tick hound, frozen stiff, except for the tip of his tail, which was vibrating from the strain. He was looking at Blanche like he couldn't believe it. They stood that way for about a minute, and then the blue-tick just folded in on himself and stepped off into the bushes at the side of the road, very slowly and deliberately, with his head over his shoulder looking at Blanche and his tail between his legs. Walt knew then that he had picked the right dog.

For the most part, Walt left Billy Coon alone, paying attention to his complaints, and trying to get things fixed up to suit him only when he insisted. For the rest, he would look at him out the window as he passed, waiting on the customers, or glance over when he went out in the front to pump gas. Walt liked having the coon around, but he didn't handle him any, nor did he seem to need to even be close to him very much (Maude was the one who fed him and took up the most time with him directly). Maybe there had been enough of that in the first place. It had cost Walt to get Billy to begin with.

He still had a scar on his finger that Billy had given him when he caught him. Walt had been going out along the logging road to pick blueberries for Maude, because she loved to have them for breakfast in the mornings with sugar and milk. It was the middle of the morning of a Monday in June, and the snakes were out—racers —sunning themselves in looping, black coils on the fence railings. Walt was looking at them, when a movement in the drainage ditch at the side of the road caught his eye. It was a pair of raccoon cubs.

He couldn't help but try to catch them. Before they saw him, he was right on top of them—reaching. They reacted fast—took off scampering in opposite directions—but Walt had gotten too close, and he made a grab for the one of them and caught him. He had to take the cub in his bare hand, and even though he was a little fellow, no bigger than a squirrel, he bit Walt's finger right to the bone. Walt tightened up his fist just enough so the coon couldn't get his head back for a second bite, and walked home with him in his hand—the cub's teeth sunk in his finger—bleeding all the way.

"Get a cardboard box, Maude," he said when he came in the store.

She saw he had something in his hand, and the blood was all over by then, dripping out of his fist, so she didn't ask him any questions, but just went and got the box and brought it to him. Walt opened his fist, and the cub dropped into the box like a wet rag. Then he closed the flaps and put a board on top so he couldn't get out, and some cans from the shelves to hold the board in place.

"Coon," he said to Maude, taking out his handkerchief and wrapping it around his hand, which was covered with blood.

"He bit you bad, Walt," Maude said. She took him in the kitchen and washed his hand off. Then she put some turpentine on the bitten place to keep it from getting infected, and bandaged it with a clean handkerchief that she tore up into strips.

"Always wanted a coon," said Walt, and they went back out where the box was on the counter and took off the board to look in on him. He was still lying there in the bottom of the box, wadded up in a corner. But Walt could see his sides pumping as he breathed, so he knew he would be all right if they could just get him to eat. He had been very careful not to mash him as he carried him back.

He put the board and the cans back on top of the box and went out into the yard and spent the next three hours making a cage for him out of two-by-twos and chicken wire. Then he put a pan in for water, and another one for food, and a piece of a tree limb so he would have something to climb on. When he finished, he brought the cage back in and set it on the counter next to the cardboard box. Then he tapped the side of the box with his knuckle. He could hear the cub scurry around inside.

Walt didn't want him to get away, so he put him into a croker sack, then worked him into the cage from that. The cub tried to get out through the wire all around the four sides, and then he backed himself into one of the corners and just sat there glaring at Walt every time he made a move. He was wild and sad-looking, with his fur all matted and crusty, sticking out in tufts that were black and stiff from the blood.

Walt was afraid he would starve to death if he didn't get him calmed down soon so he would eat. He took him into the back bedroom where it was quiet, and put him in the darkest corner of the room, with some milk in the food pan in the cage. And then he closed the door to the room and went off and left him by himself. When he came back in a couple of hours, the cub was still in the corner of the cage, and it didn't look like any of the milk was gone. That afternoon he went down to the bridge on the logging road where the Negroes came to fish after work, and he traded two cigarettes to a Negro boy for a little bream he had caught. Then he went back and put that in the cage. The next morning most of the bream was gone, and some of the milk.

Walt left him alone all the rest of that day, and when he went back with another bream in the evening, Billy had cleaned most of the blood off, so he was looking more presentable. But he still backed into the corner and glared at him when he opened the door to put in the bream.

The wound in Walt's finger had bled enough that it didn't get infected, but he had to leave the bandage on for a week, and the soreness didn't work out for three weeks more. It bothered him that he couldn't use the hand for that time.

Walt was a big man anyway, and strong. But his hands were strong out of all proportion to his size. They were hard and puffy, with swollen fingers that looked like walnuts on a string—and just about as hard. He had worked a callus on the tip of his right thumb, so he could open a beer bottle with it—holding the bottle by the neck in his hand and forcing the cap off with his thumb. He used to do the trick for the customers every now and then, saying it was good for business. He also had another trick he would do sometimes. Between the first and second fingers of his right hand he would place a pecan, with the fingers sticking straight out from his hand. Then he would slowly make a fist and crack the pecan. He didn't strain when he did it. He would just close his hand, and the nut would crack, most of the time so the halves could be taken out in whole pieces. It wasn't nearly so much of a feat as opening the beer bottles, but there was more showmanship to it, since he didn't have to strain to bring it off. And also, because a number of his customers could almost do it themselves, they tended to pay more attention to it, thinking to learn the technique. The trick of opening the beer bottles was so inconceivable to them that they stopped paying attention to it after a while.

In the evenings the men from the Two-Oaks community would come down to Shotford's store and sit around under the shed in front on upended Coca-Cola cases, drinking Spearmans Ale and talking. While they talked, Billy Coon would be out there on his run, working at the contract, going back and forth, and keeping just enough tension on the chain so it wouldn't be dragging on the ground.

Only two men could stop Billy walking his run in the evenings. The two men were Jessie Wight and Anse Starkey.

Anse had once thrown a firecracker at Billy as he walked by going into the store. It had scared Billy so he had almost broken his neck when the chain caught him running away and slammed him down on the ground. Walt had eaten Anse out about it, so he never threw a firecracker again, but he would often jump at Billy as he walked by, yelling at him and scaring him.

Anse had been mean to animals all of his life. As a child he had always been tying cans and firecrackers to the tails of dogs and cats. Or soaking a corn cob in turpentine and then rubbing it back and forth under their tails to watch them run. Those were common enough tricks for all the boys around the Two-Oak community, but Anse had a different attitude toward them. The thing was, they never seemed to make him happy. The other boys would laugh and giggle when they sent a hound off up the road with a string of firecrackers going off behind him, because they knew they were doing something that they ought not to be doing, and it made them happy. But Anse never laughed when he did those things. He would just do them, in an offhanded way, as if he wasn't really taking an interest in them, and didn't care one way or the other.

As he got older, he would occasionally trap wild animals— squirrels and possums and sometimes a bird or two—and put them up in cages or tie them to a stake in the yard. He would poke at them with a stick, or mistreat them some other way for a while after he first caught them. But then he would get tired of that and stop paying attention to them, and he would go off and leave them alone. Sometimes they would die, especially the birds that he kept in cages he made out of Popsicle sticks glued together. Most of the bigger things he caught would finally get away and go back into the woods. One possum he kept for almost a year, but then he got mad at it for hissing at him and he beat it to death with a stick.

He never had a pet. Never seemed to need to have one. For about five years, beginning when he was around thirteen or fourteen, there was an old, starved-looking hound that would follow along behind him wherever he went. He never claimed him as his own dog and following Anse around seemed to be all the hound's idea, because Anse never paid any attention to him. No one ever saw Anse feed him, nor pat him, nor show him any sort of kindness at all. But, unsatisfactory as the relationship seemed to be to everybody else, the dog evidently found something satisfying in it, because he continued to hang around anyway.

Once in a while, at Christmas and New Year's and Fourth of July, Anse would tie a string of firecrackers to the dog's tail and send him running off up the road hollering and jumping around, trying to get away from the noise. But after the string of firecrackers burned out, he would be back in the yard like nothing had happened, and Anse would go back to ignoring him again.

One Christmas Anse tied the string on his tail too tight, and the hound couldn't bite it loose after the firecrackers burned out. He went around with the string on until the part of his tail beyond the string died, and the end just dropped off. Before that happened, Anse hadn't called the dog any name at all. When he wanted him to come to him for some reason, he would just whistle and pat his leg and the dog would come, since he was always waiting around for Anse to notice him anyway. But after the end of his tail dropped off, Anse started to call him Halfass. Mostly he just called him that to talk about him. When he wanted him to come, he would still whistle and pat his leg. Halfass went on following Anse around until one day in July when Anse was eighteen and he went down into the Dorchester Swamp, trying to find an alligator, so he could kill it and sell the hide. Halfass got lost in the swamp and never came out.

The men under the shed could tell when Anse Starkey was coming just by watching Billy Coon. He always stopped pacing as soon as he got wind of him. Not at the end of the run where he took his usual rests, but just wherever he happened to be at the time. He would stop and sit back and look down the road. After a while Anse would come in sight, and Billy would keep on watching him until after he had gone into the store and come back out with his bottle of Spearmans to sit under the shed and talk to the men. It got to be such a customary thing that the men would stop talking when they saw Billy watching, and so Anse felt called upon to do something, since they were all looking at him. But he was scared of Walt Shotford, so he settled it by giving a jump at Billy as he went by, making him flinch and rattle his chain. Walt didn't like that either, but he didn't say anything, since it wasn't hurting Billy.

When Jessie Wight was coming, Billy would let them know too, but in a different way. So the men under the shed could always tell which one of them it was. Billy Coon didn't stop pacing for Jessie.

But he would shorten his circuit to just a step or two each way, and faster than he usually went. Until Jessie came up out of the grave-yard behind the Golden Rainbow African Baptist Church across the road from Shotford's, and then he would stop and sit there waiting for Jessie to come on up and give him his egg.

Jessie was a tenant on Case Deering's place, and he had a hen-house for the extra money he got selling the eggs to Shotford. Every day in the evening he would come down with the eggs to the store, and he always had a nice big one picked out especially for Billy Coon. So the coon would shorten up his circuit when he smelled Jessie coming, and then when he could see him in the graveyard be-hind the church, he would sit very still until Jessie came up and gave him his egg. He would take it to the pot that caught the drip under the hydrant, holding it in both his hands, and he would wash it off all over and crack the end and suck on the egg. Sometimes Jessie would watch him washing off the egg and then opening it up and sucking it, standing there with his arm hooked through the handle of the half-bushel peach basket that he carried the eggs in.

Then he would go on into the store, and Walt would pay him for the eggs, and Jessie would get himself a Coca-Cola, or some-times an R-C Cola, and if he had an extra egg, maybe a couple of Lucky Strike cigarettes. Then he would go out under the big live oak tree by the side of Shotford's store with the other colored men and squat down on his heels and drink the Coca-Cola and smoke one of the cigarettes under the shade of the oak tree.

One evening in August the men were sitting around under the shed in front of the store, drinking their Spearmans and talking as they always did, when Jessie came up through the graveyard with his eggs. Anse had come in already and was sitting there under the shed on a crate with his back to the road. He hadn't yet gone in to buy his Spearmans. It was Thursday, and he only had fifty cents un-til payday on Friday. He was also out of cigarettes, so that meant just the one Spearmans with the package of cigarettes. He was saving it for a little while.

Walt called to Jessie from where he was standing in the door-way under the shed. "Can't stand a suck-egg coon, Jessie. Billy Coon ever gets loose, he'll be heading straight for your henhouse and suck up ever egg you got. It's going to be all your own fault when he comes down there and sucks up all your eggs, so don't you come blaming me when it happens. You the one gave him the taste to suck eggs, Jessie. It's going to be all your own fault."

Anse couldn't hardly stand it that Walt showed he liked the old Negro so much.

"Makes my ass pucker like it wants a dip of snuff," he would say.

Jessie had caught Anse once, down in the woods when he was fifteen, pulling himself off, and he had been afraid for years that he would tell on him. He didn't much think he would anymore, because probably the old Negro had forgotten all about it since then, but he had carried the fear and resentment around with him so long that he couldn't shake it off. Whenever the old Negro showed up, the feeling would come on him again, and Anse would get choked and sullen, just looking at the ground and not talking, waiting for the old man to let out the secret and betray him.

After Walt spoke to him, Jessie left Billy and walked over under the shed. Anse wasn't looking at him, and just as Jessie came up, Anse shifted his foot and tripped him. He didn't mean to do it, but it looked like he did. All the men thought it was done on purpose. Jessie fell forward, trying to catch himself with his arms, but the one hooked through the basket caught, and when he hit the ground it sank down into the eggs, breaking most of them.

"God damn you, Anse," said Walt, stepping out from the doorway of the store, "what you got to do a mean thing like that for?"

Anse looked at him, surprised. "I never did," he said.

"I seen you when you done it, damn it," said Walt. "What you mean you never did?"

Jessie was getting up by himself. None of the men under the shed looked at him. They sat there holding their Spearmans bottles in both hands, looking down at the ground between their feet.

"I mean I never did trip him a purpose," said Anse.

"Shit you say," said Walt. "I seen you."

"What'd I want to go and do that for?" asked Anse.

"How'd I know what makes you do any of your mean tricks?" said Walt. "Some people just born with a asshole where their heads ought to be." The men all laughed at that, and Anse glared at them.

Maude had come out to see what was happening. She gave Anse a sharp look. "You hurt, Jessie?" she asked.

"No'm," he said. He was holding the basket in his right hand now. Yellow egg yolks smeared his arm.

She took him into the store.

"How the hell would I know what you got in your mind when you go pulling your shit-eating tricks, like tripping that old nigger there, and fooling around with Billy Coon? You tell me, Anse. How come you always got to be taking it out on somebody, fooling around with Billy there and throwing firecrackers at him?"

"I done that *one* time," said Anse.

"You got to always be jumping at him and scaring the shit out of him," said Walt. "Whyn't you leave the coon alone, Anse? Ain't nothing you do but just make him mad so I can't hardly get near him after you been jumping at him and scaring the shit out of him. I ain't never going to tame him good, long as you got to keep coming up and throwing firecrackers at him and jumping out at him so you get him all excited and scared."

Maude came to the door again. "Jessie's all right," she said. "I sent him in the kitchen to clean himself up some. Ain't many eggs left."

"How much we pay him last night?" Walt asked.

"Dollar," Maude said.

"Give him seventy-five cents," Walt said.

"What about the Co-Cola?" she asked.

"Give him a Co-Cola, too," he said.

After Maude had gone back into the store, Walt looked at Anse. "You wouldn't be feeling like you ought to pay some of that?" he said.

Anse fingered the fifty cents in his pocket, looking at Walt. "Maude's a fine-looking woman," he said, his eyes looking steady at Walt. "How come you got to be always spending your time with that coon when you got a fine-looking woman like that to keep you busy?"

Walt looked at Anse. "Some more of your half-assed bullshit on the way, Anse," he said. "I feel it in my bones."

Anse cut his eyes away from Walt to the men, then back to Walt. "You got some kind of hot pants for that coon, Walt?" he said. "You got some kind of hot pants for Billy Coon, and I'm spoiling your fun? Seems like you ought to be saving it for Maude and not using it up on that coon there. She'll take all you can give her, if you just save it up and don't waste it. Man your age can't waste it no-how. You got to save it up and be careful so you can do Maude like you ought. Lest you want somebody else to do it for you."

Maude was thirty-seven, but she looked like twenty-five. Her face was a little sharp-featured and hard, more like the face of a handsome man than a woman. But the men liked it well enough. All of them thought they could tell she would be good in bed from the way her eyes looked. Walt was forty-nine, and they liked to kid him about it.

"Here it comes, boys," said Walt, stepping up into the doorway. "Get your feet up off the ground. When a shithead starts to running off at the mouth, there ain't but one safe thing to do. Hold your breath and get your feet up off the ground."

Anse didn't say anything.

"Seems like you the one got the hot pants for Billy Coon there," Walt said. "You the one always got to be fooling around with him and wouldn't let him alone. Whyn't you go get you a nanny goat or something, and leave Billy Coon alone?"

All the men laughed. Anse had been caught with a nanny goat once when he was fifteen. Everybody had been shocked and thought of it as queer, even though all the boys in McAfee County sneaked down to the cow barns at night, and some even went into the pig pens. But goats were scarce, and the novelty of it worried them. They were afraid that Anse might be turning into a pervert. Anse didn't like to be reminded of it.

Three things he couldn't stand to be reminded of. The nanny goat, the time Jessie caught him pulling himself off down in the woods and the way the older boys had yelled at him when he was little.

When he was three and four, the big boys found out they could send him home crying by yelling, "Anse, Anse, got 'em in his pants." He didn't know what it meant, but it scared him nearly to death for

them to say it. When they did it to him, he would go home crying
and tell his mother. She never could take it seriously, because she
thought it was funny herself. His father would get mad when he
came in crying, and would make him go back out again. So he would
crawl under the house and lie there crying to himself, not even able
to start to think about what the big boys meant when they said it.
Whenever he began to get mad and scared at the same time, he
would hear them yelling it again.

"Seems like you the one got the hot pants for Billy there," said
Walt. "You the one always got to be fooling around with him and
won't let him alone."

Jessie came out with his Coca-Cola. He was also smoking a cigarette.

"You all right, Jessie?" Walt asked.

"Yas, suh," said Jessie. "Miss Maude fix me up so I be just fine."
He limped over to the tree where the other colored men were sitting.

"Whyn't you try Jessie's henhouse?" said Walt, watching Jessie
limp away. "Whyn't you just go over there and get you one of Jessie's
Rhode Island Reds and leave Billy Coon alone?"

"You want to let out a contract on Maude?" said Anse. "I be
glad to oblige you if you want to let out a contract on her. Then
you can stop saving it up and go spend all your time with
Billy Coon."

"Tell you what," said Walt. "Tell you what, Anse. You just go
on over there to Jessie's henhouse and pick you out one of them
Rhode Island Reds of his, and I'll buy her for you. You can pick out
any one you want to, and I'll buy her for you for a present. Then
you can take her home with you and leave Billy Coon alone."

"Whyn't you get you one of them Rhode Island Reds for yourself?" said Anse. "Get you one of them Rhode Island Reds and let
me have the contract on Maude."

"You can have any one you want to," said Walt, "and I'll buy
her for you. Only one thing. You got to pick out a pretty one. I ain't
going to pay for no ugly chicken," he said. "You want me to go with
you and help you pick out a pretty one?"

"I want you to kiss my ass," said Anse.

" 'Course, when you do come home with one of Jessie's chickens," said Walt, "I reckon that fist of yours is going to just turn green with envy." The men all laughed at that. "Specially if I pick out a real pretty one for you," he added.

"Whyn't you kiss my ass?" said Anse, hunching his shoulders and looking at the ground between his feet.

"Don't know what I'll do about Dee Witt here," said Walt, nodding toward Dee Witt Toomey, who was sitting on a Coca-Cola case, leaning against the front of the store and giggling. "Dee Witt's going to be mighty put out about that red chicken too."

Dee Witt giggled, looking at Walt.

"You going to be jealous of that chicken, Dee Witt?" asked Walt.

"Come on, Dee Witt," Anse said. His voice had an edge on it. "Shut up the goddamn laughing and come on. Sometimes you sound like you ain't got good sense."

"You going to share the chicken with Dee Witt?" someone asked.

"Ain't nobody pulling your chain," Anse said, looking around at the men under the shed to see who it was.

"Maybe Anse'd rather have him a rooster," somebody else said.

"How about that, Anse?" said Walt. "You want me to get you a rooster instead?"

"Then Dee Witt really would be getting jealous," said somebody.

"God damn it, shut up that laughing," Anse said, kicking the Coca-Cola case out from under Dee Witt. He flopped down on the ground, still laughing.

"Maybe I'll buy Dee Witt a chicken too," said Walt. "Just so he wouldn't get his feelings hurt."

Anse was standing near Walt, and he suddenly swung his fist at him, thinking to move fast enough to catch him off guard. Walt got his hand up and caught Anse by the wrist. Then he clamped down, and Anse's whole hand began to swell up and turn red. He twisted up his face from the pain, and Walt forced the arm back so he had to drop down on his knees in front of him. Then Walt twirled him around and gave him a kick on the seat of the pants. Anse flopped forward so he was down on his hands and knees in front of Walt, facing away from him.

"You don't move it out of there, I'm going to boot it again," he said.

Anse crawled off a little ways on his hands and knees and then got up.

"You kiss my ass," he said, rubbing his hand to get the circulation started again.

"Whistle, so I'll know where it's at," said Walt.

Anse turned and stalked away, with Dee Witt trailing along behind. The men under the shed were laughing as he went off down the road.

Across the road from Shotford's grocery, in the yard of the Golden Rainbow Church, is a big live oak tree. It canopies almost the whole of the east side of the churchyard, and under it the ground is sandy and bare. On the east side of the tree, away from the church and parallel to the road, a big limb reaches out. Moss hangs down from it, and about twenty feet out from the trunk the limb forks. It is the lowest limb on that side, but still high up. The fork is more than twenty feet above the ground. Once they lynched a Negro from the limb.

It was seven-thirty in the morning, and a small knot of men had gathered under the fork of the big limb. They were looking up toward the fork, and the morning light came in under the limb, lighting up the underside of the tree and falling on their faces, making them squint.

The steel stake with the looped eye was jammed in the fork of the limb. At the end of the chain Billy Coon hung, turning slowly in the air above their heads. His front paws hung down by his sides limply, and his hind legs were drawn up. The red collar was pulled forward on his face, so his cheeks pouched out and his ears canted forward. The chain ran out from the collar under his jaw, and his head was cocked back by it. He looked like he was sitting down and reaching for something, hanging there in the middle of the air above the faces of the men looking up at him as he turned slowly on the end of the chain.

Blanche lay on the ground under the fork, her head resting on her front paws, and her eyes cut back toward Walt, who was standing beside her.

"I know he done it," Walt said. "I know he done it just as sure as I'm standing here."

He kicked Blanche, and she rolled over on her back with her paws flopped up in the air. "How come you let him do it?" he said, looking down at her. She wagged her stump of a tail, scraping it in the dirt.

"He couldn't never get that close to Billy Coon," said Jessie.

"Oh, Dee Witt *done* it," said Walt, "but it was Anse put him up to it."

From the place where the stake had been in front of the store, a mark cut the dirt across the road and up to the base of the live oak tree. Walt looked at the line scraped in the dirt. "Anse done that too," he said, "with a stick, to make it look like Billy got the stake out and dragged it across here himself." He looked back toward the fork where Billy was hanging.

"It's a mean goddamn thing to do," he said, kicking his shoe in the dirt, erasing the part of the scraped line where it went by, going up to the tree. "Mean enough for Anse. Dee Witt don't know no better. Anse put him up to it, God damn him."

He kept looking up at Billy Coon. "What I can't figure out," he said, "is why he went to all that trouble. He must have known we'd figure out he was the one anyway. How come he didn't just walk up there and beat his head in with a stick?"

No one spoke.

"All that trouble," said Walt. "God damn the mean son-of-a-bitch."

"Billy Coon was all right," said Jessie, looking up at the limp, stretched body of the animal hanging there from the fork of the limb. Walt didn't say anything.

"Be all right if I take care of him?" Jessie asked. "I be right glad to take care of him, Mr. Walt," he said.

"Where you going to put him?" Walt asked, looking at Jessie. Then he looked away, saying, "Shit. It don't make no difference."

"I put him over there on the side of the yard," said Jessie. "He be right close there, so you can come see when you would want to."

"It don't matter," said Walt. "You can take him if you want to. You was better to him than anybody else anyway." The men had started to walk off, going down the road in different directions. Walt pulled his hat down and started to walk back to his store.

"He was all right," said Jessie, looking at Walt.

"Yes," said Walt, walking away. He stopped. "I'll give you a package of Lucky Strike cigarettes and two Co-Colas for your trouble," he said.

"Ain't no trouble," said Jessie.

When Jessie was a young boy his grandfather had told him a story about the slave graveyard on the plantation where he had lived. The story had made a deep impression on him, so that he never forgot it. When he had grown up and become a man, he passed it on to other children in his turn.

"Ever now and then one of them there graves would just . . . drop in," he would say, his voice low and serious, so the children would hang on the words and realize what he was going to tell them. "Folks that would come up and look seen the bodies down there in they grave clothes, and the women's hair was growed all the way down to they feets, wrapping them around like it was a nest of black snakes. And they fingernails was all twisty and pale and long as a butcher knife on the ends of they fingers."

It made him sweat all over just to tell the stories again, but he looked on it as his duty and obligation, out of remembrance of the feeling it had given him when his grandfather had told them to him years before. He grieved for the bodies of the dead, wrapped in the choking, snaky coils, and lying, he thought, uneasily under the sandy mounds beneath the moss-draped trees of the graveyard. It made him feel like he wanted to do something about it.

Jessie was a deacon in the Golden Rainbow Church, and because of this he had to go to all the funerals that were held in the graveyard behind the church. Every funeral that he attended brought back to him his feeling of grief about the bodies, and the sense of obligation that he was the one who had to do something about it.

When there was a funeral, the undertaker provided most of the equipment. It made a lovely show—with a dark green canopy over the grave, saying "*Beckworth & Sons, Inc., Funeral Directors*" printed in white along the scalloped edges, and a bright green mat of imitation grass draped over the mound of dirt at the edge of the grave, and folding chairs under the canopy, with a cardboard fan printed with a Bible picture in color laid out on every chair. But the markers that they supplied for the graves were small and insignificant and depressing to Jessie.

At the foot of the mound, after the canopy and the grass mat and the chairs were taken away, was a small aluminum holder, shaped like a harp. Into it, behind a cellophane window, they placed a printed card on which the name of the deceased, the dates of his birth and death, were written with a ball-point pen. At the top was the motto: "Ashes to ashes and dust to dust." At the bottom of the card was the message: "Beckworth & Sons, Inc., Funeral Directors. Fine Funerals at Economical Rates." When the funeral was over, one of the Beckworths would spear this little marker into the ground at the foot of the grave just before they left with the canopy and the grass mat. After the dirt settled into the grave and the mound disappeared, it didn't make much of a show.

John Henry's monument was the only one. And it was so big it just made the rest of the graveyard seem more empty and bare. Having it there made Jessie feel more worried and guilty than ever.

Occasionally a survivor, usually a woman, would try to do something to mark off the last resting place of her kin—bringing a painted oil can with plastic flowers in it, or a Christmas wreath salvaged out of some garbage can. One had outlined her husband's grave with blue Milk of Magnesia bottles, buried neck-down in the sand. But most of the graves just had the little aluminum marker. And pretty soon it would get stepped on, so it couldn't be seen, or it would be lost altogether. Jessie wanted to do something to make it better. But he didn't know what to do.

When they poured the new steps for the church, he found out.

The Men's Bible Class at Golden Rainbow got up a project to replace the wooden steps to the church with new ones of brick and concrete. Fulmer Johnson, who did brickwork for a contractor in Darien, directed the project. He built the brick abutments on either side, and helped them plan and set up the forms for the steps.

The next day after they made the pour, Jessie came down to

the church early in the morning to see if the concrete had set up. It had. During the night, while it was still wet, someone had taken a stick and written on the bottom step: FUCK NIGGERS—SEPTEMBER 1956. There was also a rough place where whoever it was had put his initials, then decided against it and erased them.

Jessie felt the step. It was hard. There were the letters frozen into the hard surface of the concrete.

"I be damned," he said, running his hand over the letters. "Whyn't I think about that before?"

His problems were solved.

When Fulmer poured the slabs to put on the tops of the brick abutments at the sides, Jessie watched him carefully as he set up the forms and oiled them. Later that night he came back and printed GOD IS LOVE in the wet concrete with his finger. The next morning it was set up hard. For the first time he was able to think about the bodies in the graves without feeling cold inside.

In a clearing between his house and the graveyard he made a place to work. Then he got Fulmer Johnson to show him how to make a form for the headstone and give him a demonstration on how to oil it and mix the concrete and make the pour, then trowel it off so it would be smooth. From time to time Fulmer would drop by to help Jessie and advise him, until he had gotten straight on all the details. But it didn't take Jessie long to learn how to do it. Eventually he got a headstone made for all of the graves that he or anyone else could identify. There were slight variations in the inscriptions— occasionally some relative wanted something in particular, or the circumstances of the death were unusual—but they were all pretty much the same:

   OR:

After he had made headstones for all the graves he could identify, he began on the others. He had a stock inscription that served them all:

The fact that he had only the one mold didn't seem to worry anyone else very much, though it sometimes worried Jessie.

"Seem like it make 'em all look alike," he would say. Then he would reason it out. " 'Course, they *is* all dead."

He decided that if he started making different ones, then everybody would want one special, and he couldn't ever keep up with that. So he just let it go. Anyway, the survivors would still come down and put their individual touches on the graves—like the blue Milk of Magnesia bottles, or pieces of colored glass, or sometimes just plain rocks laid out to mark off the grave.

Even if they all did look alike, at least the concrete headstones were big and solid. Better than the aluminum holders and the cards from the funeral home, which the rain washed out and people stepped on and bent down onto the ground so they couldn't be seen. It looked like a real graveyard with the headstones, instead of the park it had looked like with just John Henry's marker standing by itself in the middle.

For Billy Coon, Jessie took time out from his farming to dig the grave himself. He decided it didn't have to be as deep as for a person, but he dug it neatly anyway, squaring the sides and getting all the loose dirt out of the bottom. He put Billy in an orange crate, after he had knocked out the divider, laying him on his back and crossing his front paws. He thought that over for a while, since it was a coon—looking down at him in the orange crate and thinking that he should perhaps not put him on his back. But he didn't feel right about having him huddled down there on his stomach, so he decided to do it that way, putting in the red collar and the chain that Walt had told him to bury with Billy. Then he had laid a plank over the top of the orange crate and filled the hole back up, being careful again, and squaring off the sides of the mound when he had finished.

After he buried Billy Coon, he went down to the clearing and poured a headstone for him. He wanted to have a smaller one, which would have suited the grave better, but he couldn't make a special form for Billy either, so he had to use the regular one. When he had trowled it off smooth, he wrote the inscription into the wet concrete with his finger:

After he finished, he washed up his tools and went home to supper. It was coming on dark, and he didn't like to work on graveyard things after the sun went down.

Jessie looked down at the tombstone in the mold. It was too late to do anything about it. The concrete had set up hard. He could fill in the new inscription with fresh concrete, but he couldn't put a new one on. He would just have to throw away the headstone, wasting all the cement, and pour another one.

He sat beside the mold until the new pour had set up too hard to be changed. It was nearly midnight before he went home. Before he got there he had started to remember the snaky black hair and fingernails again.

Jessie worried about Anse making a joke of graveyard things. He thought about it the next morning while he was burying the ruined headstone. The trouble was, Anse was so mean he didn't know what to do about him. He decided to talk to Walt Shotford about it.

"I reckon it's some kind of a joke, Anse," said Dee Witt. They were standing under the big live oak tree where Billy Coon had been found. Right under the forked limb, looking down into the freshly dug grave, and then up to the thing hanging from the fork of the limb overhead. It was just sunup. The first streaks of light were coming out, so Anse and Dee Witt could see better every minute just what was there under the tree, hanging from the limb.

They had been out to the Sportsmans Lodge on Highway 17 until three o'clock that morning. When they left there, they had driven to Anse's house in his pickup. Anse had parked it in the yard and gone into the house to go to bed. Dee Witt had started home, walking down the road. As he went by the Golden Rainbow Church, he had seen the grave and the headstone, and hadn't known what to do about it. He had gone on back and told Anse.

"It's a piss-poor kind of a joke," said Anse. "A goddamn nigger joke is what it is."

Under the limb of the oak tree was a freshly dug grave. It had been dug very neatly, with the sides squared off and most of the loose dirt taken out of the bottom. The mound of loose dirt had been piled on the side away from the road, so anyone passing could see the hole in the ground. At the head of the grave was a concrete headstone:

From the fork of the limb over the grave hung a small doll. It hung by a piece of black fishline that had been tied around its neck, and then to a stick that had been jammed in the fork.

"Nigger joke," Anse said again.

They looked up at the doll, turning slowly at the end of the string. They could make it out clearly now, because it was getting lighter all the time. The doll was crude. It was made out of concrete, with rough places where the fingers that had shaped it had stuck in the concrete and pulled away little peaks and swirls. A big dab of red paint on top of its head identified it. They could see the red on the back of its head as it turned slowly at the end of the fishline.

"Get it down, Dee Witt," said Anse. "I can't stand no nigger joke anyway."

Dee Witt giggled. He looked at Anse, then up at the doll. "He done put the hex on you, Anse," he said.

"I know who done it," said Anse. "I'll fix his black ass. Now get up there and get it down."

"How'm I going to get it down?" Dee Witt asked.

"Climb the goddamn tree," said Anse.

"How come I got to climb the tree when you the one got the hex?" Dee Witt asked. "I near about fell and busted my ass last time."

"Get up there and get it down," said Anse.

"Whyn't you do it?" said Dee Witt, whining. "Maybe I fall and bust my head up there. You the one got the hex on you."

"*Maybe* you fall and bust it if you do," said Anse. "Sure as hell you going to get it busted if you don't." He looked at Dee

Witt levelly out of his pale green eyes. "I'm going to count ten," he said. "If your ass ain't up that tree when I get to ten, I'm going to make you wish it was."

"I don't like to climb no trees," said Dee Witt. "Look how high that limb is."

"You going to be a whole lot better off up there than down here when I get to ten. I ain't going to argue with you," said Anse. "One . . ."

"Here," said Dee Witt. "Maybe we can get it down some other way." He picked up a clod of dirt out of the mound beside the grave and threw it at the stick jammed in the fork.

"Two . . . ," said Anse. "We ain't got all day. Sun be up good before long. I want that mother down from there right now. Three . . ."

Dee Witt picked up another clod of dirt and threw it. It hit the stick and dislodged it. The doll fell into the grave. When it hit the bottom, it broke. The head snapped off, and the two pieces lay there in the bottom of the grave, the body on its back and the head turned over to one side.

"Now you done it," said Anse.

"I got the piss ant down, didn't I?" said Dee Witt.

"You busted it," said Anse.

Dee Witt looked at Anse. "You ain't worried, are you, Anse?" he said. "It ain't only just a doll," he said. "You wouldn't worry about no nigger joke like that, would you?"

Anse looked down at the broken doll in the bottom of the grave. He clenched and unclenched his hands, and then he wiped them on the legs of his pants. His eyes darted around, looking over toward Shotford's to see if anybody was coming.

"Get down there and fetch it out," he said.

Dee Witt looked down at the doll and then up at Anse. "You wouldn't really worry about no nigger joke like that, would you?" he said.

"Get it out," said Anse.

Dee Witt stood on the edge of the grave looking at him. "You get it," he said. "You the one got the hex on you. You get down there and fetch it out."

Anse looked at him. "I'm going to knock your half-ass off for you, Dee Witt," he said. "Then you ain't going to have no ass at all. Now get down there and fetch it out. One . . ."

"I don't like to be getting down into no grave," said Dee Witt. "Even if it ain't nothing but only a nigger joke."

"Two . . . ," said Anse.

"Fuck you," Dee Witt said.

Anse looked at him hard. His mouth was still open a little from the "two." "What did you say?" he said.

"I said fuck you," said Dee Witt. "Get it out yourself."

Anse made a move toward him, and Dee Witt ran out into the road. He was talking loudly now. "You got the hex. You fetch it out," he said.

"You going to do what I tell you?" Anse said, keeping his voice down.

"Kiss my ass," said Dee Wit. "I ain't going to get down in no grave."

Anse darted his eyes around. Then he reached down and picked up a clod from the mound beside the grave and threw it at Dee Witt. The expression on Dee Witt's face never changed. The clod exploded on his forehead, spattering dirt over his face and sticking to his lips. His eyebrows were raised a little, and he seemed to be thinking about something a long way off, standing there with his eyes out of focus. He raised his hand slowly, wiping his face, slobbering and spitting out the dirt.

"You scared to do it," he said, talking with his mouth held open, spitting and trying to get the dirt out. "I ain't going to do it for you," he said. "Not this time. You get down there and fetch it out yourself."

Anse picked up another clod. Dee Witt turned his head to the side and hunched his shoulder when he saw it coming. The clod broke on the side of his head. He shuffled off down the road out of range; then he turned back to Anse, making a megaphone of his hands. "Anse, Anse, got 'em in his pants," he yelled.

Anse stood glaring at him down the road, then looked down at the broken doll in the bottom of the grave. He wiped his hand hard across his mouth, his hand balled into a fist. He darted his eyes over toward Shotford's and up and down the road to see if anyone was coming.

"Half-ass," he said under his breath. "Goddamn half-ass."

He picked up a clod from the mound beside the grave and threw it at the doll. It hit and broke, splattering dirt into the bottom of the grave. He picked up another, then another, throwing them down at the doll in the bottom. Every time a clod hit it, the doll would jump. The head rolled away toward the side of the grave. One of the legs broke off.

Anse picked up a double handful of dirt and dropped it on the doll, partially covering it up. He worked fast, scooping up handful after handful of dirt and dropping them into the grave until he had covered up all of the doll.

Then he went around to where the headstone was, and put his foot against it at the top and pushed it over. It fell on its back with the lettering up. So he got his fingers under the edge and heaved it over where the writing wouldn't show.

"I be damn," he said. "How'd he do that?"

The back side had the same inscription as the front.

"Nigger joke," he said, sitting down on the tombstone at the head of the grave and looking into the bottom where the doll was lying covered up with dirt. He hugged his arms around his chest, rubbing his hands on his upper arms.

A clod hit him on the back of the head, exploding dirt down his collar.

"Anse, Anse, got 'em in his pants," Dee Witt sang, yelling through his hands. Then he ran off down the road.

Anse got up and shook his shirt to get the dirt out. He pulled the tails out and jiggled himself up and down, watching Dee Witt run off down the road toward Shotford's store. Dee Witt went into Shotford's side yard. As he passed the shed in front of the store, Anse heard the screen door slam. Shotford stepped out from under the shed, leaning on the pump with his arms folded and looking across the road at Anse.

Anse stopped jiggling, standing there bent forward at the waist by the side of the grave, holding his shirttails out behind him, and looking at Shotford. He looked like he was making a cursty.

He undid his belt and then turned his back on Shotford, starting to tuck his shirttails back in. Across the graveyard, on the far
edge, Jessie Wight was standing. His arms hung down limply at his
sides, but one foot was extended a little to the back, as if Jessie had
been sneaking up on him, and Anse had caught him at it and frozen
him in mid-stride. Anse froze too for a minute, looking at Jessie, with
his hand already shoved partway down inside his pants, putting his
shirttail back in. He looked back over his shoulder to see if Walt was
still there. He was there. Leaning against the gasoline pump with his
arms folded, looking at him. Walt's forearms looked enormous. Dee
Witt had gone up to the hydrant in the side yard and put his head
under it, washing off the dirt from the clods Anse had thrown at
him.

Anse turned back around, not watching Jessie or Walt, and finished tucking his shirt back into his pants. When he finished, he
took a deep breath, standing up straight and looking up and down
the road. There was still no one else coming. He spit on his hands
and rubbed them together; then he got down and began to wrestle
the tombstone up so he could get it on his shoulder. It was too heavy
for him to carry it using his arms alone.

It took a while. The stone was heavier than it looked.
Anse guessed two hundred pounds. And it was an awkward size—
too short for him to get his shoulder under it without lifting it off
the ground. So he had to kneel down and lean it against his shoulder and then pull it up with his arms until he got it in place to balance. He could have done it better, but he had to do it smoothly,
since Walt and Jessie were watching. It scraped and tore his shoulder while he was getting it into place.

When he thought he had it balanced, he straightened up, bracing it with his arms, and walked down into the road with it. He
made about fifty yards, and then his shoulder muscle rolled out
from under the stone and let it come down pinching on his shoul-
derblade. There wasn't any question of trying to stand the pain. The
shoulder just collapsed on him, and he had to let the stone fall. It
hit on its side, then flopped down flat in the middle of the road.

He stooped down and tried to get it up again, but the raw place
hurt him too much to slide it up. And the arm wasn't any use to him

now anyway. So he just had to let the stone flop down in front of him in the middle of the road.

He glanced off down the road, kneeling there with the headstone lying flat in the middle of the road in front of him. Way off, almost as far as he could make them out, two figures stepped up onto the side of the road, then turned, coming toward him, walking on the shoulder. Anse tried to get the stone up again, scraping his hands pulling at it, though he knew before he tried that he couldn't do it. All he could do was raise it up on its side, balancing it on the edge.

Finally he pushed it over flat in the middle of the road again; then he crawled up over it on his hands and knees, his arms straddled out on either side. He knelt there over the stone, panting and looking off up the road at the two men. Then he looked down at the stone beneath him, reading the inscription on it upside down. Over and over again, until his eyes went out of focus, and he couldn't see it anymore. He could hear the two men.

Without looking up, he lowered himself down onto the stone, covering it with his body. He laced his hands behind his neck and clamped his arms to the sides of his head, pressing his forehead into the dirt of the road and shutting out the light from the sides. He tried to wrap his body around the stone so that all of it would be covered up.

"Nigger joke . . . ," he whispered to himself, clamping his eyes shut, ". . . half-ass nigger joke."

A Worker of Miracles

The Rainbow Pool is a small, open body of water—some forty-five or fifty acres in all—that fills a basin on the northwest border of the Dorchester Swamp. The water is dyed black from the saps leeched out of the cypresses and live oaks that grow in it, and from the leaves shed by the live oaks. It is clear water. Scoop up a glassful to look at it, and it hardly seems discolored at all. But the tiny particles, held in suspension, accumulate and make the blackness. Holding your hand just under the surface, you can see it clearly, but if you plunge it deeper, it will fade slowly until you can see it being amputated in the tannin-dyed blackness of the water.

The pool gets its name from the colors reflected on its surface —green and gray and black from the moss-draped live oaks and cypresses growing along its shore and in the water, blue and green and yellow from the patches of open sky that come in through the overhanging branches of the trees, pink and yellow and purple and white from the azaleas and honeysuckle and wisteria on the banks. Because the trees shelter it, the surface is generally smooth as polished glass. You can throw in a stone and watch the ripples spread all the way to the opposite shore. The black undercolor gives back the reflections in a way that makes them more intense. It is a very placid spot.

Brother Fisco uses a small cove just southwest of the Dew Drop fishing camp for the baptizings of his Two-Oak Missionary Baptist Church. Strictly considered, it is not a proper place for baptizing, because of the still water. He has tried spots here and there along the banks of the Altamahatchee and Oconee rivers, but he always comes back to Rainbow Pool. He is a pious man, and he likes the stillness.

"God's down there," he says. "God's down there in the water."

He has not always been a pious man—only for the last nine years. Brother Fisco—Garnet Fisco it was then (pronounced *Gar Net*, as if it were two names)—had gotten religion at a tent meeting in the spring of 1954, when he was thirty-one years old. Gotten it for the fourth time, really. But that was the time it stuck. He stopped drinking, stopped smoking, wouldn't let his wife, Della, wear lipstick or shorts—even though she was a handsome woman— and had torn up the two decks of playing cards they had in the house. He had also joined the Two-Oak Missionary Baptist Church.

For a year he was the most active member of the congregation—sometimes stepping in to deliver the sermon when Brother Campbell, the regular preacher, was called away to remote and more deprived congregations that could not afford a regular preacher every Sunday. Then, in 1955, when Brother Campbell left to go back full time to the mobile-home business in Brunswick, Georgia, Brother Fisco had stepped in and taken over the pulpit. No one objected. Finding a preacher wasn't that easy for a congregation that didn't want to pay one.

For Brother Fisco, preaching is a full-time concern, but not even a part-time means of livelihood. He gets four or five chicken dinners a month out of it, and a certain status in the community. But he has to make his living working, just like everyone else in McAfee County. By trade he is a cabinetmaker—a skilled one. With a toolbox made to display his craft—a hideous and intricate wonder of inlays and marquetry and ornate carving—filled with small saws and chisels that have been dulled to a soft glow with use. Six days a week he follows that trade. Sundays he does God's work in the Two-Oak church. As he fits the intricate joints on weekdays, he thinks of the power he sometimes feels in the church on Sundays, and he longs to be a full-time Man of God. But he is philosophical.

"Thy will be done," he says.

The Two-Oak church is a depressing structure—inside and out. It was built by the congregation just after the Second World War— a white clapboard box, with a steeple, and regular double-hung windows with panes that are painted blue. The light coming in through the blue paint makes the inside gloomy and depressing. The faces of the congregation look like mummies, with an air of settled-in sadness and melancholy. Brother Fisco's face looks like the face of a handsome man with cancer. Ordinarily he looks like a man who is dying. In the blue light of the church—except when he stands to the pulpit for the preaching—his face looks like the face of a man who is dead.

He has used his skill with wood to ornament the church a good deal in the eight years he has been the preacher there. For that alone his congregation should be grateful. He has carved a six-foot-long replica of the Praying Hands, which he painted white and mounted on the top of the steeple. He has made a pulpit that is even more intricate and ornate than his toolbox, with scenes representing the Ten Commandments inlaid in mahogany panels with mother-of-pearl—three months to make each panel. He has also carved a good many miscellaneous scrolls and crosses and plaques with verses from the Bible to decorate the pews and walls.

But his masterpiece is the giant crucifix that looms behind the pulpit, filling the back end of the church. He felled the cypress tree himself, then adzed the beams by hand into twelve-inch-square timbers—twelve feet tall and eight feet wide. With the cross arms fitted in an intricate lap joint, locked with wooden pins, that took him a full day to make. The Christ figure is a mannequin that he found in a trash can in the alley behind Levy's department store in Savannah, patched and restored with spackling compound, and dressed in a flowing garment that Della sewed for it by hand. It is attached to the cross with railroad spikes, fitted carefully through its hands and feet, then driven into the wood of the beams. Red paint marks the nail wounds in the hands and feet, and streams down its face from the barbed-wire crown of thorns.

Still, the blue light from the windows overcomes the grandness of the crucifix—just as it overcomes everything else. And Brother Fisco is happy when baptizing Sunday comes around so he can take his congregation out into the sunlight for a change.

It is not only the cheerful yellow-green morning light, filtering through the branches of the cypress and oak, that makes him love baptizing Sunday.

The relatives always want to be there to see it, so he can count on a good turnout. Nothing like the crowds of sixty or seventy who come for Christmas and Easter and the Fourth of July. But a respectable group of thirty-five or so. Something like a real congregation. Large enough to make him feel he is doing the Lord's work.

And the music. He especially likes the music. Sung haltingly by the group spotted on the bank, dressed in their Sunday clothes, with their Sunday piety to quieten them under the trees. It lifts him and raises him, showing him that the Lord's work is not in vain.

He will stand before them with the child to be baptized, and perhaps Mr. Deering, or some other of the deacons, to help him with the immersion. His coat off, but the good suit pants on. And a stiff white shirt with a tie.

He has to be the one to start them singing, and he puts as much volume as he can into the first two or three bars, straining to pull them after him: "*Sha . . . all we . . . ee ga . . . ather at the ri . . . iver . . .*"

Just getting them started. Then his wife Della's clear, sweet alto will rise above him back of the group, lifting the burden of the song away, so that he will let his own voice slack off, and with his arm around the child, he will turn and lead her into the black water of the pool, while the chorus on the bank swells behind him: "*The bea . . . auti . . . iful the bea . . . auti . . . iful ri . . . iver . . .*"

Wading out with a little air of expectancy into the black water, wearing the pants to his good suit, feeling the sand and pebbles of the bottom as he slides his stockinged feet along. Not sure but that he will step on something that will hurt him, and knowing that if he does he will have to just step on it and keep going . . . knee-deep . . . thigh-deep . . . until the child is out above her waist, floating on her water-amputated legs—the song arching into the yellow-green light above him and leading him on: "*Ga . . . ather with the sai . . . ints a . . . aat the ri . . . . iver . . .*"

Della timing the song so that they get to the last line just as he and the child reach the right depth for the baptizing, then swelling her voice behind the chorus, shooting it out above them like the last roman candle on the Fourth of July: "*That . . . aat flo . . . oows by the thro . . . oone . . . o . . . o . . . of Go . . . od . . .*"
Then all standing silent, waiting for him to say the words.

He and the child would be facing them, Deering on the child's left. For a moment he wouldn't say anything, waiting while the song trails off through the cypress trees into the yellow air.

Then he would gather himself, not looking at the ones on the shore, nor at the child standing in the water to his left, but lifting his eyes and raising it up above them there. Saying the words.

" 'Then Peter said unto them, Repent, and be baptized every one of you in the name of Jesus Christ for the remission of sins, and ye *shall* receive the gift of the Holy Ghost.' "

As he speaks, he will raise his left hand gently, holding it in the center of her back, the fingers spread wide to give her support. Then Deering will take his position, ready to help if need be, and he will whisper to the child, "Get a hold of your nose with your left hand . . . Clamp it down tight . . . Cover your eyes with your right hand . . . ," whispering, ". . . *left* hand."

Placing his splayed right hand over the child's two, covering her face under the handkerchief. He can feel her contracting, going small between his hands . . . the size of a child's hollow rubber ball. Beginning to pitch over backward as she'd been told . . . leaning on him.

"I'll tell you . . . ," he would whisper, ". . . it ain't going to be slow."

Then again the words: " 'I baptize thee in the *name* of the Father, and of the Son, and of the *Holy* Ghost. Amen.' "

He would sway her three times, then pause, whispering, "Catch your breath, child," as the congregation responds their "Amen." Then he would be sliding her backward into the black water, watching the streaming hair waving over the white hands and the handkerchief. Only a moment before he would bring her back up sputtering into the yellow air.

The moment he would see her there beneath the water, with the strands of hair snaking across his hand, it would bring a power into him. He would feel that he might squeeze his hands together, make a motion with them, and the child would disappear. Vanish into the black water, like a magician gesturing away a cage with a live pigeon in it, as he had seen on the television.

"I am the Lord's chosen Vessel," he says to himself.

Thinking of what the congregation would say as he raised

his empty hands in a *hallelujah*—after the Lord would have taken her away.

Then she would be back up out of the water, rubbing her eyes with her fists and wiping the wet hair away. The congregation on the bank standing silent, until Della's voice would lift behind them, and they would break into the song again as he was leading her to the bank, his arm around her shoulder.

"You done fine," he would be whispering. "You done just fine."

That was baptizing Sunday in the Two-Oak Missionary Baptist Church.

The best Sundays of all.

Other Sundays, there would be the same two dozen or so faces, bland in the dead, blue light from the windows. Mostly older women, with a sprinkling of men—all of the men, except Lee Jay, there because they had official duties to perform, taking up collection and ushering. Brother Fisco tried to feel the power, but the faces and the blue light worked against him. In time he grew to hate them both. They became to him a measure of his failure, and a reproach.

The trouble was that he watched other Men of God on the television—Oral Roberts every Sunday, and Billy Graham from time to time—and he could see them moving their thousands, drawing them to the Lord in response to their call. Or he would listen to the Reverend McIntyre on the radio. And he knew that he felt the power too. But who could there be for him to move with it? Just the bland Sunday faces in the open space of the church, most of them huddled up on the first two or three rows, with here and there a solitary one sitting in the blue gloom. He knew that there was a key, but that somehow he was missing it. He should be able to make the power come out and fill the church—fill a tent twenty times bigger than the church. But he couldn't find the key. Meantime, the power went dribbling out over the stiff heads of his congregation, spreading into the woods of the Two-Oak community, missing its mark and soaking into the ground.

"It ain't easy to be a Man of God," he would say. Eight years. "It ain't nothing easy *about* it."

After the Oral Roberts program went off, Brother Fisco would leave the television set on to watch the *Mr. Wizard* program. He admired the cool, knowing way the man had. Feeling in him a certain kind of power as well. Different, but there.

On the first baptizing Sunday in the spring of 1963 the *Mr. Wizard* program was about how to use science to do tricks of magic to mystify your friends. Brother Fisco watched him as he made a candle burn under water. Made an egg drop into a milk bottle. Then Mr. Wizard did a trick that caused a bell to ring somewhere in the back of Brother Fisco's mind. He felt that he had found the key.

What Mr. Wizard did was pour some clear water into a glass and make it turn red. Then he poured it back into another glass and it turned back clear again.

He explained the trick: Water and phenolphthalein salts in the first glass. Baking soda in the empty second glass to make the alkali solution. Vinegar in the third glass to neutralize the baking soda.

"You can do it over and over again," he said.

Brother Fisco sat up. "Water into wine . . . ," he said.

"What?" said Della.

"It looks like the water into wine," said Brother Fisco. "Like the wedding-feast miracle of the water into wine."

"It's a trick," said Della. "He told you about it. Them chemicals and all."

"But that's the way it *looks*," he said. "Like the water-into-wine miracle."

"Yes," she said.

"I got to do *some*thing," he said. "They ain't really interested. Only it's a habit for them to come."

"What?" she said.

"I'll do 'em a trick, with the water into wine," he said. "To make it interesting."

"You going to tell them?" she said.

"It might be I would," he said. "It's the Lord's work, Della."

"Shouldn't be no trick," she said, "and you not tell them about it."

"The Lord moves in mysterious ways," he said.

"The Lord ain't up to no tricks," she said.

He didn't say anything.

"You be careful," she said.

"I been careful," he said. "Eight years. I'm just where I was when I first started out."

So the next Sunday he was ready with the pitchers and the glasses and the chemicals.

He read the text: "'And the third day there was a marriage in Cana of Galilee; and the mother of Jesus was there:

"'And both Jesus was called, and his disciples, to the marriage.

"'And when they wanted wine, the mother of Jesus saith unto him, They have no wine.

"'Jesus saith unto her, Woman, what have I to do with *thee?* mine hour is not yet come.' Couldn't nobody never make Jesus do nothing didn't he want to," he said. "Not even his own mother couldn't do it.

"'His mother saith unto the servants, Whatsoever he saith unto you, do *it*.

"'And there were set there six waterpots of stone, after the manner of purifying the Jews, containing two or three firkins apiece.'"

Brother Fisco set six iced-tea glasses in a row across the top of the pulpit. "A firkin is nine gallons," he said. "I looked it up. Sounds like it'd be just a little bit, but I looked it up." A murmur ran through the congregation when he brought out the glasses. "Used to be they'd drink them a lot of wine," he said. "In Bible times.

"Not Jesus hisself, of course," he added. "Just them Jews."

The people in the church were sitting up and listening to him.

"'Jesus saith unto them,'" he went on, "'Fill the waterpots with water. And they filled them up to the brim.'"

He raised a glass pitcher filled with water from behind the pulpit. Holding it so everyone could see it. The water looked blue because of the light from the windows.

"'And he saith unto them, Draw out now, and bear unto the governor of the feast. And they bare *it*.

"'When the ruler of the feast had tasted the water that was made wine, and knew not whence it was:'"

He poured each of the glasses nearly full of the water from the pitcher, and the glasses were filled with purple liquid—like communion grape juice. Not red, because of the blue light from the windows.

The group huddled on the first three rows was leaning toward him, looking at the glasses. The ones sitting in the back got up and moved down to seats closer to the front. Lee Jay stood in a fourth-row pew, leaning on the back of the pew in front of him, looking at the glasses. When Brother Fisco poured the first glass, Lee Jay's eyes got big. "I be a son-of-a-bitch!" he said.

After he filled the glasses, Brother Fisco waited until they had gotten quiet again; then he went on.

" '(but the servants which drew the water knew;) the governor of the feast called the bridegroom.

" 'And saith unto him, Every man at the beginning doth set forth good wine; and when men have well drunk, then that which is worse: *but* thou hast kept the good wine until now.

" 'This beginning of miracles did Jesus in Cana of Galilee, and manifested forth his glory; and his disciples believed on him.' "

Brother Fisco slammed the Bible closed, making the congregation flinch. Every eye was on him. Lee Jay stood leaning on the pew, his head down and the collar of his coat rising like the scoop of a coal scuttle behind him.

While they waited, Brother Fisco picked up each of the iced-tea glasses in turn and poured its contents back into the pitcher, until it was full of clear, blue water again.

"I be a son-of-a-bitch!" said Lee Jay again—louder. Several of the women looked back at him over their shoulders. "Couldn't even Jesus do that," he said. "Water into wine into *water* again."

"Do it again," somebody said.

So he did it again. And then again once more. Leaving the six iced-tea glasses sitting on the pulpit, but manipulating the two pitchers behind it so they wouldn't see. Lee Jay got up out of his seat and came down the aisle to stand right in front. Watching. His eyes were big as saucers. Brother Fisco's gestures became more expansive as his confidence grew. He embellished his movements.

"Jesus' will be done," he said at last.

"Amen," said the congregation.

"Do it again," said Lee Jay.

"We will now sing hymn number three-seventy-six," he said.

He couldn't hear Della in the singing as it filled the blue light of the church. He never did preach the sermon he had prepared to go with the water-into-wine illustration.

When the singing stopped, he said, "Will you offer up our closing prayer, Brother Williston?"

Lee Jay stood in the fourth-row pew, leaning on the back of the row in front, sinking his head down between his shoulders, so his coat collar rose higher and higher behind his head.

"Lee Jay," said Brother Fisco, "will you offer up our closing prayer?"

Lee Jay's knuckles showed white where he gripped the back of the pew. His face was turning purple under his blue hair.

"Lee Jay . . . ," said Brother Fisco.

Lee Jay clasped his hands. "O Lord . . . ," he said. "O Lord Jesus . . . Jesus . . . Jesus . . ." His coat collar suddenly sank behind his head. ". . . Jesus loves me, this I know . . . ," he said.

"How'd you do that?" said Lee Jay as he shook Brother Fisco's hand leaving the church. "I ain't never seen nothing like that before."

"Come back next Sunday," said Brother Fisco.

"You going to do it again?" said Lee Jay. Other members of the congregation were standing around waiting for the answer.

"Come back and see," he said.

When they were driving home, Della looked out the window on her side of the car. "You didn't tell them how you done it," she said.

"I feel the *real* power, Della," he said.

For the next three weeks he did the water-into-wine trick, with the congregation getting bigger every week as the word spread. Finally people began to come in from outside the Two-Oak community. Two or three came out from Kose. He worked up a sermon on the miracles and the power of faith, and they sat still for it, hoping he would do the water into wine again.

In the meantime he had sent off for a Johnson-Smith and Company catalog of tricks and illusions that he had seen advertised in *Mechanix Illustrated,* and when it came he ordered five dollars' worth of tricks to use with his sermons. By the time the water-into-wine trick began to wear out, he was ready with others.

He did color-changing handkerchiefs to illustrate the "Do-not-let-your-right-hand-know-what-your-left-is-doing" text. And red balls that multiplied between his fingers—from one to four—for the "fishes-and-loaves" miracle. He tried some card tricks, but Della complained about that, because he wouldn't let her have any real cards in the house to play with, so he stopped.

He felt the power more and more.

"There's one thing I got to do, Della," he said. Supper was over, and she was clearing the table. He sat turning his coffee cup.

"What?" she said.

"I feel the power," he said.

"Well?" she said.

"I just been fooling around. They going to get tired of it sometime, and I'll be back with the little bunch of women and Lee Jay again."

"You're getting them to come in there now," she said.

"They got to *stay* in there," he said.

"Well," she said.

"But I *really* feel it," he said. "The *real* power. I got to do something. Something that will make them be able to stick."

She looked at him from the sink. "You got to be careful," she said.

"You done said that already," he said.

She didn't answer.

"I been thinking about it," he said. "You got to *feel* it. Then you could bring it off. Not if you didn't feel it."

"What is it, Garnet?" she said. "What is it you was going to do?"

He waited a minute before he replied. "I'm going to part the waters," he said flatly.

She looked at him. "What waters was it you was thinking about parting?" she said.

He waited a minute before he answered. "Kallisaw Sound," he said. "I could do it when I feel it. I got to be sure."

"Where is it you was going to go when you done it?" she said.

"Kallisaw Island," he said. "I could walk dry-shod to Kallisaw Island."

Della looked at him for a minute. "You going to be in some real trouble, Garnet," she said.

"If I didn't feel it," he said. "I got to really feel it first. Then I could do it."

She looked at him for a minute. Then she filled a cake pan with water from the sink and set it on the table in front of him.

"What's that for?" he said.

"Practice," she said.

He looked at her; then he hit the pan, skimming it against the wall. "God ain't going to be mocked," he said. "'Oh ye of little faith!'"

"'Pride goeth before destruction, and an haughty spirit before a fall,'" she said. "You better be careful."

"'According to your faith be it unto you . . .' 'The woman is the weaker vessel,'" he said. "If you can't think of nothing better to say, you can keep your mouth shut. I got me two verses for every one you say."

She picked up the cake pan and put it on the table again. "You better practice anyways," she said.

"God . . . damn it, Della," he said.

They looked at each other for a long minute.

"I *feel* it," he said. "Ain't I done told you that? I feel it, woman. You can't put no test on the Lord. You got to just go ahead and *do* it."

She stood looking at him, not saying anything.

"I'm going to pray on it," he said, looking into the coffee cup on the table. "I ain't going to do nothing until I prayed on it."

"You better," she said.

"Eight years, Della . . . ," he said.

She looked at him. "You better pray on it good," she said.

The next Sunday he made the announcement.

"Brothers and sisters," he said. "I got something to say to you all this morning, and I want you to listen to me careful, so you are going to hear what I say."

A murmur ran around the church.

"I been your preacher for eight years," he said. "Eight years and two months this Sunday. I keep after it, but it is a discouraging kind of work. Most of you, you got yourself other business on Sunday mornings, so it seems like you can't never hardly find your way to this here church at all. You got to tend to your other business. Out there fishing and hunting and enjoying yourself, and ain't got no time to stop by His house and just drop in to give up a prayer to Him and be thankful for the good things he done give you to enjoy.

"God, He understands that, I reckon. Leastways, He's *got* to be used to it by now. But that don't mean it's right. That don't mean you should be left to walk in your ungodly ways and just get on with it like that. *I* ain't got used to it. I ain't *never* got used to it. I walked them ungodly ways myself for thirty-one years. I know.

"I'm telling you what's a fact, brothers and sisters. I know." He paused, holding on to the pulpit with both hands and nodding his head.

"But I know about something else now too." He stopped nodding and looked at them. "I know about how it is to walk in God's way. How it is to walk in God's sweet way. And that's what I'm here to tell you about this morning."

The congregation shifted uneasily. A murmur ran around.

"I ain't going to do you no tricks this morning," he said. "I been getting you into God's house with a trick, but I ain't going to do you no trick this morning."

"You ain't going to do no tricks?" said Lee Jay.

"Sit down, Lee Jay," he said.

He looked around at them for a minute without speaking. "You knowed it was a trick, didn't you?" he said. "The water into wine, and the color-changing handkerchiefs, and all the rest of it. A trick." He slammed his fist down on the pulpit.

"I got you into God's house with a trick, and that was the idea of it. But I got to tell you now that God ain't no trick. And the time for tricks is done past."

He took the glasses and the pitchers out and put them on the pulpit. "I'm going to show you how I been tricking you into the Lord's house," he said. "And we're going to bring them tricks to an end."

One by one he explained all of the tricks to them—the water into wine, the color-changing handkerchiefs, the multiplying balls. They sat rapt while he told them.

When he had explained all of the tricks, he looked at them, holding the sides of the pulpit to steady himself. Then he gestured with his right hand, sweeping all the things—glasses, pitchers, handkerchiefs, balls—onto the floor with a crash. The congregation flinched when he did it.

"Now the trick show is over," he said. "God's work is going to be done.

"You listen to me," he said. "You listen to me careful, and I am going to tell you about something I am going to do that it ain't no trick at all. Just God's power and glory. I am going to lay it on the line."

He drew himself up, holding the pulpit in his hands.

"Today is July twenty-first, nineteen-sixty-three," he said. "The year of Our Lord, Jesus Christ, nineteen hundred and sixty-three.

"Next Sunday—July twenty-eighth—at two o'clock in the afternoon, at the public landing of McAfee County, Georgia, I will part the waters of Kallisaw Sound and walk dry-shod across the bed of the Sound to Kallisaw Island. I proclaim this publicly and in the House of God. I am moved by the Spirit of the Lord, and I call on you to witness the same. . . . Ah—men," he said.

The congregation sat stunned.

"What'd you say?" said Lee Jay, standing up.

"I said," he said, speaking slowly, "that I am going to part the waters of Kallisaw Sound next Sunday—July the twenty-eighth—at two o'clock in the afternoon, and that I would walk dry-shod across to Kallisaw Island."

Lee Jay stared at him. "How you going to do that?" he said.

"I am going to do it by the power of God and the strength of faith," he said.

"What?" said Lee Jay.

"Sit down, Lee Jay," he said.

Lee Jay sat down; then he stood back up again.

"And to prove it ain't no trick," he said. "I hereby offer my worldly goods—my house, the land that house is standing on, my

nineteen-fifty-nine Ford hardtop convertible, got a rebuilt engine
. . . all my worldly goods—for sale to the first taker for the sum of
one dollar." He held up his index finger.

There was a long silence.

"Your toolbox too?" someone asked.

"All my worldly goods," he said. "My toolbox too," he added.

Several hands with dollar bills in them began to go up, waving
above the congregation.

"*After* church," he said. "Now," he said, "any of you that you
think you've got the faith that is going to sustain you, he's welcome
to come along with me. But if don't none of you come, I am going
to do it by myself.

"Let us pray," he said.

Immediately after church, Case Deering bought the property,
giving him one dollar in cash for a bill of sale written on a fan. Case
then passed the fan to Della for a dollar.

"Just in case," he said. "It ain't that I don't think he's got the
power."

"Yes," said Della. "Much obliged."

On the Sunday following, he preached no sermon. Instead, he
spent the morning in the sanctuary of the church, kneeling before
the giant crucifix and praying. Della sat on the back pew watching
him. From time to time members of the congregation opened the
door to look inside, but no one came in. At one-thirty he left the
church, and he and Della drove to the public landing in his Ford.

The *What's Up Down in Georgia Show*, a local-events program produced by station WSOU-TV of Savannah, carried the
event live.

There were two cameras and two sound men, and an announcer in a green blazer with a WSOU-TV crest embroidered over
the left pocket.

The show opened with the first camera panning around, picking up the people milling around on the oyster-shell beach of
the landing. There seemed to be an enormous number of people.
The beach was not very large. Occasionally the camera would find

an open space in the crowd through which the Sound itself could be seen, and Kallisaw Island in the distance.

". . . Not only people from the Two-Oak church," said the announcer's voice as the camera panned around, ". . . people from all over this part of Georgia. I have just been told that there is a couple here on their honeymoon from Saginaw, Michigan. Groups from Brunswick, Waycross, Pembroke, and American Legion Post Number 456 of Savannah. It's quite a crowd . . . a very large crowd . . ."

The camera focused on a group of pretty girls in shorts, slid in on telephoto, then out again. ". . . There are reporters here from all the local papers . . . the Atlanta *Journal-Constitution* . . . ," said the announcer. ". . . I've just been told that a man from *Time* magazine is here somewhere. I haven't been able to spot him yet . . ."

The camera panned around the crowd, then tilted up toward the sky. ". . . a beautiful day," said the announcer. ". . . temperature eighty-five degrees here on the McAfee County public landing, an easterly breeze of about ten miles an hour . . . Just a perfect day . . ."

The camera swung and picked up Brother Fisco's Ford edging through the crowd. A shout went up behind the announcer's voice. ". . . I believe . . . I believe . . . I believe Mr. Fisco . . . yes. Mr. Fisco has just arrived . . . his car has just arrived at the landing. We'll try to get a word with him when he gets out of the car. . . ."

A number of reporters—some with microphones—clustered around Brother Fisco as he stepped out of the car.

"Mr. Fisco . . . Mr. Fisco . . . you plan . . . Mr. Fisco, you plan to walk to Kallisaw Island? Mr. Fisco . . . let me through . . . Mr. Fisco . . . when did you first think about doing this, Mr. Fisco?"

The crowd parted to let him through with the reporters and the men with microphones. Several men were holding microphones up to his face.

"God's going to do it." His face on the television screen bloomed large, coming into the camera. Then the landscape tilted, losing the image. When it came back into focus, he was standing at the water's edge, looking out across the choppy waters of Kallisaw Sound. Kallisaw Island was a dark mound in the distance at the top of the screen.

". . . two point three miles from where Mr. Fisco is standing to Kallisaw Island . . ." The announcer's voice whispered in the background behind the picture. The camera swung to pick up the island; then the picture on the screen shifted to another camera directly behind Brother Fisco, looking over his shoulder across the Sound, with the island in the background near the top of the picture.

"We expect Mr. Fisco to begin in just a minute now." The announcer's voice was low, confidential. The noises of the crowd came up behind his voice from the background.

Brother Fisco walked up and down at the edge of the water, looking down at the ground. Just at the edge of the water line, but without getting his shoes wet. The crowd surged along with him, giving ground to make an open place for him to walk. One of the cameramen had to wade out into the water to get the picture.

". . . He made the announcement to his congregation last Sunday . . . two o'clock . . . today at two o'clock. It's . . ."— the crowd noises rumbled in the background—". . . thirty-five seconds until two."

He stopped walking and turned to face the Sound, still looking down at his feet, standing at the very edge of the water. But not looking at the water. Looking at his shoes.

The picture shifted to the second camera, showing a closeup of his face in profile. His eyes were closed, and his lips were moving.

". . . getting ready . . . ," said the announcer.

Brother Fisco started to speak, and the camera on his face slid back out of telephoto, showing his whole body in profile. He had raised his hands, and stood with his head cocked down, hips swayed forward slightly, his body making a shallow figure S.

"'And the Lord said unto Moses, Wherefore criest thou unto me? speak unto the children of Israel . . .'"

". . . he's speaking now . . . ," said the voice of the announcer. The crowd noises stopped.

"'. . . lift thou up thy rod, and stretch out thine hand over the sea and divide it: and the children of Israel shall go on dry ground through the midst of the sea . . .' "

". . . lowering his hands now . . . stretching them out toward Kallisaw Island . . ."

There was silence. The camera slid in for another telephoto shot of Brother Fisco's face. His eyes were strained closed, with his head cocked down. The breeze flapped the collar of his white shirt, blowing his tie back under his raised arm. He was wearing his good suit pants.

". . . seems to be concentrating very hard . . . Kallisaw Island is two point three miles across the Sound from this point . . ."

Brother Fisco clenched and unclenched his fists, holding his hands outstretched.

" '. . . Moses stretched out his hand over the sea; and the Lord . . . caused the sea to go back by a strong east wind . . .' "

". . . the wind is blowing from the east *today* . . . ," said the announcer.

" '. . . and made the sea dry land, and the waters were divided . . .' "

". . . the crowd is very quiet now . . . waiting . . ."

" '. . . went into the midst of the sea upon the dry ground: and the waters were a wall unto them on their right hand, and on their left . . .' "

Brother Fisco's head moved, and the camera slid back out of telephoto.

". . . he's walking into the sea!" The announcer's voice went up.

The camera followed him until he was a little over knee-deep. Then the picture switched to the camera behind him, slid in on telephoto, holding the picture on the water washing around his knees. The side camera came in again on his face. He was not looking down. Then he slowly lowered his arms to his sides and stood looking down into the water.

". . . well . . . ," said the announcer's voice. The noises were beginning to come up again from the crowd in the background. ". . . looks like . . . he'll have to try another day . . ."

The camera swung around the crowd, coming in close on their faces.

". . . Mrs. Fisco . . . over there . . . ," said the announcer. Della stood beside Case Deering, her arms folded under her breasts. The wind had blown her hair around across her face.

The camera picked up Brother Fisco coming back out of the water toward the landing.

A young man in dungarees and a checkered shirt ran into the picture, waving his arms and yelling, "I'm going to walk *dry*-shod to Kallisaw . . . Take my picture! . . . Take my picture! . . . ." He ran into the water, going hard. For two or three steps he seemed to be walking *on* the water. Then he fell down splashing. Other young men followed.

". . . try to talk to Mr. Fisco," said the announcer. The camera picked him up walking into the lens.

". . . what . . . Mr. Fisco . . . what do you think, Mr. Fisco . . . what happened . . ."

Brother Fisco was still looking at the ground. He mumbled something.

". . . what? . . . Mr. Fisco . . . speak into the microphone, please . . ." The camera jerked around, trying to catch him going by. A hand with a microphone came into the picture.

". . . I felt the real power," he said.

". . . what? . . . Mr. Fisco? . . . What did you say?"

"I felt the real power. I don't know."

"But . . . what do you *think* happened?"

He looked back away from the camera. "I didn't . . . ," he said.

"What? . . . What did you say, Mr. Fisco?"

"I didn't," he said.

". . . Is it true that you sold your house, Mr. Fisco?" said the announcer.

His head stopped, centered in the picture, filling it. He said very distinctly, "Yes . . . all my worldly goods. It was *real*, mister." Then he walked out of the picture.

". . . Mr. Fisco! . . . Mr. Fisco! . . . ," said the announcer.

After he had left, the announcer tried to find Della to get a statement from her. She was nowhere to be found. So he began to talk to people in the crowd, getting their reactions.

"Are you a member of Mr. Fisco's church?" said the announcer.

"Whose?" said Lee Jay.

"Mr. Fisco. Are you a member of his church?"

"I would have thought he could have done it," said Lee Jay.

"Where are you from?" said the announcer.

Lee Jay looked at him a minute. "Kose," he said. He pulled out the bib of his overalls and threw back his head, looking inside. "Kose . . ."—he paused—". . . Geor . . . gi . . . a," he said, reading it off the inside of the bib. "AHR . . . EFF . . . DEE . . . *Two*." He let the bib go and looked at the announcer.

". . . and you are a member of Mr. Fisco's church?" said the announcer.

"He turned the water into wine," said Lee Jay.

"What?" said the announcer.

"He done it with the chemicals," said Lee Jay. "He told us about it."

"What did you say?" said the announcer.

"Leastways the *water* was real," said Lee Jay.

"I don't . . . speak into the microphone, please," said the announcer.

"Listen," said Lee Jay, "he was *good*. I mean it, mister. He was good. I'd have thought he was going to do it."

". . . yes," said the announcer. ". . . Well . . . let's see if we can get some other reactions."

He talked to the honeymoon couple from Saginaw, Michigan. "Have you ever been in Georgia before?" he said.

"I never did think he would do it," said the man. He had pale hair and an unpleasant face. His voice was high-pitched.

"Yes," said the announcer. "I understand you're on your honeymoon."

"Who told you that?" said the man, frowning. The girl hugged his arm and giggled. She had a hairdo that looked like a sneeze that had backfired into her hair. There was some kind of shiny-looking hair spray on it that had matted it together in long, ribbony sheets, like the New Year's Eve whistles that unroll when you blow into them.

"So you didn't think he'd make it?" said the announcer.

"We've never been to Georgia before," said the girl.

"I *knew* he wouldn't make it," said the man.

"Yes," said the announcer, ". . . and you came all the way from Saginaw, Michigan?"

"Who told you that?" said the man. Then he turned to the girl. "You got a big mouth," he said.

The announcer turned to face the camera. "Good luck to our visitors from Saginaw, Michigan," he said. "Let's see if we can get some other reactions."

". . . Are you a member of Mr. Fisco's church?" he said.

"I been some," said the young man. He wore a checkered shirt, and his wet hair was plastered down over his eyes.

"Well," said the announcer, "and what is your name?"

"What?" said the man.

"What is your name?" said the announcer. "Speak into the microphone, please."

"Dee Witt," said Dee Witt.

"Well, Mr. Witt," said the announcer, "what did you think?"

"What?" said Dee Witt.

"I said, what did you think about Mr. Fisco's miracle?"

Dee Witt looked into the camera. "I'll tell you, mister," he said, pulling his hair out of his eyes. "He's full of shit as a Christmas turkey."

"You're on the *air*," said the announcer. "You're on the *air* . . ."

The sun was going down when Brother Fisco got to the Rainbow Pool. He had left the oyster-shell road from the public landing and cut across through the swamp to keep from meeting people. For five or six hours he had wandered around. For about two hours he had really been lost. Then he had gotten his bearings again and walked out to the pool. While he was walking around in the swamp a thunderstorm had blown up. It drenched him, but it made the air bright and clear.

He saw the Ford parked off under the trees, but he didn't go up to it to speak to Della. He was even afraid of what she would say. Instead, he walked down to the edge of the water.

The orange sky reflected on the surface of the pool, with the black trunks of the cypress trees cutting across the orange. Under the overhanging branches were serried black patterns, thrown by the leaves. The moss hung in dark festoons, no wind moving them.

For a moment he looked over the black-and-orange surface— still as polished metal—reflecting the sky. Then he walked out into the water and knelt down, holding his hands clasped before him under the water.

He heard the car door slam, but he couldn't hear Della's footsteps until she started into the pool.

"I ain't up to it," he said, not looking around at her.

For a moment she didn't answer. "I know it," she said. There was another pause. "What you want for supper?" she said.

"I ain't hungry," he said.

"I reckon not," she said. "You got to eat."

"I felt the power, Della," he said after a while. "I felt the *real* power."

"I know you did," she said. "I never took you for no liar."

He could hear her walking in the water behind him. Then he felt her hands on his shoulders.

"Jesus God," he said.

She patted him. For several minutes neither of them spoke. "It's pretty this time of the day," she said. "All black and red."

The ripples from her walking spread out in front of him, widening gently on the glassy surface of the pool.

"It's my favorite time of the day," she said.

"Jesus God," he said. "What we going to do, Della?"

He felt her hand patting his shoulder again. "I don't know, Garnet," she said. "It'll be all right. I didn't never take you for no liar."

He shook his head, sawing it from side to side.

Around the rim of the pool the frogs and crickets had started. Fish rising to feed broke the surface with slow, plopping sounds, like pebbles dropping into the water. In the eastern swamp—where night had already arrived—an owl yodeled mellow and soft. The evening noises coming up as the light was going away. Crooning, distant sounds. Overhead, streams of high red clouds ran in a vortex westward, coming down into the furnace glow behind the trees.

For a long time neither of them spoke to break the stillness. Garnet kneeling in the water, his head sawing slowly from side to side. Della standing behind him, looking up at the westering clouds. Then slowly he began to hear another sound, low and near. Gliding out of the evening sounds and climbing up beyond them. He stopped his head and raised his eyes, tilting back to listen. Behind him his wife's clear, sweet alto began to rise, singing the words of the baptizing song. Going away above his head like the trace of a shooting star in the rain-clear air. Over the calm, red waters and into the westering sky. Out of the cypress shadows . . . black . . . and still. . . .

SOME NOTES
ON McAFEE COUNTY

McAFEE (mak′ · ä · fē—rhymes with *blacker we*) COUNTY:
An imaginary coastal county of the state of Georgia. Bounded on the
north by the Oconee River, on the south by the Altamahatchee
River, and on the west by a surveyor's line running SSW from Fork
Shoal on the Oconee River to Spratt's Landing on the Altamahat-
chee. On the east it touches Kallisaw Sound and the Atlantic Ocean.

County Seat: Kose (kōz—rhymes with *rose*)—population
1,017. There are four other communities in the county that are un-
incorporated and of unknown size—less than a hundred. These are
Two-Oak, Rainbow, Willie, and Fork Shoal. They are pretty much
the kind of a place they sound like they would be, though the people in them have their good times too.

The county covers a land area of 428 square miles, at a mean
elevation of 16.8 feet above sea level. Population density is 14.3
per square mile.

Selling gasoline is about the leading industry of McAfee County, and there are more Standard Oil pumps than any other kind. But the Shell stations are nicer, on the average.

The 1960 census report put the population at 6,254—the fourth-highest count in the history of the county. (Highest was in 1900, when there were 6,427.) Currently the percentage of Negroes in the population is down to 58%. In 1900 it was 80%. They seem to be drifting away.

There is not a single feed store in the county, but there are three hardware stores—all of which are doing a good business. The average adult male consumes 1.8 cartons of shotgun shells per year, 21 pounds of twelvepenny nails, 149 inches of galvanized chain, 1/3 of a shovel, and 1/16 of a submersible pump.

Fifty percent of the population are twenty-one years of age or older. About 18% have completed high school, but on the average they drop out after the seventh grade. The McAfee Alligators (the high-school football team—colors green and yellow) have won only three games in the last five years. The coach is pretty depressed about it, but the team doesn't seem to mind. They like the green-and-yellow uniforms and the trips they get to take.

At present the literacy rate is 64%, but it is rising.

The county has a total of fifty-seven churches, two-thirds of them Baptist. The Presbyterians are the smallest denomination, but their church in Kose is the most elegant.

There are 1,334 families, with an average income of $2,431 a year (1960 census figure). The number of rooms per house is 4.3, and the number of people per house is 4.2—or one person per room. Thirty-nine percent of the houses have running water with indoor plumbing, but the ground water has a high mineral content, and the fixtures tend to corrode in a hurry. The sulfur in the water makes it taste and smell like hard-boiled eggs.

Between 1950 and 1960 there was a net loss by migration of 755 people. No one knows where they went. Probably to Savannah or Jacksonville. None of them ever came back to tell about it.

The average temperature for January is 55.6° Fahrenheit, and for July 82.5°. Rainfall is 55.73 inches per year.

In 1960 there were 71 deaths and 174 live births.

That's about it for statistics.

But there are other ways you could look at McAfee County.

If it were there, latitude 31° 30′ N. and longitude 81° 30′ W. would intersect at Shotford's Grocery Store and Filling Station.

If you could leap up into the air and hang there for a day while the world rolled around underneath you, you would see that it shares a parallel of latitude with Jesup, Georgia; Greenville, Alabama; Laurel, Mississippi; Nacogdoches, Waco, and Odessa, Texas; Enseñada, Mexico; Nagasaki, Japan; Nanking, China (Red China); Lahore, Pakistan; Bagdad, Iraq; Haifa, Israel; Alexandria, Egypt; and Marrakesh, Morocco.

Run a meridian of longitude up through the North Pole and around again, and it would pass through Spartanburg, South Carolina; Charleston, West Virginia; Cleveland, Ohio; Moosonee, Canada; Hudson Bay; Novosibirsk, Russia; Lucknow, India; Colombo, Ceylon; Paita, Peru; the isthmus of Panama; Havana, Cuba; and Cape Kennedy, Florida.

Those are the main places.

If only it were there, McAfee County would have a hell of a good location. Practically a crossroads of the wide world.

But, God damn it, it's not.

McAfee County, Georgia, isn't real.

So always remember. None of this is true.

I thought you ought to know.

ABOUT THE AUTHOR

Mark Steadman teaches in the English Department at Clemson University. "Annie's Love Child" has appeared in *The Red Clay Reader*. "Anse Starkey at Rest" and "A Worker of Miracles" were in the April and September 1971 issues of *Works in Progress*. He was born in Statesboro, Georgia, in 1930.